ALONE
AGAIN

Also by Marvin Noe

ALONE

ALONE AGAIN

MARVIN NOE

ISBN 978-1-5032-1044-8

Printed in the United States of America

ACKNOWLEDGEMENTS

Many thanks to Vaughn Vordahl and
Roger Van Voorhees for their help editing my story.

A special thanks to my son Daren and his wife.
They are always there when I need them.

CHAPTER 1

In Richie, Montana a small town in Eastern Montana, eighteen year old Seattle native newly married Brad Collins sat at the kitchen table drinking iced tea with his mother-in-law Marlina Burns. His new bride Alice and her younger sister Darcy had left the house and hour earlier to go shopping. "I hope you don't get bored hanging out with me while my girls are gone this morning."

"Marlina shame on you, we'll have time to get to know one another better. I find the relaxed atmosphere here in Richie a refreshing break from the hustle and bustle of Seattle. I must compliment your ice tea, you make great iced tea. What amazes me about this small town is how friendly the people are that live here. In Seattle, I don't even know my next door neighbor,"

The sound of a siren a few blocks away created a temporary lull in Marlina and Brad's conversation. "Oh no, there must be a fire somewhere. I hope it's not a bad fire. Our dry land wheat is in the drying process now."

"Then we better cross our fingers and hope the siren is a false alarm. In Seattle the sound of sirens is commonplace day and night, 24/7."

"We have few false alarms. By the sound, the sirens went out towards Glendive. I hope Alice and Darcy are able to return home after they exchange the pants they purchased yesterday. Sometimes smoke from a fire causes temporary road closures between here and Glendive."

"I'm sure the girls are intelligent enough to hold up where they are safe until they can safely return."

"The Fire District is pretty good at directing traffic away from any danger area. They also keep the fire away from town by back-burning if necessary. These back-burns help clean out combustible material near the city if the wind turns the fire towards Richie."

"Then you are saying we should be safe. We won't be asked to quickly leave the area. I would feel better if Alice were here with us."

"We should be safe. I can understand you not wanting to be separated from Alice. I've never seen her as happy as she is now. I hope and pray Darcy will be lucky enough to find her a special man someday."

"Darcy is a pretty young lady. I see her as an intelligent person. In time I would predict she will find her Mr. Right."

"You may not be aware of it but I believe Darcy wants to move to Seattle to be near you and Alice. I can't blame her. Eastern Montana has little to offer a young woman her age. These days most young women, guys too for that matter move away soon as they graduate high school."

"Then the pants exchange may be a phony excuse. They may have just wanted to get away long enough to discuss the best way to make you understand Darcy wanting to move to Seattle. If she does move to Seattle, I hope you come visit us often or consider moving there yourself."

The sound of a car stopping out front caught their attention. "If that is the girls they never got far. The fire may have turned them back."

Seconds later Deputy Sheriff Sam Owens a long time family friend came walking in. "Marlina, I have bad news. There has been an accident, a terrible accident. The car involved in the accident is believed to be that of your daughter and son-in-law. It was a yellow sporty looking car."

Sam's words caused Marlina to faint she crashed to the floor. Sam knelt to care for Mrs. Burns while Brad wanted answers. "My wife and sister-in-law were driving our car. How bad are they injured?" Sam looked up at Brad as he shook his head. "Where did the ambulance take them?"

"Both occupants were being taken to the hospital in Glendive, that's the nearest hospital. I'm sure they are not at the hospital yet. If you go racing off to get there, please drive careful. One accident is enough."

Minutes later Brad and Mrs. Burns drove towards Glendive. Driving past the accident scene clearly showed the violence of the crash. At the hospital bad news awaited. One of the girls was dead on arrival. The surviving daughter was battered and bruised with her face swelled beyond reorganization. "Alice, my wife wears a wedding ring."

As tears streamed from their eyes Marlina placed one hand on Brad's arm. "I saw Alice's wedding ring by the sink after the girls left this morning. She apparently took it off to wash dishes this morning,"

Four days later Darcy woke enough to ask if Alice was okay. Her few words confirmed Brad's young wife was dead. Unable to look at Alice's sister without crying he returned to Seattle right after her funeral. At the tender age of eighteen Brad Collins found his life had flipped upside down. He found himself alone again.

They had been married three short glorious months. Her death hit him hard. Alice's savings before they married totaled three hundred fifty nine thousand dollars was sent to her mother Marlina, and sister Darcy, in Richie, Montana. He hoped the money would help her mother and sister have a better life.

Experiencing a woman's love, and then losing her in an automobile accident so soon after getting married proved devastating for Brad. He cussed his absentee parents. They were never around when he needed someone to lean on for support. Unknown to Brad his parents were bad people. John and Mary Collins were wrapped up in transporting drugs from Mexico into the States. They never had time for their son. They were money driven greedy people he knew little about. At age five he was left in Seattle in the care of a nanny. At age fourteen a young eighteen year old nanny by the name of Alice Burns took over his care. It took four years of love, and respect, to bring him to recognize the love he felt for Alice was a deeper love than any love he had experienced in his life. On his eighteenth birthday he proposed and soon married Alice, the love of his life. With her dying in the automobile crash, his love was now gone, he found himself alone in a big cold house.

After getting home, Brad waited five days before contacting one of the few people with the knowledge to contact his father. Bill Barrett was a business associate in Seattle. Bill operated four Import-Export stores along the west coast for John Collins. The stores were John and Mary's cover story for moving illegal drug all over the world was they traveled exclusively buying items for their stores. In addition the stores were used to launder money."

Bill related Brad's bad news to Brad's father, John. "That damn kid was too young to get married. He had no business being in Montana for any reason. Thanks for the call Bill. I'll give Brad a call."

Brad paced the floor hoping his father would call. Why he couldn't contact his father direct he wasn't sure. Growing up he had been told he couldn't contact his father or mother directly because of security reasons. Wealthy people draw the attention of bad people. People like kidnappers, burglars, thieves, and the like. Direct calls are an unnecessary security risk he was told.

John's call came in two hours later. "Slow and methodical Brad tried explained the details surrounding Alice's death."

His father wasn't good at consoling anyone. "Life is tough, son. Your mother and I are extremely sorry to hear about Alice passing away. You were too young to be married anyway. There will be other women in your life. For business reasons we are unable to come visit you in Seattle. We feel it would be beneficial for you visit us in Mexico." John's words were cold and empty. When fathers were handed out Brad got the short end of the stick. The more his father talked the more his words drifted away from the comforting words of a normal father.

"Dad, I'm well aware of your exile status from the States because of taxes. At this time I don't feel like traveling to Mexico. I would be lousy company for anyone. I'll stay here and move on with my plan to start college in the fall."

"Don't get down on life and do something stupid. Alice was young. She found love a second time. Given time you too can find love again. Life has dealt you a tough blow. Now it's time to get off the pity wagon and move on with your life. It would do you a world of good if you came visit us in Mexico."

John had little interest in seeing his son, and new wife when Alice was alive. Now that she was gone he wanted his son to visit Mexico. As always Brad hid his anger towards his father. "I'll pass for now father, for my immediate future I want to be alone. I'm better off alone, the people I grow to love leave me. You and mother left me years ago. Ann, my second nanny died of cancer. Now Alice the nanny I grew to love and married died in an automobile accident. How much can one person take?"

John's anger flared. "Damn it son stop moping around, pull your frigging head out of your ass. You are not the first person to lose a loved one. Don't go doing anything stupid. Alice would expect you to stand up and be a man. Your mother and I can't fly to Seattle. A trip to Mexico would do you a world of good. There are a lot of beautiful women in Mexico, friendly women. Women who make great bed warmers, right now a good warm female companion would be good for you. There is more than one woman in this world that has the ability to satisfy that little wiggly thing hanging between your legs."

"I don't need to be set up with any of your cast off bitches. I'll stay here and prepare for college this fall."

"Well shit. Call us if you change your mind. If your mother gets a chance, she may pop up to see you for a couple days. I'm not sure of her travel plans."

To his parents Alice's death meant nothing. Their oh-well, death is a part of life attitude irritated the hell out of him. If he never saw his parents again it would be alright by him. Brad rarely saw his parents anyway. Beyond loving the money they send him each month he seldom thought about his parents. For a young person about to start college, he had a wonderful amount of money. His idiot parents apparently thought money could replace love.

Sitting alone day after day Brad had time to reflect on his young life. He no doubt had been abandoned by his parent, parents he knew little about. Unknown to him he was abandoned because of his father's work. His mother left because of her mental problems after learning a horrible family secret. John and Mary were brother and sister split up by divorce. Five years after Brad was born, John and Mary learned they were brother and sister. The news of her brother impregnating her put Mary in an emotional tailspin. From age five on his care was turned over to a series of nannies. Nannies became his only source of love and affection.

In Mexico, John wasn't satisfied with the sound of his son's voice. He placed a call to Jean Thomas, one of his local business associates at the Import–Export Store in Seattle. "Hello Jean."

"Hello John, I'm surprised to hear your voice. You seldom call."

"Yes, it's me. I have a problem in your area. My son's wife died in an automobile accident and the stupid kid is wrapped up in self-pity. The little shit needs a boot in the butt. I'm afraid he may start drinking or using drugs to ease his broken heart. I tried to get him to fly down to Mexico and be with me for a while, he refused. I need you to check on him and be certain he is okay."

"I saw her death notice in the paper. Your son and his wife were newlyweds. I'm sure her death is hard on him."

"Yes they were newlyweds. I spoke with Brad by phone, the depressed tone in his voice concerns me. I can't go to Seattle and the dumb shit won't come to Mexico. I need you to be of service to my son and help him through this difficult time?"

Jean Thomas knew when a drug lord like John Collins asked a favor, it was a command. His voice may have been soft but the undertone was an order. "I would be happy to do anything I can for your son."

"Do whatever it takes to straighten out my son. Do I make myself clear?"

"Your son will be well taken care of in the manner you are requesting. I'll personally see to it myself."

"If I'm reading his emotions correctly your assignment may require a long term effort. See to it you get the job done."

She understood his unspoken words. John Collins meant for her to find some young lady to sleep with his son, or she was to sleep with him. "You can count on me John. I'll get your son out of his depressed state."

As Jean drove over to visit young Collin's, she wondered how Brad could not realize his father was an underworld figure, a powerful Mexico drug dealer. Brad answered the hard knocking on his door. "Oh, it's you."

"Hello Brad, you look rough. Your father sent me to check on you. I'm sorry to hear life dealt you another tough blow. Having to kill the intruder two years ago and now losing Alice. It's only natural for you to be upset. At the same time you need to interact with other people."

"I will be interacting with people when college starts this fall. For now I want to be alone. I'm sure you have plenty of other things to do."

"College is a month away. Your father detected depression in your voice. He instructed me to check on you."

"Jean, I know you mean well, but just go. Why can't my father understand I want to be left completely alone?"

She took him by the hand. "Come with me, I want to show you something." She led young Collins into the master bath area. "Look at yourself in the mirror. I doubt you bathed or shaved since Alice passed away. If she were to see you now, Alice would be ashamed of how you look."

"Alice can't see me. I don't feel like doing anything." He barely looked in the mirror. "Leave me alone."

"Look at you. You are wearing dirty clothes. Alice would expect you to stand up and be a man. You can't stop living or you won't be ready for college this fall."

"I'm telling you I want to be left alone. Just go, I'll be fine. I'll bathe and clean up later today or tomorrow."

"My leaving won't satisfy your father." She shook him by the shoulders. "Are you planning to bathe and shave, or do I bring people in to bathe and shave you?" She threatened.

"I'm fully capable of bathing and shaving myself." Brad snapped back at her. "Just go! I told you I don't want to see anyone today."

"I'm not leaving until you prove you can shower and shave. I'll wait in the hall until you come out sparkling clean."

"I said I'll shower and shave after you leave."

"I'm not going anywhere until you are cleaned up. I know better than to buck a direct order from your father. He instructed me to do whatever it takes to get you out of your depressed state you are in. By damn I'll get you to clean up if it's the last thing I do."

She began to unbutton his shirt until he pushed her hand away. "Stop that, I am capable of undressing myself. I don't need your help."

"Then shower and shave, right now." She left the room only to slip back for a peek in. He was in the shower but wasn't soaping and washing. John's orders were to make sure his son was alright. She took a drastic step by removing her own clothes and joining him in the shower.

The sudden rush of cool air caused him to snap his head around. "What the hell are you doing woman?"

"I'm doing what your father instructed me to do. I'm getting you cleaned up, and see to it you look human again. "

"Stop that. I can wash my own body. Get out of here." He pushed her hands away twice more before giving up. The cascading water and Jean's soft hands gave him flashbacks of showering with Alice when she was alive. "Jean, you need to get out of here. My father never expected you to give me a shower."

"I never expected to give you a shower, but you concern me." Claiming to be fine he began to cry. His unexpected emotional outburst was the first step of mourning the loss of his young wife, Alice. Jean held him against her bare breast as he cried. Eventually they stepped from the shower so she could dry his body."

Considerable time after showering he stopped crying. "I'm sorry to be such a pain-in-the-butt baby. I'll do better from now on."

"There is no shame in crying when a person is grieving. My towel keeps slipping, may I borrow one of Alice's robes?"

"I don't have any of her things left in the house. I'm much better now. You need to dress and leave. You don't need a robe to wear. You came here to bring me out of my depressed state. You accomplished your goal. You can dress and leave now. I don't have a hair dryer or anything you can use. Just go."

"You gave all of Alice's things away, hair dryer and all. I can't go home looking like this. You shave while I make a phone call?" He stood looking in the mirror at his reflection. "Do I need to shave you too?" She asked.

"You have me totally confused. Why are you doing this?"

"Go ahead and lather up while I place my call to my hairdresser so she can come do my hair. I can't go home to my husband looking like this."

"I didn't realize you were married."

"I've been married for fifteen years to Bill Barret." Brad gave her a strange look. "Bill knows I came here to check on you. He also understands when your father gives an order we do what your father wants. The power of money can move mountains."

"Does that mean you would actually do anything my father asked of you to comfort me, regardless of what it was?" Jean nodded yes. "That's crazy."

"Yes but don't blame your father for commanding power over me. Bill and I knew what we were getting into. We also realize our jobs are not a job conducive to family life so we agreed not to have children." Jean's explanation was interrupted by the arrival of her hairdresser. "You might want to slip some clothes on before I let Kay in. She can trim your hair before she leaves."

Once Jean's hair was finished, she dressed in full view of Brad and Kay while his hair was being trimmed. "There is the good looking blonde haired Brad Collins I know. I will drop by each day to check your progress. If you need anything call me day or night. Get busy and stay active. Life without interaction is not life."

Brad's only comfort came from his massive electronics room conducting simple computer experiments. His desire to restart his subliminal message experiments grew stronger as his lonely days continued. Being alone he had absolutely no one to conduct experiments on.

Jean Thomas continued to be his only visitor bringing her to mind as a test subject. Before he could decide on an experiment he could conduct on her she arrived at the house. "Good afternoon Jean."

"You look rough Brad, are you sleeping at night?"

"I can't sleep in the room Alice and I shared. This morning I moved my things down the hall to my old bedroom near my electronic room. Hopefully I will sleep better in there."

"May I see both bedrooms, a bedroom can tell a lot about a person's well being. A person spends one third of their life in their bedroom."

"I've never slept eight hours a night in my life. Things other people do in a bedroom don't apply to me right now. If you remember I'm alone. My mate passed away."

"Sex can be a good emotional release. I suspect you are missing the intimate side of your marriage." She paused giving him time to absorb her words. "If you need help in that department please ask." Brad gave her a strange look. "I'm serious, just ask."

"I believe you are serious." He shook his head. "If I asked you to shower with me again, and spend the day in my bed, I actually believe you would. My father is a regular bastard."

"Your father pays well. Every dollar I earn comes at a price. Bill and I sold our souls long ago. You and I showering and having sex wouldn't change things. My husband understands what I must do if necessary."

"Maybe it wouldn't change you, but if we showered and had sex, it would change me. I won't be a part of harming your marriage the way my father does. He is the bastard not me. You and Bill have been great to me. I count you among the few friends I have."

"Don't be too hard on your father. He has a strange life for many reasons. He does things the only way he knows how. Once a man rises to a certain power level he must fight like hell to stay there. Your father's life is not as simple as you might think."

"You seem to like my father while I hate the man. How would you feel if your father abandoned you at age five?" Brad paused for an answer that never came. "I can count the number of times on my hands my father has come to see me in the past dozen plus years. He didn't know Alice yet he disliked our getting married."

"You only see one side of your father's life. Your safety keeps your father away. If his enemies knew John had a son they could get to him through you."

"What are you talking about? My father is a woman chasing bastard. With me around, I was an inconvenience. My father is giving you lies to cover his open lifestyle."

"Your father had…never mind. I've said too much now."

"Oh that's great, more silence. That's just what I need. Do you know my father once said I didn't have to marry Alice to have sex with her?" Again, Jean never answered his question. "I married Alice because I loved her. Love is not a word in my father's vocabulary. The man knows nothing about love, money is his power. How could it not bother you if I asked to have sex with you?" She continued to ignore his questions. "You can't answer me because he has bought you. The bastard bought you."

"You say your father doesn't know who you are. I could say you don't know who your father is. If you are emotionally down on any evening call me. If you don't like me, and need female companionship. I can arrange an escort lady. Your needs are a phone call away."

"You sound like my father, cheap sex can cure anything. I will not sleep with you or any sleaze-bag prostitute he asks you to hire. I have principles I live by. Beliefs father would never understand."

CHAPTER 2

College came as a huge relief. The first two years of college became routine. Brad dated various girls and had meaningless sex with some of the more liberal females. These easy girls he took to an out of the way motel. They did not rate high enough for the bed Alice once shared with him."

A couple times a month he would throw a party, and conduct simple subliminal experiments on his unsuspecting guests. The no beer nights where beer was available, but no one drank beer were always fun. With his limited subliminal message experiments, he wasn't able accomplish things he wanted to repeat. Even using different scenarios for these college parties proved to be of little value. He thought about having one person do something totally stupid. These new ideas were soon ruled out as being risky. His subliminal message experiments once again ground to a near halt.

During Brad's third year of college severe depression set. His grades began to spiraling downward to a dangerously low level. A new sexy girlfriend Jennifer Gardner did little for his depressed state. She was a handy sexual release and nothing more. Warnings came from two of his professors. "You are a bright young man why are you on the verge of failing your classes?"

Jennifer, a little vixen in lamb's clothing knew he had a generous amount of money, and his family had more money. "You have money, why get a degree you don't need?"

One professor who cared about Brad wouldn't give up. "Hire a tutor and crack the books. Do you know Karen Moore?"

"I do know Karen, but not well. We have three classes together."

"You need to know her. She is an excellent student who keeps perfect notes. She has tutored other students in the past. I'm not sure what she charges. I do know she might be the answer you need to improve your grades."

Knowing who Karen was ahead of time helped him approach her. "Hi Karen, I have a problem Professor Lingren thinks you may be able to help me with?"

"Hello Brad, what is it you need help with?"

"I'm in desperate trouble grade wise. Professor Lingren tells me you tutor students. By chance are you available to help me before I fail my classes?"

"I have tutored students in the past but we are so close to the end of spring quarter. You should have come to me sooner, if you were having trouble."

"I'm not totally rock bottom, but I could use a small miracle. Professor Lingren thinks you are the miracle I need."

Karen cringed. "Being this close to the end of the quarter, I can't guarantee results."

"I'm aware of my time frame. I'm in a tough spot you may be my only salvation to save my class credits. I really need your help. What do you say? I'll pay your going rate."

"You would need a weekend marathon study session with zero distractions. We are so close to the end of the college quarter you can't waste time anywhere, not even phone calls."

"If you are willing to help me, my weekend can be free, are you available to help me?"

"I'm available for fifteen dollars per hour. We can study four hours on Friday evening, eight hours each Saturday, and Sunday, making a total of twenty hours equaling three hundred dollars."

"Three hundred dollars would be fine."

"Keep in mind I am only your helper. You will be doing the work. I'm not selling term papers or doing class assignments for you."

"I understand, I will do my own work. I'll tell my girlfriend to stay away."

"Dorm rooms have many distractions. Is there somewhere besides your dorm room we can study?"

"I live off campus, my house is quiet. No one will bother us studying there. We can meet after class on Friday. You can ride the bus with me and find out where I live?"

"Very well I will meet you after class on Friday out by the archway."

He explained his weekend study plans to his fun loving sexy girlfriend. She hit the ceiling. "You don't need Karen. I can tutor you." She insisted.

"You tutoring me wouldn't work. Karen has agreed to help me study all weekend. She has tutored students before and comes highly recommended by Professor Lingren. She has time to help me, and I'm going to use her to help me."

"That little bitch agreed to help you because she is flat broke. All she wants is to get her hooks in you for money, so she can remain in college."

"Jen, knock it off. She will be tutoring me, and that is final. Professor Lingren tells me she has magnificent class notes, she is in my classes. I need her notes to salvage my class credits. Knock off the snide remarks and stay away from my house this weekend."

"Magnificent notes my ass, she has a magnificent chest. I bet you can't wait to get your grubby little paws on her huge breasts." Jennifer popped her blouse open and exposed both her breasts. "What's the matter with my breasts are you getting bored with these?"

"I don't like seeing this ugly jealous side you are showing. Karen and I are studying together all weekend starting tomorrow night. Do not call and interrupt us. I'm paying fifteen dollars per hours for Karen's help. I want my money's worth."

"What am I supposed to do while you are playing with your hired prostitute all weekend?"

Her whining irritated him. "Stop whining, our dating can wait until next weekend. You are being such a baby."

"By next weekend she will have her hooks in you good. Don't try telling me you are not anxious to get your hands on her."

"I'm warning you Jen, you better change your attitude before you ruin everything. I won't put up with a jealous girlfriend."

She continued her campaign to change his mind about studying with Karen. "Damn it Jen, I've had enough of your jealous tantrums. If you say one more word about my studying with Karen, we are through for good."

Friday after class he met Karen under the archway. Jen stood off a few yards glaring at them. "Your girlfriend is not happy I will be tutoring you?"

"Jennifer isn't very happy, but I have no choice. She can go do anything she wants this weekend. Long as she leaves us alone, I'm fine."

Karen turned out to be a wonderful surprise. Although he saw her in class on a daily basis he had never paid a lot of attention to her. She had dark hair, a beautiful smile, a fantastic looking body, and as Jen commented, beautiful breasts. He wasn't with Karen for her body. Her mind and her valuable notes is what he needed her for.

Karen was impressed by his house. "Wow, some house. Must be nice living close enough to college you can live at home."

"I chose Pacific Lutheran University as my college to remain living here. Why move to a cramped up dorm room if I didn't have to. I have all the privacy in the world. Living in cramped quarters and walking down the hall to shower with a bunch of guys doesn't appeal to me."

"I live in an all women's dorm with two other girls, and you are right. It is crowded. I'm enjoying our conversation, but we should stop wasting time. We need to buckle down and start studying."

They sat at the dinning room table and studied diligently for two hours when he began showing signs of discomfort. "Are you having some kind of a problem?"

He spread his arms to stretch his back. "I'm getting tired and stiff. Do we ever get a break?"

"We've only been studying a couple hours, and I saw your transcript. Two hours is a little soon for a break. We need to continue studying if you hope to pass your classes."

"Okay you win. When you get hungry, tell me so we can order food. There is a great little deli a few blocks away with great food, and a fast delivery service."

"We need to study another hour before eating." Studying brought slow results. "Brad, you are not concentrating. Finals are coming soon." She was becoming frustrated with his study habits.

"I need a rest break. I'm not used to studying at this pace." He continued his complaining. "Can we order our food now? I'll have more energy to help me concentrate after I eat?"

In frustration she shook her head. "Okay it's your dollar, order our food. You are not going to study until after we eat. The faster we eat the faster we can get back to studying."

"Make yourself at home while I place our food order, would you care for a salad?"

"A small salad with ranch dressing would be nice." Karen requested.

After ordering the food he excused himself long enough to create a subliminal message to help him concentrate on his studies. She heard the soft music begin. "Nice sound system."

"Music helps me study. I should have started the music earlier."

She checked her watch. "What time will your parents be home this evening?"

"My parents don't live here, I live alone."

Karen gave him a look of being shocked. "I naturally assumed your parents lived here. This house is huge. You should have a couple guys living here to help share your living expenses."

"Guy roommates are vulgar and messy. I can handle my expenses."

She glared at him. "You brought me here knowing we would be alone in this magnificent house all evening?"

"I wasn't trying to mislead you. I thought you wanted quiet to study."

"Yes but did you bring me here to…"

"…to seduce you?" He smiled a little grin. "Heavens no, I'm not trying to seduce you. If I were after sex this evening, Jen would be here and my bed would be rocking." He pointed back towards his bedroom.

She gave him a direct serious look. "Then you have no ulterior motives?"

"No ulterior motives. Had I wanted to know you better I would ask you out on a date. Come with me for a minute I want to show you something."

As he unlocked his electronics room door she balked and shook her head no. "I'm not going in there with you."

"I want to show you something."

"I bet you would like to show me something. I'm not going in your bedroom."

"How can I show you anything if you won't look inside?" He pushed the door wide open before stepping back. "At least peek in, this is my hobby room. I spend hours in here. What you are looking at is my future, the key to my success."

"Wow, what I see is how your grade point dropped to a low level. Standing here looking at your equipment we are wasting valuable time." She declared wearing a frown.

"This equipment could be part of my study problems. Truth is I find college boring, and the music helps me study. See the red switch on top of the board. That is the master switch. It stops every piece of equipment I own. If you work me to death, please turn the switch off before you leave."

"No one ever died from studying. Without a doubt you have the worst study habits of anyone I know. A college degree equals earning power." She explained. "You need to buckle down and study."

"I don't need a degree for earning power. My earning power is in this room. My college degree will be nothing more than wall decoration for others to see and impress visitors entering my office."

"I disagree, mark my words. A college degree will be more helpful than you realize."

"If history serves me correctly Bill Gates doesn't have a degree. He left college early to start Microsoft. Don't tell me though; I'm well aware he now funds a lot of educational programs. The fact remains Gates himself did not earn a degree in college. He may well have an honorary degree by now. If he doesn't he should have a degree. He is the most inspirational person I ever read about."

"So you want to be the next Bill Gates." She remarked in a smart tone.

"Heavens no, Bill Gates is a good man. He screwed up by being too well known. He underestimated his earning power. Neither Mr. Gates nor his family will ever live a normal life. His house, it is a regular Fort Knox. Think about the security people he employs."

"With your confidence, I wouldn't be surprised if you actually became a big success some day."

After eating she observed how fast and neat he cleaned everything up. "I'm impressed. You cleaned up our mess. Few guys I know clean up soon as a mess is made."

"Don't be fooled by what you saw. I have cleaning help come in two days a week. Enough about cleaning, I need to get back to studying. I do have one question for you, could you leave your notes here tonight for me to study on my own after you leave?"

"If I leave my notes here tonight you will have to guard them with your life? I don't have a backup of my notes." Karen warned as she shook one finger at him. "I can't afford to lose my notes. I refer back to these notes to keep my grades to the highest grade level I can.

"If you allow me to keep your notes, I will guard them with my life. Plus I will continue studying tonight on my own. This will allow you to go home. By the time you come back in the morning, I will know the information better."

"If you promise to continue studying, I will call a taxi and go home."

He nodded in agreement. "No wait, I have a better idea. Drive my car back to your dorm. That way you will have a ride here in the morning."

"I can't take your car." She protested.

"Don't be silly take my car. Here are the keys and I will see you around ten in the morning." He escorted her to the garage. "The button on the left opens the garage door. The button on the right opens the outside security gate. See you at ten in the morning."

With Karen gone he could intensify his studying. He quickly mixed her C.D. notes into a powerful subliminal message so he could study as he slept. With his study message playing he took a quick shower and turned in for the night. Being tired he dosed off easy. Throughout the nighttime hours his special subliminal message played over and over attacking his memory in much the same way a virus would attack a computer.

CHAPTER 3

The following morning Karen arrived precisely at ten calling out Brad's name. She expected him to be ready for a long day of studying. He was nowhere to be seen. After waiting a full half hour in the kitchen she began exploring the house looking to find him. She tapped on the master bedroom door as she called his name. The door opened wider from her tap. The room was empty. She moved on to the electronics room. No luck finding him there either leaving the remaining bedroom to check. Again she tapped and called out his name as she pushed open the door to find him sleeping sound. Thinking he was passed out from drinking she grew angry. She rushed to his bedside to punch his shoulder and shouted. "Get up, it's time to study."

"Oh hi Karen, is it ten already?"

"Ten and then some, we should have been studying a half hour ago." She scolded. "Get up!"

"I studied late last night. Can you make some coffee while I shower and get dressed?"

"I'll go make the coffee but don't you dare go back to sleep." She warned shaking a finger at him. "You should have been up and ready to study when I arrived today. This oversleeping is pure nonsense. It shows lack of character for you. I'll leave now but you better get up or I'm going home."

As she turned to leave his bedside, Karen was tackled by a screaming Jennifer completely knocking her over his bed. "I knew it, you little bitch get out of Brad's bed. I'm going to rip your hair out."

Brad grabbed Jennifer by the hair yanking her over backwards and down the floor. "Knock it off Jennifer, get a hold on yourself!"

She came bouncing up for a second round at Karen as he came busting from beneath his thin cover. To protect Karen, he pushed Jen down a second time. She struggled against his weight. "Stop this nonsense the only thing going on here is in your imagination."

"Who are you kidding I saw her get out of your bed?"

"The only time she was on my bed is when you pushed her there."

"I saw her on your bed!"

Using a handful of hair to guide her head he snapped it around. "Damn it; take a good look at Karen she is fully dressed. Not a hair out of place until you tried to rip her hair out. I'm the one not dressed. She arrived and was trying to wake me until you barged in."

"I saw you; you were trying to coax her in bed." She insisted.

"I've had it with you, give me my house key." He didn't wait to be given his house key back. He started ripping at her clothes. "Where is my house key?"

"Your key is in my back right pocket, stop ripping my clothes."

He continued to rip her pocket half off getting his key out before spinning her around to boot her fanny. "Now get the hell out of my house."

"I'm sorry, I thought…"

"…you didn't think. I don't ever want to see you again, get out."

He stood at the outside door watching as she walked to her car. "We'll talk later." She said as she opened her car door.

"Don't bother calling." He slammed the door before returning to check on Karen. "Are you ok?"

"I should be going back to my dorm room." She was near tears.

"Please don't go. I need your help." He stepped forward and took her in his arms and gave her a tender hug. "None of this is your fault. Why don't you use the master bath down the hall to straighten yourself up while I shower?"

"What if Jen comes back?" She asked with deep concern.

"She can't get in, I took her house key."

"She may have a duplicate key?"

"Then use this bathroom to straighten out your hair. I can shower after you finish."

While she fixed her hair Jen called. "Stop being stupid and don't call here again!"

"I take it that was Jennifer on the phone?"

"The stupid girl doesn't have a clue how lucky she is. You could have her arrested for assault."

"Why don't you go ahead and take your shower before the whole day gets away from us, besides you look ridiculous in your underwear."

"Oops I forgot I wasn't dressed, please forgive me. I'll shower and join you in the living room."

"Take clean clothes in the bathroom with you. I'm not leaving outside this door and if Jen returns I'm coming in."

As he showered she considered having him take her back to the dorm but she needed money. "Do I look better now?"

"You do look more presentable. Come along we lost enough time."

"I'll fix myself a bowl of cereal while you question me. Have you eaten this morning?"

"I ate hours ago." His knowledge of the material was vastly improved from the night before. "I'm impressed you did study late last night."

The one short break at lunchtime for a veggie snack was their only break all day. By seven in the evening he and his tutor were starved. "How about we take a longer break this time and go out for a substantial meal?"

Karen remained cautious. "I doubt that is a good idea. Jen will flip out if she finds out we went out to eat together."

"Who cares what that little Tramp thinks she and I are history. She has no say-so over my life. I'll eat with anyone I please, any time I please."

"Couples have disagreements all the time and get back together. She will come to her senses."

"I've already come to my senses, and I'm not taking the stupid little Twit back. She may try trapping me."

"How would she try trapping you?" Karen questioned.

"She keeps telling me I don't need a college degree to start the business I plan to start. Plus she hints at getting married and starting a family. She isn't the marrying type. Enough about her, do we go out or do we bring food in?"

"Going out would be fantastic. I haven't been out on a date all year."

"This wouldn't be a real date. It would be more like eating out with a friend."

"Dinner with a friend of the opposite gender is a date." Karen nodded to accent her statement. "I seldom get a chance to date. I count everything.

"Alright, you win we'll have a dinner date." Together they started for the car. "Oh wait, I forgot something." Using his right index finger he tilted her face up enough he give her a quick kiss causing her to step back. "I always kiss my dates when I pick them up."

She shook her head. "You are..."

"I'm what, good, amazing, creative, or wonderful tell me girl?"

"You are so full of surprises, I have no idea if you are nice or not. Honestly I haven't figured you out."

"That's because you kept me studying all day. Did you enjoy my kiss?"

"You caught me off guard and surprised me. How can I judge a kiss like that?" Her smile gave her approval.

"Then I didn't kiss you proper." He promptly gave her a second kiss. A kiss she didn't pull away from. "If I need more help in the future would you be willing to help me again, with my studies I mean."

"I can always use extra money. Long as I remain in college I would be willing to help you study." As they ate, little personal information was revealed by either. "Thank you for a wonderful dinner. We should be returning to the house for more studying."

As they stepped from the car she paused. "This is the end of our dinner date. Beyond that door it's all study and no play."

"Then I better give you a goodnight kiss here. When a date goes well a goodnight kiss is in order. I think our date went fine." He gave her a passionate kiss before going back to his studies.

Inside she was quick to point out he no longer needed her help. "You know the material well enough to score high on your finals."

"I'm not confident as you are. I believe you are forgetting our agreement. You are supposed to help me study all weekend. We can call an end to our studying for the night if you want. Tomorrow I would like for you to continue firing questions at me out of sequence. Give me a real test of my knowledge. I'll study on my own again this evening, if I can keep your notes one more night?"

"You may keep my notes if you give me a lift back to my dorm?"

"You should take my car so I'll have extra study time."

"You mean sleep time. If you remember, my taking your car last night didn't work out real well."

"My car had nothing to do with anything. A bitch in blue jeans and puffy pink top caused the disturbance this morning."

"Alright, I'll take your car but please try to be up and dressed, when I arrive in the morning."

"I'll be up and dressed but don't be afraid to wake me if I'm not."

Sunday morning Brad's alarm rattled him awake at nine. He quickly showered dressed before eating a bowl of cereal. Then an idea flashed in his brain. He slipped back to his room to make his bed look as though someone were still in it. He worked in the electronics room while waiting for Karen to arrive. Hearing the car enter the garage he went back to his bedroom and hid behind the door. As expected she walked cautiously through the house calling out his name. She peeked into the bedroom and saw the phony lumps in the bed. "Darn you, you promised to be up! Brad get up, we have studying to do. You can't stay in bed all day and pass your classes!"

She stepped over to the bed and gave the lump a big shove only to wind up flat on her face crosswise on his bed. "Looking for someone?"

"You idiot, help me up." She said with a smile.

He extended one hand to help Karen to her feet. "Easy girl only yesterday you said I was getting smarter, and now you are calling me an idiot."

"How long have you been awake this morning?"

"I've been up a long time, well over an hour."

"You waited an hour to pull a prank on me. I hope it was worth it?"

"Come on girl we have studies. If you don't get out of that bed we will never get my studying finished."

"I can see the devil lurking in your eyes today. Maybe it would be safer for me to go home before something else unusual happens."

"Please don't go home, I need your help. I'm back-sliding. Yesterday you said I was getting smarter, and this morning you called me an idiot. Seems to me that would mean I need more help."

"Then let's go to the dining room, we are wasting valuable time. I'll follow you because I'm not taking my eyes of you for a second"

Sitting at the dining room table she fired question after question at him. Each time he answered correctly. "You learned a lot in a short time."

"You get the credit for teaching me. I learned because of you and your wonderful notes." He reached out and patted her back with one hand.

"Brad, you mentioned starting a business. When you do start your business will you be hiring many employees?" He smiled at her. "I could use a challenging job. I would be willing to work in any position you need. My computer skills are excellent."

"Judging from your notes I used you have a good resume. No doubt you would make a fine employee. I will most definitely keep you in mind."

As if it was a repeat of Saturday the study session went well. Not once was she able to trip him up. "We may as well stop studying because you know the material. You should do well on your finals. Considering I've done my job would you mind running me back to my dorm. I could use a few extra hours rest before starting my next week."

He took his time driving her back to the dorm. "Here is your check for the amount we agreed upon plus a little bonus."

"This is way too much, I didn't earn half this."

"Don't be silly girl you earned every cent. I now feel I will pass my classes and salvage my class credits. Don't be surprised if I need you again near the end of our next quarter."

"If I'm available, I would consider helping you again."

"After our quarter break would you like to go out and see a movie together?" His question surprised her. "I haven't gone out to a movie is ages, probably six or eight months. What do you say?"

"Going out to a movie sounds wonderful. Seldom do I get the opportunity to go on a date anywhere. You know where to find me. Thank you very much for my bonus. You are more than generous."

"I appreciate you helping me and the chance to know you better."

CHAPTER 4

On Thursday Dirk Owens stopped Brad in the hall. "Hey buddy I hear Karen helped you study this weekend. She helped me last quarter. Too bad what's happening to her?"

Dirk's words shocked him as he feared Jennifer had done something to her. "What are you talking about, did something happen to Karen?"

"She has some type of family emergency. From what I hear she is planning to leave college immediately and go home. Isn't that a bummer?"

"Are you serious?" He questioned. "She is actually considering leaving college immediately?"

"I heard Ben, Joe and Judy talking about her leaving. Judy lives in the dorm with Karen so she should know."

He started to go find Karen to get her slant on what was happening when Jen grabbed him by the arm interrupting him. "We need to talk."

"Like hell we need to talk. Go find another guy to bully. I told you we are through. I do not want anything to do with you anymore."

He jogged across campus to Karen's dorm building. He spotted her sitting under a tree out front of the dorm building. "Hi Kiddo, are you okay?" She failed to answer him. "Your pretty eyes are puffy, have you been crying?" Again she failed to respond. "Dirk tells me you may be leaving school soon."

"My dad has been injured in an industrial accident. He won't be working for a very long time if ever again. I'm going home and get a job to help support our family."

"Why would you go now when you have only two weeks until the end of the quarter, you may want to continue your college classes someday."

"I hear what you are saying, but my father has been injured. I'm anxious to see him, and of course mother is asking me to help out financially."

"Do you know how bad your father injuries are?"

"Mother told me he was bad, and can't be left alone. She is caring for him at home leaving their only income as State Industrial Insurance.

The L&I money won't replace their income. Financially my parents are in deep trouble."

"I'm sorry your father was injured, but to give up your quarter grades doesn't make any sense. If your father is well enough to be cared for at home, you need to stay here your last two weeks and get these credits. Where do your parents live?"

"My parents recently moved to Las Vegas so my father could work construction in the area. He expected to make good money for a long time working in Vegas. There are always massive construction projects going on in Vegas, and now he can't work. I'm getting on a bus, and going to Vegas late Friday. I can't stay here long enough to salvage my class credits."

"How about I take you out for dinner tonight, and discuss your situation while we eat."

"Dinner would be nice, but I wouldn't be very good company."

"Let me be the judge of the company I choose. Be a good girl and scoot inside and get ready. I'll be back, and pick you up in one hour. Ditch your scraggly jeans we'll go somewhere special."

He returned in an hour to her dorm door wearing one of his golf shirts and a pair slacks. Marie, Karen's second roommate answered the door. "Hi, you must be Brad. Karen has been talking about you. She is down the hall getting ready. This is Judy our other roommate."

"Nice to meet you ladies, Karen told me she had roommates but didn't give your names or tell me how nice looking you girls are."

"Karen is in a funky mood worrying about her father. She may not be the best of company this evening." Marie warned.

"She saved my buns tutoring me. I feel it only fair to see if there is any way I might help her. She needs to finish her finals. Giving up those credits makes no sense. Her father is in no danger of dying if he is being cared for at home."

"You look sharp tonight. If Karen doesn't show up soon I may go out with you myself." Marie stated with a sexy smile. "I haven't been out to see a movie in a theater all year."

Karen came walking up behind him. "Hey, I heard that." She eyed him from top to bottom. "Marie is right you do clean up well." She fully expected a kiss from him, a kiss the girls could watch. With his mind wound tight he failed to kiss her. In the car was the second place she expected he might kiss her, again the opportunity slipped past.

"I've been trying to think of something I can do to help you. With my limited knowledge, I'm at a loss as to how I might be of help to you or parents. What I need is a crash course in you and your family's history."

"Why are you asking about my family, you are not responsible for my family."

"Oh come now girl, talk to me. When I needed help you helped me. There must be something I can do. You need to salvage your quarterly grades. Tell me about your family."

"First off my parents are the worst possible money managers ever. I doubt anyone can help them. Being in a financial mess is nothing new for them."

"If you will permit me to accompany you to Vegas I would love to meet your parents. We can fly down together after our finals."

"You must be joking I don't have money for a plane ticket. I bought a bus ticket, and sent the rest of the money you gave me to my parents."

"I'll buy your plane tickets, if you don't mind me tagging along to meet your parents. If I were to go with you, would you be against me encouraging your parents to reveal their complete financial picture to us?"

"My parents won't tell you anything about their financial situation unless you hold a gun to their heads. They would down play the trouble they are in."

"I've developed a unique technique to nudge people to my way of thinking. With your permission I could use my skills to gain information from your parents." She didn't appear to believe anything he was saying. "Damn it, I don't think you believe me."

"Until four days ago we were strangers. I don't know you well enough to believe everything you are saying. "

"Dang girl, you are making things difficult. Could you come over to my home tomorrow night for a live demonstration?"

"How long would this so call demonstration take?"

"Three hours maybe, I've never timed an experiment. Then again each experiment is different. I work my experiments from the bottom up. Increase the intensity ever so gradual. My technique is so new I must be careful and not rush my research."

"Your words are sounding wacky. I will come over to your house. If you are just clowning around I will be furious at you."

"Now that you agreed to come over we need two people for test subjects. Your parents are two people so I need two test subjects. Can you find someone to be my test subjects?"

"Maybe, can we use Marie and Judy my roommates as test subjects?"

"Your roommates are fine by me if you don't tell them what we are doing. Tell them we are having a going away pizza party for you. Call the girls and see if they are free tomorrow evening. I hate to rush you, but we are so short on time. We do this tomorrow night or we don't do it."

"Before I call the girls I have one question. Will the girls be in any danger?"

"They will be in no danger what-so-ever. We can have them do something unusual while you and I won't be affected by my demonstration. All you have to do is convince the girls to come over to my house."

He waited nervously as she spoke to the girls. After ending her call she slowly turned to him. "Okay, you have your test subjects. I'm still not sure I believe anything you are saying."

"Perfect, now tell me something about each of the girls. I need to know a little about their character so I can temporarily change their way of doing something."

"Marie the taller blonde girl is very feisty and out going while Judy is shy. Although both girls are nice they are different as day and night. Marie doesn't date anyone regular. She hints at the fun she has dating, but doesn't give any details. She loves yogurt, hates peanut butter, and like many girls she loves her chocolate. Judy, the shorter blonde hasn't dated for a very long time that I know of, and she never says one word about the guys she dates. Her mainstay food is Rice-a-Roni and she also loves chocolate."

"I need more information than you are giving me, how do the girls dress when they go out?"

"These are not wild girls, they dress conservative, blouse and jeans most of the time. We trade blouses to make it appear we have more clothes than we do."

"Do Marie and Judy like beer with their pizza?"

"The girls do like beer with their pizza, but being a school night they wouldn't drink more than a couple beers because both girls are serious students."

"Now we are getting somewhere, If I'm going to impress you I need to cut this evening short so I can get busy setting up my experiments."

Karen gave him a cute smile. "Am I to assume by your excitement you are no longer mad at me?"

He gave her a look of surprise. "Don't be silly, I'm not mad at you."

He dropped her off at the dorm and sped away without kissing her once all evening. She immediately called his cell phone as he drove away. "Hi, I called to apologize for upsetting you this evening."

"I just told you, I'm not upset. I'm fine."

"You are not acting fine, you didn't kiss me goodnight. In fact you didn't kiss me once all evening. I naturally assumed you were upset about something."

"Oh good heavens, please forgive me my mind was occupied elsewhere. Don't go to bed yet, I'm coming back to kiss you good night."

The girls were quick to question her. "What was that all about, did you and Brad have a disagreement tonight?"

"We had a slight disagreement. I found what he was saying hard to believe. My being reluctant to believe him he grew testy. He offered me a plane ticket to Vegas, and I don't want him mad at me until I get home. The jerk can trip out all he wants after I'm in Vegas. He is one strange guy. I can't figure where he is coming from."

"If Brad is such a strange guy maybe we shouldn't go have pizza at his house tomorrow night."

"He invited me over to his house tomorrow night, and if I don't go I could lose my airplane ticket. I have to go, and I don't want to be alone with him upset at me. I need you girls to be there so please don't chicken out on me. Please, pretty please?"

His knock on the dorm door interrupted the girl's conversation. As she opened the door he promptly kissed her. "I would love to stand here and kiss you all night, I can't. I have preparations to make for a party I'm giving tomorrow evening." With one last kiss he was gone in the night leaving all three girls looking at one another.

Judy was quick to comment. "I must admit your new friend does seem a bit on the strange side. Rather wound up tonight."

"He is a geek who has money. Wait until you see the house he lives in. You saw the car he drives. I'm using his car to pick you girls up tomorrow night."

The following afternoon while riding the bus back to the house, she questioned him about his experiments. "I'm doing a couple simple experiments at first. If my simple experiments go well, I may move on to something more complicated. The simple experiments will be for Marie to rub her left elbow as though it aches and Judy will tug at her left ear, these will be gentle settle movements. If you see something you don't like give me a signal of some kind to stop my experiment."

"I'm nervous but I'm beginning to think you may actually have something. Level with me, are you planning to hypnotize the girls?"

"Heavens no, I've never hypnotized anyone in my life. Pretty easy to see how you would look in that direction. You are a tough cookie. You ran a red flag in front of this bull, I'm about to charge. Tonight will be shock and awe time for you. You challenged me and I'm moving forward. Tonight you will see a sample of my future."

"What if I told you to stop now?"

"I would be very upset." He walked into the house and picked up the car keys, and slammed them on the table near her. Do you go get the girls, or do you want a ride back to the dorm?"

"Calm down, I'll go get the girls. Please let caution be your guide, these girls are friends of mine."

CHAPTER 5

An hour later Karen returned with Marie and Judy. "Wow, you weren't kidding this is a huge house. This is almost a mansion." Marie exclaimed.

Brad opened the door to greet them. "Welcome ladies you look lovely this evening and please make yourselves at home. Feel free to tour my home while I pick out some mood music?"

By the time the girls completed their tour they were influenced by the first experiments. Marie massaged her elbow and Judy pulled her left ear. The look on Karen's face was priceless. "What a beautiful house you have." Marie was in ah of everything. "Karen said you live here alone. Do you mind my asking where your parents are?"

He smiled. "I didn't kill my parents if that is what you want to know. My parents live in Mexico. I seldom see or hear from them. This music I chose sucks. Keep an ear out for the pizza delivery guy while I change the music."

While he started additional experiments the girls chatted about the house. "This house is a hundred dorm rooms in size." Marie pointed at the Jacuzzi. "The Jacuzzi interests me. I would think a thirty minute soak before bed would relax a person enough to get a good night of sleep."

"The Jacuzzi is nice and there is a hot tub out back." Judy added as she giggled. "This house has everything a playboy mansion would have."

He returned to point at the cupboard behind the girls. "Grab some plates from the cupboard behind you. I hear the delivery guy out front. Salad and dressings are in the refrigerator. Someone needs to get the beer out. We can't have pizza without beer."

As they proceeded to eat the two girls rejected the beer and asked for milk. "You girls don't drink milk." Karen protested. "Milk isn't good for your complexion."

"For some reason milk sounds better than beer this evening." Marie insisted.

He patted Karen's arm. "It's okay I have plenty of milk in the refrigerator."

Both girls simultaneously kicked off their shoes and popped open the top buttons on their blouses. "It's rather warm in here." Their actions concerned Karen.

"I'll set the thermostat behind you down a couple degrees, drink a cold beer and cool off." He offered.

"I'll pass on the beer." Marie restated.

"I don't have a pool or you girls could cool off after you eat."

"You have a hot tub. How often do you use your hot tub?" Judy inquired.

"These days I seldom use the hot tub. Hot tubing alone is not a lot of fun and I seldom have guests to my house. A party like this is really unusual."

"Have you and Karen skinny dipped in your hot tub?"

"I just told you I haven't been in my hot tub for months. She was here tutoring me on the weekend. We were not fooling around."

"Is he telling us the truth?" Marie wasn't certain about his answer.

"I've never been in any hot tub, let along Brad's hot tub." She declared.

Marie turned towards Brad again. "This is an ideal bachelor pad. Just by bringing a girl here you could impress, and bed, any girl you wanted."

Karen's eyes grew huge as Judy began to speak. "If I had a boyfriend who had a set up like this and he didn't allow us to take advantage of the facilities. I would feel unloved and dump the creep. With all this security around the place a girl could walk around nude all day and never fear anyone seeing her except the guy she wanted to see her. I bet the backyard is also secure."

Marie nodded in agreement. "I looked around while we were out there. I would skinny-dip or sunbathe in the nude on warm days."

He turned to Karen. "What gives with these girls you told me they were shy. They sound anything but shy to me?"

Judy piped in with her comments. "I'm with you Marie. I feel a certain comfort in this house. It's like a private fortress. What girl wouldn't love this place?"

The girls stood and begin dancing to the music. He slipped Karen a list of the experiments and the expected results as he went to the kitchen. After scanning the list she motioned for him to join her in the kitchen. "You can forget the girls skinny dipping. This is not going to happen."

"Then why are we in the kitchen? I showed you where the master shut off switch was the other day or you could have asked me to stop the music. If you wanted to stop the experiments why bring me to the kitchen area?"

She pushed his shoulder. "Why are you snickering at me?"

"You said you wanted the experiment off, yet you are making no effort to end my message."

"What were you planning to do while the girls were skinny dipping?"

"Clean up and do the dishes, same as I'm doing now."

"Wrong, go stop the experiment before you start cleaning up. I'll go check on the girls."

He caught her arm as she started away. "You may as well take some towels out with you while checking on the girls. You might also want to take a towel for yourself in case you decide to join them."

"Oh please don't tell me the experiment going on me now?"

"I gave you the list didn't you read the list?" He paused to study her face. "You had plenty of time to read everything and stop the message. You choose to follow me to the kitchen area instead."

"I'm not a weak person. I know what you are trying to do, your message won't work on me." She stomped off to find the girls.

He finished cleaning the kitchen before stopping the message. Some forty minutes later the three girls came inside and joined him. "This has been a fun evening. It's getting late could you giving us a ride to our dorm now?"

Brad automatically looked at Karen. "Yes, the girls talked me into getting in the hot tub with them."

"Then you also joined the fun. I'll grab my keys, and run you gals across town. It's been a fun evening."

"We tossed our damp towels in your washer and started it." Marie stated.

"Thank you Sweetie. When I get back, I can put the towels in the dryer before I turn in for the night."

She was quick to make a comment as they were getting in the car. "If I were Karen, I wouldn't leave this house unless you threw me out."

"The poor girl still has major reservations when it comes to me. I'm not like any guy she has ever known. My actions confuse her. I can't say I blame her for being cautious around me. I've never been a person to make friends easy."

At the dorm building, her roommates hustled inside to allow Karen and Brad a private moment. "Your experiments were impressive. How did you know the girls wouldn't try coaxing you into the hot tub with us?"

"I wasn't the target of our experiment. The message for you was different than the girl's message. Only if you went out to the patio were you encouraged to join the girls. You mentioned how risky my last couple experiments were. I only did those experiments to prove a point to you. My technique in the wrong hands could do an unbelievable amount of harm. Your silence is essential to me. We cannot discuss any of this where people might be around. This particular subliminal message technique is top secret."

"Subliminal messages, I didn't think subliminal messages worked that well. I knew mood music was used to promote relaxation as people shop. Is that a type of subliminal message?"

"I'm not real sure, I wouldn't think so. Special frequencies are the key to my success. I spent years to have limited success. My problem is I don't have enough people for experiments. I thought college would allow me an unlimited supply of test subjects. It's not happening, my experiments are still limited. I need to think beyond what I am now doing."

"There are a lot of people on campus for you to experiment on?"

"Could you get another ten girls to come by in sets of two so I can redo the experiment and fine-tune my power level?"

"No probably not. I don't have an answer for you. Tomorrow is another early class day for me so I better get inside."

"Two things I would like for you to do. Tomorrow ask the girls how they feel about skinny-dipping in my hot tub tonight. Secondly think hard about using my technique on your parents. It would be beneficial to find out how difficult their financial problems really are."

"I hate the thought of you experimenting on my parents."

"You said your parents were lousy money managers. I can change their spending habits. I can make them think before they buy things. Think it over and let me know. Keep in mind I need time to create my messages if I'm to help your parents." He gave her a tender hug.

"I will think about what you said. I don't see how you knowing my parents financial problems can possibly help them."

"I have no idea how much I can help. One thing I know for certain is I need your parent's complete situation, or I may as well stay in Seattle. Do you want to see your parents on welfare?" Karen shook her head no. "Then let me know what you think before its too late. If you really think your parents are better off on welfare you should stay in college."

"I'll give some thought to what you are asking. I can't promise anything but I'll let you know tomorrow."

On Friday Judy and Marie were normal in every way. No regrets from the night before. When it came to Karen's parents they were a different story. She had reservations about Brad influencing them. "Make your messages for my parents. I'll decide later if we use them or not. Are you only taking me to Vegas for the sole purpose of experimenting on my parents?"

"Oh for land sakes girl, how shallow do you think I am?" He shook his head in disgust. "My trip to Vegas has several things of interest for me. Vegas might be an excellent city for my type of experiments. I may get a chance to look over several businesses to advertise for someday. Eventually I'll own an advertising agency. My advertising agency doesn't have to be limited to Seattle. This is the electronic age I can base myself in Seattle, and do business anywhere in the world. I read in several papers and magazines that the city of Vegas is the fastest growing city in the nation. Advertising potential in Vegas should be unlimited."

"I'll take you at your word. We can go to Vegas together. I'm still not looking forward to you giving my parents one of your messages. Using your subliminal experiments on my parents is questionable. They have started bankruptcy proceedings so I don't see how you can't help them now?" She kept shaking her head no.

"Standing here in Seattle there is nothing I can do about their situation. In Vegas seeing a clear picture of their financial mess, we may be able to help. Even going bankrupt they still need help changing their spending habits."

"You have a valid point, their money management skills leave a lot to be desired. What you are asking upsets my stomach. My roommates are young silly girls. Embarrassing them would be different than embarrassing my parents."

"What are you talking about, I didn't embarrass the girls. I don't understand your concerns. How could I possibly damage anyone encouraging them to think before making a financial decision?"

"Alright, go ahead and use any message you want on my parents. Please let caution be your guide." She requested.

"I'll be leaving class early today to go home and make additional subliminal messages. I'll call you before I head over to pick you up."

Even being without female companionship since he dumped Jennifer, he and Karen had many distractions surrounding their relationship making frequent kisses between them, a thing of the past. Running out of time he needed to accelerate their struggling relationship. He saw no reason not to piggyback a message for her along with her parent's message. Her message was to be more receptive to his attention. Leaving his house he called Karen. "I'm on my way to pick you up." Excitement began to grow as Brad thought about the task he was embarking on."

After loading her luggage, Karen glared at him. "You beat anyone I ever saw. It's unbelievable how you twist words around to suit your needs. How is a person supposed to know what to think about you?" She snapped.

"It's not my fault you being a dark-haired beauty is distracting me. No one is responsible for their own actions today. It's your fault I am the way I am."

"I've been noticing a very unusual pattern. You talk like nothing is ever your fault. If this experiment goes bad with my parents, you will blame me."

He ignored her comment. "Are you getting anxious about seeing your parents?" He asked."

"I am anxious to see them, and nervous about my first plane ride. Karen was visibly shaking as she walked through the tunnel to board their flight. "These are our seats right here, I bought first class seats so we would be comfortable flying. By the way I've never flown before either. My parents fly around a lot."

As other passengers filled past them, she became extremely uncomfortable. The passenger to her left smiled as he reached up turning on the overhead air for her. "There you go, now relax and breathe deep. You will be fine."

"Thank you sir the air does help my breathing." She turned back to face Brad. "Why did you spend the money for first class these seats?"

"I'm sure my parents fly first class. Either that or my father has his own airplane." During takeoff they held hands so tight their knuckles turned white. "Here we go Kiddo, off to Vegas."

CHAPTER 6

Their flight from Seattle to Vegas was straight through. Two and a half hours later they were on the ground being met by Kathy Moore, Karen's mother. "Hi Honey!"

After exchanging hugs, Karen introduced Brad to her mother. "Hello Mrs. Moore it's a pleasure to meet you." Her mother looked young enough to be a sister. Seeing the mother came as a pleasant surprise. Brad smiled as he studied her youthful looks.

"How is daddy doing?"

"Your father is about the same. Our neighbor Mrs. Curly is staying with your father until we get home. How was your flight?"

"Smooth as glass, I worried over nothing. During takeoff, I almost choked the life out of Brad's hand. Later, I felt foolish."

He continued to study Mrs. Moore as he shook his head. "This was my first flight too." He looked around all directions. "Any idea where the car rental places might be?"

"Why would you rent a car, you can use our car if you need to go somewhere. For you to rent a car would be silly."

"I've never been in Vegas before. I may run around quite a bit while I'm in here. You may need your car to run your husband to a doctor's appointment, or an unforeseen emergency of some kind. I really should get a rental car. One never knows something unforeseen could happen to Vernon where you might need your car."

"Renting a car might be best. Let's see rental car shuttle bus is down this way. The bus will take you to the car rental area, and we'll meet you out front so you can follow us to the house."

Naturally Vernon Moore was thrilled to see his daughter, and meet the guy she brought home. Brad studied Vernon's face, as he tried to figure out how intense the man's pain might be. Being weathered, his face was difficult to read. He appeared to be sixty years old. Compared to Kathy's youthful looks, they were different as night and day. She was nothing short of a beautiful woman who looked to be in her mid-thirties at the most. The Moore's age difference confused Brad. Kathy and Karen looked more like sisters than mother-daughter. Mrs. Moore must have been extremely young when her daughter was born, he thought.

He wondered how good Kathy's business skills might be. One could easily see the Moore's were people in need of money, and Brad was a man in need of people. Was there a way he could help these people, and use them, without exploiting them? Many thoughts rumbled around in his head.

"Mrs. Moore caught him studying the house. "We bought this house as a fixer-upper. Our plans went astray when Vern became injured."

"I wasn't looking at the condition of the house so much as where a stereo system could be set up. I don't know if Karen told you or not, she and I are both business majors. I'll be finishing my third year of college this year. In our studies we learned mood music is often used to help people relax, and become comfortable in many situations. Office buildings, grocery stores, bars, hospital rooms, you name it, music is involved. Movies are a great example. The music helps enhance the emotion the director wants the viewer to feel. I have no reason not to believe soft music could help soothe part of Vernon's pain."

Kathy appeared to be interested in his phony theory. "You could be right I've never given any thought to why music was played in so many places."

A dear friend of mine was injured in a motorcycle accident. The hospital played music twenty four-seven for him, while he was in a coma. Doctors claimed while he was sleeping, the music kept his mind activated, so his heart would pump more blood through his entire body. Better circulation helps promote healing. I'm not a medical person, but if I get injured somebody better whip some music on me real fast. I want every benefit any medical person can give me. I don't like pain any better than anyone else."

"We don't have a stereo system, and we can't afford a stereo system. It's a moot point if music helps or not." Kathy stated.

"Stereos come in all size and shapes. A small portable stereo could be transported from room to room as needed. The music could play out here in the daytime and in Vern's room at night. For less than a hundred dollars, I could buy a portable stereo."

Mrs. Moore shook her head. "You brought our daughter home. We can't ask you to buy anything for us."

"You didn't ask, I offered to buy you a boom-box."

Kathy turned to her husband. "What do you think Vern, should we allow him to buy you a small stereo or not?"

"Honey if music would help relieve one percent of my pain. I would try music in a second. The last half hour before my next pain pill is rough." His face displayed his pain.

"Then it's settled I'll go scout around for a stereo. I could use some direction though, is there a discount store or something near this area?"

"Drive back the way we came to the house. At the first light turn right. Two miles on your left is a discount store. They have a huge sign out front."

"Wish me luck and I will go see if I can find the store and get myself a motel room for the night."

"You don't need a motel room we have three bedrooms. You are welcome to stay here at the house. You were kind enough to bring our daughter home. The least we can do is offer a bed for your stay in Vegas."

"You don't owe me anything. I needed a vacation, and I've never been in Vegas. It's I who owes your daughter. She kept me from being a college dropout. Her tutoring salvaged my grades. I won't be gone long."

"Let me give you our phone number and address in case you get lost. I would go with you except I want to stay and talk to mom and dad."

With Brad on his way to find the portable CD player he needed for his experiment. Kathy pulled Karen into the kitchen, where she could whisper to her daughter without her husband hearing. "Are you getting close to this wealthy young man like I suggested?"

"Mother, I can't throw myself at Brad the way you want. I barely know him. He is far different than anyone I ever knew before."

"You told us this young man has money. Look around you girl your father and I need money for his care. You have been at his house when you were studying together. Why didn't you turn on your womanly charms and bed him then. How hard can it be to bed a healthy college guy?"

"Brad is a nice guy, and I don't think we should con money out of him."

"If you ratcheted up your affection and marry this wealthy lad. Taking money from him wouldn't be a con. If your marriage didn't work out who cares, you would get a nice settlement. How will your father and I survive without money?"

"If I married Brad under false pretenses, I would still be conning him.

It takes time for love to develop."

"If this young man has the money you think he does. He won't miss the small amount we need. Get busy and use your womanly charm. You and he look like strangers, change that. Get Brad in bed with you."

Brad returned with the stereo to start his subliminal message for the Moore's. "There you go Vern now you are all set. I'm exhausted can somebody point me towards where I will be sleeping tonight?"

Kathy showed him to his room as Karen tagged along. "Make yourself at home. Bathroom is the next-door there."

"Thank you Mrs. Moore. Tired as I am I'll sleep like a baby."

"Please call me Kathy. We hope you do sleep well."

"Alright Kathy, I'll see you and Karen in the morning." Kathy scooted on out while Karen remained. "Is the other bedroom we passed in the hall your bedroom?"

"Yes I have a small twin bed." She stepped up next to him giving him the impression she wanted a kiss. He misread her intentions. She leaned away as he tilted his head towards her. She simply whispered in his ear. "Go ahead with your subliminal messages."

"Thank you Karen, you won't be sorry. What's the deal with your mother, she is quite a surprise her being so young?"

"Kathy is my birth mother's younger sister. When mother died she came for the funeral and stayed to care for me. She and my father married two years later."

"Now things are making sense, she is your stepmother. It is absolutely amazing how the two of you look so much alike"

He put one arm around her to give her a kiss, but again Karen pulled away. "Not here, mother might catch us."

Her total rejection caught him by surprise. He now thought about the message he made, part of the message was for her. Obviously the message wasn't strong enough to over ride the emotion she displayed. Doing without hugs and kisses is something he never anticipated. He had two choices, go back to Seattle and stay there, or go back to Seattle and make stronger subliminal message before returning. "Dang it Karen, I have to return to Seattle tonight."

"Why would you return to Seattle tonight, can't this wait until tomorrow?"

"I left a computer in the wrong mode. I can sleep on a plane tonight. If this wasn't important I wouldn't return to Seattle tonight."

Kathy was hoping by now Karen was slipping in bed with him. Her thought vanished when she heard the front door open and close. She quickly went to investigate. "What is going on?"

Karen faced her mother with a blank look of disbelief. "Brad left, he is returning to Seattle tonight. I upset him. He claimed he left one of his computers in the wrong mode. He is a meticulous person when it comes to his computers. He did not leave a computer in the wrong mode. I have no idea why he left."

"Do you know if he is coming back?" Karen shrugged her shoulders. "What the hell did you do to upset him?"

"He wanted a goodnight kiss, I backed away."

"How stupid can you be, didn't I make myself clear when I told you to get the boy in bed with you? It could have happened with a kiss." Kathy shook her head. "That young man could have been our meal ticket. Men love affection. I should have gotten in bed with Brad. You are going to let your father and I become Wards of the State. You are old enough to be in a sexual relationship. Why wait and get in a relationship with some poor clown that doesn't have two dimes to rub together?"

Karen shook her head. "Mother, I can't do what you are asking. I'm not a slut."

"Brad and his money are begging to be had. Oh get real, nice girls love sex too. You need to relax and enjoy life more."

"I don't know him well enough to know if he is the right man for me or not. I'm sorry, I couldn't do what you wanted me to do."

"Get some sleep, there is nothing we can do now, he is gone. Come morning we can tell your father Brad was called away on business."

Brad's clock chimed four A.M. when he entered his house. He went straight to his electronics room. During his flight back to Seattle he made the decision to remake his subliminal messages for the Moores. This decision was based on his quick assessment in Vegas. Seeing the hustle and bustle in Vegas made the city look to be a perfect place to expand his experiments. He raised the intensity level double on these messages. He now felt confident he could get Vernon and Kathy to spill their guts about their financial situation. He piggybacked stronger affection message for Karen. His body quivered from lack of sleep. Returning to the airport he had to lower both car windows for fresh air to keep awake as he drove.

Near ten A.M. he pulled into the Moore's driveway. "Mother, Brad came back." Karen flew out the door to greet him. "Did you get any sleep?"

"I tried to sleep some on the plane." He rubbed his tired eyes.

"Were you able to accomplish what you wanted to do in Seattle?"

"I certainly hope so, time will tell."

"Daddy woke a few minutes ago and mother is helping him shower now. She will be fixing omelets for breakfast this morning, will you eat with us?"

"I'm all for breakfast, move your father's boom-box out to the living room so I can put on the new music for him. I believe this CD will work better."

Kathy came walking through, seeing Brad she acted surprised. "Good morning you came back." She stopped long enough to give him a quick hug. "Breakfast will be ready in a few minutes. Was your quick trip back to Seattle worth going?" Kathy inquired.

"I saved my equipment. My flight to and from Seattle was turbulent making sleeping on the airplane difficult." Karen stepped up behind him and proceeded to massage his tired neck. "If you keep massaging me, I may fall asleep and crash face first in my omelet." By the time he finished eating his eyes were about to close. "Your breakfast was wonderful. If you people will excuse me, I need a nap."

Kathy motioned for Karen to go join him. Following her mother's instructions she tagged along. He stretched out on top of the covers. "You won't rest proper with your clothes on. Remove your clothes and slip under the covers." She leaned over and kissed him. "I'll skip out so you can undress, enjoy your nap." Karen went back to the kitchen. "Where is daddy?"

"Your father is doing his exercises to keep all of his muscles working properly. I'll take him for his therapy later. More importantly what the hell are you doing out here, you should be napping with Brad."

"He looked so tired. I kissed him and told him to get under the covers."

"I can't believe you. Napping after sex is always a better nap."

"I wasn't invited to join him." She responded.

"If you wait for an invitation to join a man in bed you may be living a long lonely life. You'll never have a family of your own, if you don't work at it."

"Since I didn't sleep well, I could use a nap. I'll go see if he wants company."

"Don't ask, slip in bed beside him and be friendly."

Kathy stood in the doorway watching her stepdaughter disappear down the hall. Karen paused at his door to look back. Kathy motioned for her to go in. Only when she stepped inside his bedroom did Kathy feel nature would take its course.

At one o'clock Kathy took Vernon for his therapy. By three they returned to the house. Kathy slipped down the hall to check on the younger ones. As she peeked in, her discovery made her smile with joy.

Near four while Vernon was napping she again went to check on the youngsters a second time, they remained in bed back-to-back sleeping soundly. Kathy slipped around to his side of the bed so she could lean down to touch his shoulder as she whispered to him. "Are you planning to sleep all day?"

He squinted up at her, thinking it was Karen waking him he put both arms up around her neck and drew her down for a kiss. Only then did he totally open his eyes. "Oh shit, I thought you were…I'm sorry."

She quickly placed a hand across his mouth. "It was an honest mistake." She whispered. "It's our little secret, now you wake her." She pointed beside him. With a quick glance over his shoulder he saw Karen lying beside him. "Wait until I'm out of the room to wake her."

Still in a daze he looked back and forth between both gals as Kathy quietly slipped from the room. Being caught in bed with a girl by her mother was bad. Then he noticed her clothes on the nightstand beside the bed. Chaos reigned in his mind. He grabbed his clothes before dashing for the shower.

After showering and dressing he went straight to the kitchen to apologize to Mrs. Moore. His apology plans was short lived. Vernon, Kathy and Karen were all waiting for him. Kathy broke the silent moment. "When you darted out last night you scared us. We racked our brains trying to figure out how we insulted you."

"It wasn't you. I screwed up by forgetting to turn all my electronic equipment off when I left Seattle. Thankfully I did get back to Seattle in time to salvage my equipment."

"We are pleased you returned. If you are hungry, sit down have some cold cuts with us."

"Maybe I could use a bite to eat. There is no easy way to say what I am about to say, so I'm going to dive right in. Karen told me why she was coming home. She said with Vernon laid up and you having to care for him full-time, you were having financial difficulties to the point of filing bankruptcy."

Vernon gave him a sad look. "The girl talks too much. We were struggling when I was working. We moved to Vegas so I could get a higher paying job."

"Bankruptcy could be the wrong decision. Karen and I have taken several business classes. If we knew your entire financial situation we may have a few alternative ideas, other than bankruptcy."

"Our bankruptcy was a gut wrenching decision. Our first thought was to sue the company I was working for, to collect for my injuries. That plan was short lived. The company folded three days after I was injured. There is nothing left to sue. Bankruptcy is our only way out of our financial mess."

"Mr. Moore, I'm not saying you are wrong. You may very well be correct but talking never hurts."

"Karen told us you come from money. I doubt you can truly understand our desperate situation. Bankruptcy is our only way out of debt."

"I am a caring person. I see no harm in discussing your financial situation."

Vernon glared at him. "Okay, we are down to our last eight thousand dollars and we have forty-five thousand dollars worth of bills plus the house payment."

"Forty-five thousand is not a lot of money."

"We are unemployed. Forty-five thousand is an enormous sun. If we continue to drag our feet, interest will compound our money worries."

"A new dual cab pickup would cost more than forty-five thousand dollars. I'm telling you forty-five thousand dollars of debt, is next to nothing. Did you talk to anyone about restructuring your debt load?'

"We spoke to our banker and two mortgage firms. They turned us down. We may lose our home. I will get three hundred sixty dollars a week equaling fifteen hundred dollars a month from Labor and Industry. Our eight thousand dollar saving is shrinking fast."

"If I were in your situation I wouldn't discount restructuring my bills quite so fast. Banks are not the only lending intuitions around. I have a few ideas kicking around in my head. I need to think these ideas over very carefully, and put a pencil to them. We can talk again tomorrow."

"I don't see any reason to continue discussing our financial situation. It won't do any good."

Brad turned and looked at Karen. "I need to go stretch my legs, would you care to join me on a sight seeing tour of the famous Las Vegas Strip?"

"I would be happy to join you for a tour of the Vegas Strip. Mother, how cool will it get in Vegas this evening?"

"You won't need a sweater."

Brad ran a hand across his face. "I'll go shave and be ready in two minutes."

With Brad out of the room Vernon leaned over towards his daughter. "Your boyfriend is trying to play Mr. Big-Shot, and score points with you, be careful Honey."

"Daddy I haven't the slightest idea what Brad's thoughts are. I can tell he is thinking hard about something. I promise I will be very cautious."

CHAPTER 7

Brad and Karen drove off supposedly to see the Las Vegas sights. "Karen explained how depressed her parents became when he flew back to Seattle so suddenly."

"I was depressed when I left. I wasn't sure you or they wanted me around at all. The only thing I could do was to clear out so I had time to think."

"I feel funny kissing you in my parent's house. I too was sad to see you go and happy to see you return."

"Seeing your parents was a shock. Their age difference alone threw me for a loop. Financial problems often lead to divorce. We learned that in class if you remember. One reason I returned to Seattle was my subliminal messages were too weak."

"The fact my parents told you anything at all about their financial situation surprised me. I can't help but think your message is getting through to them."

"Tonight we needed to get out of the house for two reasons. One being they need to talk among themselves. When we talk again tomorrow there shouldn't be any additional bills we don't know about. If what they said so far is correct, filing bankrupt is wrong. My second reason for wanting us out of the house is we need a quiet place to talk. Would you object if I rented a motel room?"

"Are you asking to get a motel room for business, or pleasure?"

He could read Karen's questioning mind. "I assure you at this time my thoughts are all business." Apparently his subliminal message for her remained too weak. He failed to calculate she had been in the bedroom napping with him, and not out where she could be influenced by his special message. "Believe me what I have to offer you is more important right now, than trying to get you in my bed."

"You need to enlighten me. I didn't realize anything was more important to a young man than getting a young woman in bed?"

"Give me a break. I'm talking about everyone, you, me, and your parents. Intimacy is a different deal all together. If sex is ever to be a factor between us it will happen much later."

"I don't understand. Why are you concerned at all about my parents or me?"

"If we keep driving around and talking I may wind up running into another car. We need a quiet place to sit down and talk. Somewhere we can't be disturbed."

"Get a motel room, but don't expect special favors from me tonight."

Brad made arrangements for a room at a small older motel. He began making coffee soon as he entered the room. She walked around the beds punching them for firmness. "These beds are hard as a brick."

"Doesn't matter, we won't be using either bed. Sit down at the table. I'll join you in a second." She sat quietly as he finished starting the coffee. "Your parents may be just the people I need for more subliminal message tests."

"Please don't ask me to allow you to put my parents through a battery of your experiments?" He glared at her. "Alright, go ahead and talk. I'm listening."

Brad poured each a cup of coffee. "My original idea was after I get out of college to start a business, and gear up the subliminal messages experiments at that time. I feel opportunity knocking now. In order to operate the business, and conduct experiments I would need help. Both you and your mother need employment."

"Now you are being totally stupid. Mother's job right now is to care for my father. She can't work anywhere else."

"Hold your thoughts young lady. If your mother could manage my business she would have flexible hours to care for your father. She could easily break away and take your father to his therapy, doctor's appointments, or whatever. You could record the results of the experiments we conducted along with keeping the books, plus cover for your mother when she needed to take your father to the doctor."

"Your plan would leave my father home alone most of the time. He is in no shape to be left home alone at this point. My father needs help to steady himself at times. Getting in bed, getting in the shower, going to the restroom, there is any number of times he needs her help."

Brad shook his head. "You are so quick to discard an idea. Admittedly I do not have all the details worked out. What if your father never gets any better. Do they want to be welfare recipients forever?"

"Of course my parents don't want to be on welfare. They have always been hard working people. Don't you believe he will get better?"

"I have no idea if he will get better. Help me massage my tiny idea into a workable solution for all those concerned. A small business could help with my research and do wonders for your parents."

"Let's approach this from hypothetical point. Do you really think mother could care for my father properly, and manage a business for you?"

"Yes, if we set things up to help her. First and foremost we would need to choose a business she already has experience in. Your mother doesn't have time to retrain for a job. Secondly we would need a business with lots of people capable of generating enough money to pay you, your mother, and myself. If we build a mini-apartment in the back of the business your father could be nearby. My whole idea hinges on you because you are the only person I know well enough to trust to record my subliminal message tests."

Karen thought for a brief second. "Did Jennifer know about your subliminal message experiments?"

He glared at her for asking such a stupid question. "Good heavens no, Jen was an air-head. She only had one good quality. She was adequate as a bed partner. I need a mature person to keep detailed records of my experiments."

She smiled at his assessment. "You can be very persuasive I'm being drawn to your way of thinking. A well-paying position would be great for me."

"Keep in mind our part of the business would be top secret. Your parents must never know about our method of advertising. My system must never escape our control."

"What business and how soon do you need an answer from mother and me?"

"If we were to do this the sooner we choose a business the better. For you this plan would be a win-win situation. This summer you would be helping your parents and while the place was being remodeled to fit our needs we could finish our third year of college."

"What would happen if at some point in the future my parents or I became unhappy working for you? Would we be allowed to leave the business?"

"Slavery was outlawed years ago. Anyone can leave any time they want. If we do our job properly there should be plenty of money to pay wages and quarterly bonuses. Under those conditions what person would want to leave?" He stated with a huge smile.

"Finishing my third year of college could prove valuable in the future. There is always the chance you may become disenchanted with your business and sell out. One problem about finishing my third year of college is I gave up my dorm room."

"That is a small problem. I have plenty of room at my house. You could have a room of your own. You may have another female roommate. Two roommates if you want?"

"My parents might not like my living in your house. Would I need to be leery of your subliminal messages?"

"If I were planning to take advantage of you, I would have tried something this morning when I woke. If you remember I found you in my bed."

"Tell me this, how could you get the financing to start this business? It takes money to start any business."

"I need people, and a business, not money. The people come first, without them my plans are dead. Think about the thousands of subliminal message experiments we could do over the summer. With my experiments out of the way my real business could be started soon as I finished college."

"Alright you convinced me, count me in. Mother will need more details before she gets on board."

"That's the spirit Karen. Now tell me what type of job experience your mother has held in the past."

"Mother has never been anything but a waitress."

Her words shocked him. "Please tell me you are kidding, a waitress."

"Our family moved around a lot chasing the perfect job. Being a waitress was the fastest way for mother to get a job."

"Alright, let's think this through. Your mother knows service, and that's a start. I see no reason why a fast food restaurant wouldn't give us plenty of customers to experiment on. Could your mother manage a fast food restaurant?"

"I may not be the best judge of mother's managing abilities. I better let you be the judge of mother's abilities. The last thing I want to do is miss led you into making a bad decision."

"If she were to falter in any way we could boost her abilities with a special message. It's getting late we better go walk the Strip. I'm sure your parents will ask what we saw on the strip."

As most first time viewers the young couple were in awe of everything they saw, strolling along the Vegas Strip. All the magical lights seemed to bring the night alive as huge crowds filled the streets. Along the Strip the Volcano, the Ships Battling and the Dancing Water Fountains were all impressive. "We passed a small café a minute ago would you care for a late night snack before we go back to the house?"

"A snack would be nice."

Later at the house the young couple found Kathy waiting up for them. Karen seemed surprised. "Mother I'm an adult; you didn't have to wait up for me."

"Oh Honey waiting up for one's daughter is a hard habit to break. Plus I wanted to hear what you two thought of our famous Las Vegas Strip."

"The Strip is nothing short of spectacular Mrs. Moore. I can only imagine the millions and millions of dollars it takes to cover expenses around here each day. Money flows like water in this city. In my estimation Vegas would be the perfect city to start a business. I see opportunity everywhere." He yawned and stretched his arms. "I'm really tired. We can talk about what we saw in the morning."

As he walked down the hall Kathy motioned for her daughter to go with him. She shook her head no. "I can't do what you want me to do, not in father's house."

"I should slap you silly. You have one day before he flies back to Seattle. His desire is to be with you. Don't let our gift horse ride off in the sunset. Your father has fed, clothed and educated you for the last twenty-one years. Now is your time to step up and help him."

"I get the feeling Brad is a controlling person. I don't want to be controlled all my life."

"All men want to be controllers. We have our feminine charm to keep men in check. I give up, I'm going to bed."

Brad stirred at nine but wasn't ready to get up. He lay there wishing he had a good book to read. Having limited choices he eventually did get up and shower before joining the others in the kitchen. "Good morning people, looks to be another beautiful day." He started to give Karen a tiny hug. She moved away to get his coffee.

"Sit down Brad. I'll fix you a waffle." Her mother stated.

"Thank you Kathy, a waffle sounds good."

Karen looked a little sheepish. "I told mom and dad you had some interesting ideas you might be willing to share with them."

"This is a free country. You can say anything you want. I do have a lot of ideas floating around in my head. Ideas I hope become a reality. To make a long story short I want to own an advertising agency someday. There is a lot of money to be made in advertising. My original plan was to start an ad agency after I graduate college. Now it appears I would be better off with a small business where masses of people come and go. These people could be used to do my advertising concept tests on. In other words I would be laying groundwork for my real love, my ad agency. To do this I need employees. Employees I can trust to do their jobs. I have a nod from Karen as she sees value in my ideas. Next I would need a manager for my business. Kathy, the manager's position I would like to offer to you."

"I have a fulltime job caring for Vern." Kathy protested.

"Yes, Vern needs care. If we set things up properly for you, you could manage the business without neglecting your husband. There could be an on-site mini apartment where he could rehab. During therapy or doctor's appointments Karen or I could cover for you in your absence. I see no reason you couldn't be with Vernon much as you are here at the house, and still earn a nice income. Basically you would be checking on people from time to time."

"What would Karen's position be?"

"She will be my office staff and my personal assistant. She would keep our financial records, and record the results of our test ads. She may also make bank deposits for the business. Basically she would be our Jack-of-all-trades. Nothing is set in stone."

Kathy frowned as she thought about his words. "What type of business do you have in mind?"

"Karen tells me you have been a waitress in various places. Managing members of a serving staff shouldn't be a problem for you. You know what it takes to keep customers. Am I assuming too much in thinking you might be interested in improving your financial picture?"

"Fast food managers historically do not make a lot of money."

"I have no idea what fast food managers normally get paid. What we talked about was three thousand dollars a month salary plus quarterly bonus incentives."

"Three thousand a month isn't a bad offer. If I knew for certain I wouldn't be neglecting Vern. I would agree to be your manager in a heartbeat."

"Your answer wasn't the answer I was looking for, but it is an honest answer. Why don't we hunt up a realty person who deals with business property and see what might be available. We may as well start with the phonebook."

Karen searched the Yellow Pages for information on realty firms specializing in business property. "Wow, look at the list of names. How will we ever choose the right realty office?"

"Cross your fingers and dial a number we have to start somewhere. Inquire about fast food restaurants. Burger joints with room to expand."

Vernon held out his hands. "Son you are dreaming high. You don't own any business. You never have owned a business. Don't get yourself in a financial mess trying to impress us."

"I'm not trying to impress anyone. My faith lies in my advertising system. With Karen's help we can double or triple the current business in any establishment. Serving more people means we need more room. Our mini apartment will also require room; room to expand is essential."

Karen covered the phone in her hand before yelling at Brad. "Come here a minute. I have Robin Tilly on the phone. She claims to have what you might be looking for. Do you want to speak with her? Mrs. Tilly sounds very confident on the phone. Should I tell her you will call her back in a few minutes?"

"Set up an appointment for us soon as you can. We can certainly look at what she has to show us." He waited patiently until she was off the phone. "Well Karen, how did you do?"

"You have a twelve o'clock appointment with Robin Tilly. Here is her office address." She handed him her note.

"You and I will make a great team. If I have an appointment you have an appointment. We can meet Robin Tilly together."

Vernon placed one hand on Brad's shoulder. "Listen to me son allow caution to be your guide. Wild hair ideas seldom work. Don't get in over your head."

"Vern, I wish I could convince you to be more positive about your future. In my mind I see you getting better with time. For the sake of argument let's say you never get any better. Some people have no choice but to live with pain. You get around well in your wheel chair. You may at some point want to take orders at the register, if you remain stuck in a wheel chair."

"Me, take food orders setting in a wheel chair?" Vern laughed at his suggestion. "I couldn't reach the register."

"Modifications can be made to any counter." While he was talking to Vernon, Kathy slipped around behind her husband and began massaging his shoulders. "It's time you became a fighter Vernon, you need to take part of your life back. This may be our chance to get our lives back under control."

Karen interrupted the conversation. "It's time we need to leave for our meeting with Robin Tilly. It wouldn't look good if we arrived late for our first appointment late."

"If we can put something together Karen and I can return to Seattle and finish our third year of college while the remodel is being done. Wish us luck and we'll see you two later this afternoon."

CHAPTER 8

While driving to meet Robin Tilly, Brad had a brief second thought about what he was doing. Knowing the reward would be worth the risk, his doubts disappeared fast as they came. Karen finally was showing signs of excitement. With or without Kathy and Vernon he could safely conduct subliminal massages if he had a fast food restaurant.

"You missed Robin's office. You should have turned back there, flip a U-turn. What on earth were you thinking about?"

"I was thinking about all the exciting times ahead of us." He couldn't tell her what his real thoughts were. At the Moore's house he had two subliminal messages playing. Strong messages by any of his previous standards yet the Moore's said nothing about their financial situation on their own. True he hadn't prodded them to say anything.

His second concern was the piggyback message for Karen. She remained nothing more than a friend. The slightest touch on her shoulder she still eased away.

Robin Tilly appeared to be about forty years old, projected the exact image of a typical well-dressed realty agent. She showed them three different properties on the computer. Property number two caught his interest, a run-down restaurant with an adjoining small vacant lot. "Is the small lot for sale?"

"This lot is too small for what you are talking about. Where would you expand?"

"The two properties together might be large enough for our needs. The current building is totally unsuitable. The lot would need to be leveled and a new building would have to go up fast. For our needs the building should be operational in two and a half months." Robin blinked her eyes. "Can it be done?"

His words shocked her. "What you are asking is a tall order."

"I'm aware of the obstacles in our way, so I'm willing to pay for performance. Is there any chance we can do this or do we look for a different location?"

"Excuse me while I make a quick call to a builder I know. He can probably answer your question better than I can." They sat quietly waiting for Robin to return. She returned with her cell phone in one hand. "Is it possible for you to meet the builder at my office in one hour?"

"Certainly, we'll go have a cup of coffee and come back later."

In the car Karen turned to him with a comment. "You may be asking too much too fast. Two and a half months is such a short time frame to be building any business. Houses take longer than two months to build."

Brad thought about his father. Cash money and pressure can accelerate anything. "Keep the faith, we haven't been told no yet."

When Brad met the builder Robin had lined up for them to meet. He busted out laughing. "Are you kidding me Robin, Bob Tilly is your husband?"

"Yes, Bob is my husband and we often work together. He is one of the best builders in the Vegas area for medium-sized construction or remodels. I will stack my husband's work against any and all builders."

"Pardon me if I offended you Robin, I apologize. For some reason Bob being your husband shocked me. If I were a native to the area I probably would have known the name Bob Tilly." He went on to explain his needs and the time frame he was hoping for.

"Mr. Collins do you have blue prints of your building design?"

"No I don't, we have been concentrating on the size of the building more than the design. As I see it our time frame is our real hang up. Down on Fifth Street several blocks is a family restaurant building that looks to be fairly new. I was thinking of a building about that size."

"I know the building. I am very familiar with the building you are talking about but the time frame you are talking about is unrealistic. Mr. Collins even if everything went perfectly financing would eat up half your time frame."

"Financing isn't a problem. My whole project from start to finish is a cash deal." His words put a blank look on Bob, Robin and Karen's faces. "How much will cash speed up a project?"

Bob drew in a deep breath. "A project like you are talking about could run seven hundred thousand dollars. It is unheard of for anyone to do a project like this using private out of pocket cash money. Someone with seven hundred thousand usually puts that kind of money towards a two or three million dollar project and finances the difference."

"I'm not your average man. My project must turn a nice profit instantly.

I can't pay interest to others and make the money I intend to make. This is a test project for future ventures."

"I see, if you are available this evening, we could eat at the family restaurant so I can get a better idea about your building plans?"

"Name the time, we can be available."

"We'll meet at seven. I'll duck in early and look the building over and make a few notes?"

"Excellent, we will meet you at seven this evening."

By seven Bob had the blueprints of the family restaurant. As he and Brad discussed the project. It became apparent the family restaurant building wasn't large enough for the Burger Joint's double drive up espresso lanes, a mini apartment along the back and the large overhead office with one-way glass for observation of all employees.

Robin added her comments. "I was hoping the property we toured this afternoon would work. Using cash we could have lowered our offers on both pieces of property."

"Don't get the cart before the horse Babe. I need to go over to the proposed building site and physically inspect the property before I convince myself the logistics can be met. All projects must be approached with caution when put under such a time frame. If we were to move forward with this project and couldn't complete the project on time, say it took an extra thirty days. How upsetting would that be to your plans?"

"Let me assure you a thirty day delay would be very upsetting to me. I'm willing to put up a performance bonus to get the project completed on time."

"All I can tell you tonight is this, I will go inspect the property in question and I will run some quick estimates and meet you here for breakfast at seven in the morning. At that time I will give you thumbs up or thumbs down on your project. I can tell you this, if I can't do this no builder in Vegas can."

"We will be looking forward to your findings in the morning."

Bob drove straight back to Robin's realty office. "I thought you told Mr. Collins you were going over to inspect the property we discussed?"

"I needed to buy a little time and get away from young Mr. Collins. He is looking for a miracle when miracles don't exist. This project has no legs and it's not going anywhere. As professionals we have to brush these people off in a nice way. Do we know if Mr. Collins has any money or is he trying to impress the little gal beside him? Young men have been known to exaggerate their wealth and importance to impress other people."

"Because of his age I had my secretary call Hamilton Investigations and run a quick check on Mr. Collins because of his young age. The kid has money and a wealthy family who continues to hand him more money on a regular basis."

"Then back the wagon up. I was about to write him off as a mental case. If he really has the money, heaven knows we need the work. Especially now that I have over-extended on spec houses. We better search hard for something that might keep us in the running for his project. He also used the term first of several projects. The fastest way to get into the fast food business is to lease an existing fast food operation, step in and take over."

"Mr. Collins wants to buy not lease. Bob, if you remember I get paid selling not to lease."

"Then we need a lease option to buy. If I could find a suitable property for him to lease, I could instantly start working on the remodel. It's the only way I could complete his project on time."

Robin's eyes sparkled. "I may know of such a property. The West Mall has a vacant building on the corner. It's much larger than the family restaurant. It's a new building plus some equipment has been installed. The building was supposed to be a restaurant of some type."

"Let's go take a look at the property. Maybe we can work out a lease with an option to buy deal and give his project a leg to stand on."

Bob was impressed with the building. Four times the size of the family restaurant building drew his interest. "This is nice provided he doesn't think the building is too large. The mini apartment could easily be built in the back corner or just outside that wall. The office could go up along the end there. How fast can a lease with option to buy be constructed?"

"We can construct a lease option in minutes if I can get in touch with this Alan Edgerman Agency handling the property. I'll try their number now."

After speaking with Alan Edgerman, Robin had nothing but good news to relay. "Because of the money tied up here, all parties involved are ready to deal. He gave me his asking price and the lease price. Both are under market value meaning they are willing to take some loss. If Brad is willing, we could low-ball them further and maybe get one heck of a deal."

"Call young Mr. Collins and tell him we have what we believe are numbers he will like. Be sure he needs to come to the meeting in the morning with an open mind. He must not reject our idea before he understands why things need done a certain way. Getting Collins to think our way may relieve a lot of financial pressure on us. My over-building spec houses, has put us in a hole."

Robin's call to Brad was difficult to hear. He and Karen were apparently in a Casino somewhere. She somehow managed to make him understand progress was being made.

Later when they returned to the Moore's home Kathy was waiting for them. "How did your meeting go?"

"Hard to tell, we think things went well. The realty lady and the builder are giving our project a lot of thought. They called about an hour ago and said progress was being made. We have every reason to be optimistic, but one never knows when it comes to business. I have high hopes."

"Vern and I talked things over. He and I both think you are on the right track suggesting I manage a business for you. After our bankruptcy goes through all of our options are gone. Living on welfare doesn't appeal to us,"

"Part of the words you are saying I like to hear. Cross your fingers and wish us luck tomorrow morning, hopefully we will learn a lot of information over breakfast."

Vernon came hobbling out of the bedroom. "Did I hear somebody talking about our bankruptcy again? Can't you forget about our personal business?"

"What kind of a friend would I be if I were to leave you alone when I believe you are making a big mistake?"

"All I know is I'm having trouble sleeping worrying about our money situation. I want things over and done with. With your financial resources you can't understand our desperate position." Vernon's voice showed anger.

"I do understand your situation and I wish you could understand my situation. I'm willing to invest close to a million dollars in a business. A business Kathy agreed to manage for me. Can you give me a good reason why I should risk a million dollars around people who just went bankrupt?"

"Why would our bankruptcy make any difference, we want a new start."

"Unless you are not telling me your complete financial picture you have no reason to file bankruptcy."

"We are not holding anything back from you." Vernon snapped back at him as if his word was being challenged.

Brad pulled out his checkbook. Promptly wrote out a fifty thousand dollar check for the Moore's debts. "Use this money and pay your debts off. Forget this bankruptcy nonsense."

The Moore's put up a token effort to return his check before agreeing to accept the money. "Alright, we will pay our bills off. Sometime in the near future we will set up some kind of repayment schedule."

"We'll worry about a repayment schedule at a future date. I have too many things going on right now to deal with anymore. Now if you will excuse me I'm going to bed. It has been an exhausting day and we have an eight o'clock breakfast meeting in the morning. Karen, we may lose one or two days of class time. Do you know anyone who keeps notes in our classes?"

"Marylou Vereman keeps good notes. I should be able to get her notes to study."

"I hope you know Marylou well, we may need her notes."

The following morning at breakfast Bob Tilly laid out his findings for Brad. "The property you saw yesterday would take eight months minimum to rebuild to your specifications. Robin found an alternative site in a better location that could be readied in your two and a half month time frame. If you want we can physically inspect the property after we eat."

Robin spoke next. "One of the serious hang-ups in your plans is buying property because purchasing property takes time. This property is a lease, with an option to buy. If you like the property and sign the lease, construction can begin instantly. After a couple months you can proceed to buy the property."

"Keep talking, what all needs to be done to this alternate location?"

"Add the espresso area and the mini-apartment. The property is in a mall next to a multiplex theater and other shops. I project this to be prime property for the next thirty years or longer. The building is new, is your espresso section a necessity to begin with?"

"Most definitely Bob, espresso is huge money in all cities. Lots of money can be made selling espresso."

Robin gave a big smile. "If everyone agrees, Bob can show you the property while I check financial numbers. We can meet in my office in two hours, and go from there."

"Okay Bob, let's see what you found."

Brad saw potential in the property instantly. "Great choice, I love this building. I can't wait until I see the actual numbers your wife is working on. Being near a huge mall like this is a giant plus. There is parking galore."

At her office Robin was all smiles. "We have favorable numbers. The lease is five thousand per month and a purchase price of one million. All lease payments would reduce the purchase price by the lease amount. I'm thinking we can take control for five thousand a month and seven hundred fifty thousand as the purchase price if we make a solid offer."

"You are talking my language. Go for it Robin but don't be too pushy, pay their price if necessary. I want to get this project up and running in the two and a half month time frame."

Karen and Brad returned to the Moore's house. Showing excitement she raced inside. "Mom, dad, Brad put in an offer on a business property, and lined up a builder to do a small remodel. This is a million dollar project and the restaurant is located in the new West Mall. The place is beautiful. I'm so excited I feel I'm in the middle of a dream."

"Did you insure the building today?" Kathy inquired.

"I haven't signed any lease papers yet. I have a verbal agreement with my realtor. She should keep me apprised on the insurance coverage I need. "

"Get yourself good liability insurance too. Get universal insurance coverage, fire, thief and liability."

Brad placed a call to Robin asking her to line up the insurance coverage he needed, if they accepted his offer. "I'll drop a check by your office before I leave the city."

Vern shook his head. "The financial numbers you are talking about blow me away. My brain doesn't calculate that high."

"My debt load will be so low my financial risk is next to nothing. My business project can't fail. Karen and I better gather up our things and head for the airport, we missed enough class time."

"You have had such a big day wouldn't it be better to stay the night and fly back tomorrow?" Kathy suggested.

"Mother makes a good point, I am extremely tired. Marylou's notes are good. Can one more day hurt us if we stay here as get proper sleep tonight?"

"Alright, we can fly back in the morning."

Later in bed Vern was questioning his wife as to where she thought the young man was getting his money. "Karen claims his family has money. Where the money actually comes from she didn't say, because I doubt she knows."

"What if his money is drug money, the place you are working could get busted leaving you, and Karen to face the police while he skips out." Vern remained skeptical.

"Maybe I should go down to Karen's room and have a talk with her." She quietly slipped down the hall to question her daughter. "Honey, we need to talk. Your father is concerned where your young friend gets his money?"

"I think his money is from a family trust fund of some sort."

"You father reminded me Drug Lords buy businesses with cash to launder money. What if Brad is a big-time drug dealer, our involvement could get us in big trouble."

"Mother he is leasing a building to create what he is planning to call the Burger Joint. I've been around him enough to know he does not use drugs, or make secret phone calls. Father is so far off track."

Kathy leaned over and whispered. "Prison doesn't interest me, and I don't want to walk away empty handed. We need to be certain he gets insured proper. The key to our success is we both must sleep with him."

"Mother I don't believe you just said that. You can't actually be planning to sleep with Brad?"

"Keep your voice down. Hear me out before you get excited, we both should sleep with him. That way when we do go to work for him we can sue him for sexual harassment. We clip the insurance company for a million dollars each and Brad loses nothing, the insurance company pays the money."

"How can you think about having sex with Brad, don't you love my father?"

"Of course I love your father, but I am realistic about the money your father will need in the future. I'm willing to sleep with Brad for your father. I suggest you set up the same exit I will be using. If you become pregnant you could collect double the money and get child support for twenty years or more. Your father would get proper care."

"Mother, this is wrong, we shouldn't do this. I'm positive he has old family money. Having a rich family is not a crime."

"How often does he see his parents?"

"Brad hasn't told me anything about his family."

"If his parents were giving him money wouldn't you think he would talk about his parents more? Think about it, using his insurance is a perfect way for us to become wealthy. We should milk our cash cow, and walk away smiling. I'm going down the hall and have a chat with him, care to join me?"

"Brad is tired let him sleep. Wait until morning, and then ask him questions about his family."

Kathy ignored her daughter's advice. She slipped down the hall to his bedroom. She gently tapped on the door before opening it. "Are you awake?"

"Is that you Karen, I'm awake. Come in if you want."

"It's me, Kathy. I can't help but worry about all the money you're spending. It is so dangerous for someone to start a new business."

He sat up in bed and reached out to grasp her hand. "I keep telling you my risk is not huge. I'm not over extending myself. I have the money laying in a bank account drawing chump-change for interest plus I have a fool-proof way of advertising that will make any business an instant success."

"I hope you know what you are doing." He released her hand. "Goodnight Brad." She leaned over and kissed him on the cheek. "Sleep tight."

He wished her kiss had come from Karen. At the same time he realized deep down their relationship wasn't going anywhere. She would be an employee and nothing more. With the subliminal message playing in the house for Karen, and her not responding meant she had zero interest in a relationship.

The following morning after showering he slipped off to the kitchen to find Kathy fixing a huge breakfast. "Good morning. If you two are planning to catch your plane, go wake Karen. Breakfast will burn if I go wake her."

"I'll knock on her door maybe she will wake." A simple knock did nothing. He eased on in where he kneeled down next to her bed. He gently touched her shoulder. "Good morning Karen." She slowly opened her eyes. Seeing him so near startled Karen causing her to use both hands to push him away. He lost his balance and fell over backwards crashing into the nightstand. "Whoa girl, take it easy, it's me. We need to get ready to leave early this morning."

Karen dashed off to the bathroom. Kathy heard the fuss and came running. "What are you doing sitting on the floor?"

"Your daughter wasn't ready to wake up. She knocked me over and dashed off to the bathroom." He sat rubbing the side of his head before getting up.

"Well get up, you look silly sitting on the floor. Go save my breakfast while I check on Karen."

Kathy charged into the bathroom. "What on earth is wrong with you girl. How did Brad wind up on the floor?"

"He startled me."

"You could have apologized. I found him sitting on the floor looking like a scolded puppy. How can we have a cash cow if you drive him off?"

Kathy shook her head and returned to the kitchen to see him scraping the last of her charcoal breakfast into the garbage. "Karen needs the tender love and care of a special man."

Karen eventually came to the kitchen. "I'm sorry I pushed you over but you startled me."

"We better hurry. I need to drop an insurance check off at Robin's office on our way to the airport."

Vernon came to the kitchen. "Good morning people."

"Good morning daddy."

"What happened to your neck boy, it's all scraped up?"

"I had a little accident with a nightstand while trying to wake your daughter."

"Didn't Kathy tell you to wake her from a distance?"

"Your wife failed to mention the distance thing. Karen, if you are ready, we should be moving on. As construction progresses we may be down every other weekend."

"You are always welcome."

"Luck has nothing to do with success in business. Stick with me and I'll make a believer out of you."

CHAPTER 9

Back in Seattle he reminded Karen she could have a female roommate if she wanted one. She refused his offer. "The master bedroom is yours. I'll stay in my old room down the hall." She looked at him as though she had something to say but couldn't get it out.

Alone in his bed he couldn't help but think a stronger subliminal message than the one in Vegas might get him some nighttime company.

On Wednesday they were back in class. Brad used a thumb-drive to glean Marylou's notes from her computer. As he started to board the bus for his ride home Karen announced she was taking a later bus. I want to fill the girls in on our plans. "I will see you later."

In her absence he took the liberty to create a special powerful subliminal message for their night of studying. He piggybacked a second message aimed straight at her. The message encouraged her to become relaxed and comfortable around him. With his normal power message failing in Vegas, these messages were hyped up.

Karen returned some ninety minutes later asking if she could help create their study message. "I'm sorry. I should have known you would want to help make our messages. Next time you may help create the message. I will teach you what you need to know very soon. Tomorrow is the day our cleaning staff comes so it's best not to leave any personal items lying about."

She shook her head. "Lord it must be nice to have money."

"Money makes the world go around. If it's cleaning you miss help me clean my electronics equipment."

"I'm still in awe of the amount of equipment you own. How much of this equipment will be moved to Las Vegas?"

"We need all this equipment in Vegas. The thought of doing thousands of experiments excites me."

"Have you ever been tempted to use a subliminal message on a girl?"

"What kind of a question is this, you know very well we did. Have you forgotten about Marie and Judy? You were involved in those actions."

"Those were simple crazy messages. I'm talking about using your special technique for seducing a girl."

"The answer to your question is no. You don't seem overly comfortable living here. Maybe I need a message so you will relax?"

"I'm more relaxed than I expected."

"Were Marie and Judy surprised to see you in class?"

"They were happily surprised. I must thank you for the opportunity to be here and finish my college year. Someday I hope to complete my degree. I'm tired of these tight pants. I'm going change into my pajamas and robe." She soon returned. "When can I see more experiments?"

"We'll do thousands of experiments this summer."

"Why should I wait until summer, girls are impatient. She promptly sat next to him on the couch. "What are you watching?"

"Nothing, considering how tired I am, I should be in bed." She snuggled in tight to his body. "I keep getting mixed signals from you. In Vegas the slightest touch sent you scurrying away. This evening you seem somewhat cuddly."

"I want what every woman wants, a nice tender loving relationship."

Brad used his index finger to lift her chin for a kiss. Their kiss led to more kissing and hugging. She used her right hand to unbutton his shirt. His return touches were gentle. She led him to her bed. "I'm on the pill." His message had worked. "Come shower with me."

"Showering together this late tonight is a bad idea. We might be late for class. Ask me again tomorrow evening, and we will have some fun."

Karen's idea of showering together won out. After showering and enjoying full intimacy they slept like kittens all night. Thank goodness for her radio alarm.

Karen woke up to give him a sheepish grin. "We forgot about our studies last night."

"Fear not my dear we studied all night."

She gave him an embarrassing laughed. "Body studies don't count. I'm talking about the class notes we should have been studying."

"I'm not talking about body studies. We studied Marylou's notes all night. From the minute you walked through the door last night you were studying. For that matter, even now you are studying."

"I didn't feel anything but making love, that wasn't studying."

Brad smiled and nodded. "That's the beauty of my subliminal massage system. People respond without realizing anything is happening to them. We better get moving and take separate showers, before we are late for class."

All day he wondered what evening might bring. What kind of mood would she be in? Should he play his powerful sex message again?" Deep down he knew what he had to do. No test was worth anything without a check. Being in deep thought he was exceptionally quiet on the bus ride home. She grasped his hand as they walked the last block to the house. Only in the privacy of the house did she question his mood. "I can see stress on your face. What is bothering you this evening?"

"Last weekend we played a powerful subliminal message for your parents. The results were less than I anticipated. My message was strong enough they should have brought up their financial situation. Now that I think back, I brought up their bankruptcy any time we talked about it?"

"Yes, you were the one to bring their bankruptcy up."

"Then my message was a failure. The question is why it failed, and how to correct my failure?" Brad pondered what went wrong. "This is why experiments without checks are of little use. I didn't learn anything from my messages last weekend. I need another message encouraging them to use their money wisely. Would you care to help me create a new message with me, I'll teach you how."

Although nervous her excitement was fun to watch. "What if I can't do what you are expecting me to do?"

"If you mess up stop, we can always start over. Write your message on a piece if paper first. Word the message plain and to the point so we don't confuse people."

"How about this, Vernon and Kathy, think before making any purchase?"

"Simple and to the point, I like that. Now comes the hard part we have to wait until we go down to Vegas again."

"Will we be going down to Vegas this weekend?"

"I'll check with Robin and Bob tomorrow and see what they say. It's only been four days. This may be too soon."

Karen seemed shocked at his statement. "What about the message for my parents, do we dare wait?"

"I'm not sure, have you spoken to your parents. If they happen to change their minds we need to know soon as possible so we can make other arrangements."

"Mother won't change her mind. As your business becomes more of a reality she will become more excited. Once she sees the money the business generates she will be with you for life."

"I get the distinct feeling your mother isn't a hundred percent convinced this managing position is for her. I believe she is willing to give it a try. Your father's negativity could easily work against our interest."

Karen wasn't sure what she should say. Believing there was plenty of time to talk her mother out of her ridiculous plan of suing Brad. She remained quiet. "I haven't talked with mother this week. I would think she would call me if she was having second thoughts."

"I saw you out on the patio talking to someone on the phone. I naturally assumed it was your mother you were speaking to."

"It may have been Marie and Judy were who I was talking with. I miss those girls."

"Call your mother and try to get a read on her feelings. You might learn more about her thoughts than you think."

"Are we finished making the subliminal message for my parents?"

"I haven't set the intensity of the frequency, but that only takes a second. All I need to do is move a couple switches and I'm finished. Call your mother."

Karen went out the patio door to speak to her mother. Being a cool evening her actions caught Brad's eye. Why the privacy, he hoped she wasn't discussing their sex escapade last night. She soon returned. "Your intuition was correct. Daddy is telling mother you might do your tests and sell out. What are your plans for the Burger Joint after you no longer need it?"

"Good Lord you ask tough questions. I have no plans to sell anything. My first attempt in the advertising business would be out of the same office at the Burger Joint. We better go back to Vegas this weekend. Your mother needs to see the building where the Burger Joint will be located. Call your mother back and tell her our plans."

Again she took the phone outside to speak with her mother. He hated Karen's secrecy; it made no sense at all.

With no special message for Karen playing he retired to his own room. After speaking with her mother she came looking for him. "You went off to bed without saying goodnight."

"I'm sorry I should have said goodnight."

"She is thrilled we are going to Vegas this weekend to see her and daddy." Although her words were spoken with a straight face Brad was hesitant to believe her. He had seen concern on Karen's face as she spoke to her mother. It was easy to read part of her face as concern. "I'll scoot out and let you sleep, see you in the morning." She instantly left.

Thursday and Friday night he and Karen also slept in separate rooms. Saturday morning it was off to the airport. "Let's hope this trip turns out to be worth the effort. The new CD you made should work better than the original. Where did you pack the CD?"

"I don't have the CD, I thought you brought it." She looked at him as though she were in deep trouble.

"Oh well, it's not a huge deal. We'll save the CD for our next trip. It just dawned on me why my message never worked well before. I bought a cheap stereo. Does either of your parents have a birthday coming soon?"

"They have a wedding anniversary in three days."

"Perfect, we can get your parents a nice stereo as a present. A better stereo system could insure our special messages to be successful."

On the drive from the airport to the Moore's home they made a quick stop to purchase a quality stereo. As a special incentive Brad dropped a hundred dollar bill on the counter. "Deliver the stereo today, around three."

Shortly after the Moore's welcomed them, Brad took Karen, Vernon and Kathy to tour the Burger Joint. Kathy seemed thrilled. "All week I've worried about something going wrong." She commented.

Right on schedule the stereo arrived at three. Brad and Karen received generous hugs for the anniversary gift. "Thank you very much. Why would you give us this?"

"Give your daughter the credit she told me you're Anniversary was coming up. Karen and I have dinner, and a show lined up this evening."

Out by the rental car he took the liberty of kissing Karen. She melted in his arms. The dinner and show was enjoyable. Their goodnight kiss equaled how the evening began. Inside Kathy was waiting to greet them. "Hi kids, how was your evening?"

"Wonderful." Karen answered. "Dinner was great and the show was fantastic. I'm beat mother; I'll see you in the morning."

With Karen out of sight Kathy turned to Brad. "I've been so worried and tense about our future. My shoulders and neck are so knotted up.

Feel right here." Kathy touched the back of her neck. "My muscles are knotted?"

"Oh wow, your neck muscles are hard as a rock. You need a couple pain relieving pills and a warm bath."

"I've taken pills every three hours all day along with two soaking baths. Nothing seems to help. Try massaging my neck and shoulders." His fingers grew weary after twenty minutes. "That feels much better."

"It's well past my normal bedtime. If your muscles are tight in the morning I'll try loosening them again."

Before he could pull away she grabbed both his hands and pulled them down across her breasts for a hug from behind. "Thank you, I feel much better. She kissed each hand."

With the huge changes happening in Brad's life sleeping became difficult. On their date Karen was friendly, cuddly, and kissable. Had they not been sleeping in the Moore's home, he felt they may have slept together. She no doubt enjoyed their one time sexual escapade. This made him wonder if she might slip into his room for a late night rendezvous.

His bedside clock showed near midnight when a squeak of the bedroom door woke him. He squinted towards the door to see her clear outline as she closed the door. His wish came true; Karen was coming to visit him. He welcomed her sensuous body slipping in beside him. Touching, caressing and passionate kisses built into a terrific love making session. As if a thief in the night, his silent visitor began easing from his grip. "Goodnight Brad." She whispered.

Instantly he sat up, the words goodnight did not come from Karen's lips as he thought. "Kathy is that you?"

She placed a hand against his lips. "Don't wake anyone." After one last quick kiss she slipped away quietly as she came.

Wide-awake and bright eyed he watched as she moved into the hall light. How could he have made such a horrible mistake? Did his message target the wrong person?" Sweat poured from his forehead. "The names Karen and Kathy may have been too much alike for his message to decipher? He was the first to shower and dress before waiting in the kitchen to learn his fate.

Lost in thought and jumped when Kathy walked in behind him. "Good morning!" She was wearing a bright smile as she leaned over to whisper. "Vern hasn't been in any condition to perform…"

He placed one finger to her lips. "I hear someone stirring."

"It's probably Vern. I better go see if he needs my help."

Vernon came rolling out in his wheelchair. "Good morning Vernon."

"Good morning son you have dark circles under your eyes. Did you sleep at all?"

"I didn't sleep well last night. With all I have going on my mind won't settle down so I can sleep."

"Kathy was up running around a couple times in the night too. Once she settled in bed she slept well. I still can't believe at your age why you want all this stress in your life. What drives you?"

"What drives me you ask? My father, no actually both my mother and father are who drives me. Both were and are horrible parents. At age five they abandoned me. They left a nanny in full charge of raising me." Vernon and Kathy looked at the anger on Brad's face while listening to the hate in is voice. If it is the last thing I do I'll show them how wrong they were to leave me and chase all over the world in search of the almighty dollar. They have always given me a generous allowance. I'm here to tell you money is no substitute for love. I have developed an excellent style of advertising. I'll make my wealth working from one location by using a computer. The Burger Joint will have office space enough I can work other businesses from the same office."

Karen joined the group as they ate. "Our boy Brad didn't sleep well last night. He is wound up rather tight. You best be taking better care of him." Her father warned.

"You do have dark circles under your eyes. With everything you have going on; I should have been smarter than to keep you up so late."

Vernon excused himself as Karen went to pack up. "I'll go do my exercises while Sis packs, we can visit again before you leave."

With Vern and Karen gone Brad again found himself alone with Kathy. She leaned over next to him. "I don't know why I went to visit you last night. I couldn't help going to your room." He failed to comment on her words. It's our secret, don't worry."

As they prepared to leave he was reluctant to give Kathy much of a hug.

At the airport Karen had a question. "What did you tell my parents this morning?"

"Your father asked why at my young age I had such a drive to get a business started. I want to prove to my parents money can be made without traveling all over the world. They shouldn't have abandoned me.

I was raised by different nannies. I can count the times I saw my parents each year on one hand!"

Realizing Brad was showing anger she held back the many questions in her mind. Their boarding call came at the perfect time. "You will feel better after you sleep on the way home."

CHAPTER 10

Over the next few days Karen called her mother in Vegas several times about the progress of the construction. If Brad were home her calls were made outside where he couldn't hear any of their conversation topics. Bob Tilly claimed to be ahead of schedule in construction. "Bob tickles me wants so bad to collect the performance bonus I hung in front of him."

"What contractor wouldn't want a bonus? Two hundred thousand is more than a little vacation. Shouldn't we be doing more subliminal experiments here in Seattle before we leave?"

"I'm not sure further experiments would be of any value. Soon I will be dismantling my equipment. Everything needs to be packed very carefully for the move to Vegas."

"If I knew more, couldn't I learn more about your subliminal message system and be of more value in Vegas?"

"If you know people you feel comfortable conducting simple experiments on speak up girl. Maybe we can slip in another experiment. We do not have a lot of time to fool around."

"Judy and Marie are both fun loving girls. Pizza and beer got them over here last time, no reason it wouldn't again."

"If you want invite your friends over soon. I can still pack my electronic equipment on schedule. Do you have any specific experiments in mind?"

She racked her brain but could not think of one single experiment idea. "I'm hopeless, how will I be of any use to you in Vegas?"

"Don't go getting down on yourself. Let's start at the beginning again. In detail describe Judy to me."

"Judy has beautiful dark brown hair, five feet seven inches tall and a hundred ten pounds. Well proportioned from top to bottom, although guys love being with her, few college students have money to date on a regular basis."

"Okay, let's have her complain about her hair. Have her talk about bleaching it blonde. We could have Judy complain her weight also. Rather than a diet, we can have her talk about getting a growth hormone injection so she can be taller and carry her weight better.

Brad waited while Karen jotted down notes. "How about Marie, can we do something with guys. Maybe we can get both girls discuss previous dates? Good dates or bad date, maybe breaking up with guy?"

Karen smiled as she rubbed her hands together. "Sounds like fun but we need more for Marie though." Her excitement began to build.

"Can Marie wear any of your tops?"

"While living in the dorm room we exchanged clothes on many occasions. She can wear anything I own."

"Then we make Marie become warm and ask to borrow a cooler top from you. We can tell her it's not hot and resist a little. We can see how aggressive she becomes, but don't put up a huge resistance. You can make the messages."

Again he paused while Karen made more notes. "If you get the messages completed tonight call the girls. Start by typing your messages straight on the computer this time. Remember to keep all the messages short and to the point. When you get them completed, come get me. We'll do the mixing process together."

Karen spent the better part of an hour wording her sentence structures to get them perfect. "Considering the girls will be under the influence of our messages much longer than a customer in a fast food place, I need to keep the intensity level quite low. This dial controls the intensity. To the right means more intensity, a normal level would be about here. We must separate each message so we get a clear picture of each message, and the result we get. When the controls are set, this switch starts the music."

She immediately flipped the switch. "Hold on little one, step one is to install the music. Get yourself a CD from the drawer there on the left. Put it in the computer on the left. Then flip your switch and start one message. Stop at the end and pause before you do your next message. Follow the same process until you have installed all your messages."

In a matter of minutes Karen completed her task. "I'm finished, what's next?"

He rubbed her shoulder. "Call your two lovely friends and find out when all this is going to happen."

"I can't believe how easy creating new messages is. How is it no one has made subliminal messages like this before?"

"People fool around with subliminal messages all the time by targeting people to keep them in a happy mood. Music in a grocery store is a great example. The results I am looking for in my tests are to get an individual people to purchase certain products. My computers have the intensity set so fine duplicating my exact technique is next to impossible without someone testing years and years. Most of the settings I use are stored in my head."

"This is so fascinating to me."

"Even for a computer geek, this would be one in ten million chance of discovering my process. He or she would need to know what they were looking for. Plus have the patience of a mountain lion. Computer geeks are looking for the fastest easiest way to do things. Fast is not how I found my technique."

Karen jumped up. "I need to call the girls and get our plan rolling." She started to dash out to the living room to get her cell phone.

He grabbed her arm. "Calm down, you must not tip the girls off something is going on. Have the girls over any time you want. I'll be a spectator for the evening."

She returned in a flash. "Marie and Judy will be here tomorrow night. I'm so excited how will I ever sleep tonight?"

He shook his head. "You must control your excitement. You can't give away what we are doing. Stick with me girl and I'll make you a wealthy woman. I'm investing a million dollars in our upcoming business project, and I expect a good payback. Your parents also will do well riding on our coattails. They too will become reasonably wealthy."

"Let's hope mother and daddy remain patient the next two months. They have never been long on patience."

"A subliminal message can zap your parents with patience. We need your parents a hundred percent on board. We are not playing games with a million dollar investment. They need to concentrate on their part"

Karen looked at him in a serious way. "I have a question, what does your father say about your business plans?"

"My father, Mr. Never-see-the-guy, doesn't say anything about my business plans. I am using my money and I'm not risking more than I can afford."

"Is your father aware of your special message process?"

"Oh hell no, nor am I about to tell him. He might take my process away from me, and use it for his Import-Export Stores. My father is doing well and making mountains of money on his own, he doesn't need my help."

"He must keep tabs on your spending too some degree, how is it your father allows you to spend your money so freely?"

"I'm twenty two years old and it's my money. He may have someone watching my spending, I don't really know. Father does have associates here in Seattle so he may very well know what I am doing. If they are watching, these same people will soon know how fast I can turn a profit with the Burger Joint."

Karen rubbed her hands together. "I am so excited I want to do something, would you allow me to make more messages for Judy and Marie?"

"If you will calm down enough you can make additional messages. What is it you have in mind now?"

"I wanted to get Marie and Judy to talk more about their dating experiences in more detail. I forgot to add these ideas into my message."

Brad frowned at her. He thought that was part of what she had already done. "It's your show Sweetie. Make any message you want. I prefer to know what each experiment is before you start them. If in your excitement I feel you are about to give something away, I'll kill all your experiments."

"Oh yes of course. I better get busy." Karen finished her extra messages in time to receive her nightly call from her mother."

This was a chilly rainy evening yet she went straight out on the patio to talk with her mother. He watched Karen's every expression while she spoke to Kathy. This constant secrecy continued to make him nervous. "Hi Honey. Bob Tilly insists everything is on schedule."

"When I go inside Brad will enjoy hearing we are on schedule. I talk to you out on the patio because I don't need him hearing any of your doubts."

"I wouldn't have doubts if you would cozy up and sleep with him."

"I can't jump in his bed just because you tell me to. My plan is to gently get to know him in my own time and my own way. Our conning Brad is wrong."

"We need money now. This kid doesn't know one damn thing about running a business. The place will go broke in six months. It's urgent we file our sexual harassment lawsuits soon after the business becomes operational. Be sure he is well insured so we are not hurting him financially." Karen failed to respond. "Honey this is our golden chance, don't blow it for you father and me,

"He isn't sexually harassing anybody. How is father doing?"

"I can't tell if your father is actually getting better or if he is learning to tolerate his pain more."

"I keep hoping daddy will get better real fast so your need for money will lessen. Brad isn't a bad guy and I hate the thought of using him."

"You need to help your father and me. When it comes to Brad you are blind. Brad isn't marriage material. Mark my words once the Burger Joint begins operational, if it ever does. He will become a big-time skirt chaser trying to bed every young waitress over the age eighteen he can get his hands on. Take your turn with him before he gets mixed up with all these other young girls. His money alone will draw women to him. Waiting will gain us nothing."

"I know what you want me to do, but it's hard." Karen ended her call and went off to speak with Brad. "I just spoke to mother. Even though mother said everything was on schedule, Bob needs to know what type of espresso machine you bought, and when he can expect the machine to arrive in Vegas."

"I expected Bob to order the espresso machine, seems I better get busy."

"I'm headed out to the hot tub." Karen declared. "If you care to join me grab a towel."

Twenty minutes relaxing in the hot tub did nothing to create intimacy. Brad became disappointed when she quickly went to her bedroom.

After class the next day Karen drove over to pick up her former roommates. "What kind of a mood has Brad been in lately?"

"You can relax Marie; he has been mellow as a kitten."

Brad greeted the girls as they entered from the garage. "Good evening ladies our pizza is on its way." Karen slipped off to start her messages while he continued talking to the girls. "In case you girls haven't figured out what is going on your former roommate misses the camaraderie she had while living with the two of you. I'm too boring for her."

"We miss her also but who could blame her for wanting to live here. Our dorm room would fit in your living room with room to spare."

As the four ate pizza, Marie started telling him how lucky Karen was to be living with him. "I'm the lucky person." Brad stated. "She has been a godsend for me. She salvaged my grades and helps with the cleaning."

"Karen told us about the two of you showering together." Judy offered with a smile.

"We did shower together once, but that wasn't the cleaning I was referring to. She helps keep the house straightened up. Plus she probably told you we will be working together this summer doing research in a business I plan to start."

"She has told us some about your plans. Just last night we were discussing how nice you are to her and her parents. I find that rather amazing."

"I'm not buying her parents friendship if that is what you are thinking. I'm buying a fast food establishment in Las Vegas. Her mother will be managing the business while I do advertising research. Karen will be keeping the books on the business and recording results of my experiments. It's called teamwork. I expect to be making excellent money in a very short time."

"I don't understand why a fast food restaurant would need constant advertising research."

"Marie, normally you would be right. My Burger establishment will need little advertising. The research conducted at the fast food restaurant is research for a second business. My dream is to own an advertising agency. I realize I'm short on advertising knowledge. That is why we'll be spending our summer doing research at the Burger Joint."

Marie wiped her forehead. "Is anyone warm besides me?"

"I'm not warm." Karen quickly stated. "Judy, are you warm?"

"Marie, it's not warm in here. I hope you are not getting sick."

"I don't care what anyone says I'm hot. Karen may I borrow a cooler top from you."

"I must have something you can wear. Let's go look."

While Karen and Marie went to find a cooler top Judy wished Brad luck on his business ventures. "Thank you; by experimenting this summer and next summer we can reduce the luck factor when I start my advertising agency." Marie returned wearing a tiny swimsuit top. "Feeling better now?"

"This is much cooler, I considered putting the other half of the swimsuit on as well. I can't believe I'm the only one hot in this house."

Judy pulled at her hair. "This hair of mine is uncontrollable. I'm tired of the color. I should lighten the color. Maybe I would feel better if I could lose a few pounds my face would be slimmer and my hair would look nicer." She paused for a brief second. "Actually I like my figure. I wonder if I could grow three inches taller using a growth hormone to adjust my weight?"

Brad looked at her as he shook his head. "I wouldn't advise messing around with any growth hormones. You look fine."

Karen's third message kicked in. "Remember the evening we pitched in money with Robert and Tony to buy pizza and Tony ate most of the pizza. The guys were supposed to take us to a movie later. They turned on our television for the Wednesday night movie of the week. The guys actually believed we were going to stretch out and make out all evening in our cramped dorm room."

Marie chimed in with her memory. "I went to a ninth grade dance with a boy. He had a roll of socks or something in the front for his pants. People laughed at him all evening. The guy was too stupid to realize why everyone was laughing at him."

Judy countered back. "I once had the shortest date in history. I started to go out with a football jock. The instant I slid in his car he thought my body became his personal property. I popped out of the opposite side of his car and went back in the house. I told the stupid jerk to use his hands on himself."

Marie had comments of her own. "As a senior in high school, I was dating a guy for six months. Larry and I were struggling to keep our hands off one another. Deciding we couldn't fight destiny forever we made plans to go all the way. I honestly thought he was Mr. Right for me."

"Oh my Marie, you have never mentioned dating a guy named Larry before."

"On our chosen night he forgot the condoms. Our adventure would have to wait for a week. We had a whole week for our inflamed emotions to build even higher. Saturday night I made sure he had condoms before we drove out to the old mill pond. We no more than started making out when a set of flashing lights blasted through the rear window because we trespassed on private property. The owner called the sheriff."

"Ouch, being caught by a sheriff was not good. I bet you were in big trouble."

"We were loaded in the back of the patrol car like common criminals. From the Sheriff's Station my parents were called. I had never seen my father so mad in all my life. He knew why we were out by the mill pond. I hadn't turned eighteen yet and Larry was twenty. My father made it clear if he had deflowered me he would have been prosecuted for statutory rape. Larry skipped town the next day. I never saw him again."

"I may have done the same thing." Brad stated.

"Listen to what happened to me." Judy said. "My mom set me up on a blind date with the son of her friend. I didn't care for the guy but he continued coming around. It took mom and me, a while to realize he liked my mother not me."

Brad kept hoping Karen would notice the late hour. Apparently she was caught up in the experiments so much she failed to notice him trying to get her attention. Having no choice he eventually killed the experiments.

Only then did she notice the time. "Where did the time go this evening?" With her head cocked slightly she turned to Brad. "I can't be out this late at night by myself. I'll clean up while you drive the girls back to their dorm room."

At the dorm he received generous thanks. "We enjoyed having you over. Our classes are winding down fast. If by chance we get another free evening maybe we can get together again before Karen and I leave for Las Vegas."

"Judy and I will cross our finger and hope another evening comes free, thank you and goodnight." Marie gave a tiny sexy wave as she said goodbye.

CHAPTER 11

Wrapped in a towel straight from the shower Karen met Brad at the door as he returned from taking the girls home. "What a fantastic evening. We only had the one tiny flaw, and I'm sure you didn't mind the view."

"I didn't see anything unusual happen, what are you referring to?"

"I'm talking about Marie's breasts you couldn't have missed seeing those. When she went to change, she pulled my tiny swim top off before she was completely out of the room."

"Dang it, I missed seeing her breasts. I must have been busy talking to Judy at the time. I'll try to pay closer attention next time. I do enjoy womanly views. You are joshing me. She was walking away from me there was nothing for me to see."

"She turned and looked back. Her breasts were exposed to anyone looking."

"Somehow I missed seeing her girls, dang my luck anyway."

On Friday, Brad called Bob Tilly for a progress report. "Hello my friend how are things going? Did the Espresso Equipment arrive?"

"The equipment did arrive. It should be installed by Wednesday and the good news, we are still on schedule."

"I love it when you say we are on schedule. What I called about is it necessary for me to fly down this weekend?"

"This weekend, I wouldn't think so but at some point you will need to fly down mid-week and apply for your business license. No one here can apply for your business license. Being a nonresident you must apply in person."

"You want me to come down mid-week that will be tough. We are so close to the end of our classes. Of course if I have to fly down mid-week I will. How long does it take to get a business license?"

"You can get your business license the day you apply. Come down mid-week because Mondays and Fridays are always bad days to conduct business at the city clerk's office."

Karen was quick to question him soon as he was off the phone. "What's this mid-week thing you have to do?"

"We need to fly down and apply for our business license. Bob says I have to apply in person, because I'm not a resident. So we will be making a quick one day trip down and back."

"Count me out on that trip. I'll remain here in Seattle and take class notes and welcome you back when you get home when you get here. I'm not interested in a fast trip anywhere."

"There is one bright spot. We won't be going down this weekend making this the perfect weekend to work on our term papers to get them out of the way."

All weekend he quietly struggled with his term paper. "This has to be the worse damn term paper ever written, it sucks. For what it's worth, there is my term paper."

Karen looked his paper over. "Would you like me to spruce your paper up and get you a higher grade?"

"You can't change my paper. Professor Gibbons might recognize your work on my term paper and toss it. With a lower grade, I can slip by, but a total failure would be devastating. I'll settle for a lower grade."

"Changing your term paper was only a suggestion. Do you think we can invite the girls over again before we go to Vegas?"

"Having to hustle down to Vegas next week, I'll be exhausted. Next weekend I will be packing up the equipment for shipment to Vegas. Of course you can invite them over, but there would be no need in trying more subliminal messages."

On Tuesday in Vegas Brad ran into a problem. There were unbelievable lines at the city clerk's office. Half his day was spent sitting in a chair waiting to be called to the counter. The real setback came when he was called to the counter. All he received was an appointment for Wednesday. His second disappointment came from Bob Tilly. The electricians and the plumbers are behind schedule. "We hit a snag, so I shifted half my crew to an alternate job site. When the electricians and plumbers catch up I can shift back and possibly catch up part of the time we lost."

"Things were going so well, I wondered when our bubble might break. Do the best you can and I know you will."

Without forethought he called the Moore's home. "Hi Kathy, how is Vernon doing?"

"Hello Brad. Vern is doing all his exercises plus talking his medication as directed. His actual progress is hard to judge, we think he is doing slightly better."

"That's terrific. I'm stuck in Vegas tonight. This was supposed to be a quick trip down and back same day trip. Unfortunately I can't get my business license until tomorrow"

"Then you are coming to spend the night with us."

"I was going to get a motel room near the Courthouse and be first in line tomorrow."

"Getting a room is silly, come here and stay. We are only ten minutes from the Courthouse. Come by early and I'll fry a chicken for dinner."

"It's been a long time since I've had home-fried chicken. I'll be over in about an hour. I want to go over to the construction site and see what it looks like."

"His second call was to Karen in Seattle. "Bad news Kiddo, I won't be flying back to Seattle tonight. I'm hung up here in Vegas until tomorrow. City Hall was backed up to the point I'll be going back tomorrow to get my business license."

"What about me. I don't want to be in this house alone all night.

"I just told you city hall was packed caused by some kind of computer glitch. Not much I could do. I'll fly home soon as I can. Any chance your former roommates might come over and spend the night with you?"

"I'll give the girls a quick call and ask. I will see you tomorrow evening." His suggesting she invite the girls over brightened Karen's voice.

"Good luck with the girls. I'm headed over to the construction site."

Karen called and explained her situation to her former roommates. They readily agreed to come over. Karen's mind clicked. If she could get the girls over she could create more subliminal messages for them. Something outrageous since Brad wasn't around. A girl's gone wild theme came to mind. They could do body painting and skinny dipping in the hot tub later." In minutes she completed the necessary messages. Being impatient Karen increased the intensity on the subliminal message to a slightly higher level. She smiled at her own work. Having the girls over for an overnight stay would be fun.

In Vegas Kathy was all too happy to welcome Brad with open arms. Sorry about your delay, but we are always glad to see you. Vernon is napping."

"Isn't it late in the day for Vern to be napping, how will he sleep tonight?" He asked with concern.

"The therapist upped his workout again. Each time they increase his workload. He tires easy for the next several days. Using his powerful sleeping pills Vern won't have any trouble sleeping tonight. How is it Karen didn't come with you?"

"I came down to pick up a business license and fly right back. She remained home to take class notes. Some computer glitch killed my plan for today. Being nervous about staying alone in my big house I called Karen to suggest she get her girl friends to spend the night with her."

"That's was nice of you." He observed Kathy check the chicken in the oven. Only then did he hear the music still playing. Kathy quickly realized he was listening to the music. "Yes we are still playing the music you left for Vern."

"You should change CD's Vernon may be tired of the same music."

"He loves that CD and believes it is helping him."

In Seattle, Marie was the first to feel the influence of Karen's special subliminal message. "Girls this may well be our last crazy night together for the year. Let's do something naughty and wild. Drinking is out because we have classes tomorrow. How about we body paint one another? What do you say, shall we have some fun?"

Judy was quick to get on board with her idea. "Let's do it, we can go down to the Costume Shop and get body paint that washes off easy."

A fast taxi trip to the Mall provided the body paint needed for their evening's entertainment. As the girls became aggressive, Karen became concerned to the point she thought about cutting off the subliminal message. "Get your clothes off Karen. We have all seen each other nude before. What's your hang up?" Not being artists didn't stop the girls. Soon all three were painted from head to toe. Marie laughed as she looked at herself in the mirror. "If this is a painting contest, we all lose."

Forgetting all about the security videos all three girls paraded around everywhere. Near ten Karen killed the subliminal message. "We better clean our mess up. The cleaning people will be here tomorrow."

"Let's rinse off in the shower and then get in the hot tub for a while before we turn in."

"The only problem I see is who showers first?" Marie asked.

Judy pointed to the size of the shower. "In that big shower we'll all fit together. That way we will all be certain to get the paint completely out of our hair."

Soon all three girls were laughing and having a good time showering and scrubbing one another's hair. "You two are corrupting me, tearing down my morals. Good thing Brad is in Vegas."

"Hold still I'm trying to wash your hair. Do you want to be clean or not?"

"Of course I want to be clean. In fact I'm ready to move on out to the hot tub after my shower." After a half-hour in the hot tub the girls were ready to settle down for the night. "Marie you can sleep in Brad's room, Judy and I can share my big bed."

"I'll sleep in his room if you are you sure he won't return home in the middle of the night. I don't need any nighttime surprises."

"If he were coming back tonight we wouldn't have been body painting like we were. Brad is spending the night at my parent's house in Vegas"

In Vegas, Vern was up long enough to eat his evening meal before heading straight back to bed. Brad's words of praise over Kathy's dinner put a sweet smile on her face. "Thank you, Vern never compliments anything I do."

He reached over and touched her hand real lightly. "Oh hey, I forgot to tell you. I'm changing the name on the Burger Joint. My business is now called the Burger Palace. I think the name sounds better."

"The Burger Palace, I like the name change. For such a young man you have a good business head. Along with your signature burgers will you be serving any healthy food items?"

"Most fast food places today have an assortment of health food items. We no doubt will need to keep pace with the times. The beef we buy will be all natural organic fed beef plus we can have salads, sub sandwiches even yogurt. Women today eat a fair amount of yogurt. We take our customers money, get them fed and roll them out the door happy. So they return soon."

"With Vern sleeping most of the time, I'm thrilled you came by this evening. I'm missing out on everything I used to do."

"I know about loneliness. My parents were never much to me. You will find relief from your boredom once the Burger Palace opens. You will enjoy all the people coming and going."

"Vern and I haven't gone out to a movie in months. Watching television movies alone is boring. No cuddling, no hugging, no kissing and most of all, I miss intimacy after watching a good movie. Our thick carpet on the living room floor was intended to serve more than comfort for our feet."

"Don't look at me I don't have any words of advice for you. All I have is magic fingers. I could give you a massage later." From the quick smiling look on her face he realized he may have said the wrong thing by offering to give her a massage."

Brad helped clean the kitchen as she continually teased him by bumping into him. At first he tried to avoid her incidental bumps. In a half teasing fashion he began bumping her back. "I'll get ready for my massage and join you in a couple of minutes."

Brad went to the living room and waited for her as he wondered if he could resist her aggression if the time came. She joined him wearing a short thin silk robe that showed most of her pretty legs and barely shaded her breasts. "Do you like my robe, its new?"

He could clearly see a faint image of her beautiful breasts through her sexy robe. "I do like your robe, Pink is your color. Have a seat I picked out a movie we can watch while I give you your massage."

"I would love to watch a movie with you but I can't get a proper massage sitting and watching television. I need to stretch out somewhere. It's the only way I can relax."

"Stretch out on the carpet." Brad suggested.

"The floor is hard and cold." Kathy took him by the hand. "I can stretch out on your bed." As if he were a puppy in training he trailed behind. She shed her sexy robe leaving her in a pair of pink lacy panties and nothing else as she pulled his bed sheet back to stretch out on the bed. "Unless you want to get lotion on your clothes you better shuck them off." She suggested.

"You may be right these are my only clothes with me. I wasn't planning to be in Vegas overnight."

"Then shuck your clothes and be quick. I'm getting cold laying here. Slip in here with me." Kathy peeked back with a sly grin as he started removing his clothes.

He soon lay beside her as his magic finger ignited the flames of passion leading her to turn over and start caressing him in return. He gave nothing more than a token resistance before massaging her perky breasts while kissing and nibbling at her neck. "Your hands feel wonderful."

"You are a remarkable woman extremely beautiful and very friendly."

"You are a wonderful lover. Very tender, gentle and you never get in a hurry. Karen is the luckiest girl I know."

"Karen is a strange girl. She is hesitant to allow me to pleasure her. She doesn't want to be more than to be a friend."

"Are you serious?"

"I'm serious; she and I are less than hot item. I'm not expecting any sudden change. I'm not sure what is going on with her. I can't for the life of me figure out what is bothering her. Hopefully in time I'll understand her better."

Kathy smiled as she pulled him down for a kiss. "You and I both know our love making is out of line, but what other choices do we have for our current stress relief except enjoy ourselves. After enjoying intimacy, Kathy took a quick shower before going to her bedroom."

Brad tried to convince himself their illicit lovemaking was a result of the subliminal message designed for Karen to be more acceptable to his attention."

By morning his guilt increased. "You gave me what I needed last night, thank you."

After getting his business license, Brad bought five soft music CDs discs and return to the Moore's home. "Here is the new music we may as well trash-can this old C.D it must be pretty well wore out after playing nonstop all these weeks." He paused to give Kathy a hug. "We both know my coming here last night was a mistake. When I return, I will be getting my own apartment. We can't continue our illicit activities. Nothing must get in our way and derail our business plans." Kathy frowned at him. "It's best if I no longer stay here."

"Please don't get your own apartment. Vern will be disappointed if you don't stay here at the house."

"You know very well what I'm saying is for the best, goodbye Kathy."

She somewhat nodded as if she understood. "Have a safe flight home and we'll see you on your next trip down and hopefully we can discuss our relationship further."

With a late afternoon flight to Seattle he had plenty of time to stop by and see Bob at the Burger Palace. "Good afternoon, wow Brad you look rough."

"I didn't sleep well. Telling me we were behind schedule was enough to keep anyone from sleeping. I'm making a huge investment and my payback is being delayed."

"Are you sure a woman wasn't involved in your lack of sleep?" Brad glared at him. "Relax, what happens in Vegas stays in Vegas. I won't tell anyone you were out on the town last night. Don't forget, I was young once myself."

"You worry about the building, not my personal life. Good luck at getting back on schedule but don't work anyone to death to do it. Tell Robin hello for me."

"I will pass your message on. Get some sleep. Once we get the remodel finished you are going to be a very busy person."

CHAPTER 12

Walking into the house at home, Brad saw Karen out on the patio probably talking to her mother on the phone again. The constant secrecy continued to irritate him. He waved hello before heading off to the shower. Clean clothes and aftershave helped his mood as he waited for her to come inside. She barely set foot in the door when he began to speak. "Am I way behind in my studies?" He asked.

Half surprising Brad, Karen gave him a welcoming hug. "Welcome home and no, you are not far behind on your work. I did two class assignments for you and sent them in on the computer."

"Thank you. I'm sorry about not making it home last night. Having an evening alone gave me time to think. I changed the name of the Burger Joint to the Burger Palace. Your mother liked the new name. My trip did give me heartburn. Bob's crew is behind schedule"

"The Burger Palace is a better name. Mother hasn't said anything about being behind schedule, what happened?"

"The electricians and plumbers are holding up progress."

"Then you may not be paying Bob's performance bonus then. The electricians and plumbers may be saving you a chunk of money. If they don't delay your project long you should be happy."

"I know Bob is trying. My whole trip was weird. I needed you there to keep me calm. I slept lousy in Vegas." He stated without looking at her. Did the girls come over and keep you company?"

"Yes my wild and crazy girl friends made it over. We had a great time while you were gone. I was talking to mother when you came in. She enjoyed your quick visit."

"Talking to your mother was okay. It sounds like I missed a good time here at home. What all did you girls do?"

"You didn't miss anything if you had been here we wouldn't have done the things we did."

"Your father concerns me. He was worse than I've ever seen him. He was a zombie."

"Mother told me the therapist upped daddy's workout schedule. He has these set-backs days when they up his exercise program. In a few days he will be better again." Little did Karen or Brad realize Kathy had given her husband extra pain medication, so she could spend uninterrupted time with Brad.

"Your stepmother looked stressed by his condition." Somehow calling Kathy, Karen's stepmother rather than her mother helped ease his guilt. At least he reasoned it might ease his guilt. Heaven knows something needs to ease his conscious. His actions with Mrs. Moore were absolutely a disgrace.

"She has always been such an active person. Now she is tied down twenty-four hours seven days a day week caring for him. She doesn't see any of her friends at all."

"I know all about loneliness. Growing up a single child you reach out to anyone who will talk to you. On my plane flight back I was thinking. If our tests go well this summer we could attend college again in the fall. We could make up a couple weeks of messages for your stepmother to play while we attend college. Every other weekend we fly down to make another two weeks of messages."

She didn't quite understand what he was trying to say. "I'll be working, my parents need my help."

"Your stepmother could operate the system so we can return to Seattle and continue going to college. Wouldn't you like to finish your degree?"

"Yes I want to finish my degree, but we better wait and see how things go before we plan too far in advance. Do you realize we only have eight class days left this year?"

"Eight days too many far as I'm concerned, I'm ready for a break. How long do you think it will be before your father bounces back from this current set back?"

"I just told you he will bounce back in a few days."

"Oh that's right. Did your mother say anything to you unusual about your father when you were talking on the phone a few minutes ago?" Karen shook her head no. "Is something bothering you?"

"I'm nervous about Vegas. It's a big step. I worry about our challenge of creating a well-paying business instantly. What if I fail and can't meet my responsibilities? The amount of money you are spending is staggering to me."

"To a lot of people the money amount might be staggering. Truth is I'm investing less than twenty percent of my net worth."

"Twenty percent, you're kidding. Are you worth five million dollars?" Karen couldn't believe her ears.

"Six million maybe but what difference does it make. I plan on making the money I'm investing back, plus a healthy profit in a short span of time. You will be smiling from ear to ear when you see the money begin flowing in."

"I hate to keep asking but did Robin get your insurance taken care of so you are properly insured?"

"You were with me when we left her a check to bind my insurance. If you feel I should I can double check on my insurance?"

"One would think you are covered but it wouldn't hurt to be certain. I'm also worried about mother. The last time we were in Vegas, mother received by mail a sheer sexy pink robe. I'm talking a see-through nightgown. Claimed she bought the robe for my father. Since his accident daddy hasn't been able to be intimate with her. Why would she need a sexy robe?"

"Are you saying your stepmother could be close to having an affair?"

"I'm saying mother is in the frame of mind where it wouldn't be hard for her to have an affair." He stared at her with a blank face. "I'm serious Brad. If mother does have an affair it might rip their marriage apart. Couldn't her actions affect your business?"

"Such a scenario could affect the business. If something were to happen I could create a subliminal message to smooth things over. Your stepmother is constantly caring for your father. She doesn't go anywhere but the grocery store. When would she have time for an affair?" He wiped a tiny bead of sweat from his brow.

In her own way she was warning Brad to be careful. "Daddy is scheduled for back surgery. That means an additional eight weeks without mother getting any physical attention?"

"Karen, I don't know. I'm not a doctor. She seems to care a great deal for your father."

"When we open she will be around young men at the Burger Palace?"

"I don't see a problem but you and your stepmother are close. Try talking to her. Reinforce the fact your father will get better soon."

"I'm her stepdaughter. I can't go into detail with mother about the intimacy lacking in her life."

"After our move to Vegas we can monitor your stepmother and make a subliminal message to help keep her from making the mistake of having an affair. Speaking of Las Vegas, I will be getting my own apartment when we move there."

"My parents won't like you to get your own apartment. Staying at their house is their only contribution towards everyone's common interest."

"I can't stay with your parents forever. You can remain at your parent's house. We need a break so we can return to square one. We don't have to be lovers to be business partners."

"I'm glad to hear you say we don't have to be lovers right now. We both have more stress in our lives than we care to admit. My parents are a perfect example of becoming involved before thinking things through. Their relationship started when she came for my mother's funeral. Kathy stayed to care for me while my father worked."

"An in house nanny is very common. I seldom saw my parents. I grew up with the care of a nanny too."

"Both my father and Kathy were emotionally stressed. One night they proceeded to comforted one another in an intimate way. My father seduced Kathy who was under age and she became pregnant. They were scared he might go to jail on a statutory rape charge. Before anyone found out their situation he took her to Mexico for an abortion. While there my father had a vasectomy making it impossible for them to ever have children of their own."

Brad reached out patting Karen's arm to comfort her. "Wow this is heavy."

"The instant gratification they so desired messed up their lives forever. Now I wonder if mother can handle her stress without straying from her wedding vows."

"Everyday people are faced with choices in their life." He realized Karen was suspicious of her mother's desires. Brad knew what to do, create a powerful subliminal message for her to forget about them crossing the lines of society. The key thing to do was act fast to cover his past indiscretion.

"Mother told me she has a reoccurring dream where she is with another man, a younger sexually aggressive man. A man with an extraordinary knowledge"

Feeling confident a special message could smooth things over he wasn't overly concerned. "Most people fantasize."

"I know people fantasize but mother could be crying out for help. If she is crying out for help we need to step in. If there ever was a good time for one of your special subliminal messages this might be the time."

"We can't bomb messages at your mother twenty four hours a day for the next several months. It would be ludicrous to think we could. I wouldn't worry about your stepmother until she is out working with the public."

"Do you think mother will be okay, until we become operational in Vegas?"

"Maybe we need to keep her mind busy. Call your mother and ask her to start a list for some Grand Opening ideas. It might give her something to occupy her mind until we decide what we need to do."

"Having mother working on grand opening ideas is great idea. I'll call mom this very minute." Using her same routine Karen went outside to speak with her mother. He watched out the window as they talked. Why would she need constant privacy when speaking with her mother, her actions made no sense? When calling Marie and Judy she never went outside. Throughout the conversation outside he studied her facial expressions. Her expressions changed several times from happy smiling to deep concern. Wearing a fake smile she returned forty-five minutes later. "Mother is excited. She thinks we should have a longer controlled Grand Opening. Two weeks with small specials each day."

"Her idea would allow us to promote business without working our employees so hard. It would also give more people a chance to take advantage of our specials. More families might join us for a meal out."

"Drawing in family business should help with revenue."

"There is something else I've been thinking about moving my electronic equipment. Packed properly I could ship my electronic equipment down by UPS. Then I could take a casual trip to the Oregon Coast. A mini vacation would be nice. There are a lot of tourist activities along the coast. Would you care to vacation with me as I drive down the Pacific Coast?"

"Dilly-dallying along the Oregon Coast sounds like fun. It might be our only relaxation of the summer. I've never seen much along the coast. I understand the giant Redwood Trees are a sight to behold."

"I've seen the Redwoods and the ocean on television. We could spend a week or more along the coast long as we kept in touch with Bob Tilly and your mother."

"Sounds like a trip made in heaven to me." Karen eyes sparkled.

"A trip would be fun. Every time we think we have our plans set something else pops up. Do you by chance know what type of summer plans your gal pals have?"

"Marie and Judy have part-time jobs. Why are you asking about them?"

"I need someone looking after this house for the summer. No telling what I might find coming back in the fall if I go off and abandon my house. I would feel much better if someone were staying here at night. I'll keep the cleaning staff and the yard care people. It's at night when I need someone to be around."

"If you hadn't taken all your equipment apart we could invite the girls over again and do more experiments like we did the other three times and asked the girls if they could care for your house."

"I think you are a little mixed up we experimented on Marie and Judy twice, not three times. You are supposed to be good at recording number and data. Why would you think we did three experiments on the girls?"

"You and I experimented on the girls twice. I ran an extra experiment while you were in Vegas the night you didn't come home. I'm not telling what we did." She sat looking at him with a smug smile. "We had fun."

"Did you have some interesting conversation again?"

"Among other things we had very interesting conversations." She glowed like a little kid with a secret. Marie and Judy are fun gals."

"I should have checked the security video when I returned."

"I forgot about your security equipment. You could have seen us on the security video. Please tell me you didn't check the security video." Karen looked worried. "You didn't look did you?"

"No I didn't look but I will look next time. Now getting back to the girls, when might be a good time to invite them out to a nice restaurant? I need a chance to ask them if they would be interested in house sitting for me this summer."

Karen glanced at her watch. "It's still early. I doubt they have eaten tonight."

Brad glanced at his watch. "It is early, go ahead and try calling the girls and find out if they would like to go out for dinner this evening. I can talk to them as we eat."

Her placing the call from inside the house caught his attention. After a short conversation Karen turned to him. "Here is the deal, Marie and

Judy would love to go out for dinner, but they can't house sit for you. What should I tell them?"

"You have tough friends. Find out how soon they can be ready. We'll pick the girls up and feed them anyway. It may be the last time you girls can get together for a while."

When Brad stopped to pick the girls up, Marie hesitated before getting in his car. "Judy and I are always up for free food, but if your only reason for inviting us out for dinner is too high pressure us into watching your house this summer. We can't house sit for you. We can't afford to give up any of our part-time jobs. We need all the money we can get our hands on until we get out of college."

"I can't believe you girls are turning me down before I give you all the reasons I think you should watch the house for me. What a bummer, get in ladies I'll feed you anyway. I'll even let you chose where we should eat?"

"The Green Garden is good for our waist lines." Marie suggested.

After a short drive they were at the restaurant. After ordering their food he quickly brought up the subject of house sitting again. "There is no way the two of you house sitting for me could hurt you financially. Quite the opposite, you would benefit greatly. I need people in my house at night. During the day cleaning people and the yard care people will be around quite a bit. Some type of activity in the house most nights is what I'm looking for. I will leave my car for your use, plus gas for the summer. At the end of summer I will pay you each five thousand dollars for watching my house."

He now commanded the girl's attention. "Say that again, we get what for house sitting?" Marie questioned.

"Listen careful Judy. For watching the house at night you get five thousand dollars each, plus my car to use for the summer, and fuel money."

Both girls extended their hand for a shake. "It's a deal."

"Stay on the dorm list. I will need the house again this fall when I return to college for my fourth year."

As the four finished eating Karen and Judy went off to the restroom leaving Brad and Marie talking at the table. "I hear you gals had one wild party while I was in Vegas."

"Oh my God, Karen told you what we did?" Her face flushed.

"We don't keep secrets form one another. Everything was done in fun wasn't it?" He teased. "A little fun never hurt anyone."

"Karen is an idiot. There are some things you don't tell. It was a wild crazy thing we did. We cleaned up the mess. The body paint washed of easy. It was a kind of a celebration for the end of another year of college."

The two girls soon returned. "We're back did you two talk about us while we were gone?" Karen asked with a smart tone.

"Oh heavens yes. Marie was telling me how much fun you girls had at your body painting party the other night"

Karen's eyes almost bugged out of her head. "Marie! How could you, why did you tell him what we did?"

"You already told him."

"No, I never said a word about what we did that night. It was none of his business."

"Brad led me to believe you already told him about our party." All three girls looked at him together.

"I lied. Now that I know part of what you did you may as well tell me everything."

"We have no idea what Marie told you? I guarantee it's all you are going to hear."

"Then am I correct to assume those funny colored marks inside the shower stall the cleaning ladies asked about was body paint put there by accident when you three showered together?"

"Marie, why would you tell him we showered together?" Karen was ready to ring Marie's neck.

"Calm down Karen. Marie didn't tell me you three showered together you just confirmed my guess. I'm only joshing with you girls. You had a party, and had a little fun. What's the big deal?"

"The deal is how you control people. You have a mean streak running clean through you a mile wide. I've never met anyone like you in my life. Your parents failed to teach you to behave properly."

"My parents were never around to teach me anything. I'm jealous because I wasn't involved in your party. You three had a lot of fun. Nobody likes fun more than I do."

"Forget it buddy there was no way you would have ever been allowed to join our party. We wouldn't have done what we did if you had been anywhere in the State."

"Now you really have my interest. Sure wish I had thought to check the security videos when I came home." He further teased.

Marie looked straight at him. "What security videos?"

"I have security cameras in and around my house. Every word along with every picture is recorded."

Judy grabbed his arm. "Oh my lord, are you saying our party is on video?"

"I can't very easily look back now. The system eventually records over itself. The day I arrived home, I could have easily looked back at the video. Having no reason to check the security video I never checked it. Your actions are safe."

"Are you leveling with us?" Judy asked with deep concern.

"I'm telling the truth, my house is well covered by security cameras. Only if something unusual were to happen would I look back. All cameras are carefully directed so not to show private areas."

"It wouldn't take much to redirect a camera." Karen stated.

"My cameras are for personal safety. They are not meant to spy on people. I'm only interested in security. Take Karen's top drawer for example, it contains her jewelry. You couldn't get her jewelry without being seen. Give me a break ladies, I just explained the system is not for spying on people, it's for security."

"Talk about overkill on security. Aren't you being a bit paranoid about security?" Marie commented.

"Paranoid, damn right I'm paranoid about my security!"

His loud words caused others near them to turn and look. She immediately lowered her voice. "I'm sorry, I used too strong a word in describing your actions and I apologize."

"Apologize my ass, when something is on your mind, say it! Get things out in the open! People shouldn't have to hide their true feelings! You called me paranoid, I'm not paranoid! I'm cautious!"

"I've upset you and I'm sorry. The last thing I wanted to do was upset you. You have been a gracious host to Judy and me. My words were out of line, I'm sorry. We'll call a cab, so you won't have to take us back to the dorm."

"Sit down, I'm not through talking. Karen and I have never uttered a single word about my life before I met her. For your information a few years ago had it not been for my one and only security camera being in the perfect location at the right time. I would now be doing life in prison or sitting on death row. That single camera was my only evidence of self-defense." All three girls sat silent staring at him. He pointed a finger at each of them. "You are doing the damn same thing the police did to me that day. You don't believe a word I'm saying. I can tell you don't believe me. I'll be back in a couple minutes and take you back to your dorm."

He stormed off to the restroom as the girls sat totally shocked. They waited until was out of hearing distance. "I never expected anything like this to happen."

"I've never seen him so angry." Karen remarked.

"He has been so nice to us, now I've ruined everything." A small tear formed in the corner of Marie's eye.

"Do you girls mind waiting here while I try to catch Brad in the hall?"

"Go ahead and catch him if you can, tell him I'm sorry for upsetting him."

As he exited the restroom he found Karen waiting near the men's room door. "Marie didn't intend to upset you."

"I know she didn't intend to upset me. She stated her opinion. Not one of you believed my explanation."

"I don't understand. How did we not believe you?"

"Not one of you gave any reaction when I said if it wasn't for my security camera I would now be in prison now. You brushed off my words as though I had said nothing of importance or I was lying to you."

"I can't speak for the girls but for me your statement caught me off guard. I didn't know what to say. Even you must admit your statement sort of came out of the blue. You shouldn't have left the table before we had a chance to ask questions."

"I was getting bad vibs, you were all against me. You girls called me paranoid about security." He pointed a finger at her. "Call my actions what you want. I'll not apologize for my security system."

"No one is asking you to apologize. Marie wanted to apologize. You stormed off before she had a chance to explain."

"Oh come on, you know well as I do she only wants to apologize because I grew angry. She doesn't want to apologize for not believing me."

"Speaking for myself, I could use more explanation before I let this go. In my opinion you are thinking beyond what you are saying. We heard your words, but you lost us along the way. How are we supposed to know what to think, give us a chance to understand what happened."

"Alright, let's go talk to the girls." He marched off to the table as she trailed behind.

"Brad would like a second try at explaining why he became upset. He thinks we didn't believe him. I'm confused and don't know what to think."

"That makes three of us, we are confused too." Judy replied.

The on duty manager came over to table table. "Sir, I have to ask you to leave the restaurant. You are disturbing the other patrons."

"Hang on a minute." Brad pulled a thousand dollars from his wallet. "I'm paying for everyone's meal over to that divider. The rest goes to our waitress. Now back to you ladies, I'm being tossed out. If you are finished, I will give you a ride back to your dorm or pay for a taxi, your choice?"

Marie was quick to respond. "We'll ride with you."

CHAPTER 13

The three girls followed him to the car. Before unlocking the car he turned to them. "Tonight is Wednesday, would it be possible for you to come Friday night to the house, and watch a video with Karen and me?" All three girls looked at one another. "You don't have to if you don't want to." Again all three were quiet. "The video is seven hours long meaning we would need to fast forward through much of the video. There is a running time line on the video so as we skipped large parts of the actual video you could still realize how long the events took place. I can tell by how quiet you are, I won't be getting an answer tonight but that's alright, think it over. Let Karen or myself know your answer Friday sometime."

At the dorm only Brad spoke. "Goodnight ladies be sure and let us know your decision." At home Karen went directly to her room."

The following morning she woke to an empty house. He had left a note on the table. "I took an early bus so I could get some study information at the library." She knew his note was hogwash. He never went to the library to research anything. His research was all done on his own computers. Then she remembered his computers were packed or being packed. Getting on the bus to go home that afternoon he again was absent. Finding the house empty she became concerned. Feeling the need to talk with someone she called her mother. "I blew it, Brad is furious at me."

"Oh good heavens girl what did you do this time?"

"We were having dinner last night when he made an unexpected comment about his past. Coming out of the blue his statement seemed bazaar. He caught me so off guard, I didn't answer him right away. He took my silence as my not believing him. He is furious at me."

"For lands sake girl, why judge him at all? We won't be dealing with him much longer anyway. Bed the man, sue the man, and we are gone. In a couple months he will be out of our lives forever."

"I don't want to go through with this goofy insane plan of yours, to sue Brad. Two sexual harassment lawsuits at the same time could spell real trouble for his business, he isn't a bad person."

"Damn it girl, are you listening to me. We are not hurting him as long as you make sure he is well insured. We can get a quiet out of court settlement that won't affect his business at all."

"This just isn't right. We shouldn't do this. Brad may be an odd person but he isn't a bad person."

"Get off your morality band wagon and do your part."

"He and I are not sleeping together. We did once and that was it."

"What is wrong with you, I told you we need to show a pattern of his philandering. I don't care how, but get him in bed with you again, and again, and again. Light his ears up."

"I hear him coming. I've got to hang up, bye mom. Hold on mother that wasn't him it was our neighbor's cat again. The stupid cat climbs our screen trying to get in. What I was about to tell you is, Brad is furious at me enough he may not want me working for him in Vegas."

"I don't want to hear this, make up to him. We only have a few days before we start work and then let him blow up. Who gives a damn then?"

"He is beyond furious and appears to be getting madder by the minute. He won't speak to me, and I haven't seen him all day."

"Then you have your work cut out for you. Get on you knees and apologize. Concentrate on the million dollars we each can get in a sexual harassment lawsuit. Try to get pregnant. If you are pregnant you can get two million dollars and child support for the next twenty years."

Karen slumped to a chair. "I'll see what I can do, bye mother."

After ending her call Karen paced the floor waiting for Brad to return, it was well past ten when he arrived. "You scared me. I didn't know where you were."

"I was at the park walking and thinking. Do you know if the girls are coming over Friday night?"

"They would like to come over. I will tell you they are nervous and uneasy. Are you sure you want them here?" She asked in a soft voice.

"Damn-it, I invited them! I want them here with open minds if that is possible." He stated with a harsh voice. "I want them to see my video, if they have guts enough to watch it!"

Although she didn't appreciate his snide remarks she let it slide. "Can I use your car again to go get them?"

"Take the damn car! You don't have to ask. When you go to get the girls stop at the store, get four nice steaks, a bag of salad and some corn on the cob. I'll barbecue while you girls watch the video." His angry tone continued.

"You haven't barbecued since I came here." He frowned at her. "Oops, I shouldn't have said that, I'm sorry."

"If you don't like barbecued steak, buy something else. I don't give a shit."

"How about Kentucky Fried Chicken, mashed potatoes and cold slaw? If we are going to watch a video we need to eat quickly."

"I just told you I didn't give a shit what you eat! Get whatever the hell you want!" His anger failed to diminish.

"Friday evening the girls were quick to inquire about his mood. "His mood changes by the minute. It goes from angry, to mad, and then furious in no particular order. I wouldn't blame you if you decided not to come over."

"Oh no Marie stated, he challenged us. It's time for us to prove we are stronger than he thinks. No way am I giving him the satisfaction of not showing up."

All three girls entered the house with caution. "Good evening, you can eat at the table before we begin watching the video. There are several things to drink in the refrigerator. Pick out what you want."

Judy touched the video lying on the table. "Is this the video we will be watching later?"

"That is the video. I ate earlier. I'll go cue up the video while you girls settle in to eat."

"Wow, he is still angrier than anyone I ever saw."

With Brad gone to cue up the video, Judy leaned over to whisper in Karen's ear. "His voice is ice cold. If things don't go better later this could be a long evening."

Marie responded with her own opinion. "His mood couldn't be much worse. We should relax, and see what happens. We have nothing to lose?"

"I was expecting him to eat with us. Did you know he was eating earlier?"

"I'm not sure he ate anything all day. When things bother him he sometimes skips meals." Karen started laughing. "We can't put this off any longer. May as well go see what he has to show us."

He returned to glare at the girls. "You still have time to change your mind if you want. Watching this video is not mandatory."

Marie shook her head. "You challenged me, I'm not going anywhere. We have no idea what you are about to show us. If you are expecting a quick answer, or a quick judgment you may not get one. All three of us are confused ladies. We don't know what to think."

"Bingo, that's my point. I've never given any of you a reason to doubt me. I've never lied to you. Yet you all have doubts about me. There is a saying in this country. A person is innocent until proven guilty. Don't ever believe that lie. The saying means nothing. You three are living proof the statement means nothing. When I said my video was the only thing that kept me from doing life in prison. Not one of you believed me. Watch the video, and then see what you think. This incident happened six years ago. In my mind it's as clear as if it happened yesterday. The video is in real time. You can fast forward when you want to. Keep an eye on the timeline. Here we go."

All three girls sat quiet for twenty seconds at most. All three jumped when the door came crashing in. With mouths wide open they gasped in unison. As the intruder lay still on the floor Brad stopped the video. Do you realize what you just saw, or do you need to see it again?" The girls never uttered a word. "I assume by your silence you all understood what happened. The next six plus hours are of me begging someone to believe me when I said I acted in self-defense. I'll leave you alone to watch at your own pace. Follow the time line, fast forward when you want." Brad started to leave the room.

"Are you going somewhere?"

"I've seen the video many times. I sure as hell don't need to see it again. I play it in my head every frigging time someone doesn't believe me."

"What if we want to stop and discuss something with you?" Marie asked.

"I've stopped the video a minute ago, and nobody said anything of importance yet! Are any of you girls expecting to change your mind real soon?" His question met with silence. "I didn't think so."

"Can we see the start of the video again?" Judy asked.

"The controls are in your hands watch any part of the video you want. I'll be out of the house for a couple hours or so."

Karen followed him to the garage. "If you must go will you please keep your phone with you, we may want to call you?"

"I always have my phone." He affirmed without looking at her.

Karen rejoined her friends. "I couldn't stop him from leaving. You have the controls Marie. Start the video over again, we will go from there."

After watching the initial incident a second time, Marie followed the time frame and skipped much of the repetitive begging while continuing to follow the events. Ninety minutes later they began discussing the video. "The first two officers on the scene caused all the confusion."

"I agree, when Brad was pushed to the floor by the officers they contaminated the actual scene."

"Do you know the woman who was trying to get to Brad when he was cuffed sitting on the front lawn. Her trying to get to him caused the police to handcuffed her at one point."

"I have no idea who the girl might be. I've never heard him say a word about another girl other than Jennifer. I presume the woman on the video was a friend of his. Why else was she there. All the chaos by the police is incredible."

"I keep thinking about all those hours without food, drink or a bathroom break. The police put him through hell. I'm guessing he will be anti-police for many years to come."

Even when he told the police about the security camera they wouldn't look at it for over three hours."

"What do you think Brad wants us to say?"

"I don't know Judy, the incident is history. No matter what we say won't change what happened to him. It was an ugly time in his life."

"Here he comes now, brace your feet ladies." Karen warned.

"Well ladies, who is brave enough to begin?"

Marie raised her hand. "I saw a man bust in your back door. He entered and threatened to kill you. In self-defense you put the man down with two kicks. On the video, I couldn't see exactly where his kicks landed. You definitely put the man down."

"I think all three of you would agree about one thing. The initial event took place extremely fast. There was no time to think, all I did was react. Let's take another look at the incident in slow motion."

"There, I saw a knife, I missed that before." Marie pointed as she spoke. "The first kick was to his groin area, and the second kick struck the man in the throat."

"You almost saw it Marie, I'll back up the video a bit. Focus on his knife and not the kicks this time."

"The man stabbed himself as he fell to the floor."

"Did any of you see any movement after the man went down?"

"I saw no movement after he went down." Marie was the only girl talking.

"At what point do you believe he was dead?"

"The man died instantly." She stated.

"Did my kicks kill Evan Filmore, or was it his knife that killed him."

Marie shook her head. "I don't know for sure, I think the man died from his stab wound."

"What else did you see on the video?"

"It took less than two minutes for the first two officers to arrive on the scene. In my opinion they are the people to blame for the chaos that ensued. Other officers were quick to follow their lead. It took a long time for any officer even those outside away from the major chaos, to listen to you."

He turned to Karen and Judy. "Any comments ladies?"

"No, Marie pretty much said everything." Judy answered.

"I agree Marie said a lot, certainly not everything. From this point on all the video is TV News footage. Did you notice how many television crews were in the background, while I was in handcuffs sitting on the lawn? I was positioned in different areas for their cameras. They put me on display like a damn dog. Did you recognize the officer who finally listened to me?"

"We saw him, what are you getting at?"

"I'll show you." He moved the video to the early lawn scenes. Look who I am telling about the security video. The only thing the officer was interested in was positioning me for the news cameras. The officer was after television airtime so he would look good. The creep used me to score points with the news media. Let's fast-forward some, ah here we are. Now our goofy officer is over giving personal interviews to the media. This is well after I told him of the security video." As Brad moved the video ahead to when the officer listened to his pleas the girls sat quiet. "Check the time."

"It's ninety minutes later."

"All total from the time I told this jerk of the security video and he listened was almost three hours."

"We had the time frame right. We missed the officer's one-man antics."

"Now there was one other important thing on the video. Can any of you tell me what it was?" Three heads shook in unison all indicating no. "The gal who was handcuffed along with me for a short time, her name was Alice. She was the only person who came on the scene knowing nothing. She instantly knew I was telling the truth. She was in many of the scenes fighting to free me. I'm surprised you missed the importance of her actions. She knew without question I was innocent of doing anything wrong. She was a wonderful young woman."

"We all saw her defending you but moved on to concentrate on police action. You are right; she did support you a hundred percent."

"Yes she did Marie. Let's get back to you saying I'm paranoid for having so many security cameras. One camera saved my buns while my one and only supporter couldn't save me. She did her best trying to save me. Alice was one of a kind and the day I turned eighteen I married her."

"You married this girl?" Marie looked shocked. "Where is she now?"

"Yes I married Alice. She died in an automobile accident soon after our wedding."

"Were you…"

"No I wasn't with her when she died. Alice was the driving the car. She and her sister were in the car. Her sister was banged up but she lived. Let's get back to the business at hand. I have a couple newspaper articles for you to read."

After reading the first article Marie spoke again. "I don't understand how could they put this in the paper, you were cleared of all charges?"

"Thanks to the police delay tactics the reporter filed the story before I was cleared. Now read his retraction and take note of the location of the retraction."

"This retraction is a joke. Few people would see this hided on page four down in the corner like it is.'

"Answer me this, when the intruder broke in, what would you have done?" He slowly looked at each of them.

Marie was now quick to answer. "I'm not strong as you, after throwing the hot soup. I would have raced for the front door."

"I agree." Judy replied. "Only being scared, I might have run before throwing the soup."

"What do you say Karen?'

"Men and women are different. Our choices are limited because we are not strong like men. The hot soup was a good idea. Things happened so fast I don't know what I could have done if anything. I may have frozen in my tracks. For a woman, running may have been her best option."

"Then am I to assume all three of you think like most people do. I had other options than to kill the guy?"

Again Marie fired back at him. "You never did anything wrong. Men attack while women run. In your situation you did the right thing, fast and decisive."

"I didn't hold back that's for sure. I believe I had a special force with me that day. How else would a person explain how a non-fighter like me could put a man away with two blows?"

"Tonight's discussion was triggered by my calling you paranoid. I still haven't changed my mind, but if I had gone through what you went through I would probably be paranoid myself. I fully believe we are affected by your environment."

"You spoke your mind very eloquently along with making your point very clear. All I need to know now is do you girls want the security system turned off when I leave for Vegas?"

His question seemed to shock Marie. "You still want us to house sit this summer?" She asked with a half-smile. "I wasn't expecting you to want us as house sitters anymore."

"Why not, most people think the same way you two do. They think I'm too controlling, moody, and not always believable. How would I benefit changing house sitters?"

Marie shook her head and grinned at Judy. "I'm game, how about you?"

"We need the money, count me in. It's been a long strenuous evening. Can you give us a lift back to the dorm we've done enough damage for one week. I hope we haven't damaged our friendship forever."

He turned to Karen before leaving. "I won't be gone long, no need to wait up for me. I still have packing to do tonight."

Marie broke the silence on the ride to the dorm. "Karen looks very unhappy. I hope the two of you can work things out. It was my big mouths that triggered the disagreement."

"Karen and my personal relationship have taken a severe nose dive. Has she said anything unusual to you girls about what is going on?"

"No, she hasn't said anything of any importance. In the past we always confided in one another about everything. As of late she is very quiet."

"Karen has changed a lot. Her actions concern me. I know she is worried about her father and her new job. Karen talks to her mother often but their conversation are becoming more secretive with each call."

Marie kind of slumped down in the seat, before she asked her next question. "I maybe shouldn't say anything, but could it be she is afraid of your controlling ways?"

"One could think it could be, but that is not what is bothering her. I shouldn't be discussing Karen with the two of you. She and I can work things out ourselves. Thank you for coming over tonight"

CHAPTER 14

Saturday Karen asked what day they would be leaving. "I'm wrapping up lose ends. I'll call Bob later today and see where he is with his work. My equipment can't be shipped until we are in Vegas and the office is finished. Otherwise we have nowhere to store my equipment. I'm hoping to slip the girls a few bucks so they can ship my equipment to me later."

"I'm sure the girls will be happy to ship the equipment for you. In fact I spoke to them today and they are wondering when they will be moving here. Both Marie and Judy love this house. For them living here will be like living on an exotic island for the summer."

"It might be another week. I'll call and speak to the girls."

"I don't understand, I thought this would be our weekend to leave."

"My attorney has some papers he is working for me. Why don't you fly down to Vegas tomorrow? On Monday you double check with everyone and see to it everything is going smoothly before we go wandering off on a vacation. When I get my paperwork finished in a couple days we'll have time for ourselves."

Having no choice she boarded the plane on Sunday, alone for the flight to Vegas. "I'll see you soon."

Brad's actions and the tone of his voice concerned her. Her flying to Vegas alone was never in their plans and facing her mother alone would not be easy. Kathy met her daughter at the airport. Rather than give her daughter a welcome home hug she shook her by the arm. "Why are you alone, how could you allow this to happen, can't you do anything right?"

"I didn't do anything wrong, I was an innocent bystander. Now he thinks I don't trust him. I'm walking around on eggshells afraid to say anything for fear of making matters worse."

"You said you did nothing wrong. You didn't get in bed with him. Men are a sucker for a woman's special favors. All you had to do was take off your clothes, and cuddle up close. How will we ever get a solid sexual harassment case against Brad if you keep messing up?" Kathy actually stomped her foot. "Tell me this, are you employed by him?"

"No, until he sets up his bookkeeping system there isn't any official way I could be working for Brad. I believe he is setting the bookkeeping up now. Until then, there is no way for me to get paid. He did say something about seeing his attorney, and accountant, just before I boarded my plane here. It could take a few days yet before I start work."

"I keep telling you, throw your birth control pills away. I keep telling you if you were lucky enough to become pregnant, your settlement could double. When he gets to Vegas we must insist he stays at the house, so we both have access to him during the evening and night time hours."

"Mother we shouldn't be trying to set him up for a lawsuit. He is a nice guy. Working with him we can do well."

"I don't care if he is good, bad, or somewhere in between. It doesn't make one ounce of difference to me. The mountain of money your father needs for his care over the coming years will be staggering. When we get to the house you will see your father isn't improving. When Vern sees the size of our settlements he won't care where the money came from, or who we had to sleep with to get it."

"Mother you are not listening to me. Brad thinks if we all work together we can all make a nice living."

"You said yourself he is a controller. Do you want to be under the thumb of a controller all your life? What if he gets tired of the Burger Palace and sells the place. Then where would we be, skid row that's where. His insurance will cover his loses."

"What if he is right about our sticking with him? We could all become wealthy wouldn't we be better off?" Kathy wouldn't accept anything her daughter was saying. "I have no desire to sue Brad. He is not a bad person."

"Look around Honey. This house is shabby, it needs major repairs. I'm not slinging burgers the rest of my life making chump-change, to patch this house up. I deserve better. When is he flying to Vegas?" Kathy was showing signs of extreme anger.

"I don't know, he is allowing the girls the use of his car for the summer. He may be moving them before coming to Vegas."

"I don't believe this. Now is when you were supposed to be vacationing along the Oregon Coast in the daytime, and lying in a motel bed with him at night."

"I keep telling you this is my fault. I told you what happened. His anger flared when Marie said he was paranoid about security. I tried to stay out of their disagreement by keeping quiet. He took my silence as I didn't believe him."

"Apologize anyway. Do anything you have to do to get on his good side again. I bet your so called girl friends are using their womanly charms apologizing to him right now. The deal you told me about would catch any college girl's eye except you. Honey we are so close to our goal. We are right at the finish line. Let's make this happen."

From Seattle, Brad called the girls to say they could move any time they wanted.

"Perfect, can Karen use your car to move our things over to your house?"

"Karen flew to Vegas last night." He explained.

"I thought the two of you were planning to vacation along the Oregon Coast a few days, what happened?"

"Change of plans, something came up. If you are ready to move I could come over later and haul your things for you."

"We are ready any time you want to come get us. Day after tomorrow we start our part-time jobs. Moving today would give us time to settle in."

"How about I stop by at eleven we can load your things, and have lunch on the way back to the house? Will eleven fit your schedule?"

"Eleven is perfect we will be waiting."

"That was Brad on the phone he says we can move today. Karen is in Vegas. He sent her down on a plane last night. He said there was a change in their plans."

"It could mean their relationship took another ugly turn or a problem with the business. Marie shook her head no. "Do we dare question him why she flew down early?"

"I didn't ask for fear of blowing our deal. We need the five thousand dollars he offered for our house sitting. If he wants you and me to know any of the details as to why she is in Vegas, and he is in Seattle. He might tell us."

Promptly at eleven Brad arrived at the dorm building to move the girl's things. Half of their belongings fit in the car. "Out of room girls, you will need to make a second trip will be necessary." On the way to the house he stopped at the Green Garden for lunch. "I won't get many more chances to eat here for a while."

"Karen told us you liked eating here. Oops, maybe I shouldn't have mentioned her name, I'm sorry." Judy stated as she covered her mouth."

"We did eat here a few times. Don't worry about mentioning her name. She is my problem not yours. She and her stepmother are trying to do a number on me. I'm trying to decide how best to deal with them. For some reason I don't feel Karen is as bad as her stepmother. Believe me both women are a huge concern to me."

Marie frowned at him. "Karen isn't bad. She can be silly at times, but I don't see how anyone would call her bad. Did she say something to upset you?"

He shook his head. "Maybe you don't know the girl I do. She is dancing on a thin wire. Don't forget who I am, the freak with the security cameras. There are times I see, and hear, more than most people." Both girls sat quiet as though they were waiting for more information. "The other day when I was messing around setting up the video for you girls to watch, I ran across by accident some disturbing comments between her and her mother. I was using the equipment in the security room to mark important areas to show you. The newer equipment is much faster than my old standby equipment I normally use. As a result I accidentally backed into some of the older security recording from a couple days before. I saw and heard them talking on the phone. To say the least it was a very enlightening conversation. They did not speak of me in favorable manner." Both girls heard a sad tone in his voice.

"Keep in mind she may have been upset and made her statement in anger. I know better than to say this, because I could be risking my house sitting job. She is a friend, and friends do make mistakes at times. I believe in giving people a second chance."

"Don't look at me." Judy stated. "I vote with Marie. People are given second chances all the time, who among us is perfect?" She added with sincerity.

"Please ladies, just eat. I have enough on my mind without arguing with the two of you, over her fine qualities that are not so fine."

When the first load of the girls' things was put away, he handed Judy the keys. "That didn't take long. Can you girls get the rest of your things by yourself?"

"Certainly we can get the remainder of our things, if you have other things to do."

"I do have several things I need to do. One is I need to search the internet and see if I can locate the new car I want. I can't decide if I should buy the car here or in Vegas."

"We won't be gone long getting our remaining things. If you need your car later it will be available in about an hour."

Brad found the car he wanted searching on the internet. The car he desired was metallic silver Toyota Camry. The car he so desired was available in Seattle and Vegas. Looking at cars on the internet didn't help make a decision on where to buy his car. His mind was preoccupied by what to do about Karen and her stepmother. After the girls put away their second load of personal items they came looking for him. "The car is available if you need it."

"Oh good, you girls are finished. At four the security man is stopping by. He will be changing some of the codes. All Karen's codes will be removed. I would like to leave my codes. Your codes can be added or all security could be turned completely off. Do whatever you think best."

Marie caught him by the arm as he started away. "Hold on big guy, I have a question. How does the security system work?"

He stopped and turned to face her. "Allow me to demonstrate. Let's say you have an out of control boyfriend. You can duck into any room in the house and shut the door. The door is automatically locked. Anytime a door is completely closed they are locked."

"Wouldn't we lock ourselves out by accident?"

"Not once you are coded in." He touched the palm reader and the door unlocked. "There is no problem getting used to the system. Karen and I used the theory a near closed door was the same as a locked door meaning someone wanted privacy. Any individual camera can be turned off. When the alarm guy gets here tell him what you want."

"What would you advise Marie and me to do?" Judy asked.

"Why ask me, I'm the paranoid person."

"Darn you." Marie scolded." I wish there was a way I could take back the word paranoid."

"I'm not giving you the word paranoid back." He used his index finger to touch the end of her nose as he shook his head. "So there." She slapped his hand away. "If you really want my advice, I would leave most of the security system on. If you are nervous about your bedroom and bath area, maybe cut those cameras off."

"Thank you, now that didn't hurt one little bit to give us your advice."

"Follow me girls let me show you something." He took the girls into the security room. "Here we…"

Marie stopped in an instant. "…Wow, talk about overkill!"

"There you go again, jumping to conclusions. Let me see I woke up at seven this morning. I haven't seen this video so bear with me. In case you are interested I do sleep in the nude, watch as I get up. I'll be showering, shaving and dressing."

"We are not watching you parade around the house, buck naked. Have you completely lost your mind?"

"No, I haven't lost my mind, but I do I have faith in my security system. Watch, you may learn something. These are all the high-tech cameras, sensor activated. You won't see, what you think you might see."

"Are you sure?" Judy still had her doubts.

"Yes I am sure." He paused. "I left Karen's video cued up to make a copy. Would you girls mind stepping out while I make the copies I need?" He motioned for them to leave, but they never moved. "I may need this video for upcoming court action."

"Court action?" Marie and Judy looked at one another. "I can't speak for Judy, but I would like to see the video. Don't get excited. It isn't I don't trust or believe you. Judy and I are caught in the middle. We consider both you and her as friends."

For effect he quietly pounded his fist on the table a few times. "Alright, remember you asked to see this, I didn't offer. I believe this is her last call to her stepmother, as she was making arrangements to drive down the coast." Leaving the video cued up was no accident. He wanted the girls to see and hear Karen talking to her stepmother.

The video and the conversation caused Marie to gasp. "Oh my word, they are planning to extort a million dollars each from you."

"Keep listening, the million dollars each is more Kathy's idea than Karen's idea. The problem is Karen should have come to me and told me of her stepmother's plan. Karen isn't the hard core bitch her stepmother is. In a way I would like to cut her some slack. Kathy is a different story she needs to be taught a good lesson. The father is another question, where he fits in, I have no idea."

What Marie saw and heard caused her to put a hand over her face as she spoke. "You are right, Kathy is the bad one. She actually plans on seducing you."

"She has already seduced me. Kathy is actually Karen's stepmother and not all that much older than Karen. During one of our Vegas excursions she came to my room in the middle of the night. The room was dark and I thought Karen came to be with me. Unfortunately nature took its course. I don't see how any Sexual Harassment Claim can be made against me at this time. I do have an appointment with an attorney tomorrow morning."

"Seeing your attorney is a smart move on your part." Marie commented. "Seeking outside advice is smart."

"Anyway the Moore's are my problem not yours. We got off the subject that brought us in this room. Watch the control panel. I type in today's date and seven A.M. The computer searches, locates and shows my head. Now watch as I move about." Although uneasy the girls watched. "As I go in to use the facilities the camera blanks out in the secure areas. After I shower my damp towel is taken down the hall to the laundry room. I'm still on camera but all private parts are covered because the sophisticated camera follows the high point of any movement, my head."

"Do you normally walk all over the house with no clothes on?" Judy asked.

"Normally no, but I was alone last night. Let me stop the video in the hall. Say right here you girls murdered me. There is a way by using a special code the picture could be expanded to see exactly what happened and who killed me."

"Do you have the code?" Judy continued her questions.

"The alarm company has the code, and I have a copy in the safe. I've never used the code. I think it would be fair to assume the code would work if a person was smart enough to follow the directions in the manual. If you girls took the code and tried to use it, supposedly it wouldn't work because you are not an authorized person to use the code. The code works in conjunction with the palm readers. For me a person coded in, I could activate the enhancement process if necessary."

Marie smiled at him. "I can't help but feel this is still an overkill system."

"For many people it would be overkill. For my age I have a decent amount of money. Money can attract the wrong type of people."

"People like Karen and her stepmother are after part of my wealth. There are people who would want all my money. My father is what many consider mega wealthy. He is eighty-two years old. Someday I stand to inherit more of his money. Living under tight security conditions is in my best interest. My father has bodyguards with him at all times. I hope to live under the radar more and hide my wealth. I want a more normal family life with a wife and two or three children, stupid me thought Karen wanted the same thing."

Marie answered his comment. "There was a time she wanted a normal family life. I don't understand what is going on with her now."

Judy chimed in with her comments. "Let's leave the security system the way you have it set, we I can adapt. Just remove Karen's codes."

Marie smiled. "I agree. What will we do when we start work, and you have an appointment with your attorney? We only have one vehicle."

"We made a deal, the car is yours. I can taxi around until I decide where to purchase my new car."

Marie gently touched his arm. "Good luck with your attorney tomorrow."

"Thank you. You may be wasting your luck wishing it on me. I somehow seem to make wrong decisions quite often. All my life I wind up alone."

Marie gave him a tiny hug. "You are an intelligent person. You can afford extra time from their attorney and accountant. Ask them for advice as to how to properly get your business up and running."

"I may do that. I've moved all my things to the far spare bedroom. Most of my clothes are packed away. The sheets on both beds are clean I changed them this morning. From now on the cleaning ladies will change linens for you twice a week, Tuesdays and Fridays."

"They enter through a private entrance in the garage. They have codes to enter. Once the cameras identify them they can enter the house. These housekeeping ladies are like nurses. It's not a big deal if one sees you getting dressed."

"Do we hear the voice of experience?" Marie asked with a smile.

"Yes, from some years ago. Didn't change my life or her life, I don't know though. Maybe it's not fair to say that. I later married Alice so something changed along the way."

Marie quickly nodded her head. "I think we understand what you are saying."

"Pardon me if I seem a bit edgy. I pretty much lost my business manager and my office staff all in one day. Eating lunch out and having someone to converse with was enjoyable. I have a favorite place down along the waterfront where I enjoy eating. I would love to eat there again before I leave Seattle. Would you girls care to join me for dinner this evening?"

After exchanging looks the girls agreed to join him for dinner. "Our eating out twice in one day is a real treat." He promptly made reservations for three. While the girls dealt with the security people he strolled around in the back yard thinking how best to deal with Karen and her mother."

After the security man left the girls felt more comfortable speaking to each other. "What do you think about the mess Brad is in?"

"I don't know Judy. I hate to speculate for fear of being wrong. Karen and her stepmother dealt him a crushing blow. I wouldn't want to be in their shoes. He won't take this lightly."

Brad came strolling in from outside. "Ladies, where are you?" He called out.

"We are in the living room."

"I saw the security guy leave. Did you get the alarm set the way you wanted it?"

"Yes, Karen's codes are gone and you are still in, so behave yourself." He moved one hand as he started to speak. "We're kidding! We are not worried about you being a problem for us."

"Maybe you should be worried the history of my relationships has not been without fault. I'm far from perfect, and I've never had an over abundance of friends. I'm one of a kind, I'm a certified nerd. I have many faults."

"No one is perfect. Karen opened our eyes. We certainly had her pegged wrong. I would like to think there is still some good in Karen. Kathy is a harder case, she puzzles us."

"I can deal with Kathy, the woman is history. Karen I would like to put to the test. It's time she grew up and stood on her own two feet. I'll know more about my options, after I speak to my attorney. I'm thinking right now Karen should be the spearhead to deal with her mother."

"You may be on to something. It is an interesting idea to force Karen to show her strength and loyalty immediately. You would then know if she were with you or against you."

"I doubt she would ever be worthy of loyalty, and trust again. If she works for me, she would be moved to a lower position like a shift manager. Karen could work hard and earn a nice living. I hope you girls are not planning to call her. When I confront her with this video I want her in a shock and awe situation. I don't want her making plans of denial before I speak to her. If she chooses the path of denial she will be history too."

"We are not planning to call Karen. We are not involved in this." Marie made her thoughts clear.

"She could easily call you. It's so easy to let a word slip. One single word could rock the boat. I shouldn't have told you any of this. I'm so keyed up I needed someone to converse with, someone to help lower my stress level."

Marie couldn't help but laugh at his words. "You are right. One word can change a lot. I learned the hard way."

"Yes but I learned a lot that day also. You calling me paranoid led to the discovery of those scheming women. I should get down on my knees and kiss your feet for saving my bacon, you are a hero."

"I don't feel like a hero. My stomach is turning flip flops. I was so wrong about Karen."

"None of us feel good about this revelation. It is so astonishing, it's almost unbelievable." Judy shook her head. "I thought Karen was a good person."

"I'm between a rock and a hard place. I still need you to house sit. My showing you the video was wrong, but I was afraid you might not believe me."

Marie cringed. "The video turned out to be a double edged sword for me. I needed to see it, but now I wish I hadn't seen it. It's like the old saying ignorance is bliss." Marie was all for changing the subject. "Would you mind telling us where we will be eating tonight?"

"I wouldn't mind at all. I should be telling you where we will be eating so you have a chance to dress appropriately. We are going for a Harbor Dinner Cruise." Brad proudly stated.

"Did I hear you right, we are going on a Harbor Dinner Cruise?"

"Yes, a harbor cruise, it is a casual dinner cruise lasting about three hours. We cruise around as we eat a fine meal served one course at a time. We will be looking at ships, ferries, and the harbor lights. The weather is perfect this evening. I think you will enjoy eating as we cruise the harbor."

"Casual is a broad statement. How should we dress for the evening?"

"I'll be wearing gray slacks and a golf shirt. Probably take a light jacket with me. It can get cool on the water. For you girls a cocktail dress or pantsuit of some kind would be nice."

Marie wrinkled up her nose. "Being college students we are not long on casual dress clothes. Jeans and tops is all we have."

"I don't have a problem with what you are wearing now, but I can tell you the other ladies on this cruise will not be wearing jeans. The last thing I want to do is put you girls in a position were you feel uncomfortable all evening. As I see it we have options. You can go as you are. I can cancel the reservation, and eat elsewhere, or get a new outfit. What I don't want to do is put any guest of mine in a situation where they feel uncomfortable."

"A new outfit is out of the question. This time of year we are short on funds. We fully understand your wanting to go there and eat because there won't be any harbor cruises in Vegas. That leaves us wearing jeans and a top no matter how we feel. We don't want to spoil your choice for dinner. This dinner cruise sounds exciting."

"I could advance you money on the five thousand I will owe you this fall. We have two hours before we have to leave and the Mall isn't far away."

His offer put smiles on the girl's faces. "You would actually advance Judy and me money for a new outfit?"

"Brad withdrew six hundred dollars from his wallet. "There you go, use the money if you want. Don't go overboard on my account. Choose something for many occasions. Something you can casually wear even to college next fall would be perfectly fine too."

"Brad drove the girls to the Mall, but went his own direction as they went in. "Call my cell number when you are ready to meet back here."

Their new outfits put the girls in a joyful mood. At home both girls dressed and were ready in short order. "Ta da!" Marie announced as she twirled around. "How do we look?"

"I like both your outfits. Marie, green is your color and blue looks nice on you Judy. You girls did well, very nice. You will be the prettiest girls on the cruise."

"You said we looked nice. What kind of a compliment is that, we girls expect a more explanatory compliment then just nice, do we look sexy?" Judy twirled as she asked.

"How about this, you girls look fantastic. I will be the envy of every man on the boat. You both look extremely sexy, but I shouldn't say that because this isn't an actual date. We are a group of friends going out to eat."

"Give us a few minutes to finish our makeup and we will be ready."

"No hurry, we have plenty of time. The traffic will have decreased by the time we hit the downtown area."

CHAPTER 15

In the privacy of their room the girls began to discuss what they had just done. "Marie, I feel a bit strange about our shopping spree. Ever so gentle Brad gets his way. We had clothes nice enough for this evening. At his encouragement we bought new outfits. What do you think he is after?"

"Are you insinuating he might try putting the moves on us later?"

"He is a guy, even nice guys like sex. He admitted sleeping with Karen's step mother. Some guys will do anything to get what they want. Guys buy their lady friends things to get the girls in a better mood. There is also the old standby, alcohol to loosen a girl up." Judy warned.

"Sleeping with Karen's stepmother was an accident. Don't allow your imagination to run away with you. He isn't a bad guy even though he is far different than any guy I ever encountered. There are two of us, what can he do?"

"We'll play it your way. At no time during the evening do we separate, safety in numbers."

"We are buddies all the way. Now let's go before we chicken out. Come on girl put a smile on your face. Relax and have fun."

Brad started the conversation driving to the waterfront. "I checked on the internet. There are plenty of cars available that would do quite nicely for me. There are cars available both here and in Vegas. After meeting with my attorney I will know more about my immediate destination. More than likely I will fly to Vegas tomorrow night late, and pick up a car in a day or two. I will stop by tomorrow evening before I leave and tell you how the meeting goes with my attorney. We can work out the details of shipping my equipment at that time. I hired you girls as house sitters not baby sit me. I'll be out of your hair soon as I can. It's time you earned your money."

"Will you be coming back to Seattle during the summer?" Cautious Judy asked.

"I wouldn't think so unless something unforeseen came up. I may need to see my attorney or accountant. If I do come up I might fly up and back in the same day. I can't imagine anything coming up that we couldn't handle by phone."

"We wouldn't mind if you do returned and stayed at the house. I was only asking because I was curious."

"Don't be afraid to call me if you need anything, or you can call me just to talk if you like. The telephone is part of the security system. It stays on in my absence. Make any calls you like as long as they are not out of the country."

Marie chuckled. "We don't know anyone over seas so your phone bill is safe. Far as calling you, who knows? We might call, and see how your business plans are doing."

"No wild parties. A few couples for a back yard barbecue is fine."

"There won't be any parties at your house, we are not wild girls."

"I didn't say you were wild girls. I was only clarifying boundaries. Keep an eye out for a parking space we are getting close. That's our boat right there. They have a limited menu. I hope you like pasta, tonight is pasta night."

"We love pasta, second row over is a parking space. See the car backing out over there." Marie pointed off to the right. "That's not a handicap space."

"Good eyes girl. Before we get on our dinner cruise boat, I want to thank you for agreeing to house sit for me this summer. I'll rest much easier this summer with someone I know staying at the house."

"We should be thanking you. We can use the extra money."

"Most people can use extra money and I have a little something for you girls this evening." Brad handed them each a box the size of a shoebox.

Each girl gave a cautious smile before opening her box. Each box contained a white carnation corsage and a beautiful Watch. We don't deserve these." Marie protested.

"The corsage is an addition to your beauty and the watch is to say thank you for helping me pass the time. Tonight is a night we all should relax, and enjoy. I'm doing my best to entertain two lovely young ladies. I've never been out with two beautiful women at the same time before."

"These watches are expensive watches."

"Shall we go on board before you ladies change your minds?"

"Please don't get upset, Judy and I don't know you well. We have no idea why you are the way you are. Truth is we have never experienced anyone like you before. You do things so unexpected."

"I suppose I am acting strange tonight, so how about I level with you. I wanted you out of the house tonight just to keep you busy. Misdirect your thoughts so you wouldn't be tempted to call Karen, or the other way around. If she were to call, you wouldn't be available to converse with her. My life is in a holding pattern until I see my attorney tomorrow. It would be in my best interest not to tip Karen, or her mother off. Call me cruel, controlling, or anything you want, I don't care. I've invested a million dollars in the wrong people so excuse me for being cautious."

"We won't call Karen. You could have sat home, and watched us there."

"If we had stayed home we would be doing dishes. How much fun can three people have doing dishes, let go eat, ladies."

On board the girls began to relax and enjoy themselves. "This is a wonderful setting for a romantic dinner. What a view, I can tell by the happiness on your face this is a special place for you."

"I do have special memories here. You ladies may have a glass of wine if you want. In my nervous state, and driving tonight, I'll be passing on the wine but feel free to partake if you so desire."

"A single glass of wine won't bother your driving. Join us, a glass of wine might help you relax, and enjoy the rest of the evening also."

"I can't Marie, I am so keyed up it feels like the hair on the back of my neck is standing straight up. Wine may not be good for me."

"Maybe a dip in the hot tub later will help you relax." Marie barely finished her sentence when her cell phone rang. She looked directly at Brad. He nodded it was alright for her to answer her phone. "Hello."

"Hi Marie, it's me Karen. How are you girls this evening?"

Marie pointed with her off hand to the phone. "Judy and I are fine."

"Have you seen or heard from Brad tonight?"

"Isn't he with you?"

"No, I'm in Vegas, and he is still in Seattle. At least I think he is in Seattle."

"That's odd, have you tried calling the house?"

"I called the house several times, he doesn't answer."

"If by chance we see, or hear from Brad. We'll tell him you called. Is there something you want us to tell Brad if we see him?"

"Bob Tilly our builder tells me he is three days away from finishing our project. The food venders are pushing us to place food orders. They want to know how much of what to order."

"Karen, I'm not part of your management team. I can't tell you what to do. Keep in mind Brad has never been in the fast food business before. Don't let him see you are afraid to make a decision, order some food."

"How much of what should I order?"

"Have the venders show you the last month of sales to the business before Brad bought it and go from there."

"This is a new business we have no history on food orders."

"That's right, it is a new business. Didn't you and he look at the buying a business before going for the new property?"

"We looked at three businesses."

"Choose one of those businesses and double their last months order."

"Double the order! Are you serious?"

"A larger business should mean more business. Double the food order it's a starting point."

"Don't you think it's risky for me to order food?"

"If Brad hasn't contacted you by tomorrow night, order the food. He sent you to Vegas for a reason."

"I hope you are right." Karen's words sounded skeptical.

"Good luck, bye." Marie wiped her forehead as she gave a sigh of relief as she turned off her phone. "How did I do?"

"You couldn't have done better if we had scripted what you were supposed to say. You covered my buns absolutely perfectly."

"Then you didn't mind my ordering food for your business?"

"Oh no not at all, I'm not ready to do any food ordering myself. I'm a pretty lame for a business owner."

Judy couldn't help but laugh. "I place you somewhere between lame and pathetic. I can't help but laugh at you. Can you explain why the hair on the back of your neck stood up just before she called?"

"I just had a feeling. Somewhat like a person gets in a poker game. She and I are in the middle of a high stake poker game. At stake are two million dollars and my reputation."

"When you finish with your attorney tomorrow you might want to give some thought to the food I ordered for you. Do you have freezer space, are the freezers on, that sort of thing."

In reality Karen's call lightened up the mood. "This is a neat evening cruise. We had a wonderful dinner, and a view to die for. The lights reflecting in the water make it look like a magical place."

"I'm glad you girls are enjoying yourself, thank you so much for joining me this evening. I wasn't up to spending an evening alone. Not being a tavern guy I needed company. Conning you girls into going out to dinner with me is all I could think of."

"Thank you for inviting us to join you for dinner. This is a real treat for Marie and me." Judy was finally beginning to relax.

Brad smiled. "When I was a kid with nothing to do, I would sit outside, and watch the cars go by. I would look at the people inside of the cars, and try to figure out what they were thinking. The couple over next to the big plant, they keep looking this way. Can you guess what they are thinking?"

"They are looking over here quite often. How are we supposed to guess what they are thinking about?" Judy questioned.

"Use your imagination. Make something up, you go first."

"Let's see, this is hard. The lady is trying to remember where she may have seen us before. We look familiar to her."

"Not bad Judy, your turn Marie."

"I'm going to concentrate on the gentleman. He is wondering how you managed to have dinner with two absolutely beautiful stunning women at the same time."

"Interesting, I like your story. My turn, I'm concentrating on both the man and the woman. They are thinking to themselves why are those idiot people staring at us?"

"Oh that's so lame, absolutely the worst." Judy proclaimed.

"I know, but my mind was distracted by two beautiful women."

"All I know is you were bad, and I wasn't very good, so that makes Marie the winner."

"I can't argue with your logic. The part where you said I was bad, you were dead right. Seems I need to brush up on my own game. Maybe on my way to Vegas I can practice on the airplane. I've made up my mind to fly down and buy my car there."

"I think we are docking now." Marie looked around. "Darn our evening was too short. This evening has been a fun filled evening. I'm not ready for it to end."

"All good things must come to an end. If you ladies will excuse me I think I will go use the facilities before we go ashore. I'll only be a minute."

In his absence Marie leaned over closer to Judy. "What do you think now, is he okay, or do we still need to be careful?"

"I'm much more at ease now than when we came aboard. After Karen's call he relaxed, and let his guard down. I still wouldn't want to be in her shoes when he sees her again. Pretty evident they are through. My guess is when he confronts Karen her natural instinct will be to deny anything is going on."

"I know it's stupid for me to say this. Since Brad will be leaving I hate to see him go. I wish I had the chance to get to know him better."

Brad returned in time to catch the end of Marie's statement. "Are you talking about Karen?"

"No, we were talking about you. We are still puzzled by you. There is no time to dice you up, and take a look inside, and study what makes you tick."

"I wouldn't recommend you look too hard or too deep. You might not like what you see. My track history has been on the rough side. Unfortunately my life doesn't appear to be getting better any time soon."

"You could be wrong. I might like what I saw." Marie warned in a teasing manor. "I plan on looking anyway."

"Your friends might think you need your head examined. The scary part is those people could be right. The departing line is thinning out. I think it's time for us to get back to our land loving ways."

On the way back to the house he stopped off at a motel. Judy gave him a dirty look while Marie was quick to ask. "Why are we stopping here?"

"I have a room here for the night. I thought I explained things to you earlier. You girls were hired to house sit only. I'm not part of the bargain. I don't need someone babysitting me."

"You don't have any clean clothes with you, not even a toothbrush." Marie pointed out. "There is no reason you can't stay at the house tonight. Karen stayed with you and nothing unusual happened."

"Hotels have complimentary toiletries so please don't argue with me. I'll taxi by the house in the morning after you girls have gone off to work. I can shower, and change before I go see my attorney. As I told you earlier today, I will see you tomorrow evening before I leave for Vegas. Goodnight ladies and thank you again for your great company this evening."

"Wait, we haven't thanked you properly." Marie was doing her best to keep him from leaving.

"The sparkle in your eyes has thanked me many times this evening. Again I bid you a goodnight, sweet dreams ladies."

Judy did the driving as they rode home in silence. Only in the house did she speak. "Brad is a man of many surprises." She commented.

"Never a dull moment and tomorrow when he leaves, will I still have many unanswered questions where he is concerned? Judy, don't be shocked by what I have to say. I find him extremely interesting."

"You have been wearing those feelings on your face all evening. I'm pleased you recognized the feelings yourself. You might not have believed me if I were to tell you how you looked. Where Brad is concerned be cautious. If he had come back to the house, and asked you to join him in his bedroom what would you have told him?"

"Now you are being silly. He didn't come back to the house and he has no reason to call the house."

"Brad looked at you the same way you looked at him. He may be lying in bed staring at the ceiling trying to think up an excuse to call you this very moment."

"Wow, some imagination, now you are playing Brad's game again. In my book you out did yourself, that makes you the winner this time."

Judy's thoughts were remarkably accurate. He was lying in bed thinking about Marie. He was comparing her to his departed Alice. He and Alice had connected instantly, yet it took four years, to allow their connection to evolve into the love it became when they married. He felt a similar connection to Marie. Could it be possible she might be the one for him. He desperately wanted to experience the enjoyable memories of marriage like he and Alice shared again. If Marie were the person he thought she was, some other guy could easily steal her love before he had a chance to know her better.

Near eleven Marie's phone rang startling her enough she jumped. "Hi Marie it's me again. I'm worried I've tried calling Brad all day. He doesn't answer his phone. Where are you girls now?"

"We are at the house. The security people coded us in earlier so we could move in. Odd as it seems Brad isn't here, but his car is in the garage."

"He isn't in Vegas, not yet anyway. Wish I had thought to call his attorney earlier. I bet his attorney knows where he is. I'll keep trying to track him down tomorrow, Bye."

CHAPTER 16

Mid-morning the following day Brad's meeting with his attorney Al Claymore didn't go as he expected. "If these two women are not currently working for you, don't put them on any payroll. You have no choice but to end your association with both these women fast as possible. We still have time to thwart their efforts. A two million dollar extortion attempt is a serious crime. I'll call the authorities."

The attorney's words surprised him. "Hold on a second, can't we handle this without the authorities being involved?"

"No, we could be accessories to attempted insurance fraud if we don't call the authorities. You may as well sit down and be patient while I make the call. I'm sure the authorities will have questions for you to answer."

"Hold on a minute. Give me a chance to think. Is there a chance we could wait one more day before calling the authorities?"

"Why should we wait one day?" Brad's attorney looked at him rather suspicious.

"You mentioned calling the authorities. Does that mean you would be speaking to more than the Seattle Police?"

"Certainly it means more than the local police. An extortion of two million dollars across state lines would be a Federal crime involving the FBI."

"I thought as much. My security system would be thoroughly checked for further evidence. What if there was something the FBI shouldn't see on the security system videos?"

"Are you talking about pornography?"

"No I'm not talking about pornography. I'm talking about a party while I was out of town. Karen had a couple of her former female roommates over. They did some body painting and skinny-dipping in the hot tub. No drugs or alcohol involved just three girls having a fun evening while I was gone traveling."

"Have you seen this portion of the security video of their party?"

"No, I heard about the party, and I know my security system. I would never intrude on the girls privacy unless there was some emergency to do so."

"Even though the girl's party might be viewed as pornography you don't dare tamper with the security video. I can wait one day to call the authorities if you would like to inform the girls as to what will be coming down. It's the best we can do. They wouldn't be shocked so bad if you informed them ahead of time your security videos will be gone through."

"These are nice down to earth girls. They were only having fun. I hate putting them in this awkward position."

"As your attorney I can only advise you not to tamper with the security system. If the authorities realize you tampered with your security system they won't like it."

"I already have tampered with my system part of the evidence against Karen and Kathy is in your machine. Why would they need to look at more of my video recordings?"

"I'm hoping you won't further tamper with your security video. If the Feds realize you tampered with the security video a second time, well after you realized a major crime had been committed they would make your life a living hell. You should leave well enough alone."

"Alright Mr. Claymore, call the authorities before I do something stupid."

"I can request two agents, one male and one female for the investigation if that will help. Wait here while I place the call." Claymore returned in minutes. "Someone will be coming over from the FBI Office in a few minutes. We'll soon know how aggressive the agents might be."

"Don't forget I need those women slammed out of my business fast. I have food in the freezers that needs to be sold. I don't have time to play around with these people."

Special Agent Jim Walters along with Special Agent Ann Sherman showed up in their Navy blue suits. After studying the video the agents were not as excited as Mr. Claymore. "This is an attempt of a crime that can be prevented. No crime has actually been committed. It would be a waste of our time to pursue what you have time to prevent. At best we have a case that will likely end in a suspended sentence. Our suggestion is for you, and your attorney Mr. Claymore to handle these ladies."

This news was music to Brad's ears. After the Special Agents left Brad took charge of the meeting. "Write up a letter explaining extortion across state lines is a Federal crime. Advise them any further attempt at continuing this extortion attempt will result in Federal Prosecution to the full extent of the law. I'll make copies of this video and deliver both your letters and copies of my video to both ladies in person. Can your letters be ready today?"

"I'll have the letters ready by four today."

"Thank you Mr. Claymore."

From the attorney's office he taxied over to Avis Car Rentals so he could rent a car to get around Seattle easier. Once he had his rental car he made two calls. Call one was easy, Marie answered the first ring. "Hi Marie, I need to intrude on you girls tonight."

"You won't be intruding on us. Come over any time you like, and stay long as you want."

"It's two now and I need time. I may be at the house when you girls get home this evening."

"If you finish early please don't leave before we get home. I do want to see you before you go. I'll come home after work fast as I can."

His second call was much tougher as he called Vegas. "Hello Karen, how are things going in Vegas?"

"My nerves are shot. I've called and called trying for two days to get you, where have you been?"

"I left my cell phone in my attorney's office and didn't know where I left the dumb thing. I met with Mr. Claymore an hour ago. He didn't remember to give the phone to me until I was leaving his office a few minutes ago. Believe it or not I have to go back and see Claymore later today for a second meeting. I'm trying to set up a limited partnership for the Burger Palace. Lots of tax advantages to a limited partnership?"

"When are you coming to Vegas?"

"I'm hoping to arrive in Vegas tomorrow afternoon. My attorney doesn't get in any hurry. I'll keep you posted as to when I'm coming. I bet Bob Tilly probably thinks I've abandoned him. Before long he will be screaming for more money. By the way how are your parents doing?"

"Mom and dad are great, we are all anxious to see you."

"Tell your parents I will see them soon, and I have a surprise for everyone. I have an appointment with my accountant in a couple minutes so I better let you go."

"Thanks for calling."

Brad drove straight to the house where he began unpacking and reassembling his electronic equipment to enable him to make copies of the video. At four he dashed back to pick up the attorney letters. Then it was straight back to the house to continue reassembling enough of the electronic equipment to make the video copies he needed. When the girls arrived home they came looking for him. "Good heavens, what a mess. Pray tell what are you doing now?"

"Because of privacy issues, I needed my equipment."

"Oh, I see. May I be of any help?" Marie asked.

"I won't turn down help. Very carefully unpack those boxes by the number. Leave the packing supplies by each box. My equipment will be repacked soon as I finish what I'm working on."

"Are you doing something illegal?"

"The short answer is no. My attorney left me no choice, but to deal with both Karen and Kathy the same way, swift and hard. Extortion of two million dollars across state lines would be a Federal crime. I need to end their plans before it actually becomes a Federal crime. I can't see twenty years in a Federal prison for Karen. Twenty years for Kathy wouldn't bother me all that much. I need to work fast with my own equipment and kill their plans."

"Brad, you are rambling on. Do what you have to do. Maybe someday you will trust Judy and me, enough to completely confide in us."

"As they continued unpacking both girls continued frowning at him. "Okay girls, here is the bottom line. If the Feds get involved they will confiscate all my security videos and all my equipment. I need my equipment in Vegas for the Burger Palace. Along with my equipment they would confiscate all my security videos, including a video of three girls having a party. The confiscated video would be gone over with a fine tooth comb. You video could be seen as pornography. They wouldn't miss one inch of anything. How many Federal agents do you want them seeing your girl's gone wild party?"

"We don't want any Federal agents seeing that video. I thought you said our video was gone?"

"For all intent and purposes your video is gone. Using the enhancing system the Feds could restore your portion of the video. I need my equipment to make copies of this video to end the threat against me. If the actual crime is committed, I can't tamper with my equipment. Once I have accomplished my goal of making the copies, I will repack this equipment and send it to Vegas. The FBI won't have any way of knowing I've been meddling around because they have no idea this equipment exists."

"You can talk all night and I still won't completely understand the danger. We'll leave you alone."

"Thank you Marie." He checked every connection twice before starting to make a powerful subliminal message for Karen. Her message carried a secondary message designed so she would be influenced to forget about his subliminal message process. Feeling confident he placed the new CD in a case for transporting. He made three copies of the security video of Karen talking to her mother before starting to disassemble the equipment.

"Wow you finished, I'm impressed. Can you stay for dinner this evening, Judy has a guy joining us and you can be my date." Marie suggested.

Brad winked at her. "No young man would turn down a free meal with a beautiful fun loving girl. You never mentioned Judy had a male friend we could have taken him on our dinner cruise the other day."

"Judy met her guy a few weeks ago. They have gone out on six dates. She finds Rob interesting and invited him over for dinner. May I give you a hand repacking your equipment?"

"Certainly Marie, your help would be well appreciated."

As they finished repacking the equipment Judy called them for dinner. "Oh hey, you packed everything back. Your timing is perfect, dinner is ready."

"We'll wash up and be right with you Judy."

Marie patted his hand before going to wash up. "Remember you are my date this evening."

"Careful what you wish for, I have rules about dating."

"I'll have you know I also have rules about dating. I only date guys I like. I'm not usually this forward. We only have this evening for a date. I see something in you I like."

"I hope I can live up to your assessment of me. I would certainly feel badly if I were to disappoint you. May I ask when our date officially begins?"

"Far as I'm concerned our date has already started."

"Oh no our date couldn't have started. I know when my dates start. My dates start with a kiss. One of my little rules I told you about." He eased Marie into his arms and took the opportunity to give her a sweet tender kiss. "Now our date is official."

"Nice rule, I like it. Let's go eat. We don't want Judy's food getting cold."

Joining Judy and her date, Marie started the introductions. "Rob this is Brad Collins. Brad this…"

"…Rob Benson!" He said finishing her sentence. Brad reached out for a handshake. "How are you Rob?"

"How do you two know each other?" Judy asked.

"We did a year in high school together. Rob was pretty much my only friend that year. At least we were friends most of the time."

"Good to see you Brad. Pardon me, but I was under the impression you and Alice tied the knot a few years ago?"

"Your memory is quite correct, we did get married. She passed away in an unfortunate automobile accident shortly after we married."

"I'm sorry Brad, I didn't know. Alice was a nice gal, you guys made a wonderful couple. I thought a lot of her."

"How about you Rob, what are you doing these days?"

"I'm a meat cutter for a local grocery store."

Judy served her dinner temporarily interrupting the conversation. "I'm confused, help me out Brad. How do you know these girls?"

"We had classes together in college. I dropped by this evening to say my goodbyes. I'm moving to Vegas tomorrow. I'll be living in Vegas all summer, possibly longer. I'm at a crossroads in my life and there are several directions I could go. I have one year of college left. I would love to finish my degree. At the same time I feel a business opportunity is at hand."

"If I had an interesting business offer, I wouldn't bother getting a degree. Money makes the world go around."

"There are not enough hours in the night to bring you up to speed on my life. I screw up on a regular basis. If you ever need lessons on screwing up, call me. I can give you advice on how to screw up quickly."

"Think I'll pass if you don't mind. I'm not sure I like those dark circles under your eyes. If I had to guess I would say you need to sleep for a week."

"Very close assessment of me my friend. Unfortunately I have more unpleasant things I need to handle in Las Vegas tomorrow. Once it's over, I no doubt will sleep much better. I'll still be busy, but I will sleep far better. Vegas is such a vibrant city. I can't wait to get my business going."

"I'm sure the girl's wish you well on your business venture, and so do I. I never had the pleasure of being in Las Vegas. I hear it is an exciting city."

"Thank you Rob." He turned to Judy and gave her a wink. "Your dinner was excellent thank you for inviting me to stay, and eat with you. I better get on over to my motel, and get some sleep."

Marie walked him to his car. "I wish you didn't have to leave so soon."

"Right this minute I hate going myself. Unless I slip you in my suitcase, and take you with me there isn't much I can do." He took the liberty of kissing her goodbye. His kiss took her breath away. "You made quite an impact on my life these past couple days. I may make a nuisance of myself calling you."

"Please do call. I'll be waiting your calls. Take care of yourself, get some rest." After one last kiss she stood watching him drive away wondering when she might see him again.

After saying goodbye to him, Marie rejoined Judy and Rob. "How well do you know Brad?" She enquired of Rob.

"I doubt anyone knows him well. He and I were in high school together. Like most people I find him interesting. He can be an extremely vengeful man. Don't ever get on his bad side. His mood can change in an instant. He sees things different than most people. You might be well served to steer clear of him. In school he had virtually no friends."

"I don't see him as a bad person."

"I didn't say he was a bad guy. I said he had a bad side, he killed a guy once in a split second."

"Yes he killed a guy once, but self-defense isn't a crime."

"Then you know Brad's story."

"We both know the story, we saw the video also. I will not judge Brad on his actions that day. I believe any guy would have fought back when threatened as he was."

"Sorry I upset you Marie. Where most people in his situation would have run, he refused to give up control. He could have a dangerous side. For that reason I believe people should be cautious around him, or when dealing with him,"

"Our deal with him is simple we are sitting his house for the summer. How can we get hurt house sitting for him when he is fourteen hundred miles away?"

"You girls are house sitters, now I'm really confused. It's not like him to walk off and leave two nice looking girls. He becomes attached to women rather easy. I noticed your watches earlier. Your watches are identical. If I were to guess, I bet he bought those watches for you girls."

"So what if he bought these watches, what difference does it make to you?" Marie was quick to challenge Rob.

"This is exactly how your hero Brad operates. He controls people with money. Money is his power. Small gifts could lead to larger gifts. Each calculated step brings him closer to your beds."

"Neither Judy nor I have been intimate with Brad, so your comments are way out of line and not appreciated."

"Oh come on girls, even you must realize he doesn't make friends easy. I'm probably as close to being a friend as anyone can be to him, and I don't know him well."

"I'm tired of arguing with you. I'm turning in for the night, you two do as you please. You can talk all night if you want."

"Easy Marie, even an idiot like me can see you are hung up on the guy. Listen to your mind not your heart. The watches you are wearing are expensive. Next time you are out shopping at the Mall and check the price tags. Each time you check your watch you will think about him. That is the actions of a controlling person."

"You are entitled to your idiot opinion." She snapped back at him.

With Marie gone Judy challenged Rob. "What pleasure do you get out of badgering Marie?"

"I'm willing to bet in the fall when Brad returns, he will have a golden path laid all the way to her bed?"

Judy shook her head. "You have been watching too many goofy movies. It's time for you to leave. You might want to study up on how to act when out in public before we go out again."

"You are right. My comments were out of line. Brad was raised different than most people. The only love and affection he received was the love of the money his father sent him. All other love he demanded from those near him. Alice his nanny was a classic example. She was four years older than him. Yet she was the woman he married."

Judy began to laugh. "Don't feel bad Rob, you are not the first person to be jealous of someone who was born with a silver spoon in his or her mouth." Judy promptly escorted him to the door. Don't bother calling, jealous people irritate me to no end."

CHAPTER 17

Arriving in Vegas Brad went straight to Ceasers Casino and Resort to check into a room. The following morning on the advice of his accountant he was off to the Employment Security Department Office. He was given a seven-name list of management personal leads. He needed to choose a qualified bondable person to run the day-to-day operation. An office manager would be chosen the same way later.

Two steps inside the Burger Palace, Bob Tilly spotted Brad. "Well, look who is back. We were about to put our flag at half mask, and list you among the missing."

"I haven't been missing, I have been hiding out. I don't want Karen or Kathy Moore knowing I'm here yet. I have a couple things to do before I call those two misfits."

"Are there unforeseen problems, I should know about?"

"My problems are strictly with them, and nothing to do with you. The problems will be cleared away by the end of the day. The Burger Palace looks great you have done a magnificent job."

"Three days and my crews will be finished and out of your hair."

"Fantastic! How about the sound system, can it be used?"

"The sound system has been finished for two weeks."

"Excellent I love music it allows me to think better. I'll scoot around and look things over while you go right on with your work. I'll check the office out in a few minutes."

He made a complete lap of the Burger Palace before busying himself in the office to start the subliminal message he made for Karen. Once he assured himself the sound system was working fine it was time to call her. "Hello Karen! I hear you been trying to call me."

"I've tried calling a dozen times today, where are you?"

"I stopped by the Burger Palace. I thought you would be here. The place looks great. Bob has done a fantastic job."

"I'll be there in a half hour, don't run off." She ran to tell her mother the good news. "Mother, Brad is at the Burger Place. I'm going to meet him now."

"It's about time that damn punk kid showed up. What kind of a mood does he seem to be in?"

"He sounds happy as I've ever heard him."

"Give him a big hug and a kiss for me. I'll fix a special dinner tonight for the four of us. Time for a celebration Honey, I can feel the money coming our way. Your father will have the best of care."

"I've got to go mother he is waiting for me. Remember what I told you mother, he has been dealing with his attorney. I think he was working on a Limited Partnership Agreement for us. You and I may become partners so we won't have any reason to sue."

"I didn't hear the words you heard, but being a partner could make a difference. Remember be nice and no matter what don't disagree with him on anything."

Playing it cool Brad greeted Karen with a welcoming hug. "Things are looking great around here. As I look out the office window down on to the working floor I can visualize all the activity soon to be down on the floor."

"I have a few pieces of furniture coming for the apartment later today."

"Good for you, I'm testing the sound system now. I've walked around to various locations in the building. Not one dead spot in the whole building. Listen how clear the music comes through. We have top of the line sound equipment. I may have to do some tweaking on my equipment to match what is here but I don't expect any real problems or delays."

"I know how you are about skipping meals when you are busy. Have you eaten lunch today?"

"I'm too excited to eat anything."

"Why don't I go get us something to eat, what would you like?"

"Why chase around. We can have pizza delivered. You can stay here and talk to me. Let someone else do the work." Thirty minutes later the combination pizza arrived. The delivery man looked shocked at Brad's tip. "I wonder if that delivery guy is going to school and delivering pizza to make extra money or is he a born loser?"

"What a strange question, why would a delivery man concern you at all?"

"I care about people. Some people go through their entire lives looking for the perfect get rich quick scheme only find themselves flat on their fanny. In the end and wind up with nothing."

"I have other things to do besides worry about other people."

Although her comment angered him he was careful not to show his anger. "I've been watching Bob work. I'm surprised to see him do anything except oversee the project. I feel bad about him missing the bonus. Do you believe he did his best to stay on schedule?"

"I believe he gave it a fair attempt. Why worry about Bob, you saved a bundle of money. You should be thrilled and dancing in the aisles to this lovely music. By the way mother is fixing a special dinner this evening for us. She feels like celebrating."

"I can't make dinner tonight. I'm having a business dinner meeting with Bob and Robin Tilly. We may be doing other projects in the near future. It will be nine, or so before I can come by the house." Her lack of concern for the pizza man and now the lack of concern for Bob missing his performance bonus wouldn't leave his mind.

"Then I better call mother and have her hold off her special dinner until tomorrow evening. We'll leave the cork in the wine bottle. Mother bought a hundred fifty dollar bottle of wine for the occasion."

"By all means call your mother and tell her dinner sounds wonderful but I can't make it." While she was on the phone the apartment furniture arrived. "Karen your furniture is here."

"I've got to go mom. The apartment furniture is here, bye." She hustled down to show the delivery men how to arrange the furniture while he had quick conversation with Bob to arrange a dinner meeting. She soon returned near him. "Is there anything else that you know of I need to do today? If not I have a ton of errands needing done."

"It looks to me like things are pretty well in hand. I see no reason you can't skip out if you want. I have calls of my own to make. I will swing by and see your parents a minute after my dinner meeting this evening."

"Daddy will be sleeping before nine, but mother and I will be anxiously waiting your arrival." She stated with a fake cute sexy smile. "You are welcome to stay at the house tonight."

"Waiting up for me would be perfect, I will see you later." His calls consisted of the seven potential restaurant manager names given to him by the employment office. He set up employee interviews for the following two days. Late afternoon he started on his second list. The secretary list was shorter list but equally important. Brad chose five people for personal interviews. Four women and one man's name appeared in the interview times.

Having dinner with the Tillys was a pleasant evening for him. "You may be wondering why Karen didn't join us this evening. I can't explain my situation this evening. Tomorrow I may be able to fill you in as to our less than wonderful situation."

Bob smiled at him. "I watched the two of you today, and you were all business. It's a smart move on your part to separate business and pleasure. You notice even though Robin and I are married but we don't compete with one another. We work together but in separate areas, never do we compete directly."

"You make a good point. Let's concentrate on this evening. I'm extremely pleased at your efforts remodeling for me. I'm sure you are aware you missed the performance bonus by one week."

"I am well aware I missed out on the performance. There is no need to rub it in. I missed out on a good deal. There was no place we could cut a corner and save any time."

"Although I do not owe you the performance bonus, I would like to pay you your bonus. I believe you made an intense effort to finish on time. You tried hard."

His offer startled Bob for a second. "Paying me the bonus is more than I should expect."

"You worked hard and your work looks perfect."

Ninety minutes later at the Moore's home a brief moment of joy was followed by shouting, anger, and crying as he laid out his evidence against Karen and her stepmother. "We are not doing anything to you!"

"In those packets you will hear the evidence, I heard. Karen, in your packet is a check for twenty five thousand dollars to cover anything you ever did on my behalf. I bid you ladies goodbye. Have a good life."

The instant he left the Moore residence Kathy ripped into her stepdaughter slapping her several time leading to an all out brawl. Neighbors called the police to end the brawl in the Moore's house. Police officers stood guard as Karen packed a small bag, and left for the night.

The following day was a new experience for Brad. He had never interviewed potential employees before. With tension high it was a long exhausting day for him. On day two of the interview process a fifty-four year old red-haired woman stood out well ahead of all competitors as the secretary he needed. Her interview was still being conducted when he realized he found the person he wanted. Wendy and her husband operated a small construction business for twenty-five years. Their business became bogged down in regulations. It was time for their construction company to get big, or get out. Nearing age sixty wasn't a time she and her husband, wanted to go heavy in debt to grow larger. He was straight forward with Wendy. "I need experienced help. This is my first attempt at operating a business of any kind. You could fill my needs very well." Out the corner of his eye he saw Karen enter the Burger Palace.

Wendy saw the look of concern on his face. "Is there a problem of some sort Mr. Collins?"

"Someone I thought I knew but didn't, will be coming to my office in a few minutes. Sit tight while I send her on her way."

"Wouldn't it be best if I stepped out for a few minutes?" Wendy rose to leave.

"Sit tight this person won't be here long." Karen knocked on the office door before entering. "Hello Karen, I saw you walk in."

"Can we…Aunt Wendy! What are you doing here?"

"I'm applying for a job, we folded our business. Regulations were killing our profit line. Joe was spending more time dealing with red tape than working."

Karen turned back to Brad. "Can we talk?"

"There isn't anything you can say I want to hear, except goodbye. Please leave my office before I call the police, and have you physically removed."

"I stopped by to return your check." She held out the check he gave her. "I don't want your money."

"Keep the damn check you are going to need it. It's a settlement suggested by my attorney Al Claymore. Cash the check and move on with your life." She hesitated before leaving. He waited until she cleared the outside door before turning back to his conversation with Wendy. "I'm sure you are wondering what that is all about. I've been doing some wondering myself. Did I hear Karen call you Aunt Wendy?'

"She is my niece. Her idiot father and I are brother and sister. That's because you can't disown your relatives. Vern is a less than honest man. His phony accident ended our business. He was injured moonlighting after work not injured on our job site as he claimed. How do you know Karen?"

"We attended college together. I fell into a trap of my own where she and her parents are concerned. They clipped me for a hundred thousand dollars."

"Oh boy does that ever sound like them. I'm sure with the family references I have this interview is over. I thank you for your time Mr. Collins."

"Hold on Mrs. Olsen we are not finished, are you bondable?"

"Oh certainly, there are no skeletons in my closet."

"Then we should continue this interview if you are still interested?"

Wendy's eyes brightened. "Of course I'm interested Mr. Collins. I need a good job."

"Then let's proceed. I'm new in the business world. No doubt I need excellent help. An experienced person like you could keep my accountant happy. He thinks I've lost my mind buying this place. I'm thinking once he sees the money we can generate from this facility, he will be amazed."

"Mr. Collins I can certainly do the job of keeping your books straight. When it comes to the actual service and sales end, I may not be of much help to you."

"I will have a good restaurant manager working down below. I will be encouraging sales from up here by running promotions and daily specials." After working out the pay agreement he asked the obvious question. "Mrs. Olsen when can you start work?"

"When I start is your call Mr. Collins. I can start as soon as you want me."

"First we need a computer system suitable for bookkeeping, inventory, and ordering. I normally use computer products that are user friendly, and have good tech support. Do you have time to go down to the office supply store today?"

His words put a bright smile on Wendy's pretty face. "Certainly, I can go today, but may I call my husband first?"

"By all means call your husband, be my guest. Use the phone on the desk if you want."

Ernie Meadows a nice looking thirty five year old black gentleman, was hired as the restaurant manager. With Ernie's management skills he pulled together a fine group of assistant managers and employees in less than a week. Training became priority one. Ernie seemed to have the ability to take a clumsy person, and turn them into a decent employee, in a very short time. He created instant respect among the Burger Palace employees. "Opening day was a proud moment as a giant weight had been lifted off Brad's shoulders. By mid-morning he went down to congratulate Ernie on the fine job he was doing. In about a week I will install more electronic equipment in the office. The equipment is designed to help promote sales. I will be pushing you and your employees. As business increases, add more employees as you need them."

Later that same evening Brad called the girls in Seattle. "Hi Judy, how are things in Seattle?"

"Hello Brad, it's good to hear your voice. Things are going fine here in the great northwest. We were wondering when you might call. What happened with Karen and her parents?"

"We parted company. There wasn't much they could say. I learned a lot myself during the ordeal. I held actual job interviews for all my current employees. My key people bonded into a fine workforce. The Burger Palace is running smoothly, and in front of me taped to the wall is the first dollar we made. Of all the dollars I touched in my life, I'm most proud of this dollar. Is Marie home this evening?"

"She is in the shower. Let me walk back that way. I'll see how long she will be in the shower." He listened as Judy called out her name. "Brad's on the line. Do you want to speak to him now or should I ask him to call back in a few minutes?"

Dripping wet, she stepped out of the shower to take his call. "Hi, it's about time you called."

"I've been busy putting together a management team, and yes the Burger Palace is open and operating smoothly. I'm anxious to do some experiments in advertising. I'm ready to have my equipment shipped. "

"I can ship your things any day you want. Tell me about Karen, you know I'm dying to find out what happened?"

"She and her stepmother didn't say much to me. I laid the proof before them and left. One day later Karen came to the Burger Palace wanting to talk. I told her we had nothing to discuss, and asked her to leave. Tell me about yourself, how are you doing?"

"Now that you called, I feel great. I'm as sexy as ever and I miss talking to you. Your kisses were nice too."

"Oh please stop, you are making me homesick. I'll be crying my eyes out tonight if you don't stop."

"Yea right, there are a million beautiful women in Vegas. I'm sure you can have your pick of girls, any day you want."

"There are no girls here in Vegas as pretty as you." He countered.

"Now you are making my heart flutter. If you were here I would give you a big hug and a kiss for such a nice comment."

"Please don't tempt me. I might fly home some weekend just to collect that kiss. A man can never get too many hugs and kisses."

"You know where to find me. Fly to Seattle any time you want your kiss. I'll be waiting. If you kiss me real nice, I may give you more than one kiss."

"You may see me sometime in the near future. Right now before I forget, use the credit card I left with you to use to pay the shipping on my equipment and insure my equipment for fifty thousand dollars."

"Will do captain, how is the Burger Palace operating?"

"The place is doing very well. I need to get my electronic equipment operational. I want to conduct advertising experiments, before our new business shine wears off. We are still working out small bugs, oops, bad choice of words. I shouldn't use the term bugs around a restaurant. How are your jobs going?"

"Thank goodness for our house sitting job. One of our part-time jobs fell through. We are looking for a filler job now. Tavern waitress is all that is available. I do not want to work in a tavern serving drinks to drunks and have my fanny pinched all the time."

"Don't get depressed Marie, you gals are helping me immensely. I will cover any financial shortage you incur."

"Don't be silly our finances are not your responsibility."

"Easy girl, friends help friends. You my dear I consider a dear friend. We can work this out. In the meantime don't worry." Over the next two hours they exchanged information and pleasantries. "I shouldn't be taking up your evening."

"I'm glad you called you made my day. I hope you call often. I want you to keep me apprised as to how you are doing with your business. I can only imagine how fun it is to watch your dream grow into reality."

"It is fun. If I call too often be sure, and tell me. I'm in the action city of Las Vegas, but I've never been lonelier in my life. I have no friends here."

"You will become friends with coworkers. If you are not somewhat friends with your coworkers, how could a person work with them?"

"Doesn't matter how natural befriending a coworker is. I can't afford to become personally involved with any of them. I hired a fifty four year old lady to be my secretary, a woman old enough to be my mother. Thankfully Wendy was the most qualified. Please excuse me I shouldn't be whining to you about how lonely I am."

"I don't consider your conversation as you whining. Talk to me anytime you want. Our conversations are always interesting. I have broad shoulders anytime you feel like talking please call. Tell me a little about Wendy."

"Wendy is a nice well developed female who doesn't show her age. It's easy to see she has taken good care of herself over the years. She has red hair and dresses appropriately for office work. She wears business suits or a nice mid-length dress. Wendy and her husband ran a company of their own until regulations forced them to get big, or get out. She is very professional in her approach to work. I think we'll be working together for many years."

"Wendy sounds nice. Now I have a mental picture of her. Send me a picture if you get one."

"Why would I have a picture of Wendy, I don't have a picture of any females."

"Oh heavens, that will never do. I should send you a picture of me."

Her words were music to his ears. "Please do send me a picture of you. I'll put your picture on my bed-stand next to my bed. Speaking of bed, I better say goodnight, morning comes early. Remember the dark circles under my eyes, they haven't left yet."

"Get more rest silly, you were bragging on your fine employees. Take a morning or afternoon off once in a while, and get the rest you need." She suggested. "Everyone needs rest."

"Yes mother, I'll try and get more rest."

"Stop that, you are insulting me."

"I'm only kidding Marie. I will try your advice and get more rest. Maybe if you were to tuck me in, then you could monitor my rest."

"My arms are too short to tuck you in so tuck yourself in very carefully, and stay there eight full hours. Your body will love the rest."

"Okay angel, I better let you go, goodnight."

"Call anytime, goodnight. I'll be thinking about you."

Over the next three weeks Brad installed his equipment, and began creating his subliminal messages. Wendy checked inventory each day allowing him to make the daily adjustments to keep sales at the desired levels, and food fresh. Each week Ernie made one healthy food change in the menu. Using subliminal messages, and the employees hard work profits increased. A health insurance plan was added for key personnel. Ernie was astounded at the steady business. As a cover Brad used some of his subliminal messages on the radio ads. He wanted people to believe radio advertising was responsible for the steady business. In reality he was encouraging customers to purchase extra food items, along with returning to the Burger Palace more often. The process being so easy left him unchallenged. With each passing day he grew more bored.

Looking for boredom relief he called Marie three times a week. "Marie, how would you like to go to a movie, or dinner one of these days?"

"I would love to go out for dinner with you, but I think you are forgetting something. I live in Seattle you live in Las Vegas."

"Thanks to the Wright brothers, I can arrange a flight to Seattle. In three hours I could be on your doorstep."

"Fly up first chance you can. I'll be waiting with open arms, and the kisses I promised."

"How about I fly up this Friday night and spend the weekend together?"

Marie's heart raced. "Friday night would be perfect."

"I'll call and give you my arrival time later. See you soon Marie, save those kisses for me."

"I will save many kisses for you." Brad always felt good after speaking to Marie. If only she lived closer to him they might have a chance at a real loving relationship.

If he were to ever get time away from work he would need to plan well ahead or take a loss in sales while he was gone. He could stock up on music laced with subliminal messages to promote certain products. He could leave instruction for Wendy to play certain music on certain days.

CHAPTER 18

Making his weekend date plans with Marie wasn't enough to keep Brad from being bored. Wendy observed his mood change as he slid into a state of depression.

"Mr. Collins something is bothering you, what is it?" He turned and looked at Wendy. "I'm a good listener if you care to talk."

"My employees are doing so well, there is no challenge in my being here. I have one hour of productive work each day. The rest of my day is pointless, and boring. Since I'm not a golfer, what am I supposed to do all day?"

"The money this business is bringing in is nothing short of fantastic. Most people would be dancing on the roof top with the income we are generating. In a very short time you have created one of the most successful small businesses in this city. I don't understand how can you be bored?" Wendy touched the back of his neck. "Wow, your neck muscles are knotted something awful. No wonder you don't feel good. I'll finish counting this money in a minute, but first let me massage your neck."

As Wendy began massaging his neck he thought about his new promise not to mix business and pleasure. He immediately reached back and stopped her hands. "Please don't, I'll be back later." He left the office in a harried rush.

His reaction to a simple touch came as a shock to Wendy, leaving her with questions. She felt confident a simple touch wasn't wrong. Why would her touch bring such a response? She watched as he left the building. Outside in the parking lot he strolled around as if in some sort of trance. Occasionally he stooped over to pick up a stray piece of paper. Clearly he was struggling with an emotional problem. Without looking where he was walking Brad stepped directly in the path of a car.

The car swerved but clipped him enough to topple him over. Wendy raced out to see if he was okay. She found him standing next to the car apologizing to the lady for scaring her. "What on earth were you doing, are you on drugs of some kind?"

"No Wendy, I'm not on drugs or medication of any kind." He turned and started away.

She grabbed his arm enough to jerk him around to face her. "Come back here. Don't you dare walk away when I'm talking to you? Something is wrong, and I want to know what it is."

"I'm okay Wendy. I came out here to be alone so I could think."

"Do your thinking in a safe place, not in the middle of the traffic in our parking lot."

"You are making a big deal out of nothing that lady barely bumped me. I'm not hurt, and I apologized for scaring her. Let's just drop the whole incident."

"You were not injured because the lady was paying close attention by looking where she was driving and swerved. Had she been looking at parking spaces rather than where she was driving, you would be in the back of an ambulance on your way to the hospital. I saw what happened from the window. Come back up to the office where we can talk."

"Wendy, you don't understand. I hate that flipping office. I feel like a damn caged animal sitting up there. Plain and simple, I do not have enough to do. If you insist on talking can we go for a walk to do our talking?"

"How far are we walking?"

He gave a short laugh. "Depends on how long you want to talk."

"I haven't been walking much lately. These high heal are not made for walking. Add in my fifty four year old legs, and you may have to carry me back if we walk very far."

He glanced at her shoes and then at her legs. "You do have nice legs, walking will be good for them. I love it when you wear dresses. Too many women these days hide their legs."

"My husband Joe might not like you discussing my legs. We came on this walk to talk about you not me." He steered her into a store." Why are we going in this store?"

"This store sells shoes. You need walking shoes."

"I didn't bring my purse. I can't buy new shoes."

"I'll pay for your shoes."

"Now hold on a minute, why are you buying me shoes?"

"It's very simple in five short years of sitting in our office your beautiful legs will be fat as a butterball. Your husband won't like that either. From now on each morning before it gets too hot, I want you to take a fifteen or twenty minute walk. The exercise will do you good."

"Mr. Collins is my walk mandatory?"

"It's getting warm now. You could walk in the cool of a morning. It would be good for you."

"What if I don't like walking alone?"

"Grab one of our employees to walk with you."

"Or I could grab you for my walking partner?"

"You and I won't be walking together each day. Our walking together each day wouldn't look proper, and people love to talk."

"I agree our walking together each day could draw suspicion." Walking with new shoes made a world of difference. "These shoes are much better for walking, but we should be turning back. It's been a long half hour, are you going back with me?"

"I'll go back with you, but I haven't done anything to ease my boredom. Guess I'll have to think of something later. Wendy if you don't want to walk each morning we could turn the apartment into an exercise room."

"The apartment in the rear of the Burger Palace is new, you can't tear it apart." Wendy protested.

"It is doubtful the apartment will ever be used. My plans changed a great deal since I built the apartment."

"I'm puzzled. I've seen the inside of the apartment. It is a nice apartment. Can you tell me why you are not living in the apartment?"

"I don't live in the apartment because I'm spoiled. I live where other people wait on me, and I like activity around me. In the apartment I would be alone, so I have a suite at the Ceasars."

"Wait a minute are you serious, you actually live in a suite at Caesars?"

"I live in the hotel connected to the Casino. It's one of the best bachelor pads in the city. All the place lacks is a fine lady friend."

"You don't appear to be the type of guy who would lack for female attention. Look around; there are nice looking young women everywhere."

"Shows how wrong you can be. I have problems with the opposite gender. I become attached way to fast for my own good. Patience is not my best trait."

Wendy nodded her head. "Are you talking about Karen?"

"She would be a perfect example. I met her and wound up liking her better than she liked me. My misjudgment of character almost cost me two million dollars. She and her idiot mother were setting me up for a sexual harassment lawsuit. I accidentally caught on to their scheme and foiled their plan."

"That sounds like the Moore family. Wait until we get back in the office and tell me more about what she and her idiot mother were up to." The Burger Palace was busy as ever as they returned to the office. "Now sit down and tell me about Karen." Wendy changed her shoes back to her high-heals.

"Karen isn't important anymore. She isn't who I'm worried about now. My dealings with her are over and done with. It's the next girl I met. She seems to be a nice wholesome girl. Unfortunately she lives in Seattle. How can I…"

"…the money, the money is gone!" Wendy screamed looking around like a wild woman.

Brad's head snapped around. "What money is gone?"

"I was counting money when you almost got hit by the car. I ran out to see if you were okay. I forgot about the money, it's gone. The money was lying right here on my desk, it's gone." She patted her hand on the desk where the money had been.

Brad glanced across the desk. "How much money was there?"

"I would think there was six or seven thousand dollars, maybe more. I'll cover your loss but we better call the police."

"No don't call the police, call Ernie on the intercom. See if any of our employees left early before their shift ended." He waited as she checked. "All our employees are working. I better call the police, our money went somewhere. A crime has been committed."

He placed his hand on the telephone preventing her from picking it up. "Forget calling the police, we don't need any police."

"We have to call the police, we've been robbed."

"Wendy we don't need bad publicity. I don't want people thinking we are an easy place to rob. Let me try something before we call the police. I feel our robber could be an employee because customers shouldn't know this office is up here." Without giving any thought to Wendy observing his actions he mixed the most powerful subliminal message he ever made with a music video. It was then he realized he had made the special CD, in full view of Wendy. "Call Ernie and tell him not to allow any employee to leave the building. If any employee tries to leave have Ernie stop them from leaving until I talk to the employee."

She quickly followed his instructions. "You really believe an employee stole the money, and will try to leave?"

"If you stole seven thousand dollars wouldn't you want to leave early?

I'm going to nudge our suspect a touch. Let's change the music to a new tempo. Now Mr. Thief, if you are in the building your ass is mine." He stated with excitement.

Wendy was in the state of confusion. "What on earth are you doing?"

"Something you shouldn't have seen. Since you did see me do something, you may as well watch for a result. Keep an eye on our employees, if I get the reaction I'm looking for. One of our employees should become rather nervous real fast."

"Watch Jason over there in the corner, is he the man you are looking for?"

"I do believe Jason could be our thief. Look at how nervous he is. Come on Jason follow instructions from the music. Look at him Wendy he keeps looking up here as he works his way back towards Ernie. He may soon ask if he can leave early because he isn't feeling well."

Wendy couldn't believe what she was watching. Jason had a quick word with Ernie causing Ernie to bust out laughing. He picked up the intercom phone. "Hello in the office, is anybody up there?"

Brad answered the intercom. "Hello Ernie, what can we do for you?"

"Are you missing a little money by chance, a few thousand dollars perhaps?"

"Ernie, we are missing more than a little money, we are missing several thousand dollars to be exact."

"The money is down here locked in my cash drawer. I sent Jason up to the office earlier with a receipt. He found the office door was wide open and the money lying in plain sight. He brought the money back to me for safe keeping. Do you want to hear something funny, Jason got a strong weird feeling you were thinking he stole the money. How is that for a good laugh?"

"It's a laugh alright Ernie."

"I'll send Jason up with the money now, if you promise to take better care of our hard earned cash."

"Thanks Ernie we were worried for a while. You can count on us taking better care of our money in the future." He turned towards Wendy as he patted her shoulder. "We got lucky girl, the money was safe all along. Change the music back to what we were playing."

Jason came jogging up the stairs before Wendy could ask more questions. Brad cut the music off, and replaced the CD. "Hello Jason, thank you for taking good care of our money. We appreciate your help."

"I was shocked to see this money lying in plain sight, and no one here. I checked the restroom, but not finding anyone all I could think of was to secure the money. I took the money back to Ernie for safe keeping."

"You did the right thing, and we are proud of you. Wendy left the money lying out when she saw me get knocked down by a car. She ran out to see if I was alright. She cared more about me than my money. I hate to lose money, but I'm glad she was more concerned about my welfare than my money."

"I've got to tell you Mr. Collins when I remembered the money it was as though a bolt of lightening hit me. I was scared you would think I stole the money. My fingerprints are in this office on your chair, the desk and the restroom door. They are everywhere."

"Jason all is well that ends well."

"I better get back to work before Ernie comes looking for me."

"Hold on a minute, doing the right thing deserves a reward. Wendy, count out two hundred dollars out for Jason."

Jason blinked his eyes. "Thank you Mr. Collins."

"You are welcome, keep up the good work." Brad sent him on his way with a pat on his back.

After Jason left the office, he turned to a very relieved Wendy. "I can't believe I was that careless. I am so sorry and it won't happen again."

He rolled his office chair over next to her chair to place one hand on her hand. "Relax, there was no harm done. I think I'll go back to my suite and rest. Can you make a bank deposit later? "

"I would be happy to make the bank deposit for you if you trust me with your money?"

"Of course I trust you and I will see you in the morning."

CHAPTER 19

The following morning Wendy was still apologizing for the money incident. "I'm sorry about the missing money yesterday. I cannot believe how careless I was. There was almost seven thousand dollars, I lost for you. I'm surprised you are taking my stupidity so well."

"Why worry about money that isn't missing. What do I have to do to get you to relax, get a masseuse up here?"

"Last night as I went to bed I would have welcomed a masseuse. I was so upset about losing your money, I couldn't go to sleep. My husband Joe is out on the road when I need him to comfort me."

"Is your husband a salesman of some type?"

"Joe is a truck driver. When we closed our business he took one of our trucks and started long hauling. He says the truck is geared wrong to be fuel-efficient and wants to sell our truck. He thinks driving for someone else might be better. I'm leaving the decision about selling our truck to him. He knows more about driving trucks than I do."

"Has he thought about driving local for someone so he would be home each night?" She gave him a sad look. "There should be local truck driving jobs available. Delivery trucks, construction trucks, sanitation trucks are all local jobs. Any one of those type jobs would allow him to be home each night. I'm thinking you would love having your husband home each night."

"Driving local is a problem, because much of the construction work in Vegas is done around the clock twenty-four hours a day. He hates driving truck at night. As a new hire he would no doubt be on graveyard shift if he drove local. Even some of the sanitation trucks run at night in the alleys around the business district and the casinos."

"I see your point. Joe working at night wouldn't be very comforting to you either. Urge Joe to keep looking for a local job. There has to be something he would like besides running all over the country. Now about business, it's important we keep our food supply fresh. Can you do a quick inventory check for me?"

"We are long on the Mexican Food Ernie brought in."

"Do you have an inventory printout I can look at?" After scanning the printout he chose the next daily special to be Mexican Food. Although some distance away she watched him out the corner of her eye, as he mixed his food subliminal message with a music CD. Soon the promotional ad started with different music.

"I'm almost afraid to ask, are you using the same technology to make in-house advertising as you used on Jason yesterday to locate the missing money?"

"Would you be upset if I said yes?"

"I don't know, I saw Jason jolted hard but I don't know how. I also saw Jason perfectly fine in a matter of minutes."

"I didn't intend for you to see anything. Please don't say anything to anyone. We'll talk about this in depth, some other time."

Wendy wasn't about to wait. "Are you doing anything dangerous?"

"I'm not hurting anyone if that's what you mean. I've been experimenting with encouragement advertising. Basically I'm encouraging customers who are not sure what they want, to make a faster choice so our order lines keep moving at a more rapid pace. I also check inventory to find any excess product and promote that item. By pushing slow moving items, I'm keeping all food items fresh. Good food, and fast service is what every fast food customer desires. Otherwise our customers would go to a standard sit down restaurant. Our customers win and we win so everyone benefits from what I'm doing."

"Are you breaking any laws?"

"No, my encouragements are extremely weak in general. Let's say you are allergic to fish, and I'm promoting fish. My weak message wouldn't over ride their knowledge of being allergic to fish. I only target the undecided. A person coming in for a burger will still order a burger. The undecided person who stands reading the menu a dozen times holding up the order line is who I help make up their minds."

"What about Jason, his message didn't appear weak?"

"You are right Wendy. I panicked, thinking I was targeting a thief. I didn't want our person to exit the building where I couldn't influence them, so I cranked up the intensity to the highest level I ever used."

"You jolted poor Jason big-time. Left little doubt in my mind something you did worked. Long as you are working lawful. I do not have a problem with what you are doing."

"Then we are cool, while you handle things here in the office I want to check out the neighborhood. I'll be gone a couple hours or so. I hope you understand, by what you saw yesterday my technique can be extremely powerful. Used improperly the results could be dangerous. This has to remain our secret. The Burger Palace is my testing ground."

"What results are you expecting from your fish promotion today?"

"Seven percent of our trade should order fish. During light customer times the boost might be up to ten percent if they hang around longer."

"I'll be watching for the results later today." Wendy paused long enough to answer her phone. Her call brought instant panic to her, she screamed and dropped the phone and covered her face.

Thinking her husband Joe had been in an accident, Brad snatched the phone from the floor. "Hello! You startled Wendy. Start over and speak very clearly, so I can understand you." He soon learned Wendy's daughter Carol had been beaten up, raped, and left for dead sometime during the night. Only now had she been found, and was being taken to a local hospital in critical condition. Brad wrote down the address and phone number of the hospital before hanging up the phone. "Let's go, I'll drive you to the hospital." On the way out he yelled at Ernie. "We have an emergency. I'll call you later!"

At the hospital he comforted Wendy as she waited for more information about her daughter. "Would you like me to call your husband?"

"Joe is in his truck out on the road."

"I know, but we should call him. What's Joe's number?" He dialed the number she gave him. "Joe, Joe Olsen. This is Brad Collins, your wife's employer. Wendy has been called to the hospital. Your daughter has been injured. We haven't seen her yet, so we are not sure how bad your daughter has been injured."

"I'm on my return trip to Vegas now I should arrive in Vegas two hours. I'll be at the hospital soon as I can."

"We may have more details when you get here."

Wendy's husband never arrived at the hospital in time to listen to the doctor's report. "Carol has been through a terrible ordeal. She has been brutally raped. In time her physical injuries will heal. Being raped, beaten, and left for dead is every woman's nightmare."

Wendy was quick to ask when they could see her. "The rape evidence collection team is still working with her. After they finish their work you may see your daughter. She will be heavy medicated. She may not respond to you seeing her. She will need a lot of rest, love, and attention in the coming weeks."

In a light comforting manner Brad rubbed Wendy's back. "You heard what the doctor said. I'll get an Office Temp to cover for you while she is rehabbing. The Burger Palace will survive, and don't worry about money. I will continue paying you during your time off."

Considerable time later Wendy's husband arrived at the hospital. "Here comes my husband now. Joe this is my boss Brad Collins."

"Hello Mr. Collins, nice to meet you."

"Nice to finally meet you Joe, I wish we were under better circumstances. I should be going back to the Burger Palace. Keep me posted on your daughter's condition."

Brad called an office temp firm before talking to Ernie to fill him in on Wendy's daughter's situation. With the Office Temp set up for the following day he began counting the money for a bank deposit he planned to make on his way home.

"In his suite that night he needed a sympathetic ear. He tried calling Marie in Seattle, Judy answered the phone. "Hi Brad, Marie isn't home yet. She is working until eight tonight."

"Dang I always get anxious and call too early."

"How are things in Vegas?"

"Every day brings new challenges. Remember the old saying sometimes the best laid plans go astray, that saying is very true."

"Oh come now how bad can it be. You sound normal to me."

"Tonight I don't feel normal. How are you and Rob getting along?"

"Rob and I keep having disagreements over you. His views are laced with jealousy. I believe he realizes his problem. Why he doesn't work on his problem I don't know. All I know is, I'm getting very tired of arguing with him."

"Don't give up on Rob, on my account. Many people have different ideas about me. Use you own scale to measure him."

"I will, shall I have Marie call you when she gets in?"

"Please do have her call. It's nice talking with you, behave yourself."

He was in the shower when Marie called. Dripping wet he answered the phone. "Hi Marie, how are you tonight."

"I'm fine, Judy tells me you are in a down mood tonight, what happened?"

"It's been an unbelievable day. A car in the parking lot knocked me down. We lost seven thousand dollars for a short time. Wendy is off work because her daughter is in the hospital, and I'm dripping water all over the floor. Other than that I've had a wonderful day."

"Why are you dripping water all over the floor?"

"I was in the shower when you called."

"Dry yourself off silly. When you called me the other day, I was in the shower. I dried and put on my robe while talking to you."

"I'm not as clever as you are. It's hard to dry my back off with one hand. I'm not putting this phone down. "

"If I were there with you, I could dry your back for you. Since I'm not there you need to put you phone on speaker. Set it on the bed beside you so you can dry off and talk at the same time."

"Oh Honey don't say you would dry my back, now I feel worse than I did before."

"After I dried your back I could give you a massage. I give great massages. You better dress before you freeze your fanny off."

"Freeze in Vegas, not a chance. I might sunburn my fanny, but I won't freeze. Few clothes are needed here, what I really called about is our date Friday night. With Wendy at the hospital caring for her daughter Carol, I'm in a bind. I can't leave Vegas."

"Oh no, I was looking forward to seeing you. What happened to Wendy's daughter?"

"Carol is fighting for her life. She was raped, beaten, and left for dead."

"She was raped, oh my Lord how terrible. Will her daughter be okay?"

"Doctors seem to think in time she will recover physically. Emotionally will be a separate struggle. The emotional toll on her may affect her for a very long time. The doctor is warning her parents it may take a lot of counseling, before she is anything close to normal. Her doctor stated she may never fully recover."

"I can't imagine something as devastating to a woman as being raped. You mentioned getting knocked down in the parking lot by a car, how did that happen?"

"I stepped right out in front of a lady as she was leaving. Wendy was looking out the office window, and saw me get hit. She was counting money at the time. In her excitement to see if I was alright. She ran out without locking the office leaving seven thousand dollars lying in plain sight. When we went back up to the office the money was gone. All this happened right at lunchtime. We worried about the money for over an hour. Come to find out one of our employees brought a receipt to the office, saw the money, and took it back to my restaurant manager Ernie for safe keeping. My whole day was bazaar."

"Were you hurt by the car?"

"One small bruise on my leg but nothing serious, I'm alright."

"If you are not careful, I'll have to come down to Vegas and take care of you. If I could afford a trip to Vegas, I would fly down and see you right now. I may not be a lot of help. I could dry your back and give you a massage."

"You might want to reconsider your thoughts. If not I will buy you a plane ticket to come see me."

"I don't need to reconsider my thoughts. I've never been to Vegas. What girl wouldn't like to see Vegas, and the guy she misses more than you will ever know?"

"Then we better put our minds together, and see what we can work out. What does your work schedule look like?"

"I work Wednesday through Saturday. I could trade shifts on Saturday I could be off work by noon on Saturday and in Vegas by evening."

"I love a girl with a plan. How about Judy, she would love Vegas also. I have plenty of room for both of you?"

"You are a persuasive guy. Judy and I shouldn't be taking advantage of your generosity."

"Please don't worry about taking advantage of me. Talk things over with Judy. See what you can do and let me know. I have a two-bedroom suite. Being short handed at the Burger Palace, I will have to work a couple hours each day. I could work early while you sleep in. Judy would be with you, in case I had to work more than I anticipated. There are plenty of things to do within walking distance of my place. Call me back after you talk with Judy."

"I'll call back soon as I can. Don't forget to dress before you go out."

"Very funny Marie, you need not worry. With all the trouble I now have I don't have time to be arrested. I'll be waiting for your call, bye Honey. Do your best to convince Judy to fly down with you."

"Let me run your offer by Judy. I'll call you back soon as I can." Marie charged through the house yelling Judy as she looked for her. "You will never guess. Brad wants to fly you and me to Vegas this weekend and see him. What do you think, can we go?"

"He wants to fly us to Vegas."

"You would be keeping me company while he is working. His secretary is on leave because of a family emergency, leaving his schedule very unpredictable."

"I know you are excited, calm down a second. I understand you going to Vegas to visit Brad. It would give you a chance to know Brad better. I vote you should follow your heart. My going to Vegas would disrupt your time with him."

While visiting the hospital, Brad learned what he expected. No change in Carol's condition. "It's still early in her recovery. Be positive, patients can sometimes feel the emotion around them. Do you know if the police caught Carol's attacker?"

"The police do have a convicted sex predator in custody. The creep has a long history of sexual violence. The police keep hounding Carol's doctors about questioning her. She is in no condition to make a statement."

"Our court system is a joke, sexual predators can't be cured. They progressively get worse. The only way to stop them is put them six feet underground. The faster these people are put to death the better."

"Joe and my only concern is Carol right now. We can worry about her attacker later, when his trial comes up."

"I better scoot on down to the Burger Palace. Call me if you need anything. Try to keep a positive attitude. I'll see you tomorrow."

"Your boss is a nice guy, very caring." Joe commented. "He certainly doesn't think much of the police. I hope he is wrong about them. This creep they have in custody needs the book thrown at him."

"Let's hope for a swift trial. Long trials can be emotionally draining. Carol has had all the stress she can handle."

"I cancelled my load for tomorrow. I can't hang around the hospital very long. Our truck needs to be on the road earning money."

Wendy disagreed with her husband. "Carol's health is all that's important right now. We can work on money issues later."

At the Burger Palace, Brad found things were going well except Ernie was still working. "Hey buddy you shouldn't still be here. You put in your hours long ago."

"My evening manager has a special event going on for a couple hours. I'm covering for him. Everything is fine except we have way too much money on hand this evening. Can you make a late cash drop at the bank tonight to secure the money?" Ernie showed extreme concern.

"If someone walked in and robbed us now we would lose over twenty thousand dollars."

"Sure I can make a bank run. We need to get a huge safe in here and have an armored truck to move our money around. These evening bank runs are dangerous especially late at night like this."

"Check my numbers before you make the bank drop. The money is in the cash drawer by my desk."

"Brad used his office to recount the money. As always Ernie's numbers were correct. He entered the money count in Wendy's computer before starting for the bank. Marie called before he could get out the door. "Hi Baby, what did you learn about Judy coming to Vegas with you?"

"She thinks I should fly down and see you. I've given your offer a lot of thought. It's a very generous offer. Are you sure we should do this?"

"You and Judy will love coming to Vegas. All you have to do is use the credit card I left you to purchase your plane tickets. I would make the arrangements for you, except I don't know what time would be best for you to fly out."

"I told Judy you have room for us. She still doesn't think she should fly down to Vegas."

"That is a bummer. Other than thinking she might be in our way, did she give any other reason why she doesn't want to fly to Vegas?"

"She has several good reasons. As I said, first she thinks she would be in our way. Her best reason for not going to Vegas is her parents wouldn't appreciate it. She hasn't been home in almost three years. Her parents would see a trip to Vegas as a waste of money. So you are stuck with me as your single guest for the weekend."

"Wonderful, I can't wait to see you. Wear the lightest clothes you have and bring one change of clothes. No need to tote extra luggage around. If you need more clothes, we can buy you clothes down here."

"Alright, I'll see you Saturday, late afternoon. Hold on, I hear Judy on her cell phone screaming. She has to be talking to Rob. I think the guy is all but gone. She just hung up on him. I should hang up, and go see if I can console her."

"Would you mind seeing if Judy would talk to me for a minute?"

"How about I go ask her, and call you back later?"

Brad waited in his office checking inventory and making small adjustments in his subliminal food promotions. The girls called back much faster than he expected. "Hello Brad, Marie tells me you want a word with me."

"I would like a word with you. Marie mentioned you haven't seen your parents in three years. I'm sure you miss them."

"I haven't seen them, because I haven't been home in three years. I can't afford to waste my education money on travel."

"I understand, money rules everyone. Marie also thinks you believe your parents would be upset if you came to Vegas with her."

"I know my parents would be furious if they ever found out I went to Vegas. Marie will need to fly down and see you by herself."

"I think I can handle her by myself. I don't want to do anything to upset your parents. So I have a different idea. Would you allow me the honor of buying you a plane ticket, so you to go visit your parents?" The phone was dead silent. "Judy, did I lose you?"

"I'm trying to figure out why you would do this for me?'

"I'm willing to buy you a ticket for several reasons. You won't enjoy staying in that big house alone while Marie is in Vegas. Second, your parents would love to see you. Third, Marie tells me you are struggling with your relationship with Rob. A brief separation might help both you and Rob."

"You are dead on, where he is concerned. While Marie was talking with you earlier, I was telling Rob I didn't want to see him anymore. I would love to get away for a few days. I will repay you for my plane fare. It's the only way I will accept your offer."

"Very well, you can pay me back whenever it is convenient for you. Using my credit card, Marie can get your ticket when she gets her ticket. Most important, have fun girl."

"I will have fun and thank you very much."

"Then we have your trip settled. May I speak with Marie again?"

"She is standing beside me with the biggest smile you ever saw. I think she heard part of our conversation."

"Hi again, Judy said I was smiling. You should see her face; whatever you told her put a smile on her face."

"I gave her secondary idea she liked. When you get your plane ticket get one for Judy. She is going to visit her parents while you come visit me. Where do her parents live?"

"Her parents live in Fairbanks, Alaska and you have made her a happy girl. When I get to Vegas, we need to talk about you buying me things all the time. You can not keep doing this."

"Now you just hold on young lady. Some guys continually buy their dates flowers, fancy dinners, and movie tickets when they go out. Flowers are expensive. They cost fifty to seventy five dollars for a dozen roses so it's no different than me buying you clothes except your clothes will last much longer than roses. Tell me Honey, who is the more practical guy, them or me?"

"I swear you beat all I ever heard, you have words for all occasions."

"Everyone has words for all occasions. All you have to do is be smart, and use words to your advantage. When making a good point, be direct."

"What are you doing this minute?"

"I'm sitting in my office. Talking to the prettiest gal in the world, wishing I were there with you."

"Why are you still at the office this late at night? You should be in your apartment relaxing not working. How do you expect to get rid of the black circles under your eyes if you don't get proper rest?"

"Unfortunately I work for a living, we had a profitable day. I'm counting the money so I can make a bank deposit later tonight before I go to my room. I'll check food inventory one more time, before I leave tonight. With Wendy off caring for her daughter I have more than ever going on."

"What do you call a profitable day? Did you make four, five hundred in profit?"

"We make more money than that on espresso sales each day." He checked his watch as the Burger Palace was closing for the night only then did he realize how late it was. "Oh my word, look how late it is. I still have my bank deposit to make, dinner to eat, and a shower before bed. It will be late before I get to sleep tonight. When you learn your flight schedule call me. I have to go Honey, see you soon, bye."

"Goodnight Brad, sleep tight."

"Now that I know you are coming to see me I will sleep much better."

"I can't wait for Saturday to get here."

"That makes two of us anxious for Saturday to get here."

CHAPTER 20

Each day Brad's first stop was at the hospital to check on Carol's progress. Wendy remained optimistic as her daughter's medication was reduced. "If she continues to improve the way she is, I may be able to return part-time, and help out at the Burger Palace before long."

"You returning to work would be very beneficial to me, but don't neglect Carol. I'm pleased to hear she is progressing. Has she spoken to the police yet?"

"Two female officers have interviewed her twice. They say with her testimony the rapist will get the maximum life sentence in prison. Her doctor warned us not to allow the authorities to push her too fast."

"How well is she interacting with her father?"

"She has improved a lot since Joe left on the truck two days ago. I think he will be surprised when he returns next week. Just the same if I could get my hands on that rapist, I would choke him to death with my bare hands."

"Knowing the police the way I do. I would not advise allowing anyone to hear you say, you would like to kill this assailant they have in jail."

"You're right I shouldn't have said anything about killing Carol's rapist but this whole business angers me. As a tax payer, I'll wind up paying for the defense of a man who harmed my daughter. I would rather spend my dollar on a bullet and shoot the bastard. None of this should have ever happened to Carol."

"I need to get on with my work at the Burger Palace. Even though our Office Temp is doing what she can. My workload has increased considerably."

"After Carol goes to sleep. I may slip over to the Burger Palace tomorrow evening, and help out for a short time. I need a break away from the hospital."

"I'll hang out until you get here. Be sure and call me if you change your mind and don't come."

The following evening around eight Wendy came to the office. "Hello, I was about to give you up. How is my favorite red-head doing this evening?"

"I'm doing okay, but I can't stay long Carol is very restless tonight. A therapy doctor came by to see her today. In her opinion Carol may need years and years of therapy. She seems to think there is little chance Carol will ever lead a normal life."

Brad wrinkled his brow. "That's not good news. Seems her doctors should be more positive around her. Can you keep a secret for the rest of your life?"

"Why would I want to keep a secret for the rest of my life?"

"If something were to happen that was unusual, and nobody else should know, could you keep the information to yourself?"

"My secrecy may depend on what it was and how it affected me. What is it you are trying to say?"

"If I did something that affected someone else, could you keep our secret?"

"Stop beating around the bush and speak English, so I can understand what you are trying to saying?"

"Let me give you a hypothetical question first. If you and I had an intimate relationship could you keep our affair a secret for the rest of your life?"

"My husband is a nice guy. I wouldn't want to hurt him by telling him of our affair, so I would never tell Joe. Is that what you wanted me to say?"

"I don't care what you say one way or the other. All I want to know is if you can keep a very important secret for the rest of your life." He tapped his finger on the edge of his computer. "Right here is the answer to Carol's problem. You and I can help your daughter, if you can keep a lifetime secret your daughter can lead a normal life."

Wendy seemed confused. "I don't understand what you are trying to say."

"Before you were called to the hospital, we were discussing Jason's reaction to my experiment." Wendy nodded her head. "We could use the same technology slightly different and block the memory of Carol's rape from her mind." Wendy's eyes grew large. "It's true, we can block her memory of the rape."

"Then we should block her memory, how do we start?"

"Before we do this you must remember every action has a reaction. You and I would have a lifetime secret to carry. No religious confession in the coming years. Our lips would be sealed for life."

"Carol deserves to live a normal life. We must do this for Carol's sake."

"Our actions would change everything. With Carol's memory of the rape blocked she could not testify against her attacker. The prosecutor may choose to drop the charges against the rapist. How would you feel then?" He paused briefly allowing her time to think. "Would you trade your daughter's mental stability for the possibility of some other woman getting raped, and murdered in the future?"

"Oh my Lord, you ask tough questions. I need time to think over what you are proposing. Can we continue this conversation tomorrow?"

"Thinking is always good, Take your time, and think things over very careful. Do not discuss this with anyone but me. Once we begin there is no way of turning back. One thing I should point out before we make our final decision on blocking her memory. I should see Carol's condition for myself."

Wendy took him by the hands and drew him to a standing position where she gave him a motherly hug. "I agree, I think it's time you met Carol."

Even knowing how bad her condition was, Brad never expected the reception he received from Wendy's daughter the next day. As he met Carol he naturally extended one hand for a shake. She screamed and covered her head. "Get out, get out of here, help I'm being raped!" Nurses came charging in as he backed away from her bedside.

"Sir, wait outside in the hall you are disturbing the patient."

"Calm down Honey, that was my boss Mr. Collins. He wasn't going to hurt you. He wants to help you."

"That man isn't touching me for any reason." Carol's body continued to quiver. "No man will ever touch me again."

"Honey my boss is a nice guy. He gave me all this time off to be with you. He won't hurt you."

Carol's whole body continued to quiver. "That filthy man tried to touch me. I don't want any man touching me."

The head nurse gave Carol a powerful sedative shot. "Calm down Honey, I'll be right back." Wendy located Brad waiting in the hall. Before saying anything they walked further down the hall. "I never anticipated her to have such an adverse reaction to you."

"Her reaction was a sudden surprise, how is she around other men?"

"Carol hasn't been around any other men."

"What about her father, the doctors or male nurses?"

"Joe left with our truck before her medication wore off. He called tonight as I was driving back here. He is in town and will see Carol in the morning before heading out with his next haul. Her doctors and nurses are all women."

"Well shit, do you know the name of your daughter's assailant?"

"Wendell Carpenter, the newspaper listed his age as sixty. His picture was in the paper."

"Dang, I missed Carpenter's picture in the paper. I wish I had seen the creep's picture in the paper."

"He is a leather skinned creepy looking sixty year old bastard."

"Did you by chance keep the paper you saw his picture in?"

"I may still have the paper at the house."

"If you get a chance look for the picture, I would love to see a picture of this Wendell Carpenter. When Joe comes in tomorrow you better have him approach Carol slowly."

"I doubt she will react to her father the way she did to you."

"Carol will react to her father. Exactly how much she will react is the question." He paused giving Wendy time to understand his words. "She could surprise me and welcome him with open arms. Then again she could be very cautious around her father. Carol is nothing close to her normal self. Don't forget what I told you if we block the attack from her mind she cannot testify. Without her testimony the police could release Wendle Carpenter. We have no idea why Wendle Carpenter chose her as his victim. He could come after her a second time."

"Please don't do this to me you are clouding my mind and making our decision more difficult. We can't possibly cover every scenario."

"He pulled her close for a hug as he whispered in her ear. "You say we can't cover every scenario but we can cover every scenario. How far are you willing to go to help Carol depends on how large a secret can you keep? We have no limit."

"To help Carol, I can keep a secret to the ends of the earth. Physically she is doing well her mental state is my concern."

"Are the police still trying to question her?"

"I'm not sure you can call what the police are doing to Carol is questioning. It's more like she is being coached. Coached to see what kind of a witness she will make."

"I know their drill. Here is the deal Wendy. I have a guest flying in from Seattle this weekend. We need time to think this clear through. Can we put our final decision off on how to handle Carol until the first of the week?"

"I don't need the weekend to make up my mind. I would sleep with the devil himself if it would help Carol."

Brad smiled and grinned. "You won't have to sleep with me."

"I wasn't calling you the devil."

"There are people who would disagree with you. I'm sure your niece Karen and her stepmother are two who would call me the devil. I seem to remember Kathy saying something to that effect when I booted them out of my plans. When, and if, we do block Carol's memory we must be ever so careful not to block more of her memory than the actual rape. In order to do this she must be monitored. As of now she doesn't want me near her. I need to observe Carol undetected plus this has to be done without Joe or my Seattle guest's knowledge. My guest will be leaving Monday."

"Your friend, what time Monday is he leaving?"

"For starters my guest is a she, a very pretty she. Marie will be leaving late Monday afternoon. If we knew one another longer I wouldn't let her leave at all."

"Then Tuesday we decide on our plan of action. I'm counting on you, don't let me down." Again she gave Brad a motherly hug.

"I'm glad to hear you are not afraid of any adverse reaction Carol might have."

"I saw you absolutely jolt Jason, in a few minutes he was fine. I've watched Jason each day since. He is normal in every way. After seeing him recover so fast, I have little doubt you may be able to help Carol with her mental instability."

"Keep in mind we must precede with caution."

Brad couldn't tell if she genuinely believed he could help Carol or if Wendy was a desperate mother willing to try anything. "Wendell Carpenter still concerns me."

"Give me a gun Brad, I will kill the bastard. Carol shouldn't have to live in fear of this creep for the rest of her life."

"I agree it doesn't seem right to let him go free. Still we need to move forward with caution. First we need to concentrate on Carol. For now stop threatening Wendell Carpenter. Others must never hear you make threats against him."

"No woman should have to go through what Carol went through. That dirty-old man should pay with his life." Wendy spoke the words of a caring mother as small tears trickled down her cheeks. "Just the thought of him drawing a breath irritates me."

"I had better scoot on home to get my beauty sleep. You try and get some rest too. I'll check in with you periodically this weekend. If you care to meet Marie I'll bring her by. She is a neat gal, I was going up this weekend to see her until Carol had her problem. Marie quickly agreed to switch and agreed to come see me. This girl could easily be the Miss Right I'm looking for."

"Miss Right, that's saying a lot. I can't wait to meet this mystery girl. While I have your attention, how are you getting along with your Office Temp?"

"Rose is doing the best she can, but she is no Wendy. I miss your positive attitude and smiling face in our office."

"What is Rose like?"

"Rose is very pretty, jet black hair, five ten, adequate figure, beautiful smile. She is young and lacks confidence. Given time she will make a good employee for someone. Don't worry your job is safe."

"I'll be looking forward to meeting your special lady."

CHAPTER 21

Waiting for Marie on Saturday made the day seem long. Brad checked his watch every five minutes. Rose noticed his strange actions. "Am I doing something wrong to upset you?"

"You are doing fine. I have a special friend flying in late today. A female friend I haven't seen in weeks. I'm so excited. I had a tough time sleeping last night. Speaking of time it's time for me to drive out to the airport to pick her up. I'll see you Monday sometime."

Marie was wearing a huge smile, a pink top, and jeans as she arrived at the airport. He welcomed her with a generous hug. "It is so good to see you I've never missed anyone so much in my life." Again he hugged her.

"I missed you too, when does our weekend date start?"

"Now of course, I'm pleased you came to see me."

"Then stop neglecting me and welcome me with a kiss."

His welcoming kiss was borderline indecent. "There you go Sweetie do you feel better now?" She answered by burying her head in his chest as she hugged him back. "Baggage claim is down this way. The Vegas sights are beautiful but they have not one site to match your beauty. Her eyes sparkled as they drove down the Vegas strip towards his suite. "We'll swing by my suite and drop your luggage off before we go eat."

Marie was in awe of everything. "The architecture of these buildings is magnificent. It must take a fortune to keep this city moving forward."

"Las Vegas Boulevard is beautiful after dark. The whole place sparkles with lights at night. This city never sleeps."

"Brad's suite impressed Marie. "Wow this is where you live? Judy will never believe this. I'll need pictures to show her what she missed by not coming with me."

"We can grab post cards as we walk around and take few pictures. Your room is on this side, do you need anything before we go out?"

"I went to the airport straight from work. Would you mind if I took a quick shower and freshened up?"

"By all means go right ahead and shower. It's been a stressing week, I'll take a little rest while you get ready." Lying down on the bed was a big mistake, he went into a deep sleep.

Marie was very disappointed to find him in such a deep sleep. She sat down beside him and touched one shoulder expecting him to wake. He never moved. She bounced the bed some, still he never moved. Marie checked her watch and determined he had slept over an hour. Not one to give up easy she kissed his cheek. He smiled slightly, but did not wake. By now it was getting towards the eight o'clock hour, and she had not eaten lunch. Having little choice she called room service and ordered dinner for the both of them as poor Brad continued to sleep. She knew how much he was looking forward to her visit. For him to drop off into this deep of a sleep, he had to be exhausted. She resigned herself to eating alone before lying down next to him on the bed. Near ten he stirred to find her napping snuggled in next to him. He squirmed around enough to wrap his arms around her, his cuddling woke her. I'm so sorry I didn't mean to fall asleep."

"It's okay. I had a nice little nap myself. We are quite the lively pair. Judy would have a big laugh if she could see us now."

He blinked as he looked at the bedside clock. "We missed our dinner show! Darn it all, anyway, I drag you all the way to Vegas to impress you, and all you get is to watch me sleep. There is a lifetime memory if I ever heard one." He gave her a tremendous hug and a loving kiss. "Vegas never sleeps, let's go find something to eat and then we can catch a midnight show somewhere."

"I grew hungry while you were sleeping. I ordered room service and had a snack while you were snoring away. At best I can only eat something light."

"It's not much of a romantic dinner but we can eat down stairs at the buffet. That way we can eat fast and be on our way to see the night lights on the famous Vegas strip."

Marie enjoyed sampling the food at the buffet although she couldn't eat much. Brad seemed nervous. "Relax, I'm enjoying our date. I have great food, and good company. What more could a girl ask for?"

"Most girls like soft music, a candle light dinners, diamond rings, long white gowns and a wedding cake."

"You forgot cars, kids and a house with white picket fence."

"Wow kids on our third date, you expect a lot from a guy."

"A girl has to aim high…" She teased. "…doesn't she?" She asked with a sparkle in her eye.

"How many kids are you thinking we need?"

"Two would be nice. Three would be alright. Beyond three, I would need to think about what we were doing."

"Then we better go for a stroll on the strip because I need exercise to build up my strength if expected to father children."

"You have plenty of time to build up your strength. The children can wait a year, maybe two." The beautiful night lights fascinated her. "What a place, Vegas is a giant fantasy land."

"In Vegas people can kick up their heels and have fun. One of the famous sayings in Vegas is what happens in Vegas stays in Vegas. Personally I doubt much of anything stays here beyond people's money."

The Battleships at Treasure Island captivated her sparkling eyes as she stood watching the show wrapped in his smooth arms. He enjoyed peeking around to watch her face more than watch the Battleships. The flaming Volcano and the Dancing Waters along the Vegas strip were also a joy to see. Further down the famous Strip the roller coaster high atop the New York-New York sent shivers up her spine. "How can anyone ride that contraption so high in the air?"

"They simply buy a ticket and hang on. Would you care for a ride?"

"No way would I get on a mechanical devise that high in the air. I would wet my pants."

"How about a Gondola ride at the Venetian, we could cruise around slow and peaceful as we kissed and hugged traveling through the waterways winding through the tunnels."

"Now you are thinking, a Gondola ride sounds interesting, a little more my speed. Would I need a life jacket?"

" Oh no Honey we cannot put a life jacket. We don't want to cover your beautiful body anymore than necessary." From the New York Casino they crossed over the Vegas Strip towards the MGM Grand. A brief pause on overhead crosswalk gave a magnificent view up and down the Strip. Brad pointed off to the east. "We could have eaten at Hooters down there."

"I don't think so. I'm not into competition. Call me greedy or whatever but I demand your full attention. You can eat at Hooters when I'm not around. Is their food good?"

"I've never eaten at Hooters. People say the food is good. I'm inclined to believe them because I haven't had a bad meal in Vegas since I came here. I'm surprised but even Mickey D's on the strip is extremely busy."

She turned to face him square before giving him a funny look. "Be honest now, are you telling me the truth, you have never been in Hooters?"

"Other than where I am staying I've never been in any of these buildings. Like you this is all new to me. I've driven the Strip many times but this is my first time strolling around. It's a special place to see and share with someone you love." He pulled her close to him. "Having you with me is like being in the middle of a dream."

"You are right. This does feel dream-like. I can easily visualize I'm floating on a cloud and about to be kissed." She giggled in anticipation of a kiss.

"Please allow me to complete your dream." In a split second she found herself on the receiving end of a long deep kiss. "How about we go to the midnight Comedy Club over at the Tropicana?"

"I'm game for anything." After an hour of rib splitting laughter at the Comedy Club the happy couple headed back to his suite. "That was a racy show at the Comedy Club." She stated. "I blushed several times."

"Don't feel bad Honey. I'm sure everyone blushed at some point during the show. Few people escape the wrath of a good comedian."

"This is a crazy city. I love all the excitement. I can see why you chose Vegas for your restaurant venture. There certainly is no shortage of people."

"There isn't a more money driven city anywhere in the world. People bring millions of dollars here each day."

"I've read a lot about Vegas but the Vegas Strip is well beyond anything I expected."

"Look around you, the entire city is busy and growing by leaps and bounds. Some experts say this city is beyond recession. I tend not to believe them. This city is built on fantasy, alcohol, and fun. If the economy drops, Vegas will be hit hard. People can easily cut back on their entertainment."

"Is your business stabilized so you can return to college in the fall?"

"I thought so early on, but this week when I bumped into a snag concerning my secretary's daughter. I'm not sure how that is going to work out."

"Caught up in the city's beauty, I forgot about Wendy's daughter. You told me on the phone she was raped, how is she?"

"Carol is not good. The poor girl has been through hell. She is getting good medical care. Wendy has taken off work to be with her daughter. I hired an office temp until she returns. The office temp is a big help to me but she isn't Wendy. Carol continues to improve physically but her mental health gets worse with each passing day. She hates men."

"I'm sorry to hear she isn't doing well. What does her doctor say about her condition?"

"Her primary doctor says she will recover physically but she will need extensive counseling for many years. The poor girl is absolutely terrified of men. I can't visit her at all."

"Did the police have any luck catching her attacker?"

"The police do have the man in custody and what I think is a lot of evidence. Still they want Carol to testify. Right now she is unable tolerate the prosecutor, let alone face her attacker. Without her testimony this Wendell Carpenter character could receive a short sentence or walk away free. There is no way of knowing if her getting raped was a random act, or if the man targeted her specifically. If he is allowed to go free he could come after her again."

"Wow the poor girl, what a life to look forward to."

"The authorities did say this Wendell Carpenter has a history as a sexual predator in the LA area but this is the first time he has been picked up in the Vegas area. When Carpenter goes to trial the jurors will not be told of his prior sexual predator history."

"That doesn't sound fair, what is wrong with our court system?"

"Our court system is not fair to the victim. Carol may be facing years and years of mental counseling while her attacker could easily go free. The criminal has all the rights while the victim has no rights. "

Marie stopped to draw in a breath. "My legs are giving out you are walking me to death."

"You are in luck. I know a cure for tired legs, it's called a taxi."

In minutes they were entering the suite and he was preparing for their goodnight kiss to end their evening's date but Marie had other ideas. "I haven't been up this late in ages. Probably the night I graduated high school. Our time passed so quickly. It's almost four AM, did you notice daylight is breaking outside."

"Don't look at me that way Honey. I wasn't a party animal until you came along. Land sakes girl, I was an ordinary hard working young man until you corrupted me. My night owling is your entire fault."

She laughed as she playfully slapped him. "I wonder if you know the meaning of the word corruption."

"I believe I know the meaning, but I'm open for a demonstration. Give me your best description." She suddenly pushed him backwards causing him to fall across his bed. Equally as fast she pounced on him. "Whoa girl, I'm fragile, be nice."

"Shuck that shirt; I owe you a back massage." She gave him a sexy smile before seductively unbuttoning his shirt. One kiss on his chest accompanied each button she opened. "Roll over so I can massage your back?"

"I like your technique." He began opening buttons on her blouse. One kiss for each button opened where given in return." Further tender kisses ignited their passion to a fevered pitch ending with a beautiful lovemaking experience allowing sleep to come easy for the young lovers.

Straight up twelve she woke still snuggled in Brad's arms with him smiling at her. 'How long have you been awake?"

He gave her a gentle kiss. "I don't know, only a short time. I was enjoying every minute watching your beautiful breasts rise and fall with each breath. Wish we could stay here all day. Unfortunately I have a business I need to check on. I can't afford to go broke because I have a guest in town."

"Staying here would be nice but I'm a realist, what exactly is on our agenda today?"

"My most important mission today, is to love you. But as I said I have some work to do. How would you like to go shopping here at the Mall while I do my work, we can hookup again in a couple hours/"

"I would rather spend my day with you at work, if you don't mind?"

"I would be proud to have you with me at work. You might find what I do boring. First on my list is checking in at the Burger Palace. I need to see how things are going there and checking food inventory. Before we leave the office I need to prepare a bank deposit. We can eat breakfast at the Burger Palace if you like?"

"Maybe we can have a little afternoon corruption before we go out this evening. Several places we visited last night I saw signs identical to the one in your bathroom encouraging people to conserve water. We should follow their instructions and shower together."

The warm cascading water reignited the flames of passion leading to another joyous lovemaking session, further delaying departure to the office. "Honestly Honey. I must shower for real and get dressed so I can take care of business. Do you want to be responsible for me going broke in Vegas?"

"You can't totally blame our delay on me. Give me a chance to shower first and I will be ready in twenty minutes. I'll hurry much as I can."

As the energetic couple stepped out the door Brad's cell phone rang. "Hi Ernie, what's up my friend?"

"We have a problem at the Burger Palace. Wendy is here, she is crying hysterically. She won't say what is wrong? Several people have tried talking to her. She won't say anything she just sits on the office steps and keeps crying."

"I'll be there in ten minutes Ernie. Do not allow Wendy to leave before we get there."

Marie heard part of the conversation. "Is there a serious problem at the Burger Place?"

"Wendy is at the Burger Palace, and she is extremely upset. We better hurry and find out what her problem is."

When they arrived Wendy was sitting on the second step leading to the office with several people were gathered around her. "Please move back people give us some breathing room, go about your business." He took Wendy upstairs into the inner office as Marie naturally followed them up. He momentarily forgot Marie was with him. He held Wendy tight in his arms to console her. "Can you tell me what upset you?" She tried speaking but was totally incoherent. "Take a few slow deep breathes so I can't understand you. He turned his head slightly and saw Marie's shoes and realized she had followed them to the office. "Marie, go into the restroom and get a damp washcloth, we need to wipe some tears away."

He continued to soothe and comfort his upset office manager by massaging her neck and upper back. He motioned for Marie to use the washcloth on her face.

Marie understood and obeyed his instructions. "Here let me help you Wendy." She gently wiped away the tears along with her smeared makeup. Together their tender care helped Wendy regained her composure. "Can you tell us what upset you?"

"Someone from the prosecutor's office called the hospital. I spoke to them on the phone and told them not to come to the hospital. They insisted on coming over to interview Carol. I told them she wouldn't be able to testify anytime soon." She repeated. "Two stupid men came charging in unannounced while Carol was getting her sponge bath. They saw her stark naked and she freaked out. It took four hospital staff members to hold Carol down so they could give her a shot to sedate her."

Brad shook his head. "I don't understand what makes law officers refuse to listen. What a bunch of morons. Country wide law officials are all the same, they never listen. Why they train officers to treat everybody as a suspect I'll never know."

"Earlier this morning we had other bad news. Carol's doctor told her and I there was no physical reason to keep her in the hospital much longer."

"Oh shit, let me guess. The doctor suggested a different facility for her, a mental rehab facility." Wendy nodded. "I had a feeling they wouldn't keep her in the hospital long. Is there a mental facility in the Vegas area?"

"Sunshine Rehab, they deal mostly with drug rehab people. From what I understand they deal with a lot of young men. How will Carol survive in a facility like that?"

"She couldn't survive in an environment of that type. Marie how would you like to run down and order us some food?"

His plan to get Marie out of the office for a few minutes failed as Wendy cut him short. "No need for her to go downstairs to order food. I'll call our order down, what would you like?"

"I'll have the chicken salad and a diet soda. Marie doesn't know our menu. She might want to walk down and see a menu."

Marie wasn't about to leave the office and go down stairs. "I'll have the same food as Brad is having."

"Get something for yourself Wendy. I doubt you have eaten all day either and have Ernie send up the cash bag when our food comes up. I haven't made a bank deposit today." He reached over and held Marie's hand as Wendy ordered the food. "Ladies please excuse me. Marie this is Wendy my valued office manager. Wendy this is Marie my dear friend from Seattle, who thinks enough of me to fly down for the weekend visit. She hopes to keep me on the straight and narrow long enough to see if I'm marriage material or not. She may have her work cut out for her."

"I can save you time Marie. You could search the world over and not find a nicer person than you have right here. Brad has a little anxiety now, and then, but he has heart of gold."

He looked into Marie's eyes. "I've been brainwashing her."

"Certainly appears that way, here comes our food."

"Where is your office temp today?"

"Rose had a dentist appointment this afternoon. I'm not sure if she is coming back this afternoon or not."

Marie raved about the food. "No wonder the Burger Palace is such a success, this food is fantastic. I was looking down at your menu while waiting for our food. You have food choices for everyone. Our food was ordered, made fresh and it came fast."

"Ernie is responsible for the menu and the preparation. You can thank him on our way out later. People we have work to do, I have some security cameras to check. Wendy we need a phony set of transfer papers for Carol to be moved to the Sunshine Rehab Center. Go ahead and make the papers we may need them in a hurry. Marie, I have a job for you. Count the money and check Ernie's numbers for me."

"Are you serious, you actually want me to count your money?"

"Why not, you can count can't you?"

She smiled and pushed at his shoulder. "Yes smarty, I can count."

"I won't be gone long ladies."

Marie and Wendy talked among themselves in his absence. "Wendy, do you have any idea what Brad is up to, I sure don't?"

"If I were to guess, I would say he is planning to help me keep Carol out of the wrong rehab center. He is coming back now, don't question him he has his own way of handling things."

"How well I know." Marie acknowledged.

Wendy showed Brad the phony transfer papers she created on the computer.

"These documents are good, they should do quite nicely. You would make a great crook. On Tuesday show these papers to the hospital staff right at eight when the shift is changing. When you get Carol out of the hospital bring her to the apartment here. If we are to help her, she must be where we can keep an eye on her."

Wendy smiled at him. "Keeping her here at the apartment does make more sense than putting her in Sunshine Rehab Center. I love the way you think."

"We'll make it work. If you could stay with her a few days it would help. Sometime between now, and Tuesday stock the apartment with food you will need. We'll have a lot going on next week. How are you doing with counting our money?"

"Ernie's record is still perfect. His numbers were correct, eleven thousand fifty four dollars and thirty two cents. I could go shopping for weeks if the money were mine."

"Easy girl, we better get on with our bank deposit and sock the money away to cover our bills. Good luck Wendy and try not to worry. You do understand why we need the security cameras don't you?' Wendy nodded. "With her not allowing me to see her personally it's my only choice to observe her. I hope you understand the down side is the cameras will be rather intrusive."

Again Wendy nodded her head to indicate she understood. "I should be getting back to the hospital. The shot they gave Carol to sedate her could be wearing off soon."

As Wendy started to depart he gave her a tender hug. "Remember, I have my cell phone with me at all times. If you need our support don't hesitate to call me."

Driving to the bank Brad and Marie discussed Carol and her problem. "I don't imagine you feel very good about my plan to spy on a young girl. I don't feel great myself, but I have little choice."

"I'm not sure what you hope to accomplish by spying on her. By the way Wendy was acting when we met her today this is a complex problem. Meaning, you have your work cut out for you. Are you certain isolating Carol is the right thing to do?"

"How can I be totally certain she will get better care here than any other place? I'm torn between telling you and not telling you what we plan to accomplish with Carol. You might find this a little hard to believe." He gave Marie a trusting look. "Wendy and I plan to block part of Carol's memory by hypnotizing her. Thus I need to observe her up close, and personal without Carol knowing it."

"Have you ever hypnotized anyone before?"

"Certainly not to this extent, our goal is to block the rape from her mind so she won't be afraid of men. If we don't block her memory of the incident she may be institutionalized for life."

Marie gave him a serious frown. "Are you being honest with yourself, do you really think it is possible to block the memory of a rape from someone's memory?"

"I most definitely think it is possible. If I can block her memory, is another question. It's common for people, children especially to block certain unpleasant things from their memory. You can be certain Wendy and I will proceed with caution. Part of the reasons for bringing Carol here, is so if Wendell Carpenter is released on bail he won't know where she is living. I'm hoping Wendy will stay at the apartment with her daughter while she is here."

Marie shook her head. "Whatever you are planning you never cease to amaze me. Without a doubt you are a caring person. All those people were trying to calm Wendy without success. When we came in, single handedly you took charge and calmed her in seconds."

"I wasn't alone. You helped me calm Wendy. Don't give me all the credit. I'm not a miracle man. Some might even say I'm a meddling bastard."

"I used a damp cloth to wipe away tears and smeared makeup. Even then you had to tell me to get the washcloth. Few people are the leader you appear to be. I'm impressed."

"Marie, I checked the things I needed to check here in the office. Once we make the bank deposit our work is finished for today. What would you like to do?"

"Surprise me and treat me like a queen but don't walk me to death. My legs won't take another long walk."

"How about something new, we can go for a Grand Canyon Helicopter tour?"

She shivered with excitement. "I've never flown in a helicopter but it sounds exciting. Do we need an appointment?"

"I can call and find out if they have room on the next flight out to the Grand Canyon. A helicopter ride does sound exciting. Keep in mind you will be higher than the roller coaster at the New York."

"I know but a helicopter ride sounds wonderful. I've never seen the Grand Canyon and I've always wanted to see it."

"I have not seen the Grand Canyon either. This will be another first for the two of us Honey." The canyon tour took two full hours. What a beautiful site by air. The canyon was full of magnificent rock formations formed over thousands of years. They observed tiny specs on the canyon trails who were hikers going up or down the canyon walls. "Some of those hikers camp in the canyon ten days or longer."

"I would like to stay in Vegas ten days, but not out here in the bottom of the Grand Canyon. My legs tire out walking on sidewalks what would they feel like down there clinging to the side of a cliff?"

After their Canyon Tour the young couple drove to the Orleans Casino and ate dinner in one of Vegas' premier prime rib restaurants.

"Mister, you are spoiling me. How will I ever be happy going back to my normal life of a poor struggling college student?"

"I'm not spoiling you on purpose. All I want is to love you. I feel cheated because Wendy stole two hours from our weekend. Two hours represent six hugs and ten kisses. How do I recover lost kisses?"

"Finish eating and drive me back to your suite. We could try your Jacuzzi while recovering part of our lost kisses. Who knows what might happen after that. We'll play it by ear and see where we go."

"I wanted to escort you to one of Vegas' large Broadway type shows. The dancers wear fancy costumes, bright lights, and the women are topless. Although I've not seen one, I'm told these shows have everything."

"Would you be satisfied, if I were to dance topless in your suite?"

"There you go corrupting me again. What am I going to do with you?"

"How about you love me, now and forever?"

After Brad and Marie had their late afternoon rendezvous she had more questions for him. "Do you mind if I ask a serious question, a question having to do with Wendy and Carol?" Marie didn't wait for a response to her question. "This Carol business, it's not totally on the up and up. You can't legally spy on anyone. You are taking too big a risk doing anything concerning her."

"Yes, there is some personal risk to me. I'm not worried about what we are thinking about doing to help Wendy's daughter."

"I hope you are right. You could get in a lot of trouble."

"Wendy sort of put me up to spying on her daughter by asking for my help. I can't help Carol without observing her so technically you are right, but what else can we do?"

"I'm trying to understand your position. Is there any chance I could meet Wendy's daughter before I return to Seattle?" Brad cringed. "I might feel better if I could see how bad Carol is for myself. I know I'm asking a lot. Wendy may not want me seeing her daughter."

Brad instantly flipped open his cell phone and made a call. "Hi Wendy, how is Carol this evening?"

"Very restless, her nurse told me the massive shot they gave Carol to sedate her should have knocked her out for six to eight hours, she was fully awake in three hours."

"Wow, three hours is not very long. Marie would like to see and meet Carol. Would you mind if I brought her by?"

"Did Marie say why she wants to meet Carol?" Wendy asked with concern.

"Hold on, I'll ask her. Honey, Wendy is wondering why you want to meet Carol."

"May I speak to Wendy myself?" He handed his phone to Marie. "Hi Wendy, I have something eating away at me all afternoon. I can't explain the feeling I have. It's an urge to meet Carol, so I can put a face to her name and see her condition for myself."

"I don't see any harm in you seeing Carol come by and enter her room cautiously and be prepared for anything. She may not take kindly to a stranger entering her room."

"Thank you Wendy, we'll see you in a few minutes. I hope you don't mind our going to see Carol. I have a severe urge to meet her, why, I don't know."

"I don't mind you seeing Carol. You have a strange feeling about what you heard Wendy and me talking about. Our conversation left you confused. Seeing her might help you understand why we are planning to do an illegal intervention. Admittedly Wendy and I know little about this type of intervention."

It was a short drive to the hospital. "Carol is in room two sixteen. Take all the time you need in her room." He released Marie's hand at her hospital room door. This is Carol's room, I'll wait out here."

"Why am I going in alone, I thought you be going in with me?"

"Honey, I can't go in. Carol won't tolerate me in her room."

Marie drew in several deep breaths before entering the room. She spent thirty minutes trying to converse with Carol, while Brad paced back and forth in the hallway. She exited the room shaking her head. "That girl is in a bad way. It's easy to see why Wendy is concerned for her mental state. She is beyond anything close to a normal person mentally. Hypnotizing someone in her state could be next to impossible. She is not concentrating on anything. The life has gone out of her, she is in a zombie like state. I don't see how you can possibly help her. Without her concentrating, you have nothing to work with."

"Wendy and I understand the challenge ahead of us. Would you mind going back into the room and ask Wendy to step out here for a second?"

When the girls returned he had a very serious look on his face. "Ladies we all agree Carol needs help. Wendy you saw how she reacted to me the other day, so my question is more for you. How would you feel about me going in her room again today?" Wendy's face showed concern. "I need to know if she has made any progress from when I saw her before."

"Oh please, you are asking a lot." He nodded in agreement. "Alright, enter easy and leave fast, if she becomes upset." Wendy's face clearly showed she wasn't certain he should enter Carol's room.

"If Carol reacts to me again like she did before. I need to know how long it takes for her to settle down."

"I hate this, but you are right. We do need to check. Let's give it a try."

"Marie, go ahead in with Wendy. You need to observe her reaction to me. Be sure and warn Carol I am coming in, we don't need to startle the poor girl."

Both ladies were apprehensive about his going into her hospital room. All three expected some kind of reaction from Carol. Unfortunately they received more than they expected. She instantly screamed and began throwing everything she could get her hands on at Brad. Thank goodness most of the things she managed to grab were plastic. He exited the room much faster than he entered. Wendy grabbed at her hands. "Easy Honey, Brad won't hurt you."

"He's a man. Keep the son-of-a-bitch away from me. Men are filthy pigs. No man will ever touch me again. I don't want men around me."

Marie quickly joined Brad in the hall. "We should go, I've seen enough." Not until they were in the car did she say more. "You have your work cut out for you. Before you begin trying to help Carol set benchmarks, be honest with yourself. Don't be disappointed if you can't help this girl."

"I can help the girl but helping her we create another problem. We may be allowing a rapist to go free. By blocking her memory she will not be able to testify against the creep."

"It is amazing how fast life can become complicated. All you can do is concentrate on Carol. How long do you expect to keep her hypnotized?"

"Long as it takes to clear her mind about her rape, forever if necessary. Together Wendy and I will monitor her very closely."

"You can't stay awake for days to monitor her. Do you want me to stay a few extra days and help monitor Carol's progress?"

He touched Marie's hand. "Honey I know your offer comes from your heart. You know we won't be operating totally legal. You shouldn't get involved. Seeing me watch a young woman might give you a lower opinion of me. Voyeurs rate slightly above a pervert."

"Don't put yourself down. What you are about to undertake is nothing less than brave. Think about my offer, you could use my help."

"Don't worry about me Honey, when I get tired I can alternate, twenty minutes napping, twenty minutes awake. In a few short days we should know if we can help her or not. At that time we can make a decision about what comes next."

Marie gave him a concerning look. "You still have dark circles under your eyes. Even without Carol's problem you have enough on your plate. Take the advice you gave Wendy. Take deep breaths, relax, and allow people to help you."

Without comment he parked in the suite parking lot. He walked around the car and opened the door for her. He pulled her tight in his arms for a sweet hug. "I wish things were simple as you make them sound." He gave her a kiss before releasing his grip. "We are wasting our last evening together."

"Being with you is never a waste. I'm enjoying every minute, day and night when I'm with you. I wish I could stay longer."

For a brief instant he considered allowing her to stay the extra couple days she requested. Yet he knew there was no way he should allow her to see his powerful subliminal messages in action. "It's been a crazy weekend Honey certainly not at all the weekend I expected. Let's go up to our room and change before we go out for dinner?"

"You amaze me, now you are a mind reader. If we skip going out we could order room service and try the Jacuzzi in your room."

"I like your idea. I'm anxious try the Jacuzzi."

After their soothing soak in the Jacuzzi they never made it to the shower until after another bedroom tussle and a lengthy nap. Near ten PM the cozy couple showered and dressed before going out for a late night snack. "This city amazes me. It's zeroing in on midnight on a Sunday evening and crowd of people still roaming the streets are unbelievable. It is unbelievable, does anyone ever sleep in this city?"

"They must. This is the perfect place for my experimental advertising research. I've accomplished more in five weeks than I expected to accomplish in the next two years. I've progressed to the point I get bored. Let's grab a snack here it looks like a quiet place to talk."

CHAPTER 22

Inside the quaint little snack bar in the Casino, Brad asked about Marie's family. "I come from a middle-income family. My father works for the city of Salem, in Oregon. Mother is a receptionist for a dentist. My younger brother Tom attends junior college in Portland. He plans to transfer to a larger college after I get my degree. We have wonderful family holidays at Grandpa and Grandma's house. They live twenty miles outside Salem. Anything else you want to know?"

"I would love to meet your family."

"I also have many Aunts, Uncles and Cousins who are nice people." Marie stated with pride. "We do have a family Black Sheep. Uncle Bernie is an alcoholic. Where does your family live and what do they do?"

"I know so little about my family. If we have a Black Sheep I don't know who it might be, unless it's me. My parents seem to live in Mexico a good part of the time. They do travel a lot. They search the far corners of the earth buying merchandise for their Import-Export Stores. I seldom see, or hear from either of my parents. Over the years I've grown to accept them being absent from my life. They have this strange misguided belief money can replace their love. I do receive a nice allowance each month. The people that cared for me and those around me are where I get the love and attention I need to make it through each day. How about we go find a lounge and put a little romantic dancing into our evening?" His words brightened her pretty smile. "We can have a drink and take a twirl on the dance floor."

"I love dancing, let's go before it gets too late. I couldn't wish for a better trip than you bringing me to Vegas."

"It's been a pleasure for me too. Once I get this Carol business out of the way and Wendy is back working full-time. I would like to fly up to Seattle and see you on a regular basis, twice a month maybe."

"Come anytime you want, and stay long as you want. I can't believe how fast our weekend is slipping away. We have what is left of tonight and part of tomorrow. We should return to your suite and let you rest.

After stealing your valuable work time, you will be very busy after I leave. We should be at the Burger Palace earlier tomorrow than we did today. I came to Vegas so I would get to know you better. My plan is going well. I've seen you do more in three days than I ever imagined. I now understand how busy you are."

The following morning Brad and Marie arrived at the Burger Palace around nine to find Wendy working away. "Good morning Wendy, what on earth are you doing here?"

"I'm trying to put in some of the hours you are paying me for."

He patted Wendy high on her shoulder and then gently rubbed her back. "You don't need to make up any hours. Your daughter is the person who needs you. We are getting by in the office."

"I'll leave by nine-thirty and be at the hospital about the time the nurses finish giving Carol her sponge bath."

"Why isn't she showering herself?"

"I'm told giving her a sponge bath is part of her therapy. Female nurses are the only people allowed to touch her for now. The therapist thinks people bathing and showering her will change her outlook about being touched."

"I'm glad you told me people showered her. It shouldn't make a lot of difference for what we are planning except if she needs touched, you may need to bathe Carol a time or two. By late next week she should be near normal again."

"Before you go running off today take a good look at this. We will be out of all fish products before the day is over."

"This young lady on my left has been distracting me. I've been neglecting my duties. You better change to standard music number nine."

Wendy understood his instructions loud and clear. He wanted plain music with no messages. "You two run along, and enjoy the rest of your day. I'll finish up here and make a bank deposit before I go back to the hospital."

"Brad, I would like to gamble. Twenty dollars, that's my limit. Have you won any money since being here in Vegas?"

"I haven't tried my hand at Lady Luck. I've been working. My plan is to make an honest living, and avoid getting hooked on gambling."

Walking through the Casino on her way to the Mall area Marie spotted a slot machine Marie liked. Her twenty dollars soon became forty dollars. She bounced, screamed and hugged Brad. "I'm a winner! Let's go shopping before I lose my money."

Moving on to the Mall shopping was soon delayed. She balked at the high prices in the Casino Mall. "If you want to buy me clothes we better find a different shopping area. I'm not paying these outrageous prices for my clothes. I'm hungry. We should have eaten at the Burger Palace while we were there. I love the food there."

"You are in luck I know the owner of the Burger Palace. I can get us a great window table. Plus I'm sure you are right you will find clothes more to your liking in the Mall near the Burger Palace."

From their leisurely meal and shopping spree it was time to think about getting her to the airport. They stopped by the suite long enough to get her luggage and pack her clothes. "I feel funny about you buying me clothes. No man has ever bought me clothes before." Her objection was coated by a huge proud smile. "You are spoiling me."

"Your father bought clothes for you."

"You have a way of twisting people's words. My father buying me clothes doesn't count. All parents buy their children clothes."

"I'm just giving you a bad time. I happen to think you should fly down and see me three maybe four times before your fall quarter starts at college."

"What will people think if they know you bought me a bunch of clothes and paying me to fly to Vegas so often?"

"They will think I love you."

Dilly-dallying around putting her clothes away at his suite set Marie behind schedule. She had to hurry at the airport. Heavy traffic ate up valuable time. They barely had time to kiss good bye, see you soon Honey!" He fought off the overpowering urge to call her back. Knowing his tendency to fall in love with women too fast, he had to allow Marie to fly back to Seattle.

From the airport Brad hustled back to the Burger Palace to finish setting up tiny spy cameras in the apartment. The bathroom stool was the only place in the apartment he could not observe the occupants. Another concerning factor was the Office Temp. He could not allow Rose to see him spying on a female, Rose was dismissed. Around ten in the evening he called Seattle to make sure Marie arrived home. "Hi Honey. I miss you. I wanted to be sure you made it home alright."

"Except for crying on the plane, I made it home alright. I miss you too."

"You can bet your life I will move mountains to see you soon as possible. What about Judy did she enjoy her trip?"

"She had a fantastic weekend, as did I. I do want to warn you next time I see you be prepared to tell me what you are really doing with Carol. I find it hard to believe you are hypnotizing anyone." The phone fell silent for several seconds as she waited for his response. "Did I lose you?"

"No, I'm here. Please don't ask any questions. Cell phones leave records. I'll call again soon, bye."

"Dang it all, he hung up on me."

"Why would Brad hang up on you?"

"I was asking a question he wasn't prepared to answer. He said cell phones leave records then he hung up. He is working on a special secret project concerning Wendy's daughter."

"Tread easy when you are talking to Brad. He likes his space, don't push him." Judy warned. "Don't press him about anything."

He felt bad about hanging up on Marie. What else could he do? By midnight more intrusive cameras were installed and checked in the apartment. He then began making subliminal messages for the young girl. Being alone in the office gave him time to create these messages, read them over and change words when necessary. He searched his mind until he came up with the exact words he felt confident would be beneficial to her before going back to his empty suite.

What a difference a day makes, twenty-four hours ago he was the happiest guy in the world. Now his suite felt cold, he was alone again.

Straight up eight the following morning Brad entered the Burger Palace. On his way up to the office he stopped for a quick breakfast and conversation with Ernie. "Wendy's daughter will be moving into the apartment for the time being. As you know she had the problem with that creep Wendell Carpenter. Knowing the police as I do, they could release her attacker on bail. The girl needs to stay somewhere he can't find her."

"Wendell Carpenter is a bad dude he needs to be lethally injected into his next life. The world would be better off without him."

"You surprise me Ernie. I never expected you to believe in capitol punishment." Brad patted him on the back. "Keep up the good work, quarterly bonuses are next week."

"Excellent, my wife will be thrilled with a bonus check. Did you happen to see the article in the paper yesterday about Carol's rapist?"

"I didn't see the paper. Marie was my focus yesterday. Is the article something I need to read?"

"According to the article Carpenter is a decorated War Hero. He was in the Special Forces did three tours in Vietnam and wounded twice. Until six years ago he was a loving family man. The reporter quoted a doctor that thinks his aggression against women can be controlled with medication."

"If Carpenter was wounded in Vietnam he was shot in the frigging head. He isn't mentally right. I better get on up to the office before Wendy fires me."

Monday became a complete blur as Brad tried to catch up on work enough to handle things without his office temp. On Tuesday from breakfast to the time Wendy and Carol arrived at the apartment seemed like an eternity. His messages for Carol were strong, but not the intensity of the message he used on Jason when the money was missing. He would be observing her, and could make adjustments on an as needed basis."

At ten, Wendy and her sad emotionless daughter arrived at the apartment. Carol's head hung low, shoulders sagged. She was the very image of a severely depressed person. He shuttered at the massive challenge before him. From the safety of the office he carefully observed her as she went to the bedroom. There she stripped to her panties and put on a robe. After changing she rejoined her mother who was channel searching for something to watch.

"Honey will you be alright, while I go check inventory on my computer?" Carol completely ignored her mother's words. "I won't be gone long." Wendy hurried to the office. He killed the bedroom and bathroom monitors before she arrived. "Brad, I'm scared. Are we doing the right thing?"

"Get a hold on yourself Wendy. We can't expect instant results. It's too late to change our minds now. Carol is here. Go back to the apartment and relax."

After dashing to the office and back Wendy did a better job controlling her anxiety. Her near lifeless daughter began to brighten. She and her mother soon carried on short conversations and shared an apple as a snack.

Realizing his subliminal message was starting to work put a smile on Brad's face. Remembering his words to Wendy about staying with the plan he fought off the urge to increase the power to speed up her recovery. Early evening Carol headed off to the bathroom as he spied on her from high above. She disrobed, dropped her panties and stepped in the shower. A twinge of guilt wasn't enough to keep him from watching the young girl shower. He periodically checked the other monitors to make certain Wendy didn't slip off and come to the office.

Carol was exceptionally uncomfortable with her body as she showered. She was scrubbing her delicate skin far too hard. Red blotches began to appear her body. He could only imagine she was trying to wash away the filth of the rapist from her skin. After her long scrubbing shower her tender skin could only be patted dry. She soon settled down with her mother to watch more television. "Honey I need to check some things in the office. Will you be alright for a few minutes?" Carol nodded. "I'll be right back." He switched off the restroom cameras. She came charging up the stairs and flew into his arms giving him a motherly hug. "Your message is working you are an absolute miracle worker."

He couldn't help but laugh. "A miracle worker, I don't think so. You need to control your emotions. We still have a lot to do before Carol gets back closer to normal."

"Don't sell yourself short. Joe and I now will have our daughter back. She will again be a productive individual."

"Speaking of your husband, will he be coming over to visit Carol tonight?"

"No not tonight Joe is out on the road."

"How would you like to check our bank deposit, you could do the counting in the apartment. Have Carol help you count the money if she will. We need her doing various things so we can check her memory on different subjects. Remember keep the television on, or the stereo on at all times. The sound can be very low while the two of you sleep but our messages must remain constant. Support Carol best you can. Tell her music encourages healing."

"Having her count money is a great idea. I'll grab the money bag on my way back to the apartment. Thank you again for your help."

He began to reflect on Wendy's strange actions she shouldn't be the target of any message. Her two hugs and the kiss was out of character for her. Her unusual actions were most likely nothing to worry about. He passed them off as a simple thank you gesture for helping her daughter.

He tipped back in his chair for a brief rest. Marie was right staying awake around the clock would be difficult. Although he wasn't big on espressos by morning he was certain espressos would be needed to survive day two. By noon he found it difficult to concentrate as his mind continued to drift back to Marie and her visit. She wanted to stay, he wanted her to stay, but it was too soon with his track record. He could ruin a great relationship before it could fully blossom. He hated being alone. Karen was living proof of what happens if a person thinks they can force someone to love them. With Marie, he vowed to proceed slowly.

Ernie brought him a chicken basket, small salad and a diet soda to the office for his dinner. Super hungry he ate his tasty food while watching the ladies discuss the movie as it ended. With each passing hour Carol interacted better with her mother. He continued to check his watch. At eight in the evening he planned to call Marie. Over anxious he dialed too early, Judy answered the phone. "Hello Brad, your call is early. Marie isn't home for another half hour."

"Darn I always call to early. We had such a terrific weekend I miss her."

Judy could easily detect the excitement in his voice. "One only has to see the glow on her face to know you both, had a great weekend. She missed you so much she cried herself to sleep last night. I incorrectly assumed the two of you had an argument."

"I hugged my pillow several times in the night myself. I'm in a tough spot where Marie is concerned. I love her dearly, yet my history has been to become involved with the opposite gender faster than I should. Our relationship needs to grow at a slow steady pace."

"Don't be confused. Marie is no Karen, she loves you. You could be a penniless bum and she would still love you with all her heart." Brad laughed. "Don't snicker, I'm serious. She loves you."

"Do you really believe her love for me is that strong or are you overjoyed to see she had a nice weekend?"

"Yes I believe her love for you is strong. Next time you talk to Marie, test her. Tell her your father pulled all his support and financing from you, and had to put the Burger Palace up for sale, basically leaving you broke. Then listen to what she says."

"Oh good heavens girl, I couldn't do such a thing to Marie. She is too sweet to play games with."

"Hold on a minute, I hear her coming now." He waited patiently while Judy shouted out for Marie. "Brad's on the phone!" Hearing her footsteps getting louder put a smile on his face. "This isn't a good call, he is in a funk tonight. His father clipped his wings and closed his bank accounts plus he put the Burger Palace up for sale. Brad is really down emotionally."

"Give me the phone! Brad, are you still there?"

"Yes Honey, I'm here."

"Judy told me your bad news. I've got six thousand dollars I can send you. We can sell your car if that money will help."

"Whoa slow down Honey, your roommate was being funny. The girl is pulling your leg to prove a point to me. My finances are fine, but if you really want to help me swat Judy on her fanny a few times for me. She pulled a very naughty joke on you."

"Why that little rotten stinker, I'll deal with her later."

"Don't be too hard on her she lied to prove a point. One of those little white lies deals. We were discussing you and how you and I felt towards one another. She explained how you arrived in Seattle with tears in your eyes. I confessed my tears to her. She couldn't understand if we thought so much of one another, how I could allow you to leave. I reminded her of my track record of becoming attached to a woman before I knew her well. She insisted you would love me even if I were broke. You walked in at the precise moment for Judy to test her theory."

"She can be quite the scoundrel at times. I'm relieved to hear your finances are normal. You have such a fine business going it would be a crime to sell it."

"When you offered me your college money she proved her point. Now that we confirmed I don't need your money, there is something I do need."

"Name it and you have it."

"I need hugs and kisses. I could use all you can spare."

"Hugs and kisses don't mail well. I can save them until you come see me. How is the Carol business going, are you able to help her?"

"There are early positive signs we are helping her. It's far too early to truly access our progress. Wendy is getting well ahead of our progress. She sees Carol as completely well. Believe me she isn't normal yet. She has yet to interact with anyone beside her mother. I keep urging Wendy to go slow."

"As her mother I can understand her anxiety. If what I understand you are saying right, you do need to proceed slowly."

"I believe she is showing definite signs of improving. Not as much as her mother thinks but she is showing some improvement. I plan to move forward with great caution. This is all new territory for me."

"How are you doing? I worry about the dark circles under your eyes. You had the dark circles before you started this Carol project and now with less sleep how will you get by?"

"I'm doing alright. You were right about staying awake and how hard it is. Earlier this evening I dozed off for a full hour."

"I told you I'm needed in Vegas."

"You might be a distraction for what I'm doing, please don't ask for details. I'm not ready to go into details at this time. I see Ernie bringing cash bag up to me. This means I need to get back to work. I'll call you tomorrow night Honey, I love you."

"I love you too, bye."

CHAPTER 23

Ernie took one look at Brad as he handed him the cash bag. "Hey man you look beat you shouldn't be working so late at night. If you keep working these hours you will die a young man."

"I need to catch up on our bookkeeping. Don't worry my friend. I'll be fine. I stole a few hours sleep earlier and given the chance, I may soon nap again soon. I won't have this schedule much longer."

Ernie shook his head. "Please don't stay all night again you look exhausted. It's too hard on your body."

"I'm fine and soon as Wendy returns to work full time. I'm taking some time off. I'll be going to Seattle for a few days and see my lady friend."

"You are planning to see Marie. She is a beautiful lady and very smart. Count the money careful. I better get back to work."

With Ernie gone he resumed his secret monitoring. Carol was actually joking and laughing with her mother. She soon retired for the night and Wendy immediately came charging up to the office for a quick word with him. "Today's progress was amazing." In her excitement she hugged Brad. "Go home and get a good night's sleep. Carol will be fine tonight. You look rough, you really need to go home and get proper rest. If anything changes, I'll call you."

"My concern is she could have a nightmare. Calling me might work except it takes me an hour to dress and get back here. I better stretch out on the floor and nap here."

Back in the apartment Wendy went straight for a shower. The proper thing to have done would be to turn off the intrusive shower camera. By leaving the cameras on he could get a comparison video to see how a normal woman showered. Brad opted to watch as she undressed. Wendy's body looked to be in remarkable shape for a fifty year old woman. Drawn to her beauty he never looked away until she dressed in her nightclothes. Being tired he stretched out on the floor hoping to sleep. He woke several times during the night to check on Carol who hadn't moved. Around seven Wendy woke him as she entered the office. "You should have gone home like I suggested, Carol did fine all night. You are the one who had a rough night." Wendy paused in mid-sentence. "That's my daughter you are watching shower."

He glanced up at the monitor. "She looks very normal this morning."

"I know but you are watching my daughter, shower!"

"I am watching your daughter shower from a safe distance. The camera shows her general actions not the close up details. Any female showering would look much like her from this distance. We talked about how intrusive the cameras would be. Making sure she is comfortable with her own body is exceptionally important. This is all in her best interest."

She gave him an angry look. "Are you sure?"

"I'm very sure. I have a comparison video." From the drawer he produced the video of her first shower. "Let me show you a video from sixteen hours ago." Brad installed the video. "In this video Carol is about to scrub her skin off. Look at the reds spots where she rubbed so hard. After watching her first shower I adjusted the intensity of my subliminal message to a higher level. You can easily see at this point an adjustment needed to be made."

"You most certainly were not lying when you said your cameras would be intrusive. Carol wasn't the only person to shower yesterday. Did you spy on me as well?"

"I felt a comparison video would be helpful. I'm guilty as charged."

"Did you enjoy spying on us?" She asked still looking angry.

"What a silly question. Men are visual animals. In this case there were over-riding factors driving my attention. Watching the two beautiful women shower wasn't all bad."

"If your mother were here she would slap you up the side of your head."

"My absent mother and father never cared enough about me to slap me. They pawned me off with a nanny at an early age. If you feel I need a good slapping, slap away. I thought our sole purpose for bringing Carol he was so we could help her. To help her we must observe her."

Wendy leaned down as though she was about to slap him across the face. She changed her mind at the last minute as she gave him a light pat on the cheek. "Promise me when this is over we can destroy these videos."

"Soon as we determine the videos are no longer of value, we certainly will destroy the videos."

"I'll take your words as a promise. The reason I came up here this morning is to invite you to breakfast with Carol and me." Brad gave her a questioning look. "It was her idea to invite you to breakfast. She thinks eating here would be fun. Our breakfasts are good."

"In less than twenty four hours going from not tolerating any male person to inviting a male to breakfast makes me suspicious. Are you sure this was Carol's idea?"

"Carol is a different person now than she was when she came here. Wash your face and join us. I think her progress will impress you."

"I'm going to stay here until I'm certain she will be alright in the Burger Palace. If she seems anything close to normal. I will come down and join you for breakfast."

"Don't wait too long to join us. Carol is not the person you saw in the hospital. She will be fine."

"Let's hope so." As Wendy exited the office he dashed in the restroom failing to completely close the door. She thought of one more question and turned back. Seeing the door partially open she thought he was washing his face and walked in to see him urinating. "Oops sorry, I thought you were washing your face."

After draining his system he stepped out into the office. "I wasn't expecting you to return so soon. What's on your mind?"

"What do we tell Carol if she asks why she is recovering in your apartment, or if she asks what she is recovering from?"

"The Burger Palace is no place to discuss her situation. Later today we may be able to ease into her condition with her. When that time comes we can only tell her what we believe she is ready to handle."

Before going down to join the girls he took time to study Carol's reaction to other males around her. She did better than he expected although she was cautious to keep distance around her. He knocked on the door jam for good luck on his way to join the women. "Good morning ladies, I hope you found the apartment to your liking?"

"Yes Mr. Collins your apartment is comfortable. Mother thinks I should thank you for allowing me to stay here. There really isn't anything wrong with my other apartment unless you know something I don't. I was living comfortable in my old place."

"It's best we don't talk about why you are here in public. Let's order breakfast I'm starved. We can possibly talk later. Wendy can you get my usual Omelet Sandwich while I get us a table by the window?"

As she started to eat Carol inquired why she was at this apartment. "You are here for your own safety. For now the fewer people know you are here the better. This is not a good place for private conversations. People shouldn't hear your story until you understand your story. Then if you want to tell people your story at a later date, it's your decision."

"According to mother it was your idea for her to bring me hear. I came to breakfast hoping you would tell me more than my mother is telling me. Seems I made a mistake. I'm not getting any information from you either."

"Let me assure you your mother, your father, and I want what is best for you. You have been out of the hospital one day. We all must guard against any type of setback."

"All I'm getting from you and mother is the run around." Carol clearly showed her anger. "Information should not be withheld from me."

"I'm sure all this bait and switch business is confusing to you. Believe me we have good reason to treat you as we are. We would rather error on the side of caution, if we error at all. How would you like to make a deal young lady?"

"I don't need more run around if that is what you have in mind?'

"Hear me out before judging me so harshly. We all agree this morning you are doing remarkably well. We don't know if your progress is temporary or permanent. Give your mother and me one more day while you recoup?" Carol frowned at him. "Your part would be easy, hang out in the apartment and rest. You can do whatever you want long as you remain in the apartment."

"Do you promise to tell me what this is all about tomorrow?"

"Hold on little Missy, tomorrow will still be a maybe. If your mother and I still believe you are continuing to do well. Some information can be given to you. Not your complete story. We must do this in steps, so we don't mess up your recovery. Depending on how you handle information given to you will be the determining factor when additional information is given to you."

"Then you are saying one more day and I will learn something?"

"It can be soon as one more day. Everything hinges on how you react to situations and people around you. This is no time to throw caution to the wind. You surprised me this morning by having breakfast in public. Yesterday I would have bet money you couldn't be out in public like this. Being out here is a good sign, an excellent sign in fact. We are proud of you."

"I'll accept your deal. You better come up with some answers very soon. Otherwise I'm out of here."

"Easy girl, nobody is holding you captive. You can walk out anytime you want the door is right behind you. Your mother and I would like the opportunity to continue helping you by giving you a private place to recover fully. When you looked in the mirror this morning you had to see the bruises on your neck indicating you need time to heal physically. Emotional healing also needs time to heal. We are asking you to be patient."

"I do have a strange feeling inside. A feeling I can't describe."

"I'm guessing if you are patient in a week from now your uneasy feeling will be a distant memory."

"I'm hearing more of your double talk." Carol snapped back.

"I hope you choose to stay here. Either way I have bookwork to do. I bid you ladies goodbye."

She remained quiet until he was out of hearing distance. "There goes a strange man mother. How on earth did you ever start working for him?"

"He comes from a money background making him different. Thinking he can help you, I asked for his help. With your father on the road so much and you not improving in the hospital, I had to do something."

"I find it hard to believe you asked for this guy's help."

"I did ask for his help. I wasn't sure he would consider helping after the way you treated him at the hospital."

"Mr. Collins never came to see me in my hospital room."

"Honey, he was there twice. Both times you threw things at him. Thank goodness he understood the stress you were under. One thing I am certain of is he won't give up on you, long as you don't give up on him."

"One more day mother, if I'm not given information. I'm out of here. I'll go straight to the hospital and check my hospital records. Then I'll know what is going on."

Following Brad's lead from earlier Wendy followed suit. "Honey if it will tear you up to wait one more day, take my car, and go check your hospital records. I may as well go back to work since you are not willing to work with us. I've wasted a lot of work-time already."

"Don't get excited Mother. I'll go back to the apartment and wait one more day as I agreed. Tomorrow I want answers."

"Coming out here for breakfast was one of the setbacks we needed to lookout for. Since coming out here you have showed some anger. Your mood change hasn't been in your best interest."

In the comfort of his office Brad busied himself editing security videos making two separate versions. One video showed Carol's progress while in the apartment. The second video contained the shower scenes of both women. Exhaustion was catching up with Brad. He could not continue at this sleepless pace. It became time to take a chance. He went straight to the apartment. Carol answered the door. "Do you have a change of heart and decide to level with me?"

"I came to see your mother, may I speak to her?"

"She is in the restroom. You may come in and wait if you like."

"Thank you, are you sure it's alright if I come in. You are looking at me as though I'm some sort of a monster."

"Yes you may come in. I'm studying you carefully trying to figure you out."

"Not much to figure out about me. Didn't your mother tell you I am a Warlock with special powers?" He reached out and touched Carol's hair. "Will you stop with the Mr. Collins bit and call me Brad."

Wendy's appearance ended the verbal duel between them. "Wendy, I could use a favor. I'm very tired this morning. If I went to my suite and rested could you make a bank drop for me after lunch?"

"Certainly I can make the bank drop for you. Carol should be fine while I'm gone."

"Take Carol with you she might like a breath of fresh air." He pulled four crisp one hundred dollar bills from his wallet. "Here, you girls can do some shopping while you are out." He glanced in Carol's direction. "If I get to feeling better, I may see you ladies later this evening have fun."

He skipped out before Carol could question him. "I'm lost mother what just happened here?"

"Brad is testing you. He wants to see how you react to everyday people."

For Brad his suite was a welcome sight. He hung out the do not disturb sign, showered and shaved before bailing under the covers. He never moved a muscle for six hours. Thinking about the work piling up at the Burger Palace was the only reason to get up."

For the second straight day sales were down. This Carol business was taking a toll on profits. At the same time it was a clear signal to him before starting the advertising business the office would need additional equipment. Only periodically did he check the monitors to see what Carol was doing. Around five he called the apartment. "Hi Wendy, how did our patient do on her excursion today?"

"Carol did fine. We had great time shopping."

"Will Joe be in town tonight?" Brad inquired.

"Joe should be in Salt Lake area tonight."

"In that case would you and Carol care to join me for dinner this evening? We can make a second bank drop while we are out. Call me when you decide."

She called back almost instantly. "Carol agreed to go out for dinner."

"Then how about we let Carol decide where she would like to eat, she may have a favorite place she likes to eat."

Carol chose Tony Roma's, a restaurant that is traditionally busy and noisy. "Mom and I had fun shopping today. It's been a while since we were shopping together. We didn't get back until four."

"How about you Wendy, did you have fun shopping with your daughter?"

"I always enjoy shopping with my daughter. I'm not sure what Joe will think. He gets nervous when we buy things. I'm not sure he will like you paying for our shopping. "

Unable to contain herself any longer, Carol looked straight at him. "What was your real reason for buying our outfits?"

"You appeared to be doing better. Your mother and I, needed to see how well you do out among people. Basically we are doing the same thing here at Tony Roma's. We let you choose the restaurant to see if you would choose a nice quiet out of the way place, or a noisy place like Tony Roma's."

"So all day you have been controlling me?"

"Your mother and I are not controlling you. We are testing you. When you complained we were holding you captive. I gave your words some thought. We are allowing you to show us how well you are doing. On the surface it sounds as though you did fine."

"If I'm doing so well, why are you holding things from me?"

"I won't lie to you Carol even with you doing well today. Tomorrow will be another slow progress day. Please be patient with us. There are delicate matters ahead that may affect the rest of your life. In time there are things you won't want to hear or see. Unfortunately these are things you must see and talk about. If it takes one more day, or ten more days to know your full story, does it really matter. Ten days is nothing in a person's life."

"I'm not waiting ten days for my answers. Tomorrow you are telling me something. At any rate I thank you for the dinner date."

"No, no, no, our dinner was a dinner among friends not a dinner date."

"Oh gee mother, now our friend has standards."

"What a terrible thing to say, Brad is trying to help you."

"I'm kidding mother, he kids me, why can't I kid him back?"

"Listen to me Carol. I have a special little gal in Seattle where my primary home is. It would be very inappropriate for me to call this a date or spend excess time with you."

"Mother told me about Marie, I met her at the hospital, she seems nice. What is this about your primary home being in Seattle? You live and work here in Las Vegas?"

Brad made a mental note about Carol remembering Marie being at the hospital. Earlier in the day she acted as thought she didn't remember having visitors at the hospital. Oh well, maybe he misunderstood. "I am a college student in Seattle who bought a business in Vegas. I want the Burger Palace running smooth, so I can return to Seattle in the fall. My desire is complete my college degree. This business with you is already eating into my social time. When your mother is able to return and work full time. I plan on flying to Seattle for some quality time with Marie."

"I don't see any problem why you can't go see your lady friend. Tell me everything you are holding back. Mom can return to work, and you can fly to Seattle." She bent her arms up at the elbow as she held her hands wide open. "Everyone would be happy."

"I wish things were simple as you think. In time you will understand why we are being cautious. In the end you will know every last detail. Now I have a stack of payroll checks to sign. Oh darn, I forgot to stop by the office supply store. Wendy is there any way you and Carol could drop me by the office and then go pick up some blank CDs for me?"

"I can go get your CDs. How about you Carol, do you want to go with me?"

"I may as well go with you. I'm not ready to be put back in my cage for the night."

Once the girls left Brad went into the girl's apartment and showered. He cleaned up every sign he had been in the apartment before leaving. Upon return Wendy brought the supplies to the office. "What was all this CD nonsense about you have drawers full of these things?"

"Your nosy daughter was asking too many questions. I needed to get away from her, and get her mind on something else."

Wendy nodded slightly. "You are right she is pushing hard. I better get back to the apartment before she comes up here looking for me. Will you stay here again tonight?"

"I'll see how my work goes before I decide to go home or not. I also have my daily Seattle call I can make before I leave."

"Goodnight Brad, I'll pray for your sins." Wendy relayed with a slight grin. "Carol did so well last night and today you need to go home after you finish signing the payroll checks." Brad glared at her. "Don't give me that look. You know what I'm talking about."

"Pray for my sins, what have I done that is so bad?"

"Come on, spying on women taking showers has to be a huge sin."

"Male doctors look at naked women all the time, are they sinning."

She looked shocked by his response. "Excuse me, you are no doctor."

"I'm sort of like an honorary degree doctor except I have an imaginary doctor degree. I'm a sweet loving phony."

"Oh brother, now I've heard everything. I better go see Carol."

With anxious fingers he made his call to Seattle. "Hello Marie, how was your day?"

"My work is very boring and I miss you. I'm very lonely. How is the Carol business going?"

"The girl appears to be doing remarkably well. So well in fact she is rebelling, and demanding more information than we are comfortable giving her. She went out twice today, and did get along well among a mixture of people. Her deathly fear of men has eased considerably. Before you ask, my sleep is still limited. When I do try sleeping, I dream about you."

"In your dreams am I the only person in your dreams?"

"Just you Honey, I can see you now standing in the shower washing your long flowing dark hair." The vision he described was Carol showering in the apartment below. "You are a vision of beauty. I can close my eyes and picture you showering as you gently wash your smooth soft skin. I get chills up my spine wanting touch your beautiful body."

"You are a typical man, what would you do without women?"

"I'll not argue with that statement. Without a good woman, men are nothing. If you must know, I'm addicted to you?"

"I hope you remain addicted to me until I see you again. Before I forget Judy has a new boyfriend. Rob is history. He found out you paid for her plane ticket to see her parents and wigged out. Here is the funny part, he was convinced you and Judy were having an affair."

"Oh shit, I should have known he would be upset. Judy did the right thing dumping him. Jealousy can lead to abuse. She is better off without him."

"Her new guys name is Sam Anderson. A guy she dated two years in high school so they know one another quite well. He is a better match for her than Rob. He isn't into the casual sex business like most young guys are today. He talks of wanting to get married someday."

"The casual sex thing you mentioned, I'm not like that either. My problem is I become attached to the opposite gender too fast. True love needs time to grow. One of the hardest things I ever did was to let you leave Vegas. At the same time it may have been dangerous for you to stay. With Carol showing great progress I may be about to fly up and see you sooner than I originally thought. I guarantee I will come to Seattle soon as I can. For now I have lots of work to do so I better get busy. See you soon Honey, I love you."

"I love you too."

He paid bills on line and checked inventory before retiring for the night. His call to Marie relaxed him to the point sleep came easy.

CHAPTER 24

By eight the following morning Brad was at the office editing videos to show the ladies when Carol pushed for information. The edited video compared her emotionless arrival to her current condition. The difference was dramatic. By nine thirty Wendy called the office to remind him, Carol was anxious to speak with him. "Will you be coming to the apartment soon?"

"I think it would be best if you and Carol came to the office. Could I impose on you to bring me a breakfast sandwich and my diet soda, on your way to the office?"

Minutes later Carol came busting into the office all smiles. "Okay Big Shot, today is the day."

"Wendy your daughter seems a little wound up this morning. A very good sign I might add. Question number one is…"

"…no, no, no, hold on buster, I didn't come here to answer questions I came for answers."

Brad pointed a finger at her. "Listen to me young lady without questions, there can be no answers. Let's try this again. Question number one, do you remember where you were working when your problem began?"

"I worked as a clerk in the Mini Mart on Eighth and Olive. I was employed there six months. In fact I should be working there now."

"Your mother and I are not sure you should be working just yet. Do you remember an incident concerning you at the Mini Mart?"

"I wasn't involved in an incident at the Mini Mart."

"You were involved in an incident. You were roughed up right at closing time."

"I wasn't roughed up at work. I should know more about what happens to me at work than you would."

"Carol, listen to me careful. Where do you believe your bruises came from?" She remained quiet. "According to the Mini Mart security camera your attacker hid inside the Mini Mart until you closed at midnight. He

199

brutally attacked you. This guy's name is Wendell Carpenter. He is an older gentleman. Do you recognize his name?" She shook her head no. "Carpenter is a bad guy, one mean low-life bastard. He is a criminal who is getting progressively worse. Here is the newspaper picture of him study his picture careful. See if he looks familiar to you."

"I've never seen this guy before in my life." Carol insisted.

"According to the security videos you have seen this character before. There were clear pictures of you coming face to face with him a split second before he attacked you. Watching the security video is how the police caught your attacker."

"If I were robbed, I'm glad they caught the robber?"

"This Wendell Carpenter guy is in custody. Robbery wasn't his main goal. You were his main target. He has a long history of sexual assault. He beat you and left you for dead."

With a look of concern Carol looked to her mother. "Mother, is Mr. Collins telling me the truth?"

"Yes this filthy man assaulted you. Then he tried to kill you so you couldn't testify against him, if he were to get caught. By the grace of God, you being young and with Mr. Collins' help you are doing quite well." A single tear trickled down Carol's cheek. Wendy hugged her daughter. "You were an emotional mess, and not getting any better at the hospital. I asked for Brad's help. He was very hesitant to try helping at first. He tried to visit you in the hospital."

"You told me Mr. Collins came to visit me. I honestly don't remember him being there. If I insulted you, I'm sorry."

"I tried visiting you twice. The second time you threw things at me. Thank goodness those things were plastic. I scooted out faster than a rabbit getting to his hole. In the past your mother had observed some of my intense advertising. My technique can have amazing results. She asked if I would use these techniques to help you. After several long discussions with your mother, I finally agreed to give you my best effort. So far the results have been amazing."

"Now wait a minute, hold on. Let's get back to what you were saying. The actual word for what happened to me is rape? I was raped?"

"The modern day term is sexual assault. The two-word combination covers the physical beating along with the unwanted intimate act. In your case Carpenter should also be charged with a third crime, Attempted Murder."

"Honey you have made a remarkable recovery in a short time."

"Then I should be thanking you, Mr. Collins."

"It isn't necessary to thank me. My technique was very intrusive. Only because your mother thought you could become suicidal, did I agree to help. Your father wasn't part of our discussion. Your doctor was preparing to send you to the Sunshine Rehab Center for long term therapy. Your doctor said you would need years and years of therapy. Coming here you were able to go out and deal with the public in a matter of two days."

"We did go shopping, and out for dinner. I must be fine, meaning your work is finished."

"Carol this is where caution comes in. I've never used this strong a technique on a person before. I have no history of the long-term effects. Furthermore I have no reason to believe you will have any problems in the future. None the less we should not take any chances by allowing you to rush anything."

"I'm sure my whole ordeal is over and done with."

"We still have your attacker you need to be careful of. We know so little about the man, except he is a dangerous Sex Predator. Why he chose you is still a mystery. The police think you are going to testify against him. We blocked your memory so there is no way you can testify to anything."

"Whoa, hold on. That means this creep could go free?'

"I don't see a snowballs chance in hell of your attacker going free. With your testimony the prosecutor expected him to get a life sentence, without your testimony he may get 10 to 20 years. Who knows what goes through the mind of a Judge. In my opinion the security video and the DNA will show enough evidence to still get a life conviction."

"You could be wrong. To be certain he gets the maximum sentence, I should testify against him. Unblock my memory until after the trial."

"Honey unblocking your memory won't help at all." Wendy insisted. "The mental state you were in a good defense attorney would hammer at you until you had a full-scale emotional breakdown. Sexual Assault trials are ugly regardless of what is on the security video. You would be accused of asking to have relations with this Wendell Carpenter, and changing your mind at the last minute."

"Are you of the same opinion as my mother?"

"I do side with your mother. One healthy Carol is worth a billion Wendell Carpenters. If I were your mother I would kill the man myself before I would allow you to go through a trial of this type. If you testify at his trial you could be living the Sexual Assault over and over."

Both women looked straight into his eyes after his statement. Carol was first to speak. "If you were my mother, you would actually kill him?"

"In a heartbeat, that creep did everything in his power to kill you. All mothers in the animal kingdom protect their young. Why should your mother be any different?" Carol gave no reaction to his statement. "She loves you. I suspect if the need arose, she would lie to save your life."

"Brad is right Honey, if I had a chance to kill him without spending the rest of my life in prison. I would kill him."

"If my attacker gets a short sentence he may attack some other woman?"

"Your mother and I can only do one thing at a time. For now we choose to concentrate our efforts on you to make sure you are okay. Later we may testify on your behalf at the actual trial. We can tell how you were and now how you are blocking the incident out of your mind. We can easily bring the doctor and nurses from the hospital to testify to your condition. Wendell Carpenter will not get away with what he did to you."

"I'm fine and healthy now. I should be the main person to testify against my attacker."

"Hopefully you will continue to be fine forever. You need to be honest with us about how you feel. If any of your current feelings change tell us. Above all else don't worry about your attacker. His actual trial won't come up for a year or more. You have time on your side. We've covered more than I expected today. I think this would be a great time to take a break. You think about what we talked about and after lunch we can talk again if you want. I eat around two o'clock."

Carol couldn't wait, she and Wendy returned to the office fifteen minutes early. "I've thought about what you said all morning. I've made up my mind. I definitely want you to reverse the process so I can testify against my attacker."

Her callous words shocked him. "I see you didn't listen to one thing we told you this morning."

"What's it to you one way or the other what I do, it's my life."

"I'm a friend of your mother. She asked for my help yo keep you out of Sunset Rehab Center. Do you want to be confined with brain dead druggies?"

"Oh please stop, no way was I that bad. You are exaggerating my condition."

"You amaze me. I don't think you listened to anything we said." He gave her a look of disgust. "You are a hard person to help. Why would you want to risk your mental health again?"

"You and mother said I was an emotional mess and suicidal. That is not true. I've never been suicidal in my life."

"Your mother said possible suicidal, didn't want to take any chances with your life. Do you remember how you were emotionally before Carpenter attack you?"

"Of course I remember how I was before living in my apartment. I was fine then; I am fine now, so I am going to testify."

"I honestly don't know if you are fine. You are angry, pushy, and not listening to anything we are saying. I've done everything but beat my head against the wall to get you to accept our words as to your condition before my involvement. I think it's time we allow you to see what our concerns were. Slide your chair back; turn a little this way so your view is clear to see the monitors."

"Monitors, you have been monitoring me?"

"Hell yes I've been monitoring you." Brad's voice boomed with anger. "We have been telling you all along we are observing you. You are not listening to us at all. Our observations were very intrusive. Of course we shouldn't expect you to know this because you have not been listening to one damn thing we said. Maybe this video will make our point." He pushed play. "This is you coming from the hospital. Two days ago you were a frigging zombie." Anger continued in his voice. "Could you testify in a sexual assault trial walking around as a zombie, hell no you couldn't."

"No, I couldn't testify in a drugged up zombie condition. I'm ok now. The medicine they gave me at the hospital is out of my system now."

"You weren't drugged up at that point. The hospital was about to transfer to a long term mental facility. We stole you out of the hospital. Any mother who saw her child in the condition you were in would do anything to help you. Your mother chose a method of action she knew could work in a short span of time." He pointed a finger at Carol. "Are you close to what you just saw in the video?"

"You know I'm nothing close to the person I saw on the video. I'm thinking about my attacker's next victim if the man goes free. He will certainly attack another woman and likely succeed in killing his next victim."

"To hell with Wendell Carpenter or his next victim, they were not our immediate problem. Have you ever climbed a flight of stairs?"

"What kind of a question is that, everyone has climbed stairs?"

"Did you take the top step first?"

"Stop asking stupid questions of me!"

"You took one step at a time to get up those stairs because it was the way to climb stairs! When a house is built they don't build the roof first! Your mother's first step was to help you return to normal! She and I will not apologize for our actions! His voice remained angry.

"Were your actions legal?"

"Damn it girl our actions are close enough to legal for me."

"What if I called the police and tell them about you and mother, what would they say?"

"I have no idea what the police would say. Here use my phone! Call the police you ungrateful little wench!" Brad's anger continued to flare.

"I didn't say I was calling the police. I asked what they might say if I did call them?"

"Your mother and I are dealing with your life. You are playing silly frigging games. You should be on your knees thanking your mother for caring. Don't bother thanking me. I did this for your mother not you. Now get out of my office." He pointed towards the door. "I have an enormous amount of work to do."

"We haven't finished talking. Nothing has been settled."

"For now we have finish talking! I've had it with you! Get out I have work to do!"

Once the women left his office he called the Office Temp Agency and inquired about getting Rose back. Luck was with him. She was available and arrangements were made for her to come immediately. Second he checked stock inventory so he knew how to direct sales. This continued loss of business was unacceptable. Towards evening Wendy returned to the office. She was surprised see Rose back in the office. "What is Rose doing here?"

"I'm losing money, and we are wasting time on your daughter. This is a situation I cannot tolerate any longer. I've had it!"

"Are you replacing me?" Wendy questioned.

"I don't know. We'll see how it goes."

"I don't blame you for being upset. I came up to ask if Carol and I could have another conversation with you today."

"No more conversation today or any other day during business hours." He snapped back at her. "Eight o'clock tonight or before seven in the morning, take your choice." With Rose's help on the bookkeeping he could concentrate on his next subliminal message for Carol. He wasn't about to allow the little wench to call the authorities on him.

"Near six he went down for dinner and ran into Wendy as she was picking up a couple sodas. "Carol had a change of heart." Although he didn't say anything he felt like screaming you bet your ass she had a change of heart. I zapped her ass with a strong message. "She feels bad about what she said to you earlier. She never had any intention of calling the police."

"Tears don't carry any weight around me. If she wants anymore of my time tell her to leave the tears behind."

"I'm sorry I got you involved." Wendy looked sad.

"Don't blame yourself for your daughter's actions. You did what you thought was right. Me, I may have been too easy on Carol from the get go. Never in my wildest dreams would I have thought your daughter would act so ungrateful to you."

"Unfortunately she would like to speak with you again this evening. I wouldn't blame you if you said no."

"I'm not afraid to see her. Tell her to come prepared and keep our meeting short. I have a lot of work backed up in this office. I'm trying to cover our short profits of the last several days. I need to get things back in order so I can fly up to Seattle before Marie forgets who in the hell I am."

Wendy realized he was still furious at her daughter. "Will you need me to work next week?"

"Rose will be here, if you have some time to help out, come up and help. Don't neglect your daughter. Do what you can for the ungrateful little wench."

Wendy left without further comment. Upon her return she gave Carol a stern look. "I'm neglecting my job. I think Brad is planning to replace me. He brought Rose back into the office."

"Did Brad say for sure he was replacing you?"

"I can read between the lines. I've never seen him so upset, his voice is full of anger."

"I've made a mess of everything. Will he see me again?"

"He agreed to see us this evening. He said to come prepared, keep your talk short, and no tears. It's up to you Honey can you be civil to him?"

"Yes mother, I will be nice to Mr. Collins."

At six when Rose left he set about making an additional Subliminal Message for Carol. The message was strong and simple. Calm down and accept what he and Wendy were saying. He struggled over the exact wording allowing time to get away from him. Before he knew it the ladies were coming to the office. He installed the new video and set it to play in the office. As the ladies entered the office he excused himself to go get a diet soda. "You ladies need anything?"

"No thank you. We came to…" Carol watched as he stomped off. "You are right Mother, he is extremely angry." Upon his return she began talking before he sat down. "If you had the same choice to make today would you do the same thing?"

He glared at her. "Not if I knew the outcome ahead of time. Given the same information I had then, hell yes. I would help your mother again."

"May I see more of your intruding videos?"

"You don't like our words. I don't believe you will like our videos either. These videos are more intrusive than any words you can ever imagine. Of course they had to be intrusive. That won't matter to someone like you. I gave up two nights sleep watching you sleep to be certain you were not having nightmares. Talk about wasting two good nights."

"You watched my every move?"

"Absolutely I watched both you and your mother's every move. Damn it, listen to us. I didn't know you, and I'm not someone who spies on young women on a regular basis. I had no other way of comparing your actions. Thus your mother became a victim herself, a victim of me. Hearing Wendy say she was willing do anything to help you, I took the liberty to spy on your mother too! Good heavens girl, use your brain!"

"Stop shouting at me! Play your video?"

"You don't like listening so I doubt you will believe what you see either. I've edited out dead time because I don't have days to waste." Again he glared at her before starting the video. The video clearly showed Carol to be in a very depressed mood. She was offered food but wouldn't eat. It showed her mother trying to interact without success. "You may stop the video. I was in a depressed state."

"Your mother and father spent days at the hospital watching you lay there in a zombie like state. For days they took the doctor's advice and constantly talked to you. As you saw on the video talking didn't help anymore than talking to you now. Your folks were at a loss of what to do. Willing to do anything your mother turned to me. Now I'm going to restart the video. Try to refrain from being shocked. Watch the video from the standpoint of you wanting to help the girl you just saw in her zombie state. Hold your comments while you are watching the video. We can discuss everything later."

Her shower scene soon appeared on the screen. She gasped and covered part of her face but said anything. The video clearly showed her scrubbing excessively until she had red scrape marks on her body.

"If we had allowed you to continue showering in that manor you would have been bleeding by your third shower." As the video progressed it showed her mother showering as any normal woman would. "Your mother isn't scrubbing hard like you were." When Brad's shower scene popped on the screen Carol looked at him and raised her hand as though she wanted to say something. He motioned her to remain quiet. "Keep watching." Only after his shower scene did he stop the video. "You saw two normal people shower and you saw yourself shower. Would you say your shower was a normal shower for you?"

"You know very well I wasn't showering normal."

"In your shower scene I saw a person abusing her skin. At that point I intensified your treatment. Now between your shower and going to bed you improved, watch and listen."

Restarting the video Carol could see the progress she made in a short time. "Wow, there is a big difference."

"Let's jump ahead to your next day shower. Notice how calm and at ease you are with your body this time. Not comfortable as your mother when she showered still improvement is always good. You went out twice that day and did well. This is your shower the evening after being out twice. Again you can see more improvement."

"I can see my improvement. How long are you planning to video my showers?"

"I think we have all seen enough. You deserve your privacy back."

"Thank you, would you mind explaining why you video taped yourself in the shower for us to see?'

"It was another test for you. A man abused you. We needed to see how you would react to the sight of a naked man. Who else could I video besides myself?"

"You beat all I ever saw everything is a test to you."

"Yes, a closely monitored test. I would never allow you to be in physical danger while trying to improve your mental mix up."

"You and Mother have helped me. I thank you for your efforts. I feel funny about not remembering enough to testify against my attacker. He should be put away for life."

"The only people who would disagree with you are the Judge and the Attorneys. Long as they can recycle criminals everyone gets paid over and over."

"That's not right."

"No it's not right. Wendy you have been quiet for quite a while. What are you thinking?"

"I'm so happy to see Carol progressing. It is hard for me to think about her attacker just now. I have the same question Carol had, how long will you be keeping the video showing the three of us showering?"

"We shouldn't need these videos anymore unless Carol needs a second look."

"I don't need to see the videos again." Carol quickly stated. "We can destroy them. If my father ever saw those videos you would have bigger bruises than I had."

"I can drive down to the hardware and get a hand held propane torch so we can melt the videos. You ladies can wait here, or I can call you when I get back." Carol was quick to agree waiting in the office.

In his absence the gals watched the edited video a second time. "Pretty easy to see how you came to the conclusion I needed extreme help. Just the same his spying on us was over the top."

"Honey had Brad realized we could get you out of your depressed state so fast I doubt he would have used the shower camera. I'm guessing he felt uneasy and decided to video himself. I'm extremely glad to see you watching him, a man showering, didn't upset you."

"I found watching him shower odd but not upsetting to me."

Brad returned in twenty minutes. "I have the torch ladies. Let's go outback by the garbage. One by one each video was melted into flat plastic pancake. The plastic mass was allowed to cool before they were tossed in the garbage. "That does it ladies, no more videos."

"I'm glad the videos are destroyed. Do you have more information to tell me?"

"Come along and find out." The ladies were relieved their shower scenes were gone and were now smiling. "Carol, it's time you return to work but I wouldn't advise you to go back to the Mini Mart. May I be so bold as to suggest you work here at the Burger Palace until you find other suitable employment?"

Carol laughed at his idea. "Is this a charity offer?"

"Take a look out through the glass. You won't see any charity workers out there. Ernie runs a tight ship, he keeps our employees hopping. You don't have to work here. I believe you should continue living in the apartment here until the authorities decide what to do with your attacker."

"Why are you doing all this for me?"

"I'm a friend of your mother, and it's natural for her to want you near her for awhile."

"Should I speak to Ernie tomorrow?"

"Talk to Ernie any time you want."

"What about me?" Wendy asked. "When may I return to work?"

He placed a hand on Wendy's shoulder. "Come to work any time you want. We'll keep Rose until we are totally caught up. I'll be busy setting up new equipment. This ordeal pointed out how short I was on equipment. Then of course I want to get away for a short vacation. Marie is waiting for me to visit her in Seattle. Carol is coming around enough we can move forward. If I can get the equipment I want, tomorrow night I may be working late."

CHAPTER 25

Being dead tired, Brad slept late the following morning. Half the day was shot before he went equipment shopping. He purchased some new equipment to take with him and ordered other equipment. Buying new equipment insured he would be working late into the night setting up the new equipment that couldn't be installed while others were working in the office. By working late nights and sleeping days calling Marie was next to impossible.

He did take the time to do an e-mail explaining how busy he was. His simple e-mail along with no phone calls left her wondering what was going on. Mid afternoon while he was making a bank run his cell phone fell from his pocket landing on the hot blacktop in the parking lot. He picked up the phone placing it back in his pocket without checking its working capability. Marie's repeated attempts to call him never came through.

Judy did her best to console Marie. "Don't give up on Brad. He has quite a mess on his hands dealing with Carol and her unrealistic daughter."

"He does have a lot going on but why doesn't he answer his phone. I may be history as his lady friend. He may have found a local girlfriend in Vegas he likes better than me."

"Don't think that way. Brad's e-mail said he was installing new equipment."

"Installing new equipment could be nothing more than an excuse to avoid calling me. One would think he would be man enough to call and tell me if he didn't want to see me again."

In Vegas, Brad was working late when Wendy came looking for him. "It's after ten, why are you working late?"

"I'm almost finished for tonight. Two pieces of my equipment haven't arrived yet."

"What I came to see you about is Carol was hoping to speak with you again tonight."

"Oh my, I'm dead tired any idea what she wants this time of night?"

"I would rather she spoke directly to you rather than my saying anything. As a mother I should stay neutral."

Hearing Wendy say she wanted to stay neutral seemed like an odd statement. "Use my cell phone and have her come up now, not much point in putting off the inevitable. Rose will here in the morning. Do you realize how late it is?"

Wendy tried using his broken phone. "Your phone isn't working, it's completely dead and the case is broke. You dropped your phone some time or other. I better walk down and see where Carol is."

Carol brought him a diet soda on her way to see him. "Well, thank you girl. I can use a little pick me up, what's on your mind this evening?"

"Do you think I will be able to interact with men again one on one?"

"I think so but you should proceed with caution. You should get use to guys slow so they don't read you wrong. I know patience is not your thing but I urge you to be extremely careful when it comes to guys."

"If I need help dealing with men will you help me again?"

"This is a switch you asking me for help." Her words made him smile. "I have no idea how you were with guys before your assault. Then there is the physical aspect to consider. You were injured in a sensitive area. Emotionally I may be able to help you. Physically, I wouldn't know where to begin." Carol gave him a serious but sad look. "I'm no doctor. My suggestion would be to get your medical records at the hospital. Then go over your records with a doctor. Be certain you understand what he or she is telling you. Why not consider a physical examination at the same time. The more information you have about your body the better."

"What you are saying makes sense. It's a good place to start but I might still need help. Are you willing to help me further?"

"Your mother and I both want what is best for you. We'll do what we can, if we feel you need more help later."

Long after Carol was sleeping Wendy returned to the office. "How did your talk with Carol go, did you agree to help her?"

"We left my helping her as a maybe. She is going to check her hospital records and learn all she can about her current physical condition first. If she needs help later I may consider helping her. I'm not sure how receptive she will be if we try to help her further?"

"Suggesting she get her medical records is good. Is that all you discussed with her?"

"I think so, our conversation was very short this evening. Unless you know something I don't?"

"I think you may have missed something during your discussion. Whatever the case I'll leave it to her to ask you what she wants when she is ready."

Wendy hinting her daughter had more questions made getting a good night of sleep near impossible. What more could Carol ask for?

The following day Wendy was in a great mood. "Look at these numbers. Yesterday we had our most profitable day ever."

"Those are words I love to hear. You will appreciate numbers like that when quarterly bonus time comes tomorrow. Five percent goes to you and Ernie will get his five percent. The rest comes to me to pay down my investment."

"I bet your father will be proud when he sees the profit numbers you are turning in the Burger Palace. This place generates more profit than I ever expected a fast food place could."

"Our profit is the result of a good management team. We all contribute and work well together. Far as my father goes I doubt my father will even notice the money we are making. He never has time for me. Why would he change now?"

"We may have a problem with Carol. She thinks you agreed to help her find out how she will react to personal contact when she deals with men on an intimate level. She thinks you are willing to interact personally in this manner."

"Holly shit. I can't have a personal relationship with Carol. I have a budding relationship with Marie. Why would she ask such a thing of me, if that is what the girl wants she is out of line. Wendy you are her mother didn't you voice an objection?"

"My daughter is an adult. It's not my place to interfere with her personal choices in her life. She needs to make her own decisions."

"Marie and I haven't made a deep commitment but I think we are headed in that direction. I can't afford to mess up my relationship with her."

"I side with Carol on this. You and Joe are the only males who know of her assault. Joe is out because he is her father. That leaves you as the only male who knows of her fragile emotional state. I know you would be gentle and considerate of her feelings if you were to become intimate with her."

"No, no, no, a thousand times no. I can't help her."

Rose arriving for work thankfully ended any private conversation about Carol. Much like the previous day business at the Burger Palace boomed making another extremely profitable day.

At the end of the day Rose announced she had a new job lined up. Her new job was set to start the following Monday. "You have been a life saver for us and we certainly appreciate your help. I knew there would come a day you would find full-time permanent employment. You are too good of worker to keep doing temporary work. Good luck on your new employment."

Once Rose left for the day, Brad sat at his desk rubbing his forehead. "Did I give you a headache?" Wendy asked.

"Yes you gave me a headache. I feel like I've been hit in the head with an ax. Getting hit by a car in the parking lot never shook me up badly as what you told me this morning."

"I'll run down to the first aid kit and get you something for your headache."

Watching Wendy go down stairs to get pills for his headache he noticed Carol working. As Wendy returned she saw him watching her daughter. "Carol is enjoying her work. Getting active again has been very good for her. She gets off work at six this evening and hopes to share the hospital record information with you."

"I've already had a rough day. I'm not looking forward to that in-depth conversation."

Wendy patted him on the back. "Things are not complicated as you think. You being a college age guy, you are not a virgin. Carol is not a virgin, so I don't see a problem." Wendy left the office before he came up with an adequate response to her statement.

Synchronized to the second her shift ended Carol came charging to the office. "Mother tells me you may have misunderstood our previous discussion. Can we go down to the apartment and look over my hospital records. If I entered from the inside and you walked around to the outside entrance no one would notice our being together."

"Going to your apartment is a bad idea. Bring your records to the office we'll discuss them here."

Carol returned to the office in minutes. "These are my chart notes and the actual reports. Right here it states little internal damage, light bruising only. My external bruises have healed so I would expect my internal bruises to be healed."

"Air doesn't get to the internal bruises. I would think internal healing might take considerable longer."

"You are making an excuse. You are the only man I trust. You know my situation so I know you will be gentle with me."

"There you go rushing things again. When patience was handed out you were standing in the wrong line. I can't have intimate relations with you, not now not ever."

"I've had days to think about this. You have distant lady friend, someone you don't see often. You are not engaged, or married. That means you are still able to play the field for a short period. Our actions would not affect you and Marie's relationship."

"Marie and I's engagement could happen faster than you think. Before I became so busy we talk daily on the phone. Working on your problem stole valuable time with her."

"No proper thinking young woman living in Seattle can believe you live in Las Vegas, the original sin city, doing without female attention. For all you know Marie may have a bed-warmer of her own. Helping me wouldn't cause you a problem. How about we start with simple touching and caressing?"

"If I were to touch you tonight by tomorrow night you would be pushing the intimacy issue again. We are not close to being best friends."

"Get off you're golden pedestal, you are not God. You are the one who made me dependant on you. If we were to approach intimacy, I could trust you to back off if I became uncomfortable?"

"I keep telling you I can't do this. I think Marie and I have a future together. Cheating on her would be wrong."

"Take a day or two, but you know I'm right. Shall we shake hands on my agreeing to be patient?" Carol extended her hand. Without thinking he responded by shaking her hand. "See how calm I am. You are the first male to touch me since my ordeal."

"A handshake doesn't mean anything. People have rules to live by. I shouldn't endanger my relationship with Marie to help you. Why would I want to risk destroying my relationship with Marie by experimenting with you?"

"What I need could be finished before your relationship with Marie becomes more serious. You had three dates with Marie. You are not ready for a lifetime commitment with her. Only you and I would know if you helped me."

"Your mother would know."

"Mother doesn't count. She would never say anything to anyone."

"I need a week or so to think this over." His only out appeared to be stalling for time to create a subliminal message for Carol to find her male interest elsewhere."

"I can wait one week and then we will talk about setting up a place and time for you to help me."

He kept an eye on Carol as she exited the office. As she crossed through the Burger Palace she stopped briefly to chat with one of the male employees. She spoke to a young red headed shift supervisor by the name of Rusty Cramer. Being a new shift manager Brad knew little about Rusty except Ernie thought enough of him to promote the young man to a shift manager. Smooth as the Burger Palace was running convinced Brad that Ernie knew what he was doing. Rusty might be the guy he needed to distract this wanton girl. Not wasting a second he hustled down to speak with Ernie. "Hey Buddy! I need a favor. Can you spare Rusty for a few minutes?"

"Certainly, what's up Mr. Collins?"

"I need a private word with the young man, and it would be better if others employees didn't see us talking. Send Rusty out with some trash I can catch him outside where we can talk without others guessing what we are talking about. I won't keep him long."

Rusty was surprised to see the head boss waiting out by the trash bin. "Hello, did Ernie tell you I wanted a private word with you?"

"No, Ernie sent me out with some trash, am I in trouble?"

"No trouble at all Rusty, I noticed you talking with Carol. Was your short discussion a general conversation or business?"

"We weren't goofing off. We were clarifying her work schedule."

"Damn, I was hoping your conversation was of a personal nature. She is my office gal's daughter."

"I'm aware she is Wendy's daughter. Carol is a good employee who works hard every day."

"I'm glad she is working out. Pardon me for rushing but someone else may come out here and interrupt us. Do you have a steady girlfriend?" Rusty shook his head no. "Are you married?"

Rusty laughed at the order of his questions. "No, I'm not married. I don't understand what you are getting at. What else do you want to ask me?"

"Would you consider asking Carol out on a simple date, a movie, dinner somewhere, or dancing perhaps?"

"She seems nice, but I haven't given any thought to asking her out on a date. Is there a company policy on employees dating?"

"We have no policy about employees dating one another. Some stupid guy roughed her up a while back and her parents are concerned she might be afraid to date now. She needs to get back in the dating game to build her confidence again."

"Then her parents want me to ask her out?"

"Wendy and her husband are not aware I'm talking with you. When I saw Carol and you talking she looked comfortable with you. You might be the perfect guy to ask her out. If you were to take her out treat her gentle. If you go to kiss her, use your index finger to tilt her head up so your action doesn't come as a shock. You know, stuff like that. No sudden unexpected moves."

"I better get back to work before Ernie comes looking for me. I'm glad we had this talk. I think I will ask Carol out."

Returning to the office he found Wendy waiting in the office when he returned. "What did you tell Carol when she came to see you?"

"Marie is my girl. I don't want to jeopardize my relationship with her."

"I can't agree with your line of thought. I think you are over-analyzing a simple situation. You have done a lot for Carol why stop now?"

"Wendy, have you ever cheated on your husband?"

"No, I've never cheated on Joe. Hypothetically speaking if my cheating would help our daughter I would most definitely cheat on him. I can't help her and you can. Marie knows you are not virgin, you were married before. You can't expect her to be a virgin. So a short interaction with my daughter would be nothing more than another experiment for you."

"You women are going to be the death of me. I'm going to Seattle soon. We can talk again after I get back."

"Can you do one thing before you go anywhere, go by her apartment and give her a hug? I want to demonstrate you touching her won't affect your relationship with Marie."

"Alright I'll go hug, Carol right now. I'll set the monitors so you can watch but it won't change my mind." Without calling ahead he marched straight to her apartment. Carol answered the door on his second knock. "Hi, your mother challenged me to give you a hug. I'm on my way to

Seattle this evening and your mother insisted I come by and hug you before I leave."

"This isn't how I envisioned we would be hugging."

"Can we please pacify your mother for now and see what happens later." As he stepped close he wrapped his arms around her quivering body. He now realized she did indeed need more help, help from somebody.

She apologized for her uneasy hug. "You caught me off guard. I wasn't expecting any hug from you this evening. I thought simple touches would come first."

"My error, when your mother challenged me I came out swinging. I'm not sure how long I'll be in Seattle. We can talk and possibly hug more when I return."

"Enjoy your weekend. You deserve a getaway weekend."

Back in the office Wendy was quick to thank him. "Have a nice trip to Seattle, tell Marie hello for me."

"I will, good night Wendy."

He busied himself creating Subliminal Messages for both Carol and Rusty. Messages he had no intention of making an hour earlier. Her message, relax around Rusty. His message was to be gentle with her. He killed all advertising and started the messages he created for them. He left Wendy a note telling her to go back to normal advertising at ten AM.

From the Burger Palace he made a stop at the phone store. "This idiot phone doesn't seem to be working proper. I need a new phone but I want my same number." In twenty minutes he had a new phone. His first call was Marie. "Hi Honey."

"Brad!" She shouted. "You haven't called for three days."

"I haven't called because I'm stupid. I've been busy, too busy to think straight. Wendy borrowed my phone to call her daughter and the dumb phone didn't work. I've been struggling for three days trying to call you with a phone that didn't work. I just picked up my new phone."

"You had me worried when you didn't call. I tried calling your cell several times, no answer."

"I thought my phone was working it made all the right sounds. Good thing Wendy was smarter than I am. I was thinking you found another part time job and wasn't home in the evenings. Sweetheart, how would you like a visitor this weekend?"

"How soon are you coming to Seattle?"

"I was hoping to get away today, but it didn't happen. I'm not going near the Burger Palace tomorrow. For all those people know, I'm gone now."

"What time can you be here?"

"I'll fly in and pick up a rental car and be at the house by five tomorrow giving us plenty of time to eat out somewhere tomorrow evening."

"Now you have me all excited how will I ever sleep tonight or concentrate on my work tomorrow. I have a million hugs and kisses saved up for you."

"I'll be there in one day save those kisses for me. I love you, bye."

"I love you too, bye." Her hands trembled with excitement as she put his phone away.

CHAPTER 26

The following day Brad rested all morning before going to the airport. The flight to Seattle was glass smooth. On final approach at Sea-Tac he began to smile. In about an hour he would be holding his love tight in his arms. "Excuse me sir, time to get off the plane."

"He hurried through the airport and cursed though heavy traffic until he arrived at the house to find the girl he loved waiting in the driveway. "Oh how I've missed you. I should have been here two weeks ago, but I find it so hard to trust people in my absence."

"Come inside and stop worrying about what was. Let's deal with the here and now. I have dinner waiting for us."

"You didn't have to cook. We could have gone out for dinner."

"I wanted to cook for you to showcase my talents. We have the house to ourselves this evening. Judy is out on a date with Sam Anderson. After we eat I'm taking you to the hot tub for a relaxing soak to relieve some of your stress. I have a chicken casserole and salad waiting for us. Let's go eat before the casserole gets cold. I'm anxious to hear about everything you have been doing."

"The good news is I haven't been arrested and put in jail yet."

"Then you must be doing something right."

"I hope I'm doing a lot of thing right. Lead the way my dear the sooner we eat the sooner our hot tub adventure begins. Judy may not be gone all evening. Your dinner looks wonderful. This is my first home cooked meal in weeks and it tastes great."

"Tell me about Carol, how is she doing?"

"That idiot woman is the challenge of a lifetime. She has zero patience. Here is the real kicker she has improved, but these last steps need to be taken slowly. Slow is not in her vocabulary. Sometimes I would like to grab her and shake some sense into her. She wants to testify against her attacker. We have blocked her memory she can't possibly testify. She has it in her head we can unblock her memory long enough for her to testify. Then she wants to block her memory again later. Talk about a stupid

219

girl. I had videos showing her condition before our interference. She saw those and agreed her condition was bad. Thinking we had cured her, we destroyed the videos."

"Why would you destroy the videos?"

"The videos were extremely intrusive. If someone were to get a hold of those videos they could wind up on the internet. Worse yet I could be sent to jail for tampering with a witness."

Marie laughed thinking he was joking. "Were the videos all that bad?"

"To an outsider, oh you bet they would be considered extremely bad."

"Would I consider your videos extremely bad?"

"I hate to think of you as an outsider. In the same breath, I venture to guess you would think our videos were truly obscene. In this instance you are better off keeping your hands clean of the whole mess. I have been doing things I'm not proud of. I put a couple things in motion and ducked out of Vegas like a common criminal. I came straight here thinking you could hide me out for a few days. Will Judy interrupt us as we hot tub?"

"She won't bother us. We are safe to skinny-dip and fool around all we want. Would it matter all that much if someone walked in on us we will be submerged in bubbling water."

Hand in hand they walked out to the hot tub. "You are so beautiful. I can't believe it took me this long to come see you. This Carol business has been eating up my valuable time. I do have other news to tell you. I was about to say when I get back to Vegas. I will be starting my advertising agency."

She looked shocked. "What about college?"

"Don't get excited, I haven't ruled out college. It's a matter of experience; I need to start dabbling in the advertising field. My ad agency needs to start slow. I don't want to create mistakes and cause setbacks. Robin Tilly the realty agent who helped me with the Burger Palace deal. I'm thinking she would make a good customer for me. I've tossed enough business her way she has to listen to me. Getting people to listen to me has been a major problem most of my life. With her I already have an in."

Marie gave him a sad look. "It sounds very much to me as though you are not returning to college this fall?"

"Honey starting my ad agency wouldn't be the end of college for me."

"I disagree with you. This advertising agency has been a dream of yours so long once you start the business you won't be able to shut it down. Returning to college will be the last thing on your mind. I know you won't come back. Starting another business will make it harder for us to see one another. Once my classes start, I can't fly down and see you until Thanksgiving break."

"Alright, I'll admit it. I'm not sure college will be that helpful to me. Think back to last year. Messing around with my simple basic experiments caused me the need a tutor. "I have a feeling the time is right to start my Ad Agency. I know there is money to be made in advertising, and I know how to make money advertising on a small scale. You helped count money at the Burger Palace. If using my advertising technique to sell burgers creates revenue like that. Think what I could make selling houses?"

"I'm sad to say you know the answer to your question well as I do. No doubt you would make a lot of money. I was so looking forward to you returning so we could see one another on a daily basis."

He pulled her naked body tight against him. "Honey, I've run every scenario through my mind time and again. There are pros and cons to all decisions. I'm sure by now my father is seeing the money being generated from the Burger Palace. He may be wondering why I didn't choose a different more lucrative business. My father is very money oriented. I want to prove to him I can make a good living, and raise a family at the same time. He chose to give up his family to amass his wealth. To me what he did is a crock of BS."

"This is a very fascinating conversation but I'm turning into a prune. Can we get out and dry off and continue our conversation in the house?"

"Your wish is my command, lead the way angel. Where do your parents live and when do I get to meet them?"

"My parents live in the Portland, Oregon area. They are on vacation visiting family in the Midwest."

"Dang it all, I wanted to meet your parents. Oops, here allow me to dry your back for you." He moved in exceptionally close and kissed the back of her neck. She quickly spun around to accept his second kiss on her pretty lips. He picked up her silky smooth robe and wrapped it around her. "It's a shame to cover such a beautiful body."

"Come inside, we can uncover it again." Together they spent a passion filled night. By ten the following morning they were eating cereal at the kitchen table."

"What are our plans for today?" Judy walked in before Marie could answer his question. "Good morning."

"Hello stranger, Marie has spent days pacing the floor waiting for you to call. Were you hiding somewhere?"

"My life is a circus. Sometimes I feel I'm standing in the middle of a tornado. No matter where I step, I'm bound to spin around."

"I have a question for you big guy. Think hard before you answer. If you had to do things over would you buy a business in Vegas again, or would you start a business here in Seattle?"

"Vegas any day, the Burger Palace is an interesting profitable experience. We generate a nice profit each day seven days a week. If I had additional room to build on I would expand the restaurant."

"Then stop complaining, and enjoy yourself. You only live once." Judy suggested. "You still have dark circles under your eyes, but you look happy as I've ever seen you look."

"I'm trying to enjoy life, if you could spend one day in my shoes you wouldn't be making fun of me. The dark circles under my eyes come from my life in Vegas. My happiness comes from being here in Seattle with Marie."

"I'm not making fun of you. What I mean is slow down, take a few deep breaths, and enjoy life as you go." She repeated.

"Hey girl that's cheating, you are tossing my own words back at me. Marie told you about my dealings with Wendy."

"So what if she told me about how easily you calmed Wendy down. She only told me because she was proud of how you handled her situation. Besides I enjoy harassing you. I would love nothing more to sit here and argue all day but I must go to work. I'm covering for a friend today. Can I trust you two to behave while I'm gone today?"

"It's Marie who corrupts me. You should be lecturing her not me. I'm an innocent bystander." Judy gave him a funny little smile. "Why are you looking at me so funny, have I ever lied to you?"

"I've got to run, if she gets out of hand and you are in fear of your life, call 911 or call me at work. Someone will save you."

"Do you think if I married Marie I could control her better?" He turned and winked at Marie who was smiling ear to ear. "We can get a ring later Honey."

Judy shook her head. "You two have a good day." She dashed out.

Marie laughed. "Since Judy has been going out with Sam, she has been walking on air. Like you, I've never seen her happier than she is now."

"She does look happy." Desiring more affection he drew Marie tight in his arms. "Where shall we begin our glorious day?"

"You are my guest, what we do today is your choice."

"Let's see, to get our day started off right, we could kiss and hug or we could hug and kiss. I'm not sure what would be better."

"We should try it both ways, see what works the best." After several exchanges of hugs and kisses she declared it didn't matter. Either way warms my heart. What else are our plans for today?"

"I do my experiments many times. When we return we'll try kissing and hugging again. The weather looks to be nice out today. How about we go to the Woodland Park Zoo? I haven't been to the zoo in fifteen years or longer. We could walk and talk as we looked at the animals and the people watching them."

"Going to the zoo sounds fun. Long as we are together, I don't care where we go or what we do. I've never been to the zoo here in Seattle. My parents took us to the Portland Zoo several times but never here. This will be a new experience for me."

His reason for wanting to go to the zoo had nothing to do with any animals. He wanted to observe Marie's actions as they watched families enjoying their outing. "I was seven last time I was here. Ann brought me along with one of her granddaughters. My father stripped a gear when he found out Ann had taken me to the zoo. He claimed I could have been kidnapped very easily. Not only was the zoo out. There were many places I couldn't go. That's a whole different story and certainly not what I care to discuss today. I didn't fly here to complain. Let's talk about pleasant things, see the couple with the two kids over there by the fence. Look at the happy faces on the children. I want to do things like this with my family some day. I'll make time for my family and enjoy their smiles."

"You are right those people are having fun as a family."

"People today don't spend enough time with there children doing the little things. Look at those kids over there they are having as much fun as any kid in Disneyland. Even lower income families can go visit any zoo on any day. This is not an expensive event."

"My folks took me to the zoo, the museums and out to Cannon Beach. We had what I consider a normal family. Both my mother and father worked. We were far from rich. We did short trips and took a two-week vacation each year."

"That's because you had parents that cared about you. I was an accidental error to my parents. I became an inconvenience to them. So they abandoned me."

"Accidental error, I don't understand. You have a bad habit of coming right up to important words, and stopping short before clarifying anything. I think you want to confide in me but are afraid I will disapprove. You need to trust me more."

"I know deep in my heart what you are saying is true. My family has a deep dark secret. I've been trying to find the right words to explain things so you would understand. The right words never come to mind. Maybe I need a more private place to talk."

"There is a bench over there under that tree. Would that bench be private enough, if not we could return to the house?"

"The house would be more private. We can talk more there later. Let's finish looking around at the zoo first."

It was a quiet ride back to the house. "Shall I fix us a sandwich before we begin our intense talk?"

"I'm not hungry." Brad was nervous and botched his family story as he spit it out fast. "My father graduated high school and uncertain what to do with his life so he went to work in an Import-Export store for his father. He met my mother working there. I don't know if they were married when she became pregnant or not. I suspect not because my grandfather who was an older single gentleman never liked my mother. With mother's pregnancy she couldn't travel as much. Father did continue to travel but much less than he had before. My mother's mother came to visit my mother one day and all hell broke loose. My mother's mother and my father's dad had once been married. My father and my mother were brother and sister separated at an early age who now found themselves back together with a child." Small tears formed in his eyes.

Marie caught the brother and sister part. "Wow, your parents had no way of knowing they were brother and sister."

"Originally, I was to live with my mother. She had a nervous breakdown. My father traveled, so a nanny came to care for me. Mother returned a few times but couldn't handle the memories I will always believe my father should have came home and cared for her and me both. The bastard didn't."

"On the surface I would agree unless work was the only thing keeping your father from having a breakdown himself."

"No I don't think so. I don't believe that to be the truth. Father loved money and other women more than he loved mother or me. History cannot be changed. My goal is to prove to my father I can raise a family, and make good money. I want to be a full time husband and father. I want to be a husband and father who receiving love and respect from his wife and family each and every day."

"A goal many would admire, including me. You are doing an excellent job with your life so far."

"If I'm doing such a wonderful job or not is yet to be determined. Somehow during my father's travels he fell behind in paying his income taxes and as a result he cannot enter the US more than a few days a year. He is no longer a citizen of the US. He slips in and out of the country like a thief in the dark. That's only part of what I wanted to tell you. This Carol business is the rest. I'm not proud of my actions. Explaining my actions isn't easy."

"From what I saw of her condition nothing concerning her would be easy. Hopefully someday you will trust me enough to tell me, or show me what you really did to help her. You did say she was making good progress so whatever you are doing is helping her."

"It's so hard for me to tell you everything. Carol is very impatient, well beyond anyone I ever met. I'm at such a disadvantage because I never met Carol before her unfortunate incident. What Wendy tells me may be one-sided. As long as her daughter isn't locked away in a mental facility she is happy with any progress."

As Judy returned from work she walked into the living room causing Brad and Marie to pause in their conversation. "Hello people, am I interrupting?"

"You are not interrupting, sit down, and rest your weary body. Tell me about this new flame of yours."

"Sam is not exactly new to me we dated two years in High School."

"Oh that's right, Marie did tell me you were recycling guys now."

"No, I didn't say she was recycling guys. You made that up."

"Me make up a story, why would I make up such a wild story? I think you have me mixed up with someone else."

"Sam is a nice guy and I don't mind recycling a nice guy. Sam is not a college student. He is six foot tall, nice looking, clean cut, and business minded. He hopes to be a real estate agent soon. Sam is working on passing his real estate exam as we speak. I'll also add he isn't a big tease like one guy I know."

"My teasing is all in fun. I don't have any siblings to joust with. Be honest Judy, what's a little harmless kidding now and then? It lightens up the heart."

"In a way I suppose it does. I better scoot to my room and let the two of you continue with your conversation."

"Hold on, don't be too hasty. I'm guessing you and Marie will discuss everything she and I talk about later anyway. Stay if you like. We were discussing my dealings with Carol. I was explaining I'm at such a disadvantage because I didn't know the girl prior to her assault. It was Wendy insisting I help her daughter by using my advertising technique. She realized the same technique had the capability of helping her daughter."

"Any mother would have asked for your help knowing you could help." Judy replied.

"I've never used my technique quite this way. To be safe I needed constant intrusive monitoring. My tiny cameras were more intrusive than you could ever imagine. Wendy seemed to understand my position. Watching Carol day and night exhausted me."

"If you remember, I offered to stay in Vegas and help with the monitoring of Carol." Marie added.

"I know you offered to stay. It was a generous offer but I couldn't get you involved in what I was about to do. Needing some sort of a baseline, I observed Carol's every move for the first two days. I also watched Wendy's every move. I was using the highest level of intensity I ever experimented."

"Carol must be better or you wouldn't be here. So the increased message worked, I fail to see a problem?" Marie gave him questioning look.

"I'm not a natural born voyeur. My spying on women didn't sit well with me. We did attain our goal of blocking part of her memory. Thinking we had no further need for the recorded videos they were destroyed before anyone besides Carol, her mother and I saw them. Now she insists we restore her memory of the assault. She wants to testify against her attacker."

Marie looked rather surprised. "She was in no condition to testify. If you were able to restore her memory wouldn't there be a huge danger in her going half-way insane again?"

"Of course it would be a huge danger. You know it, Wendy knows it, and I know it. The stupid girl saw how bad she was on the video. She still refuses to understand how serious her condition was. I'm having no luck at changing her mind so I did a couple things and skipped town and came straight here for a break."

Judy looked deep in his eyes. "Could you restore her memory so she could testify and block her memory again later?"

"Wendy and I tampered with a witness. Any more action on my part could land her and me behind bars. No way can I allow her to testify against her Rapist. Plus I have no desire to go through the spying process again. Men are visual animals I felt like a total creep watching those women do personal things."

"Stand your ground and don't restore her memory. Why put yourself at risk any more than you have?" Marie didn't totally understand what she was hearing.

"Your suggestion sounds easy. I've tried a dozen different angles to discourage her but she keeps asking to have her memory restored. She even threatened to call the police if we didn't do what she wanted. No way can I allow her to call the police."

As Judy grew more interested in the conversation she sat down. Marie had more questions. "In hindsight would you destroy the videos this soon again?"

"Oh hell yes, we didn't have any choice. We couldn't keep videos of people showering." Both girls' mouths fell open. "Don't look at me like that, I told you my videos were intrusive. I watched Carol shower and needing someone to compare to so I watched Wendy shower. That's when I upped the strength. A couple days later I videoed myself as I showered, so I could get Carol's reaction to seeing a naked man. When she watched the videos she handled seeing the videos fine, thus we destroyed them."

Marie shuttered as she thought a few moments. "Sounds as though you did what needed done. I can understand why you don't want to go through anything like that again. Once finished you stopped soon as possible, so why are you second guessing yourself?"

"If I did everything right why don't I feel better?"

"You were treading in a very unfamiliar area any result would feel strange to you." She suggested.

"I was extended beyond my experiments and operating with limited information. Further adding to my stress, were the slumping profits at the Burger Palace while I messed with Carol's problems. I'm not about to allow slumping profits to happen again. I purchased more equipment and installed it before coming to Seattle. I should have had equipment capable of handling her situation and the Burger Palace's advertising at the same time."

"Now I get it, your new equipment explains why you want to start your ad agency now."

"There is more than new equipment involved in my decision. My work at the Burger Palace is very profitable, but I am bored to death. I need to be doing something more challenging. The Ad Agency could fill this void in my life for the time being. It also would get me off to a good start for next year when I want to run full bore with my idea."

Marie shook her head. "If your jump start goes well I doubt you will return to Seattle this fall for college. You have all the skills needed to make the money you desire. If you choose college in the fall you would soon be bored. I'm not slamming you. In your position I too would find it difficult going from a successful business owner back to a college student. College is all about becoming a success in life. A goal you already attained."

"In the business world when opportunity knocks you grasp the opportunity because the same deal may never come around again. Add in personal relationships and outside problems and I have a mess. A mess is how I would describe my life at this minute. Coming to see you these particular days was no accident. I'm running from a few problems in Vegas."

"This conversation is getting deeper and deeper." Judy stated. "Would you mind if I called a time out long enough to shower, and change, before we talk further? I don't want to miss any of this."

"Go ahead and do what you need to do. We are not going anywhere. We will stretch our legs in the back yard while you shower and change."

CHAPTER 27

Out in the fresh air behind the house, Brad held Marie tight. "Being cooped up in my office so many hours I miss the privacy this yard provides. When I first moved here there was a little rabbit living in this back yard. That rabbit became my first pet."

"I grew up with two dogs."

"I don't have time for a pet. Maybe someday when I have a family I might have a pet. I enjoyed our time in the hot tub last night was fun. When I get a house in Vegas I will put in an indoor type hot tub in a temperature controlled room for year around use."

Several minutes later Judy joined them outside. "Sorry to interrupt but you said you came here running away from problems in Vegas. Pardon me for saying this but that's stupid, you should handle your problems one at a time."

"I wish things were as easy as you make them sound. Let's go back inside someone might hear our conversation out here." Inside Judy was waiting for them. Brad and Marie joined her at the dining room table. "Okay ladies take your best shot, where were we?"

Marie set out ingredients to make a nice salad or a nice sandwich. "We can eat while we talk."

Judy touched his hand. "I was about to say maybe you are not approaching things right. Take a piece of paper and write down each problem. Then number your problems in the order of importance. If you are uncomfortable that someone might see your list. Make your list a mental list, we can respect privacy."

"Alright Judy, I'll try your list idea. Do you have a piece of paper I can use?"

"Right behind you, in the top drawer is a tablet."

He couldn't help but laugh. "See how my mind works I lived in this house several years. I knew where the tablets were kept, but my mind didn't compute I had to ask for a tablet."

The girls watched as he drew a large octagon on his paper. At each point of the octagon he wrote one problem, Marie, Burger Palace, Father, college, Carol, ad agency, Pam Tilly and last Sam Anderson. Judy wrinkled up her nose.

"Marie, take a good look at this list. I've never seen anything like it. Brad made his list in a circle. Lists are usually written up and down. You have never met Sam. How can he be a problem for you?" Judy was defending her man, before she gave Brad a chance to explain anything.

Marie pushed his shoulder. "Never mind explaining about Sam, what is my name doing on your list, I don't mean to be a problem for you."

"First of all my topics are in no particular order. They all interconnect because they take valuable time from me. Let's take Carol for starters, in a week, two at the most. Her situation should be cleared up. Second is the Burger Palace, The Burger Palace has surpassed my expectations in generating income. Marie can testify to the money coming in from that business. The problem is my working at the Burger Palace is boring to me. Beyond Carol, there is no challenge at all. You girls claim to have simple meaningless jobs yet you come home happy beyond belief. I come home feeling dead tired. I need to turn the day-to-day operation of the Burger Palace over to someone else. Wendy is in charge while I'm in Seattle. I plan on leaving her in charge when I return. Having her in charge should allow me to spend more time with Marie, here or in Vegas. So that helps three of my problems. Number four is college. If I'm getting well paid for being at the Burger Palace and still bored, Marie was right earlier saying college may not hold my interest." Brad paused for a few seconds. "Come on ladies. A conversation should consist of two or more people."

"I didn't realize we were having a conversation. My understanding was you were giving an explanation. Isn't that the way you understood this to go Judy?"

"Absolutely, I'm still waiting to hear how poor Sam became your problem."

"Okay girls, we move to number five, the advertising agency. I need Robin Tilly working with me selling real estate in the Vegas area. Getting her to work with me shouldn't be hard. I gave her lots of business already. She would be number six on my time consuming list. Sam Anderson would be number seven. He is about to become a real estate agent in the Seattle area. His being new in the business should give me the upper hand on Sam. Anything I could do to make Sam an instant success should be very impressive to him. Having sales people working in both cities, we could generate tons of cash for everyone involved."

"Okay that leaves your father as number eight. Is he doing things different?"

"Judy, I feel my father's presence watching my every move. I haven't spoken to him in six or eight months. His arrangement with me has changed a little. My father is sending additional money to me. I haven't spoken to my accountant on specific numbers. I wish my father and I could communicate more often. Something feels wrong when I think about him."

"Then get off you duff and call your father. Talk to him about how you feel." Marie stated in an almost scolding way.

"Honey I can't call my father direct. Bill Barret one of his local associates is whom I would call in an emergency. If I call in a non-emergency situation the best I get is a handful of words about how busy my father. Nothing about my father is easy to understand."

Marie shook her head. "You have the strangest family I've ever heard of in my life. I've never heard of so many self-serving individuals in my life. Their actions make absolutely no sense at all."

"I don't have a family, I'm an older orphan. There is no reason to feel sorry for me personally, I'm doing fine. I get upset at how my father treats me but the old dog kicks a lot of money my way. I would be a fool to push my father completely out of my life."

"I'm almost afraid to ask." Marie stated. "How soon will you be going back to Vegas?"

"I don't know exactly, I'm waiting for a call from Wendy. She is setting up a business meeting with Robin Tilly for me. If she doesn't call soon I may go back to Vegas anyway. I can't leave this Carol situation hanging the way it is much longer. It's time finish dealing with her. Don't look so sad Honey we won't be apart long, I promise."

The phone barely rang before Judy snatched it up. Sam was on the line. "Excuse me I'll take this call out to the patio."

Marie leaned over to whisper in his ear. "Judy is expecting a proposal from Sam very soon. She thinks the proposal will come after he passes his real estate exam. As you can see it's beginning to appear I will be attending college alone this fall. I won't begrudge Judy for falling in love. It's every girl's dream and I'm happy for her. I believe she has something special going. Sam is a nice guy. You on the other hand are looking very uncomfortable and edgy. Is there something else on your mind?"

"It would take a full year to tell you everything that is on my mind. How long do Sam and Judy talk?"

She checked her watch. "I would say those two will talk a good hour anyway."

"That is quite a while yet. Do you know if her family owns anything she might inherit some day? If she is thinking they might get married, has she said anything about a prenuptial agreement?"

"Why would she and I talk about a prenuptial agreement?"

"With the high divorce rate in today's society prenuptial agreements are very common. You should discuss a prenuptial agreement with her. My father is a big believer in people protecting money. The internet is full of information about prenuptial agreements."

"Did you and Alice have a prenuptial agreement?"

"We had a basic prenuptial agreement, nothing fancy. Fifteen percent of my holding before our marriage and half of what we accumulated while married. The settlement check I sent to Alice's mother was three hundred eighty five thousand dollars."

"I don't understand. You were the surviving spouse. Wasn't the money automatically yours?"

"You are correct. The money was rightfully mine. Alice came from a lower income background. She did a lot of nice things caring for me when she maybe should have been home caring for her mother. I felt her mother could, and would use the money wisely. So I sent the money to her."

The call Brad had been waiting for from Wendy came. Marie watched with interest as he spoke to her. "Then I'll be in the office at ten on Saturday, thank you Wendy."

"This visit is too short." Marie stated in an unhappy tone. "You will be leaving tomorrow. You are making me tear up."

"Late afternoon tomorrow I will be leaving, but I won't be gone long. I may be in and out of Seattle a lot the next few weeks. Starting my advertising agency I will be meeting with my accountant and my attorney several times in the coming weeks. Tuesdays through Thursdays would be my guess. You may see more of me than you like."

"If it wasn't against the law, I would hold you captive. You could be my slave." She wrapped her arms around his body before giving him a big kiss. "Can't you stay in Seattle and deal with Robin by phone?"

"Sorry Honey I can't stay in Seattle and do my work. I need the use of my computer equipment. I wouldn't leave Seattle yet if my meeting wasn't vitally important. Opportunity is knocking now. I can't pass this up as if it's nothing important."

Their hours together passed all too quickly for Marie. Saying goodbye as he left for the Airport was no easier than when she left Vegas.

One would expect walking through the Airport without luggage should have been a breeze, it wasn't. A passenger without luggage drew lots of attention. He was called aside and questioned in length. Airport authorities called Marie in Seattle and Wendy in Vegas to check his story. "We get some dual residents but they usually have at the least a carry-on luggage." After excessive questioning he was allowed to board his flight.

From McCarron Airfield in Vegas he drove straight to Robin Tilly's office. "Good morning Mr. Collins. I've been wondering when I might see you again. You created a nice business. Is it time to sell and cash in the profits?"

"Oh heavens no, the Burger Palace is a little gold mine. I'm not about to sell out yet. I'm here to talk about helping you sell houses."

"Well this comes as a surprise. Do you have a realtor license?"

"I don't want to sell houses myself. For a small fee I want to advertise houses for you to sell. Before you toss me out as a kook, let me explain my thoughts. I'm willing to prove my services are valuable to you. Do you advertise on the internet?"

"Of course, all realty agencies advertise virtual tours of houses on the internet."

"Here is the deal. Pick any house you want in the standard price range. Allow me to enhance the video and the house will sell fast."

Robin studied the serious look on his face. "I can choose any house I want?" She thought for a second. "Then I choose a new house Bob recently completed. Our money is pretty well tied up in three spec houses he built." Robin smiled as she handed him the video of the house. "I hope your special advertising works. Our cash flow has shrunk to a dangerously low level. We overextended ourselves expecting a house to sell by now."

"It's eleven now, can you swing by the Burger Palace around four and I'll have your video ready. I'm planning to start my advertising business in a couple weeks. I'm looking for customers like you. My fee once I become operational will be one and a half percent of the selling price. This first house is a free gratis demonstration."

After his meeting with Robin, Brad called a flower shop. He ordered a dozen long stemmed red roses, to be delivered to Marie in Seattle along with a short note. "I miss you Honey, see you soon." Three hours later a phone call followed up the flowers. "Hi, are you missing me yet?"

"I missed you before you made it to the Airport. How are things in Vegas?"

"Absolutely wonderful, Robin is on board with one test house. My friend's problem child Carol is dating a nice young man. Wendy did a fantastic job in my absence. I'm happy, unless you tell me no. I am coming to Seattle late Monday."

"I'm not telling you no. In fact I may even store up a few kisses for your arrival."

"Can you do me a favor before I get to Seattle? Try and find out when Sam is taking his realty exam."

"I already have that answer. Sam tested today."

"Oh wonderful, then Sam is a realty agent."

"No, he failed his realty exam and unfortunately he failed it in a big way. He and Judy were very disappointed. Watching those two mope around this evening hasn't been fun. She blames herself for his failing because she took up a lot of his time."

"Dang Marie, you said they were getting very close to marrying after Sam passed his realty test. This had to put a kink in their plans and my plans too. Don't worry, my plans have many fingers. If one finger fizzles, I'll switch to another plan. I have many different directions I could go. Fact is I should be doing something right now. Can you find out the information Sam is studying for his realty exam? A copy of the manual he is using to study may prove helpful to me and Sam, not to mention Judy."

"I'll do my best to acquire the information and get it to you. Thank you for the flowers. The roses you sent are beautiful."

"Beautiful flowers for a beautiful lady. I'm going to move heaven and earth to be in Seattle on Monday. This Sam business could work against me. I'll burn the midnight oil, and see what I can do. I better run Honey and remember I love you. If you get any information on Sam's studies let me know soon as possible."

CHAPTER 28

With Brad's plan set for Sam and Judy to study the real estate exam it was time to move to further business. Carol hadn't given up on testifying against Wendell Carpenter. In order to deal with Carpenter he needed a diversion. "Wendy, we need to have an employee of the quarter. We could give our winner a certificate of achievement, a nice iPod and a hundred dollar check. Ernie could choose the employee we honor. You could present the award. I'll have a word with Ernie while you buzz out and pick up some iPods, get four iPods. I may want one for myself. He planned to make special messages for Carpenter."

During Wendy's absence Brad began making a subliminal message for the creep. He knew dealing with Carpenter would be a huge challenge. His plan was simple if he could pull it off. To pull his plan off he would need to download the subliming messages to an iPod and keep the intensity level high enough to affect Carpenter in a short span of time. Posing as a freelance reporter he hoped to talk his way into an interview with the sex offender.

Through diligent work and a few hundred dollars he was able to set up a meeting with the rapist and his attorney. The personal interview could only be on previous charges. The sexual assault charge in Carol's case could not to be discussed. Brad could care less what case they talked about. In ten minutes he could nail this Carpenter creep with his super powerful subliminal message. With the interview set for Monday afternoon his plan to be with Marie Monday evening went out the window. He called Marie to explain he would be arriving in Seattle Monday later than expected. "Hello Sweetie."

"Oh hi, I was about to call you. Sam has been studying his real estate questions on an internet site. I emailed the site to you, have you seen my email?"

"No I haven't seen your e-mail but thank you. What I called about is Monday evening, I will be delayed. I have a very important meeting on Monday afternoon that will throw me off schedule. I'll catch the first flight out after my meeting. I may arrive in Seattle in the middle of the night so I will get a hotel room and see you Tuesday morning."

"You will do no such thing. Call me from the airport when you get here and come straight to the house. I'll be waiting at the door to greet you."

Her insisting he come straight to the house regardless of the time made him feel loved. "Okay Honey, I better get back to work. Wendy is pulling on my arm. I love you Marie, bye."

After ending his call he turned to Wendy. "What is it you need?"

"I never meant for you to end your call. I'm sorry to interrupt but it's time for me to go home. My husband is coming in this evening. I'll see you in the morning."

"Good night Wendy. Tell Joe hello, and enjoy your evening."

He watched until her car was out of sight before opening any iPods and preparing Subliminal Messages for Wendell Carpenter. Knowing he would only have a small window of opportunity for his special message to influence Carol's rapist he made the message extremely powerful. Although the intensity level was less than when the money was missing the subliminal message was many times more intense than standard advertising messages.

On Sunday Wendy stopped by the Burger Palace to pick up a bank deposit. She found Brad working. "What are you doing here, it's Sunday?"

"I had a few things I wanted to check before my business meeting tomorrow afternoon. After my meeting I'm flying up to Seattle. I'm hoping to meet Marie's parents this trip."

"Certainly explains your good mood. I do have one suggestion for you. Why don't you marry Marie, you are a basket case without her. You are cantankerous and moody when she is not around."

"Thank you for such a glowing review, you made my day. I really needed to hear, I'm cantankerous and moody."

"I embellished a little. How about mean and ornery, does that sound better?" She paused to laugh. "When Marie is at your side you are a much calmer person, and a far more likable guy. You love her, why waste time playing silly games. How long will you be in Seattle?"

"Long as I can, you have my number. I'll be in Seattle several times in the next few weeks working with my accountant firm and my attorney. I'm setting up my advertising agency. You are handling the Burger Palace well so don't expect me to return soon. There is not a lot of need for me to waste my time watching you work." She sat staring at him with a blank look on her face. "Is something wrong, out with it lady?"

"I'm surprised. I knew all along you wanted an ad agency. I thought that was next year or the year after. Will you be selling the Burger Palace?"

"I'm starting the ad agency right out of this office. My new equipment is here."

"Are you really going to Seattle to start the new business as you say or are you avoiding Carol?"

"Both actually, I think Rusty is showing enough interest in your daughter to keep her attention. With me gone she should concentrate on him more than I was hanging around."

"I'll warn you now she plans on cornering you when you return. She still wants to testify against her attacker."

"Carol can't testify without endangering herself along with you and me. We may need an additional subliminal message for her but we have no reason to be hasty, unless she forces the issue. For her own good she needs to make correct decisions herself."

Seventeen hundred miles north in Seattle the girls were discussing Brad's last visit along with his upcoming visit. "Marie you can't blame him for shying away from college. You know his heart is not in getting his degree."

"I know but I was looking forward to seeing him on a daily basis. Judy, don't look at me that way. I'll not show my disappointment to him. There is something else bothering him. He shows signs of wanting a family soon but is afraid of making another mistake. At the end of his last trip, he suggested I advise you to sign a prenuptial agreement if you and Sam get married."

"Sam and I do not have enough money to worry about a prenuptial agreement. Wake up girl that message was for you. He is planning to ask you to marry him. You said he wants a family. By starting the ad agency he wants to feel he is providing for his family not just living off his father's money. Think about it girl friend, you may be getting a marriage proposal very soon."

"Brad did indicate his net worth was close to two million dollars, enough money he would want to protect his money. I didn't tell you this but when his wife died he was legally entitled to her share of their money. He sent Alice's fifteen percent of their holdings to her mother. He sent her a check for three hundred eighty five thousand dollars. If I pushed the right numbers on my calculator the check is fifteen percent of two million dollars. Add back the money he is now making he could be nearing the two million dollar net worth again."

"I'm thinking you better be ready with your answers. Would you marry him and would you sign a prenuptial agreement?"

"Your questions are easy to answer yes on both counts, I will and yes I would sign a prenuptial agreement in a heartbeat. My only hesitation would be if he asked me to live with him. If Brad is family orientated as I believe, living together won't cross his mind."

Judy dashed for the ringing phone. "Hi Honey!"

"Hello Honey to you also Judy, how are you this fine day?"

"I'm sorry Brad. I thought it was Sam calling. Hold on I'll get Marie."

"Wait, I have a question for you before I speak with her. I understand Sam is struggling with his real estate exam and you are wondering if he is spending time with you is affecting his studies. Tell Sam not to worry, I have the perfect solution for him. Now my question for you is simple, do you personally have any interest in becoming a real estate agent yourself?"

"I haven't given any thought to becoming a realty agent myself. I will admit becoming a realty agent would be a nice career."

"Then I'll set things in motion for you, and Sam to study together. Is Marie near you?"

"Marie is right here but hold on I need an explanation."

"I'm short on time. I'll explain when I get to Seattle. Please hand the phone to Marie."

"What on earth did you say to Judy, she is scowling at me?"

"I asked her a question and told her I would explain everything to her when I get to Seattle the first of the week. Maybe she has the Carol syndrome, and is short on patience. All I asked was if she had any interest in being a real estate agent herself someday? She wasn't sure so I'm making a CD for Sam to study and since Judy didn't officially object. She will be included in the study. Could you do me a favor and see to it Sam spends the night with Judy at the house, while I'm there, like he does when I'm not there."

"How do you know Sam spends some of his nights here at the house?"

"I saw a few men's clothes in the laundry room when I tossed my towel in the washer."

"We weren't sure how you would feel about hiring us to house sit, and her having a live-in boyfriend with her. Sam hasn't been here all that long, two and a half weeks."

"I checked the refrigerator and the garbage. I didn't see any alcohol or drug containers so I don't have a problem with Sam living with Judy. I see Robin Tilly walking this way, and she has a big smile on her face. I'm betting the house I enhance advertised for her, sold. She is striding with pride. This may be a nice conversation we are about to have."

"I better let you go so you can get your work finished. Bye, see you soon."

"Robin Tilly was walking on air. She grabbed Brad around the neck and gave him a giant hug. "I sold three of my husband's houses. They were alike except for the outside color. If I understood you correct. One house was free and upon closing I will owe you for the other two houses. Bob is thrilled to see his houses sell. Three hundred fifty thousand dollars was the selling price for each house. Your commission will be ten thousand five hundred dollars."

"Congratulations Robin, nice job. Stick with me and we will make a great team."

"Those are words I want to hear. When can you enhance more house videos for me?"

"I'm leaving for Seattle tomorrow and I expect to be in Seattle most of the week. I could enhance one house for you in the morning before I leave if you have the video here early."

"Thank you, I'll deliver you a video early tomorrow morning."

CHAPTER 29

Monday afternoon Brad grew remarkably nervous walking into the jail area of the courthouse to meet with Wendell Carpenter and his attorney. Could he actually con the attorney and the sex freak into believing he was a freelance reporter, only time would tell?

Meeting the rapist came as a surprise. Brad introduced himself as Mr. Abrams. Attorney Don Macintyre and Carpenter were wearing double breasted suits making the rapist look as if he were a banker. The unshaven man pictured in the paper was not in the interview room. Even so Brad wanted to puke at the sight of the Wendell Carpenter. He settled for setting his emotions aside to concentrate on the business at hand. "First off I would like to thank you for granting this interview. I believe I understand the ground rules. If I get out of line with my questions feel free to stop me. I have a small recorder and a camera. I also play soft music to help people relax while conducting my interviews. Where you were born?"

"Austin, Texas." The attorney answered the question while the rapist himself showed no emotion. Question after question the attorney answered. Brad hid his disappointment of getting answers from the wrong person. In all honesty, it didn't make any difference who answered his questions. He was buying time for his subliminal message to affect Wendell Carpenter. Childhood questions were asked, was he an only child, did he play with neighborhood children. In time questions were asked about his school years and two pictures were taken. Ninety minutes elapsed. "Well gentlemen I believe we have covered enough for our first interview. Please understand nothing can be published without written permission from the two of you. I can work with what we have so far, and then give you a call. This will give you a chance to see where I'm going with the story before we scheduled our next interview."

Don Macintyre, Carpenter's Attorney followed him out to the parking lot. "We won't be signing any release forms for your story. Mr. Abrams I thought you were a reporter writing about a war hero having a difficult time readjusting to civilian life." Brad had given them a false name. "You are an impersonator, you may want to be a reporter but you are not. I advise you to find a new occupation."

"Geez man, I have to start somewhere. Why get upset, nothing can be printed without your permission. How can you turn down my request before you see my material, this isn't fair at all. No way should you have led me on believing I was getting somewhere."

"You are unprofessional so don't waste your time whining or writing this article because we are not signing any release."

"Alright, you are the person in charge. I'll not waste my time"

Brad couldn't help but laugh, as he left the parking lot. In all honesty his questions were so horrible he could have been tossed from the room after the first question. He felt confident his powerful subliminal message for Wendell Carpenter would put an end to Carol wanting to testify against her attacker. She can't possibly testify against a dead man. From the jail he drove back to the Burger Palace. "What are you doing here?" Wendy asked. "I thought you were on your way to Seattle?"

"I just finished my business meeting. Cross your fingers I believe my meeting went well but in the process I missed my plane." Checking on line he was able to secure a first class ticket on Alaska Airlines leaving late in the day. He promptly called Marie. "Hi Honey. I'll be at the house late this evening."

"Don't worry about me getting up to meet you. I'll nap before you get here. I may not look my best when I answer the door but I'll be waiting at the door for your arrival."

"Okay Honey. See you soon, bye."

Wendy smiled at him. "I love the smile on your face each time you talk with Marie."

"Why shouldn't I be smiling, this is a special trip. I'll be gone four days minimum maybe longer and my next few days will be exceptionally busy. Please don't call me unless there is a national emergency. Did Robin stop by and get her video?"

"She dropped by about an hour ago."

"Then I'm out of here and I'll see you in four days."

Even knowing the world would be better off without the likes of a Wendell Carpenter he felt strange as his stomach was queasy about encouraging the rapist to commit suicide. There were few choices to deal with these types of people and the courts are no help.

His queasy stomach remained at the airport until his boarding call came. The Alaskan Airlines first class seat allowed him to drift into a deep sleep almost before the plane left the runway.

Being exhausted it seemed only minutes when the stewardess touched his shoulder as she whispered in his ear. "We are at our destination." As he cracked an eye open, he couldn't help but jump. Again she repeated, "We are at Sea-Tac."

"Thank you." Gazing around Brad realized he was the last person on the plane. I'm sorry Miss." The watch on his wrist indicated it was ten PM. From the rental car desk he called the house. Marie answered on the second ring. "Good evening Honey, I'll be there in about an hour."

"I'll meet you at our door." Her voice sounded weak and sleepy.

She lay awake watching the minutes tick by awaiting his arrival. Hearing his car pull up she raced to the door. As Marie opened the door she pressed one finger to his lips and whispered. "We must be quiet so we don't wake Judy and Sam." He smiled and followed her to the bedroom before kissing her. "Sorry I'm so late Honey. I couldn't help being late."

Without further words she began undressing her suitor. Together they quietly slipped beneath the bed sheet. On certain occasions words are not needed. After a quick comforting love session sleep came easily. Mid-morning the next day he woke alone in the house. Marie, Judy and Sam had all gone off to work. His meeting with his accountant was set for two P.M. leaving him time for a hearty breakfast in a restaurant near the attorney's office.

At the appointed hour he walked into the accounting firm where he was introduced to a new member of the firm, Darlene Smith. She appeared to be well qualified. Multiple college degrees hung on the wall behind her. "Hello, nice to meet you Miss Smith." Without further delay he laid out his plans to start his advertising business.

"You surprise me for such a young man you are developing a real business mind. Still I believe an advertising firm will be a huge challenge for you."

"I welcome new challenges whole heartedly. The advertising business will have greater potential for higher earnings. My plan is to start slowly and work out of the same office as I operate the Burger Palace."

"Please allow me to caution you on not neglecting business at the Burger Palace. You have done a remarkable job with your first business in a very short time."

Brad paused as he studied the female accountant. She wore a green business suit that hid her average sized breasts. She looked to be in her mid thirties with medium length brown hair, she wore glasses and a petite build. "I have a more than capable assistant who will be watching the day to day operations ate the Burger Palace. I also have a favorite gal I plan on asking to marry me. So I will have a built in partner for my new venture."

"Congratulations, I wish a long happy marital life."

"Thank you Miss Smith but please my friends call me Brad."

"Alright Brad it is, do you have a name chosen for you new venture?"

"I don't want my name on the business directly. My advertising business is the type of business I won't need a lot of exposure to lure in new customers. Hand choosing is how will get my customers. I know this sounds stupid but I like the name Burger Palace so why couldn't I name my ad agency the Ad Palace?"

"The Ad Palace will be a catchy name. I'll work your corporation papers up in that name. If you change your mind about anything, call me soon as possible."

"Is there anything else you need right away, if not I'll duck out and leave you to your work. I have an appointment at four with Al Claymore my Attorney."

In Claymore's office he explained his intention to ask for Marie's hand in marriage. "She is a great gal and what I need from you is a prenuptial agreement. My father would never approve of my getting married without a strong prenuptial agreement. I have one successful business now and plan to start another. I want my new wife to be a full partner in my new business."

"Smart thinking, you are right about how your father thinks. I'm sorry to here about your father's deteriorating health. I know this must concern you."

"What is this about my father's health being bad? Nobody said anything to me, what are you hearing?" Claymore gave a funny look. "I haven't talked to my father or any of his associates in eight or ten months, he never calls anymore?"

"Then you should call your father personally. I don't have a lot of information regarding your father. Bill Barret mentioned your father's health when he called about some paperwork your father wanted done. Haven't you noticed the money transfers to your account are considerable larger than before."

"I haven't paid any attention to the money transfers. I've been busy making my own money. Tell me what you know about my father health."

"I told you my limited information."

"Well shit, I'm calling Bill Barret." Like Al Claymore if Bill had other information about John Collins health he wasn't forthcoming with the information.

"A standard prenuptial agreement is fifteen percent of your previous holdings such as the money coming from your father and money earned thus far at the Burger Palace."

"Draw up the papers soon as you can. I'm moving on to a new business venture and I want my new wife to be a full equal partner for our new business. If you have any questions later call me."

"Then I better move your prenuptial agreement to the top of my list of things to do first. Congratulations, I'll be looking forward to meeting the future Mrs. Collins."

"Thank you, now unless there are more questions for me I will be on my way. You have my cell number if anything comes up."

"Eventually I will need personal information from your intended spouse to complete the paperwork for your prenuptial agreement. When is your wedding date?"

"Our wedding date hasn't been set yet. I'm still building up courage to ask Marie for her hand in marriage."

"Don't try feeding me that story you of all people do not lack courage." Brad smiled as he left Al Claymore's office. "Good Luck young man. Step up and ask her to marry you."

By the time he rushed back to the house it was well past six when he arrived. Marie welcomed him with a kiss. "We were thinking you might be lost."

"I wasn't lost, just busy. Time flies when you are having fun." He was promptly introduced to Sam Anderson. "I've been looking forward to meeting you Sam. Ladies do we have any dinner plans for this evening?" The girls remained quiet. "If you will allow me, I would be happy to take the four of us out for a nice dinner. It would give Sam and me a chance to know one another better."

Sam turned to Judy. "What do you say shall we join them or allow them their privacy?"

"We should join them. Brad mentioned something earlier he wants to share with us. While eating dinner he could explain what is on his mind."

"Marie, called the Olive Garden and get us a table while I wash up?"

After making the dinner reservation she found him in the shower. "We have a seven thirty reservation. I laid out clothes for you?"

"Thank you Sweetheart." He stuck his wet head out of the shower long enough to kiss her. "I love you."

In the kitchen Sam was questioning Judy. "Do you know what Mr. Big-Shot has on his mind? Could he be upset I'm living with you in his house?"

"Most of his ideas have to do with making money. He also has a strange way of saying things. He is not the easiest person to understand at times. It's okay to ask questions but try not to irritate him."

Brad and Marie rejoined Judy and Sam's conversation. "Is anybody hungry as I am? If you are, let's go eat?" Being a weeknight the Olive Garden wasn't super busy. After ordering he turned to Sam. "When did you become interested in becoming a realty agent?"

"My mother has been a real estate agent for twenty years. She has strange hours at times but those strange hours produce a nice income. On Saturday I tested and failed. This was my second failure and my mother is very upset with me. She lays most of the blame unjustly on Judy, for my failing my state exam. Mother claims Judy is stealing my study time."

"I can put a quick end to your failing the real estate exam. I have a proven study method. Use my study method and you will pass the realty exam on your next try and that brings me to you young lady." He pointed at Judy. "I set the preliminary details in motion so you could study at the same time Sam does. The two of you could pass the realty exam on the same day if you choose to test." All three dinner guests looked at him as though he was crazy. "I know, don't tell me. You are not the first people not to believe me. If you will excuse me I need to use the facilities."

"Wait, hold on Brad. I didn't..."

"Relax Sam; I'll be back in a few minutes."

"Darn it all, you warned me he acted different than most people. Now I've made him mad. I was waiting for more explanation. I'll try his study method."

Upon returning Brad jumped to a new subject. "Ladies I have the checks for your summer wages." From a vest pocket he produced two envelopes. "Along with your checks I would like to thank you personally for taking care of my house this summer."

"Wow, these checks are too large. Why the extra money, unless I'm mistaken these checks are two thousand dollars over our agreement?"

"Anyone putting up with me earns extra money."

"That's the silliest thing I ever heard." Judy protested.

"Is it silly as a new study method?"

"Now hold on a minute." Sam declared. "We didn't put down your study method. Your words came as a surprise. I'll try your new system, I have nothing to lose." Sam further stated with a huge smile on his face.

"I doubt you will give any credit to my system when you ace the realty exam because you look to be a very intelligent person. Sam, my guess is you are close to passing the state exam on your own. This girl…" He pointed at Judy. "…is the one who interests me. Judy passing her realty exam is when you might believe I'm onto something."

Judy showed her excitement. "If you actually believe I could pass the real estate exam using your study method, tell me what I should to do. I'm all ears."

"Finish eating for starters." Her excitement pleased him. "We'll set things in motion back at the house." Judy's expression of excitement was over-shadowed by Sam's confused look. "Wish I had a camera Sam, your facial expression is priceless. I'm not leaving you out Marie, tomorrow is your day off. I plan on devoting the entire day to you." His words put a smile on her face.

At the house he pulled out the special subliminal message CD. "In my hand is the study method the two of you will benefit from. The process is very simple. Play the CD and go about your business. Play the CD twenty-four hours a day even while you sleep." Both Judy and Sam looked at him in a strange way. "Give my study method a try and find out together, shall I set the CD for you?"

"Do you mind if I watch?" Sam inquired.

"Come along Sam, Judy you go into the bedroom and listen. We need the sound at a low enough level so you can hear the music but not so loud it keeps you awake." In less than a minute the sound adjustments were made. "Your study notes are mixed with the music. In this case you study as you sleep, very simple, very effective."

Sam chuckled. "Study while we sleep. I've heard of everything now, how can people effectively sleep and study at the same time?"

Brad patted him on the back. "Live and learn my friend. Marie, take me to the hot tub. I've had an exhausting day, I need to relax."

"Come along we won't need a swimsuit. Judy and Sam can use the Jacuzzi inside while they studying. We can fix something to drink before we go out to the hot tub."

"Isolation and seduction, I like that. You seem to be a girl after my heart." He promptly gave her a hug and a sexy kiss. I have some special things going on tomorrow all in a very unpredictable order. My head is still spinning; it's too full of plans. I'm over taxing by brain."

"At some point you will have to take charge of your life and put a stop to the constant chaos surrounding you. If you don't take charge of your life you could die at a young age." She reached up and touched his cheek below his eyes. "You still have the dark circles under your eyes, you need a long rest."

"I'm trying to take charge of my life. Tomorrow I hope to clear up some of the chaos surrounding me. Today at my attorney's office I learned my father's health might be failing. There is no way I can call my father direct. When we speak he calls me. I placed a call through my normal channels for him to call me but he hasn't returned my call. All I can do is wait for him to call or someone to call on his behalf to. Speaking of family I hope you remember I haven't met your parents. Half my day is shot with meetings I hope to have. I would be pleased to have you at my side tomorrow."

"I was thinking we could drive down and see my parents tomorrow. Our having meetings tomorrow changes things. My parents live in Oregon so it's quite a drive to see them. I've driven down and back the same day before but I'm not anxious to do it again. You will need to meet my parents another day. Out of curiosity how many days do you expect to be in Seattle?"

"This minute, I have no idea today but after we see how tomorrow goes. I should know more about when I have to leave." His voice trailed off.

"How early will we leave the house tomorrow?" He sat staring off in space. "You seem preoccupied, and the dark circles around your eyes scare me. Are you worried about your father?"

"Of course I'm worried about my father. He is not a young man. He is well into his eighties. When you talk about someone in terms of failing health it is very concerning. He lives in Mexico and I'm hoping mother is with him. I called Bill Barett to have him contact my father for me. So far father hasn't called. After Alice was killed in the automobile accident he lectured me about marriage. Father said I should never get married."

"Your father actually said you should never get married?"

"His exact words were if I wanted female companionship. I should hire an escort girl and he was serious. I disagreed with my father. No prostitutes for this kid. I want a wife and family. I'll buck my father forever if that is what it takes. I'll take a wife and family over his money any day. You asked how early we needed to leave the house tomorrow. I've been stumbling for the right words to decide when we should leave."

She smiled. "You never struggle with words, what's up with you?"

"People confuse me. I've been called a controlling person many times by many people. When I try to choose my words careful they don't always match my thought process, does that make any sense?"

"I'm not sure, can we go inside my skin is starting to wrinkle?"

As they dawned their robes and went inside Judy was waiting for them. "I forgot to thank you for helping Sam and I." Along with her thank you she gave him a generous hug. "Goodnight."

"You are very welcome."

In the bedroom Marie turned to him. "Do you realize if Sam passes his real estate exam and Judy marries him, I may be attending college alone this fall?" Again he remained quiet, lost in thought. "You beat all I ever saw, your concentration level leaves a lot to be desired this evening."

"Honey, you used the term if he passes his test? I guarantee he will pass. I also expect Judy to pass if she follows through and takes the real estate exam. My system works beyond belief. Mr. Claymore my attorney is drawing up paperwork for my ad business. One of my meetings tomorrow is with him. Then my accounting firm is another stop tomorrow. What time does the mall open? There are things I may need to do at the mall."

"Most of the stores open at ten. You lived in Seattle long enough to know the Mall stores opened at ten. You were raised in Seattle."

"My attorney suggested I move straight forward. It appears he may be right. Being stupid I thought I could come up with the perfect way to do things myself. It's plain to see my way isn't working. Do you think I should try Claymore's way?"

"If your attorney's idea is a good idea, why not go for it?"

"Alright, straight forward it is. Marie, will you marry me?"

Marie flew in his arms as she showered him with hugs and kisses. "Yes! Yes! Yes! I will marry you under one condition. First we draw up a good prenuptial agreement." She continued to hug the daylights out of him.

"A prenuptial agreement of fifteen percent would keep my father in check and protect you. The prenuptial agreement would only apply to my family money and what I now have personally, not what we will earn in the future."

"Sounds perfect to me, when do we marry?"

"Claymore can draw up papers for our prenuptial agreement. He will need your information to fill in the blanks where your information goes and let you take the prenuptial agreement to your lawyer for approval before you sign."

"I don't have a lawyer. I trust you or I wouldn't be marrying you."

"Honey Mr. Claymore may insist on you having an attorney of your own. Our prenuptial agreement wouldn't be legal if you were not represented by an attorney. It's very important we do things right from the get go. Our Wills are another thing needing changed."

"This marriage business is a whole new experience for me. I have never had a Will in my life."

"That's alright. I'll clue you in ahead of time our Wills should be different. In the event of my death, half goes to you and the second half will be split equally among our children in a trust fund format."

"Can't my Will be the same as yours?"

"Certainly your Will could be identical to mine but if I were you I would give half to our children and the other half to your parents if they were still alive or to your brother if your parents are gone."

"All this legal talk is depressing. Can we forget all this legal stuff for tonight and concentrate on more pleasant things like loving me?"

CHAPTER 30

Marie came bouncing into the kitchen the following morning happy beyond belief. She grabbed Judy by the shoulders to dance her around a few times. "You were right, Brad asked me to marry him."

"Congratulation, I told you he was working up the nerve to ask you to marry him." Hearing Brad enter the kitchen Judy turned to him. "Here comes the man of the hour now. Congratulations you are getting one fine lady." She pulled him in tight for a three way hug. "I love you both and wish you many happy years together. Any idea when this blessed event might take place?"

"We haven't talked about a date. Wedding plans take time." Marie commented.

"Excuse me Honey, our wedding needs to be soon. I know we haven't talked about our options. I want the ad agency operational within two weeks. For you to become an equal partner in our new ad agency business from the start we must be married before we sign the paperwork. Would you consider getting married in Vegas and have a formal wedding ceremony up here near your parents later when we have time to plan a nice wedding?" She gave him a questioning look. "I know I'm asking a lot but everything is snowballed on me. Trying to impress my real estate connection in Vegas I enhanced a house video as a test for Robin Tilly. I wanted her to be ready to go forward when I needed her. I laid out my plan and she chose the house. The first house was done free of charge. Other houses we worked together on later our business fee would be one and a half percent of the selling price. Robin is a sharp woman. She sold three houses off the one enhancement. To get paid the money she owes us the Ad Palace has to be in business and I want you to be a full partner at that time."

"Two weeks is very soon. Do you mind if I think this over before I agree or disagree?" She shook her head. "Getting married in two weeks is unheard of in my family."

"Honey there is more to consider than the ten thousand Robin owes me. The very day the Ad Palace becomes a business it has a value. Say

250

a couple hundred thousand. If we don't marry first you risk losing a hundred thousand dollars or more."

"Stop throwing dollar numbers at me. My mind is going in circles. I care about you not your money."

"The money and I come as a package. I screwed up, I should have asked you to marry me six weeks or a month ago. Plus I shouldn't have enhanced the house video for Robin Tilly. This whole mess is my fault, I take full responsibility but now the rush is on."

"Pardon me, I don't mean to interrupt but are you expecting my Sam to sell houses in Seattle using your advertising agency?"

"I would like both Sam and you to sell houses in the Seattle area using my system. Together you could do very well selling houses using my proven enhancement advertising. Your personal wealth could grow by leaps and bounds."

"How many sales people are you expecting to work with in each city?"

"I haven't discussed this part of the business with my partner. I believe we could work with four agents in each city and still have plenty of time to devote to ourselves. There is no point in making good money if we can't enjoy the money."

Marie sat a bowl of cereal in front of him. "Thank you Honey, let's use a conservative number. Say each agent sold two, two hundred thousand dollar houses each month. Multiply by six, times that by twelve months and the Ad Palace makes over four hundred thousand dollars a year."

"On average houses sell for more than three hundred thousand. These are big numbers you are throwing at me. If I'm following you right the earning potential could be unlimited for everyone."

"Not all houses sold would be sold using my system. Any house sold in a standard way, the agent would retain all the commission."

"I wish Sam hadn't left so early this morning. He needs to hear your projected potential. In the mean time do everything you can to get your ad agency operating in case I do pass the real estate exam because I'm getting excited about making money. I'm on board soon as possible."

Marie hugged her friend. "Sounds like you want me to marry him today."

"We can't marry today. We have rings to purchase and prenuptial papers to sign. We will have a full day so we should be getting dressed."

Marie placed a hand on his shoulder. "Do you mind if I call mother and tell her my good news before I get dressed?"

"By all means call your parents. Tell them I anxious to meet them."

With her off making the phone call Judy stepped up and gave him a nice hug. "These plans you have are nothing sort of amazing. I wish you all the success in the world." She ended her hug with a kiss to his cheek.

"When a person makes plans there are always kinks in the plans to be worked out. Be patient and keep the faith. Working together we can accomplish our goals. My first challenge is to convince someone to be the Broker in the agencies I work with. Broker and all there should only be three or four agents. Everyone in the agency should get the opportunity to use my sales technique if they so desire."

"Sam's mother might be the broker you need. She could work same as her agents. When I pass my realty exam I could join the sales staff. I feel as though I'm in the middle of a dream, pinch me."

"Pinches leave bruises."

Marie covered the mouthpiece on the phone before calling out to Brad. "Mother wants to know when we are going down to their house so they can meet you."

"Good heavens another tough question. Tell your mother we will see them within the next ten days." He turned his attention back to Judy. "I don't know Sam well, how does he feel about my being so forceful?"

"He has no idea of what to make of you." She stated with a smile.

"At some point after Sam passes his real estate exam. I should meet Sam's mother. A lunch meeting with her would be nice. This project needs to involve everyone if we are to be successful."

"I'm not Carmen's favorite person so I think Sam should be the one to set the lunch meeting for you to discuss your business proposal with her."

Marie's eyes were sparkling when she returned. "Mother is thrilled with our news. Daddy wasn't there but mother can't wait to meet you. I better go shower and get ready."

"We need to look at rings. If you don't find a ring to your liking we can look more in Vegas when we get home."

"What about my job?" She asked. "What should I tell them?"

"Another decision for you Honey. If it won't leave your employer in a bind just explain you are moving to Vegas to get married. If you think that might create a problem ask if they can find a replacement for you." Marie nodded okay before dashing off to the shower. He turned his attention back to Judy. "What are your plans for today little lady?"

"I'll call Sam and tell him your plans. Then hang out here at the house and wait to see if he can set the meeting for us."

"Come with me dear child." Off to the security control room they went. "Right now my special study CD is only playing in your bedroom area. Go ahead and switch on the remaining switches there, all nine of them. The slide lever on the right, push it up near the center. Now we have your study information playing throughout the house. All day anywhere you are in the house you will be studying. I had you up the volume so if you were doing laundry or something noisy you can still hear your study information. Keep in mind you won't be aware you are hearing the study information but you will be studying."

She shook her head as she smile with excitement. "This is so weird it's hard to believe anyone can study this way."

Brad gave her a small hug. "Trust me you can study this way. Do you know when Sam is planning on retesting again?"

"He wants to retest on Saturday. He feels pressured by his mother and he wants to get his realty license before I do."

"Sam shouldn't feel pressured by you getting your license when he does. You both can pass if you test on Saturday. You will know the material by then."

"I've watched Sam study for months. Saturday is too soon for me to test."

"Using my study method you will be ready to test by Saturday." He reached out and touched her shoulder. "Trust me, test Saturday."

"I don't know, Sam tells me the test is tough."

"You know from your college tests to read each question completely. These so called instructors love to put in a trick question. If they can trick you with one lousy question you might mess up other questions. Sam has one of two problems he may be rushing, or he could be just on the outside edge of knowing the material well enough to keep from becoming confused by the questions. My study system will do him a world of good as it will benefit you."

She smiled at him. "However things turn out. I thank you for your effort. I better get my laundry started so when Sam comes home this evening my work is complete."

Marie wasn't prepared for the whirlwind day ahead of her. The ring shopping was stressing along with the accountant and attorney meeting.

By evening she was mentally drained. "I'm sorry, but I need to lie down for a while. This has been an overwhelming day."

Judy returned from grocery shopping in a glorious mood. "Late this afternoon I jumped on the internet site Sam uses to study. I know more of the material than I thought I would. I was amazed, I have little doubt your system is working."

"Play it cool around Sam and hide your excitement. He needs to remain confident going into the state realty exam on Saturday. Don't allow him to think you are smarter than he is."

"I see your point and I'll be careful, where is Marie?"

"She is taking a nap. I wore her out today. She had a lot of decisions to make with little time to make them. She looked at a lot of rings but couldn't find what she liked. Then we spent hours in the attorney's office working on the wording of our prenuptial agreement and our Wills. Our stupid attorney took six hours to complete those papers. Tomorrow Marie has an appointment with her attorney. She needs someone to protect her interests well as I need my interests protected. We were briefly at my accountant's office. So far the whole process is blowing her away."

"If Sam and I marry we won't have those problems. He and I have so little we won't need so much as a Will for some time."

"You would still be wise to draw things out in black and white. From my vantage point I see two successful people who in time will be worth a considerably amount of money. Don't allow wealth to creep up on you. Get yourself a good accountant. My stupid father got into tax problems causing him to leave the country. For years he has been living in Mexico."

"I sincerely hope your vision is right about our success."

Sam walked in as she was finishing her statement. "Whose vision is right about us?"

"Brad's vision, he thinks we will make loads of money in a short time."

"Wish I had half your confidence." Sam responded.

"Confidence is built one step at a time. You are on your way my friend."

Sam glanced around and down the hall. "Where is Marie this evening?"

"She is resting, we had a busy day and accomplished only half of what we expected to accomplish. Tomorrow doesn't look good either. She has an early meeting with her attorney. This will be a strange meeting for me. I've never gone to a meeting where I was the outsider before. What are we having for dinner?"

Judy smiled. "I cheated and picked up a roast chicken at the deli. We have things to make a great salad so all I have to do in make some mashed potatoes and gravy."

"Why don't I finish making dinner and the two of you go relax?"

"Are you serious?" Judy asked with a smile.

"Scoot along and relax. Dinner will be ready at seven." At a quarter to seven he went to the bedroom and kissed Marie on the cheek to wake her. "Honey, dinner will be served in a few minutes."

"Oh my, I was sleeping sound." She blinked her eyes. "Give me another kiss, and I'll go wash my face, and comb my hair before I join you in the kitchen."

At the table Marie told about her exhausting day. "Tomorrow I may face the same thing with my attorney. I now have more sympathy for Brad continually racing around in circles."

Sam had a solution for her. "Marry a poor person and you won't have those problems."

"I didn't set out to fall in love with Brad. It sort of happened on its own. He swept me away before I knew anything was happening." Marie looked square at Sam. "Laugh now Sam but when you become a successful person in the real estate field; you will need a good accountant and an attorney. Then we'll see who is doing the laughing."

"Marie's right, your day will come much sooner than you think."

"There is quite a difference in the two thousand dollars I'm worth and the two million Judy thinks you might be worth."

Marie almost panicked at his mentioning the two million dollar figure. Brad had to realize that number came from her. Brad remained calm. "Build yourself a good reputation and in a few years you will be worth two million dollars, maybe more."

Sam looked at him rather serious. "Do you know the meaning of the word embellish?"

"Stick with me, together we can accelerate your career. Either way with or without me I believe you will be successful. The method you choose to become successful is up to you. Whatever you do will require hard work. Nothing comes easy in life."

Later in the privacy of their room he asked Marie if there an airport near where her folks live? "I'm sure small planes fly in and out near them somewhere but until I met you I never traveled by plane."

"In that case we fly down to Portland rent a car and go meet your parents. I'm anxious to meet your parents. Keep in mind we can't stay more than overnight and part of the next day. You can probably come up for a proper visit soon. I have no relatives to attend our wedding so our actual church wedding ceremony should be near your folks. I'll leave the decision up to you. I'll marry you anywhere."

"After listening to your attorney today, I understand how much easier the paperwork on the Ad Palace would be if we married as you suggested and have our ceremony later. I do want a nice wedding ceremony someday."

"Plan any type of wedding you want, spare no expense. You deserve the best. Having a formal wedding ceremony will be fun."

"Our wedding won't be huge. I want a small intimate wedding filled with family and friends."

"My guest list is zero unless I invite my attorney and accountant. Come to think of it who could I get for a best man?"

"Sam could be your best man." She suggested.

"I'm not sure he knows me well enough to like me, friendships take time."

"You could use my brother Ray?"

"I don't know your brother either but young Ray might be the perfect choice though. Who will your bridesmaids be?"

"Judy for starters, from there I'm not sure, a cousin maybe?"

"Judy is a fine choice I might add. If we get married in Vegas would you like Judy to stand as your witness there?"

"I would love to have her with us in Vegas. It can't happen because she doesn't have time or money enough for a trip to Vegas."

"Money isn't a problem, we can cover their expenses. Do you know if she will be testing this Saturday when we are down seeing your parents?"

"She wants to test Saturday but Sam thinks she should wait a few weeks so she can study more."

"That blasted Sam is a true nonbeliever so I suppose there isn't much chance of my meeting his mother, Carmen Anderson this soon. If I back door him and meet her without an introduction from he may be upset. If I had access to my equipment I could handle Sam. My subliminal messages would erase his lingering doubts about me."

"You use subliminal messages! I knew you weren't hypnotizing anyone. I didn't think subliminal messages worked."

He smiled and winked at her. "They work Honey." He went on to explain in detail how subliminal messages worked and how safe subliminal messages are.

"Have you experimented on anyone I know?"

"Karen set up experiments on you and Judy. The blouse switch you did that one night. The pizza but no beer night was another. She did only harmless experiments. The girl's gone wild skinny-dipping night. I wasn't involved in that test. Karen made those messages while I was in Vegas."

"Then she knows what you do?"

"She knew at one time. I blocked her memory before I sent her packing. That's how I knew my memory blocking messages would help Carol. Basically I had no choice but to block Karen's memory of what I do. My technique in the wrong hands could do major damage. If I had money enough to do nationwide advertising I could elect you the next president of the United States."

"What you are telling me boggles my mind."

"Only if someone were to steal my computers could they come close to what I am able to do. I have several computers giving codes to one another to operate my system. None of these computers are connected to the internet directly. I have two internet computers similar to the computer I left here but they are not hooked to my subliminal message computers. Computer hackers are no danger to my system or me. When we get back to Vegas I'll demonstrate my system and how it works."

"Now you have me so keyed up how will I ever sleep?"

"It's my fault I'm pouring things at you faster than I should. I want so much to share everything with you. The important thing is we must not tell anyone about my using enhanced subliminal messages to advertise. Judy and Sam must not be aware of how I enhance house videos."

"While we are confessing, I have something I should confess myself. I owe you an apology. I shouldn't have said anything to Judy about you being worth two million dollars in assets. Had I been thinking proper I wouldn't have made my comments to her"

"Don't worry about it, no harm done. She knew I had more money than most guys my age. To be truthful I don't honestly know myself what my net worth is. Might be a little above the two million by now. I probably should watch my money closer but I don't. I'm trying to concentrate on successful business ventures ahead of me and not what I already have." Brad stated as he rubbed her back

"I love your massaging hands, they feel great but you are putting me to sleep."

"Getting you to relax is the whole point of my massage. If you fall asleep I've been a success." He gently kissed the nap of her neck sending a chill down her spine.

CHAPTER 31

The following day Marie's attorney went over and over the prenuptial agreement insisting she should get more up front. Her attorney complained over words of no importance. For three solid hours Marie sat telling her attorney she was happy the way the prenuptial read. "Don't change anything."

Then it was off in search of wedding rings again. "Why don't you choose a ring for me?"

"I want you to choose a set of rings you like. These rings we get now do not have to be lifetime rings. You may want new rings later in life. If this store doesn't have a ring you like we can go elsewhere."

"Oh my word, look at the price of these rings. I wouldn't be comfortable wearing a six thousand dollar ring set, what if I lost them?"

"If your rings get lost or stolen we would get you another set. Rings are a material item that can be replaced. Buy any ring you want long as you are happy." For himself he chose a diamond-studded wedding band. After seeing the ring he chose she took the six thousand dollar ring. "Nice choice Honey."

On Saturday while Brad and Marie flew to see her parents Sam and Judy took the real estate exam. Marie's parents Ray and Susan Richards were waiting with open arms to meet their soon to be son-in-law. "So you are the young man who stole our daughter's heart, nice to meet you Brad."

"Guilty as charged, I am the lucky guy. Your daughter is a very special lady and I love her dearly."

"She tells us you will be making your home in Las Vegas."

"I currently own one business in Vegas. Within the next few days we will be starting and second business in Vegas that will have a branch in Seattle. We have a few hurdles to jump yet. I think we will get things moving our way very soon. Living in Vegas makes the most sense."

"Marie told us you were ambitious. You are young and have your whole life ahead of you. Be careful not to spread yourself so thin you go bankrupt trying to impress others. Live and enjoy your family life."

"Mr. Richards your daughter and I will get control of our lives very soon. We fully intend to enjoy our family. God willing you will have a couple grandchildren bouncing on your knee some day."

"Easy son, you and she are not married yet. You might want to wait on having children a few months."

"Listen carefully, to make our new business start off smooth. We need to be married very soon. Our plan is to marry in Vegas on Wednesday. In about a month we will have an actual wedding ceremony somewhere near here. We would like you and mother to attend our wedding in Vegas."

"Of course we want to be at your wedding regardless of where it will be. We will certainly be there for your wedding."

Ray's words put a smile on Brad's face. "Will you be flying to Vegas or driving?"

"We have vacation time coming. No reason we can't drive over so we can stay and enjoy Vegas for a few days. I suspect we can spend five days in Vegas."

"Five days in Vegas would be wonderful. How about I set you up a room where we are staying." Ray, Susan and Marie all watched intently as he made the reservations. "You are set. Your room is at Caesars where I live."

Brad's words shocked Susan "You live at Caesars?"

"For the time being, I do live at Caesars. Sometime in the next three months we should be getting a house of our own. At any rate I set up a room for you. All meals you eat at Caesars, charge them to your room. Marie and I will pay for your stay in Vegas."

"Does your young man always toss money away like this?"

"Does this answer your question?" Marie held out her hand to display her rings. "He is spoiling me big-time."

"Wow, I agree. That ring is spoiling you. I sort of hate the thought of you living in a crazy place like Las Vegas."

"Ray, don't underestimate Vegas. There is a lot of money to be made in Vegas. We will be making our primary home in Vegas. Our goal is to have a loving family like you and Susan have. My parents were a complete joke."

The Richards found comfort in his words and pleased at their daughter's choice of a husband. Marie and Brad's twenty-six hour visit was far too short for all concerned. "Planning our actual wedding ceremony, Marie may be here at your house quite a bit. If you will have me, I'll come when I can."

"You are welcome at our house any day."

Judy called just as they were leaving her folks house. "We Passed! Both Sam and I aced our real estate exam yesterday."

"Way to go guys, congratulations. Marie relayed the news to Brad. Sam and Judy passed their real estate exams." Brad gave thumb up signal to her. "Judy wants to know if there is any way we can go back to Seattle before flying down to Vegas, Carmen wants to meet you."

"Here we go stepping into a whirlwind again. I'm all for meeting Sam's mother, Seattle here we come."

Ray couldn't believe his ears. "You are getting married in Vegas on Wednesday. Today is Sunday and you are flying back to Seattle for a business meeting on Monday. Marie said you were a mover and a shaker, she wasn't lying."

"We will be in Vegas to meet you on Monday evening when you arrive." Susan's goodbye hug by far outshined any hug Brad ever received from his mother. He loved the genuine affection she displayed towards him.

Back at the Seattle house Judy was on an emotional high. Passing her real estate exam was a highlight in her life. Being short on time Brad moved forward quickly laying out his plan for the Ad Palace.

Carmen Anderson knew an opportunity when she saw one. She quickly agreed to be the Seattle broker the Ad Palace needed. "I can't turn down additional advertising."

"Be smart realty agents and don't advertise against yourself. Don't ask me to enhance houses that are all the same. Choose different neighborhoods, different house styles, and different price ranges. Work together as professionals so all can benefit. Send only good clear house videos to us in Vegas."

"I think we understand what we need to do,"

"Our fee is one and a half percent commission on any house we help sell. We operate with a non-binding verbal contract. You may get out of our deal any day you want with a simple phone call with no questions asked?"

Carmen raised her hand. "Who tracks our accounts?"

"You do. When you collect from a sale, send us a check."

"You are very trusting. How do you know we won't cheat you?"

"Don't think I'm always a nice guy. If you decide to cheat me, don't ever let me find out. There are times I'm short on patience. Marie and I are going to Vegas and be married on Wednesday. We leave here at ten this evening. Sam, Marie and I would like you and Judy to join us on Wednesday for our Vegas marriage. Marie's parents will also be in Vegas with us." Judy and Sam kept looking back and forth between themselves. "Travel and accommodations will be our treat."

Judy reached out and touched his arm long enough to stop him from talking for a second. "Stay here tonight and fly back to Vegas in the morning when you guys are well rested."

"We are meeting Marie's parent's tomorrow evening in Vegas."

Carmen turned the conversation back to business. "When may we utilize your system?"

"When Sam and Judy fly down for our wedding send three videos down with them. I'll try to fit time in my schedule so they can bring them back when they return to Seattle. If I can't get the videos finished in time I can mail the videos when they are finished."

"If Sam and Judy were to fly down tomorrow, you might have more time. Expanding my office will require additional expense." Carmen suggested. "A sudden cash flow would be very beneficial to me."

"I will try to help by enhancing videos soon as I can. While I make a call to my right hand gal in Vegas, Marie can jump on the computer and line up tickets for your flight to Vegas."

Soon Marie and Judy were online getting tickets. Once their task was complete Judy leaned over close and whispered in her ear. "Are you sure Brad is financially stable?"

"Financially he is fine. Equally important he is not asking anyone to do anything illegal. You have a verbal contract so there is no risk to you, Sam or Carmen."

"What about you, are you giving up a college degree to marry. If he goes broke where does that leave you?"

"I don't see him going broke. If something unusual were to happen, I would go back to college and finish my degree. You should see the Burger Palace. The business is a gold mine." Marie gave her friend a comforting hug. "The only thing bothering me, I'm going to miss you."

Monday afternoon Brad and Marie flew back to Vegas. "Will Sam and Judy be staying here in our suite or getting a room of their own when they fly down?"

"Oh dang, we should have called to get Sam and Judy a room like I did for your parents."

"Thank you, I was hoping you would say they would have a room of their own. Call me greedy but I want more private time with you." Marie soon learned the hotel was full. "Darn it, the hotel is full. Sam and Judy may wind up staying with us."

"It's fine by me if they stay with us long as you don't mind."

"We'll make do."

Brad met Sam and Judy as they arrived at the airport. "What a beautiful city, look at the size of these Casinos."

"Wait until you see Vegas after dark when it really shines. The hotel is full so you and Judy will be bunking in with us. This will be your room, private bath is that way. Marie is out shopping for a wedding dress. No telling when she might return. Why don't the two of you go scout around in the casino? We can buzz your cell when Marie returns."

"You don't mind if we just take off, and scout around on our own?"

"No not at all, go right ahead, there is a lot to see. Marie wants to take the two of you out to dinner this evening. Casual dress for dinner, she wants to show you and her parents our Burger Palace."

"Why don't you come with us and show us around?"

"I want to be available if Marie calls or her parents arrive. If you brought any videos I could start looking at your videos and making a few notes."

"You wanted four videos to enhance so we brought six in case there were a couple videos you didn't like."

"Good thinking, now scoot along and have fun."

Within minutes from Sam and Judy's departure the wedding shop called to get an okay on his credit card. Marie had picked out a six hundred dollar wedding dress. "Yes, Marie Richards has my permission to use my credit card. If there are any accessories she needs put them on the card too."

Twenty minutes later she called back. "I need to have the dress fitted. Can you continue entertaining Sam and Judy a while longer?"

"They are out doing the tourist thing. I haven't seen your parents yet. Can you call Judy's cell phone and tell her you are delayed until later this evening?"

"Alright, fix yourself a snack it may be eight before we eat at the Burger Palace. Mom and dad are driving here. They may have gotten delayed somewhere."

"Try not to worry about the time we will all survive until dinner."

Brad took his alone time allotted him to call and order a new car for ther bride to be. "We have exactly what you are looking for. One car is white and the other is silver."

"I'll take the white Camry it's a present for my new Bride. I'm getting married Wednesday."

CHAPTER 32

Judy and Sam were impressed as they ate at the Burger Palace. Although it was late Monday evening the Burger Palace flourished with business. "I never imagined a burger place this size being so busy on a Monday night. This is amazing. The menu alone blows me away. When Marie said you owned a gold mine, I thought she was a girl in love, and stretching things to make the place sound better."

"We try to have something for everyone. We need enough variety so our customers return often without having to eat the same food. We actually have construction workers in the area who eat here twice each day. Our office is upstairs behind those mirrors. This whole place is monitored for security reasons."

"The Burger Palace is more of a restaurant than a burger place." Sam commented.

Brad turned to his prospective bride. "Tell us about the wedding dress you bought."

"I can't talk about my dress nor will you see my dress before our wedding ceremony. The groom isn't supposed to know anything about the brides dress until she walks down the isle. Its bad luck if the groom sees the brides dress before the wedding."

"Heaven forbid Honey we certainly don't want any bad luck on our wedding day."

It soon became dark enough to enjoy the Vegas lights. The two couples strolled from casino to casino as they enjoyed the evening. Around two A.M. the four returned to the suite for a well deserved night of rest.

The following morning as Brad was still sleeping when his bed-mate slipped out to go pick up her dress and make certain it fit proper. Sam hustled down to the casino floor to try his hand at gambling. Judy took her time showering and dressing before going down to join Sam for a late breakfast. As they ate Marie called to ask Judy if she could wake her future husband before leaving the hotel. "I will be happy to check on him in a few minutes."

Brad was awake enough to hear footsteps coming near him. Thinking it was Marie returning to wake him he lay in waiting for her. As her soft hand touched his shoulder he grabbed a surprised Judy and pulled her down on top of him and planted a huge kiss on her lips. "Good morning Honey. Oh shit, I'm sorry, I thought you were Marie." Stunned Judy lay on top of him. Her eyes were huge as she stared at him.

She placed one hand over his mouth. "I know what you thought anyone could have made the same mistake. I should have called your name rather than touched you. Marie is one lucky girl if you kiss her like that very often." Only then did he become aware she was not pulling away. He could feel her heart beat against his chest. "I better leave so you can get up and dress." Still she was slow to move.

"I answered two calls for you this morning. One call was Wendy and the other from a Bob Tilly." After a few more seconds her body began to lift from his chest. "Sam and Marie are both out this morning. They won't know of our kiss."

"Please accept my sincere apology. I honestly thought it was Marie waking me I'm so sorry."

"Apology accepted and may I say your kiss was nice." Then she surprised him by leaning down again for a gentle kiss. "Now accept my apology."

She promptly exited the room leaving him in the state of confusion. This was his wedding eve not the day to be kissing other women. He took his time showering hoping Judy would go join Sam or Marie would return. Walking from the bedroom he saw her waiting still wearing her sexy smile. "I'm going down to join Sam now."

She spoke the words he wanted to hear. "Have fun, I'm off to the office to work on your videos. Your videos are very good I might add. We can all hook up later this evening for a nice dinner. Marie's parents will be joining us. The Orleans has a great prime rib dinner I think everyone will enjoy."

"We were impressed by the Burger Palace last night. I'm like the construction workers you spoke about. I could eat there most of the time."

"Here is a hundred dollars each, for you and Sam to gamble with today." Judy held up her hand as though was about to protest his offer. "Here go enjoy your day and I'll see you and Sam later."

In the office he enhanced the six videos in less than an hour. He put a tiny 'A' sticker on each video so he would know they were Anderson videos. Three of the videos were put in the safe. Wendy questioned his actions. "For now I don't want my agents realizing how fast I can enhance their videos. They might think I'm over-paid."

Wendy's next question caught him by surprise. "How soon before Carol needs to move?"

"Why would Carol move, I thought she was comfortable living in the apartment?"

"Bob Tilly came by saying he was ready to do the remodel on the apartment."

"Oh good heavens, I need to call Bob and tell him we changed our mind." He quickly dialed Bob. "Hey Buddy, sorry I didn't get back to you before now. My life is a zoo. I've changed my mind about remodeling the apartment. It is being used now so we'll leave it alone. Again, I apologize for not calling you. "

After the quick informative conversation with Bob, he turned his attention back to Wendy. "You tried calling me several times. Was there something else on your mind?"

"My hours, I can't continue working these seventy hour weeks. I'm dead tired every night. I can't keep this schedule up."

"No one expects you to put in seventy hours. We need to find you a helper. Once our wedding and honeymoon is over, Marie and I should be around more but our focus will be on our new business the Ad Palace. My suggestion would be for you to conduct an employment search to find the office help you want."

"I took the liberty to started searching for my office helper. Carol could help me. Carol already knows quite a bit about your subliminal messages system."

"How is her…"

She gasped putting one hand to her mouth. "…I forgot to tell you! Wendell Carpenter hung himself with a bed sheet in his cell. All the pressure is off Carol to testify and she is like a new person."

"Well I'll be damned our rapist friend cashed himself in. How convenient, I think that is wonderful. Brad comment before instantly turning the subject back to office help. "If you think Carol can handle our office duties, hire her. How is she getting along with Rusty?"

"She and Rusty are fine with one another. If you will permit them to do so, he would like to move in with her." Wendy's smiled showing her approval.

"If you are cool with them living together, it's fine by me."

Wendy looked at him in a questioning way. "I can't believe you had so little reaction to Carpenter's death. I thought you would be more excited."

"Why would I give a damn about him?" Brad asked with a smile. "He was a bad dude and needed to go. Carol is off the hook and good old Carpenter can no longer hurt another woman. It's the best ending one could expect." Brad's face showed a slight smirk and a gleam in his eye.

She spotted a gleam in his eye. "You, you had something to do with his demise. How could you, you were in Seattle?"

His face clouded over as he grew angry. "Do you think our fine Justice System would have done the right thing with the son-of-a-bitch?"

"You were in Seattle, how could you do anything from Seattle?" She asked again.

"What difference does it make who did what? He can't hurt women any more. The world is better off without him."

"My Lord Brad this is…"

"…This is Justice, what you sow so shall you reap. Violence breeds violence. The world is better off without individuals of this caliber. I took no pleasure in doing what needed done. Allowing Carol to testify could get you and me in big trouble. That wasn't going to happen."

"You knew my feelings on that bastard from the start. I could have killed him with my bare hands without giving my actions a second though."

"Then enough said. We'll not speak about him again."

"I agree. A woman by the name of Darlene Smith called several times wanting to talk to you."

"She is with the accounting firm I deal with in Seattle. She called my cell several times, I didn't answer. I'll call her, but I'm not dealing with her personally until after Marie and I are married. She and my attorney, Mr. Claymore, are doing the necessary paperwork for the Ad Palace. I suppose giving her a call now wouldn't hurt."

Wendy watched as he spoke to Darlene on the phone. Ending the call he pounded a fist on the desk. "Dang it all, my father is ill and nobody tells me anything except he has upped the flow of money to me. Hell, I already knew that. These people know things, but are not telling me a damn thing. I don't understand all this secrecy. When I get back to Seattle later this week I'm going to put some pressure on Bill Barrett, Al Claymore and this Darlene Smith because someone needs to be telling me something. If I can't find anything out I may need to go to Mexico and see father."

"If your father is ill, you should go to Mexico and visit him."

"How are you and Joe getting along?"

"About the same, we don't actually fight or anything like that. My only complaint is our marriage is dull. The intimacy in our lives is becoming less and less. We have been married twenty-two years. I hear other women say their marriage is revitalized once the children move out. Our marriage hasn't revitalized. Stagnate is how I would describe our relationship."

Robin Tilly paid a surprise visit to the office ending their conversation about Wendy's personal relationship with her husband. "Hello Brad, I was hoping to catch you. Your system of enhancing houses is working great I sold house number four."

"Congratulations Robin, you are quite a little go getter. I commend you on your hard work. You are blowing away all my predictions."

"What do you need to have your ad agency operational so I can sign an exclusive contract with you?"

"Our new business will be called the Ad Palace. To answer your next question we do not have the paperwork signed so we are not in business at this time. I believe Thursday or Friday will be the signing day. Far as a contract between you and our ad agency, all we need is a verbal agreement. If at some point if you become disenchanted with our arrangement you would be free to walk away. The second advantage is you would retain the ability to sell houses in the traditional way along with my enhanced method."

"Working without a contract is not a normal way to do business."

"I realize working without a contract is unheard of in today's world, but for ease and happiness of all parties. I believe its best we operate without a contract." He went on to explain the set up he wanted in Vegas.

His explanation caught Robin off guard. "You want me as a broker."

"Robin you are a very aggressive sales person therefore I believe you will make a fine Broker capable of handling two good agents working under you. I have faith in your ability."

"How soon do you need an answer from me?"

"I can easily give you a week or two Robin. I'm getting married tomorrow night. Then it's back to Seattle to sign the business papers and I should be back in Vegas by the first of next week."

"What about your honeymoon, newlyweds usually take a quick honeymoon?"

"Marie and I will have a delayed honeymoon. A quick marriage here in Vegas is so Marie will be co-owner at the start of the Ad Palace. Then in about a month we'll have a Wedding Ceremony near her parents before going to Hawaii for our honeymoon."

"Call me when you return and good luck on your marriage."

"Thank you Robin. I'm looking forward to our working together for many profitable years."

Eventually Marie arrived to join Brad for lunch. "I have one final fitting at three and I should be finished. I didn't realize choosing a wedding dress was so involved. What are Sam and Judy doing?"

"They are off to win themselves a casino. She said something about breaking the house as she left. I have a few more things to do this afternoon. Number one on my list is to get you some transportation. When you finish your dress fitting call me and we can run you down to pick up your new car."

"Why would we buy a new car, we have a second car in Seattle, I can drive the Seattle car."

"Honey that car is five going on six years old. You should get a new car. Our cars will be a tax write off through the business anyway. You may as well get a new car."

"If our transportation is a write off, I'll take a new car."

After her final fitting for her wedding dress she came back to the Burger Palace. "Marie, I know this week is a rush-rush busy-busy week. On Thursday or Friday before we go back to Seattle, can you find a little time to help Wendy?"

"I would be happy to help her if I can, what is it she needs?" Wendy looked at him and turned her hands palm up indicating she had no idea what he was referring to.

"She needs personal relationship help with her husband." Both ladies looked stunned. "She feels Joe and her closeness isn't strong as it should be. I started thinking about things she could do to improve the situation. Number one, check their house. See if there can be some non-expensive improvements to add comfort and intimacy to the house. Make the house more pleasurably than any place Joe stays while he is out on the road in his truck."

"I'll do what I can to help Wendy."

"An outside opinion might help Wendy. Who knows something simple as a Jacuzzi tub might help create an intimate area in the house. You girls work out the details. I can probably line up a small remodel through Bob Tilly if any changes are needed. A flat screen television in the Jacuzzi area might also be a nice starting point."

"I'll do anything I can to help, after my parents leave Vegas. Speaking of my parents, they will be here at five this evening."

During the drive over to pick up her new car Marie displayed her excitement. "I've never had a new car before." The salesman approached them. "Here you are Mr. Collins, the keys to your new car." Brad failed to accept the keys. "Is there a problem Mr. Collins?"

"No problem, the car is for my soon to be wife give her the keys." After writing a check for the car she drove off to the airport to pick up her parents.

Judy was waiting at the suite when Brad arrived home. "Hi, where is Marie?"

"She is picking up her parents at the airport. How was your day, did you win any money?"

"Gambling is not my thing I lost twenty dollars in the blink of an eye. Sam is doing okay. He gets up a few dollars and then down a few dollars. At least he gets to play on his money for a while. I walked around quite a bit today before coming back here for a nap. I was wondering where everyone was. Sam should be coming up in a few minutes."

"Darn had we known you were here, we could have had you come join Marie and me for lunch at the Burger Palace."

"My day was alright, I love watching people. The shops in the Mall here is fantastic to stroll through. The clothes are too expensive for me to purchase, but I love looking at them."

"We are happy you and Sam were able to come down and stand up for us at our wedding. It means a lot to both of us. I also know Marie feels bad not getting to spend the day with you. The dress fitting was more complicated than she originally thought."

"I've enjoyed my day and if you remember it started with a pleasant surprise." She gave him a sexy smile.

"Oh come on Judy, give me a break. I apologized for my idiot actions."

"I know you apologized, your sudden kiss startled me at first. Looking back it's funny. If the room had been dark, I may have been pregnant now."

"No, I wouldn't..."

"Oh come now, you had more than a good morning kiss on your mind when you grabbed me. You can't fool me. I know when a man is excited."

"Can we change the subject, how are Sam and you getting along?"

"We get along fine. Saturday evening he asked me to marry him."

Brad smiled as he nodded his head. "Well how about that and you said what?"

"I haven't given him my answer yet. I'm thinking about marrying him."

"Ouch, I doubt that was the answer he wanted to hear. I'm sure you had a reason for not giving him a quick answer."

"The way he proposed I wasn't prepared to give him an answer. Apparently he has a condition called low sperm count as a result of mumps two years ago. Marie and I talked many time about having our children grow up together the way she and I grew up. Sam is a nice guy. If I marry him our dream of having child near in age to you guys may be gone."

"I see, have you told Marie about his condition?"

"No, I didn't want to put a damper on your upcoming wedding. Of course there are other ways to acquire children. Adoption wouldn't be for me. There are so many unwanted crack babies today. I couldn't take a chance on getting a retarded child."

"I can't blame you for not wanting to raise a crack baby."

"There are various types of donor options I should check out. I'm sure all options are expensive and carry some risk with each process. In a way I wish your bedroom had been dark this morning. Then things might be different if I married Sam."

"Judy shame on you, you shouldn't say such a thing."

Marie called from the parking lot ending the strange conversation. She and her parents had arrived. "We will drop the luggage off at their room and be to our suite very soon. Is everyone else ready to go eat?"

"Honey, have their luggage taken to their room. The hotel has bellhops to move luggage about. See you in a couple minutes." He turned to see a sad looking Judy. Don't look so sad, I'm sure you will come up with an answer for your dilemma. Have you tried looking up Sam's problem on the internet?"

"I hadn't thought about looking on the internet. It's not a bad idea." She smiled briefly. "I might get lucky and find some valuable information."

Sam came charging in further disrupting their conversation same as Marie's phone call had earlier. "I lost my hundred dollars. It took me all day to lose my money, but I lost it."

Brad patted him on the back. "You are lucky to be alive. If Judy wasn't such a kind hearted individual she would have killed you by now. You bring a girl to Vegas and then ignore her when you get here."

Sam apologized for ignoring his wife all day. "I'll make it up to you tomorrow."

"It would have been better had we spent more time together. We still have a couple days in Vegas for you to redeem yourself."

Marie's parents entered the suite happy as two kids in a candy store. It had been twenty years since they were in Vegas. "The changes here in Vegas are amazing. We planned to drive to Vegas. I had an upset stomach delaying our departure so we flew here."

Brad quickly explained there was more going on in Vegas than a person could see in a month. "Do you need to rest or are we ready to go eat?"

"Susan and I are ready to go eat."

Brad's five dinner guests enjoyed the prime rib meal at the Orleans. "People I have reservations for the ten P.M. show at the MGM. I have no idea what the show consists of other than it is listed as an Adult Show. If you would like to see a big-time Vegas show, that's great. If you would rather go do something different, that's fine too. For that matter our group doesn't need to stay together. We can easily separate and do our own thing. Susan and Ray were agreeable to the show. Brad turned to Sam and Judy. "The show should be seventy five to ninety minutes in length."

"I had a nap Sam, watching the show and milling around later won't bother me at all." Judy wanted to see the stage production.

Sam agreed. "Lead the way people, off to the show we go."

The six person group enjoyed their first big-time Vegas production. The flashy costumes mixed with scantly clad men and topless women captivated the group for a full two hours. Susan patted Brad on the back. "The show you chose was racy but enjoyable, thank you very much. We may try to incorporate another show before we fly home. I can hope anyway."

"I've been busy since coming to Vegas this was my first show. I had no idea what to expect. I visualize in two months, we may have time to enjoy more big production shows here in Vegas."

After seeing the show Sam and Judy went their separate way while Ray and Susan strolled along the famous Vas Vegas Strip with Brad and Marie. The Volcano impressed her parents. "This city and all the lights is amazing."

"Walk on down this way and you can see the Battleships fighting."

"How far is it, will my legs hold out walking there and back?" Susan asked.

"We can walk far as you want. When your legs get tired we can taxi back to our hotel."

"Then let's go." Two full hours later Susan asked where the taxi was. "I've had enough sightseeing for tonight.

CHAPTER 33

After brunch at the Burger Palace the following day the Richards went daytime sightseeing. Marie planned to have her hair and nails done. Sam irritated Judy by reverting to his old ways and wanted to hit the Black Jack Tables. "You promised to escort me around today. The wedding is at eight, it's twelve now. You come with me until four. From four until six you can play Black Jack. We are eating this evening at six thirty at the Italian place here in Caesars. Then after the wedding you can escort me around again."

In their side of the suite Marie gave Brad a kiss before dashing off to the Hair Salon. "Okay Honey, I'll see you later. I'll be checking a few things at the Burger Palace and coming back to our room for a nap. Call me if you need anything."

Since Wendy was training Carol there wasn't anything Brad could do at the Burger Palace except kill time. "Hello ladies. How is the training going?"

"Carol is doing great she thinks everything here is pretty basic."

"I enjoy working in the office. The book keeping is standard and the computer switching is easy to follow. You have a well thought out plan using this set up. The messages to balance food sales and help people make their choices are a wonderful idea. When I'm eating out I hate getting stuck behind someone who doesn't know what they want. This is certainly a busy office."

"Ladies I have a big night coming up so I think I'll slip back to my suite for a lengthy nap."

"That's right you are getting married tonight. Enjoy your evening."

"Thank you Wendy I will enjoy my evening."

Back at his suite he kicked off his shoes and stretched out on the bed flat on his back to rest. Some stupid game show was playing on the afternoon television. He did not care what was on television long as there was a little background noise so every little sound wouldn't wake him. At four a touch on his shoulder did wake him. "Hi Judy I didn't grab you this time."

"No you didn't, you were very careful. Marie has been trying to call you."

He grabbed his phone. "Oh geez my phone is off. I never turned it on all day, how stupid can a person be?"

"She is running late, something about her hair being too kinky and had to be redone. She may be a few minutes late for dinner. She still wants to be with us for dinner."

"I better call her." He immediately punched Marie's number on his cell phone. "Hi Honey, I'm told you bumped into a problem. If it will help I can call and schedule our wedding at a later time. Say nine, to give you an extra two hours to get ready if you need the time."

"That would be wonderful, I would love more time. You are so considerate. I love you more than you will ever know."

"I love you too, I'll change our dinner reservation to seven then. Relax and don't worry Honey. Take all the time you need."

"That was sweet of you." Judy stated. "I'll call Sam and the Richards with the time change."

He was relieved to see Judy exit his bedroom. After what happened before he didn't know what to expect. He walked out to the center lounge area he kicked back with a diet soda to watch a movie. Judy soon joined him. "Mind if I watch the movie with you?"

"Of course not, have a seat. Make yourself comfortable."

"May I sit beside you, with any luck I might drift off for a short nap?" Before he could respond she was beside him with her head on a pillow next to his leg. "Sam walked my legs off last night, they feel like Jell-O." He couldn't help but stroke her pretty hair as she lay beside him. In a matter of minutes she was sound asleep. Brad wanted to ease away from here. For fear of waking Judy he remained sitting where he was.

When the movie ended he slipped away to shower and get ready for dinner. Sam returned to find Judy sleeping on the couch. He gently woke her. "Why are you napping out here? A bed would have been more comfortable for your nap?"

"I was tired, my legs were jumpy and I used the television to distract my restlessness. It's time we should be changing for dinner. I don't think Marie has returned yet, I hope things are alright with her." She barely got the words out of her mouth when Marie walked in. "Oh there you are. We were just talking about you."

"Hi guys, where is my husband to be?"

"I'm not sure, he may be dressing."

Marie found him shaving, "Be careful we don't need you bleeding all over the place."

"Hi Honey, your hair looks nice." He leaned over to kiss her. "Can I see your wedding dress now?"

"I told you before grooms are not allowed to see the bride's dress before the wedding. My dress is down at mother's room so you can't see my dress until I walk in later tonight at the wedding ceremony."

"That's an old wives tale. All that business about bad luck if I see the bride's wedding dress before the ceremony is a bunch of bunk."

"Try telling my mother your theory and she will pull your ear until you listen to her. I would prefer you didn't upset her. Not every day a mother gets to see her daughter getting married."

"Is this the correct shirt I'm supposed to wear later?"

"Yes, that is your shirt and your tie is on the hanger with the Tuxedo. Be careful you don't wrinkle your shirt before the ceremony. We'll have pictures taken after the ceremony."

"I hope my tie is one of those pre-knotted ties because I have no idea how to tie one of these strangling chokers. I might hang myself."

"Give me your tie, I'll show you how to tie the knot. Put it around your neck, cross over here. Will you stop kissing me? I'm trying to show you something. Up through there and back down here, it's that simple."

Again he kissed her. "For you tying a tie is simple, do you mind telling me where you learned to tie men's ties so fast?"

"I have a father and a younger brother. I helped them tie their ties."

"Their four dinner guests enjoyed dinner at the Italian restaurant while Marie and Brad picked at their food. "Nerves do funny things to people. You two look more like someone headed to a funeral than someone about to get married." Judy commented. "You need to take your own advice, stop and take a few deep breaths."

Marie tried the deep breathing trick. A few deep breaths did help. "I still can't eat this much food." She declared, "I might not fit in my dress, we spent hours getting my dress to fit perfect."

"Stop worrying and eat something, this is Vegas. If your dress doesn't fit you can always have a nude wedding." Judy remarked.

"Judy, my parents are here!"

"Your parents know I'm kidding. Eat a little bit of something or you may get queasy later." Ray and Susan did get a laugh out of Judy's nude wedding statement.

"This is sin city." Her mother pointed out with a grin. "You know what they say, what happens in Vegas stays in Vegas."

"Very funny mother, if you are finished eating it's time I started dressing." Marie kissed her man to be goodbye. "I'll see you in the Chapel babe."

He returned her kiss before she departed. In his room he shaved a second time. Checked his eyebrows to be certain a wild hair wasn't standing out, checked his fingernails, and drew in extra deep breaths for good measure.

In the Richards room after Marie was fully dressed in her beautiful white Wedding Gown, her father began taking pictures. "You look absolutely beautiful Honey. Your mother and I wish you many years of happiness."

"Thank you father, I love you."

Judy waited patiently for Brad to come out of the bedroom so she could check his tie while he continued to struggle trying to tie the necktie. Checking her watch she knew time was getting short. She finally went to the bedroom door and asked if he was having trouble with his necktie. "I can't tie this damn necktie, it doesn't look right."

She walked on into the room offering her help. I can't believe how nervous you are. Let's see now, about there, cross over here, down this way, up here and down through here. Nope too short, let's retie your tie again." She redid the tie three times before she was satisfied. "There you go and may I say you look very handsome this evening. It's tradition for the maid of honor to kiss the groom." She placed her arms about his neck and pulled him down to her level for a long generous kiss. "I love the smell of your cologne."

"You better stop kissing me before Sam comes in and pounds me to a frigging pulp. Sam still isn't sure what to make of me."

"Sam is down at the Blackjack Table and he won't move until we pick him up on our way to the chapel. He won a few dollars earlier today and believes he can win more."

Brad checked his watch. "The time is near, we should be going."

"When I mentioned a nude wedding earlier I was kidding you might want to put your pants on before you go down to the chapel."

"Oh shit!" He spun around, grabbed his pants, and slipped them on so fast he snagged his shirttail in the zipper. "Damn it, my zipper is caught."

She quickly stepped around in front of him. "Let me see, what did you do?"

"My shirttail is caught in my zipper." He tugged a tugged on the zipper without results.

"Hold still and relax, let me try and fix your zipper."

Faster than he could say no she was down front of him on her knees tugging his stuck zipper down. "Geez I hope no one walks in here."

"There your zipper is unstuck, try it again but be careful. That's it, now you look presentable." She patted the zipper flap. "Your zipper doesn't lay quite flat but its okay."

"You are a lifesaver girl. I'll return the favor someday."

"Helping me pass my real estate exam was a bigger favor than tying a tie and undoing a stuck zipper on your pants. I still owe you many thanks."

The actual wedding ceremony went flawless. The chapel was small but luxurious. Marie made a beautiful bride in her long white wedding gown and lacy vial. Ray took more photographs while a chapel worker took a video. All six retired to the lounge for a celebration drink. As if in a dream Brad sat daydreaming about being married, he again had family ties. If only his parents had not been such idiots they too cold have joined the celebration.

A new generation has begun his children will have parents and grandparents. Deep down he knew there was no need to give more than a little thought to his side of the family. He and Marie would never be close to his parents.

After a passion filled honeymoon night Marie woke wrapped in her new husband's arms. He immediately began massaging her shoulders. "Good morning Mrs. Collins." She snuggled in tighter against him. "You have made me the happiest man in the world, I love you now and I will love you forever."

He was rewarded for his words with a generous kiss. "I love you too."

"We need to go eat before I die of starvation. I have plans for us later. First we eat to keep our strength up then we come back to bed to start thinking about our family."

"Are you kidding me or do you really want a family this soon?"

"Children should have young active parents not the old cronies like I had. I saw the gleam in your parent's eyes. I'm betting they are ready for grandchildren."

"You naughty man, I love you. Sometimes you can be very persuasive."

"All I know is if we lay here talking we'll never have children." He began kissing Marie's lovely breasts ever so gently. "I love you."

Later they joined the others for a noon time brunch. Everyone was in a glorious mood until Judy told the story about his shirttail getting stuck in his zipper. Brad turned beat red while everyone laughed at him. To make matters worse Ray wanted a reenactment so he could take a picture. Everyone agreed with Ray and put pressure on Brad for the reenactment. Come on Honey be a sport, we need a picture for our family album." Can't you keep a secret?"

"Life is full of laughs and your zipper getting stuck was a good one. The look on your face was priceless, as I was kneeling in front of you trying to free your zipper. You kept glancing towards the door to make sure no one was coming in. Can you imagine what Marie would have thought if she had walked in while I was freeing your zipper?"

"I will get even with you for embarrassing me." Try as he might he could not relax and enjoy the reenactment. He wasn't use to being the butt of any joke. The more nervous and red faced he became the more the group laughed. "I may get even with all of you except Susan. She is more civil than the rest of you, she has class. Sam what is wrong with you, can't you hear the tables calling your name?"

"You want me to play cards and miss all this fun, no way."

Later when they were alone Marie was quick to compliment her husband. "I'm proud of you for not getting furious at us for the zipper reenactment. Two months ago you would have stormed off and been gone for a week."

"Who says I'm not furious. I have a policy to never kill people with witnesses around. It's taking all the will power I have to remain calm."

"Don't be mad at Judy she was only having fun." Marie sealed her words with a kiss. "Do you feel better now?"

"It will take more than one kiss to make me feel better. Any other day you might not want to count on me being in such a generous mood."

"Maybe we girls have broken your spirit."

"If you broke my spirit then you are married a wimp not a man. I'm starting a training workout tomorrow."

"You are wrong. I married a considerate kindhearted man. A man I will love forever." She accented her point with a second more generous kiss.

"You owe me a lot of loving to make up for my embarrassment. Making me reenact my most embarrassing moment of my life was cruel."

For their late evening dinner it was a foursome, Brad, Marie and the Richards. Sam and Judy decided to go their own way for the evening. "It's nice of Sam to finally spend time with Judy. I was beginning to wonder about the two of them."

As the four ate dinner, a conversation came up about Brad's parents. "Too bad my parents are not more sociable. They could have shared in our joy. Expecting anything beyond money from my parents would be ridiculous."

Marie's father touched Brad's arm. "Marie says your father may be in poor health. That is unfortunate. We hope he gets better soon. Do you know what is wrong with your father?"

"I've not been told anything about my father's health. I have considered going to visit my father many times. So far he hasn't allowed me to visit him. It's been a long time since I've spoken to him on the phone. It's been five years since I've seen him on person." When speaking about his parents Brad looked sad.

"It's your mother I don't understand." Susan shook her head in disgust. "How can any mother not want to be at her son's wedding?"

"Susan, I did not even bother inviting my mother to our wedding. She told me her reasons for not being in my life more. I still think with a little effort and possibly some medication she could have raised me. She chose not to be a proper parent."

"After all these years your parents may never change."

"I hate discussing my parents. I would rather talk about our wedding ceremony near your house. I'm leaving all those plans to Marie. Date and time is her choice. All I want is a two week honeymoon in Hawaii. She can make those plans too."

On Thursday after Ray and Susan left. Brad, Marie, Judy and Sam all boarded a plane for Seattle. "I hope our attorney and accountant have our paperwork ready I can't afford to be in Seattle long. Marie might duck over and stay with her parents and work on our real wedding plans a few days when I head back to Vegas."

"Before we forget, Sam and I would like to thank you for the enhanced videos. We have a question."

"Fire away Judy, I'm all ears."

"What are you planning to do with your Seattle home?"

"Interesting you should ask. We haven't given the house much thought. We shouldn't need the house much longer. At the same time we have enough going on at one time. I don't want to deal with the house until later. How would it be if you and Sam continue living in the house for the next six months or so while we decide what we want to do with the house?"

"Our continuing to live there for the time being would be nice. It would give us time to build up our savings for when we begin looking for our own house."

The following morning Marie was all smiles as she walked into the accountant's office beside her husband. Introductions were made and business took center stage. "You haven't been answering my calls. I tried telling you by phone your father has upped his contributions a second time to your accounts. He also sent a note to you."

Darlene Smith paused while he read the note. "My father certainly does things differently. He say's congratulations on our marriage, and wishes us many happy years together. I'm surprised father acknowledged our marriage at all. Shit, this note was mailed here in Seattle. Bill Barrett or Judy set us this note."

Marie shook her head. "Your father is a different sort of man. I'm disappointed in him but for some strange reason I can't wait to meet him."

"Darlene gathered her thoughts. Getting back to business your complete portfolio looks good. You are showing a steady increase in net worth each month. Because of interest rates and different things it would be very difficult to say you are worth exactly this much today this minute. You have the value of your Seattle home, the Burger Palace in Las Vegas and the considerable amount of cash on hand. Al Claymore sent me a copy of your prenuptial agreement."

Marie nodded her head. "Claymore told us you would get a copy of our prenuptial agreement."

"The fifteen percent Document you signed is a very standard prenuptial agreement. With you now married it made you an instant millionaire when you said I do. The fifteen percent today is worth approximately one point two million." Marie's head wobbled enough to draw Darlene's attention. "Are you okay Marie?"

Brad looked around fast enough to catch his new bride as she toppled over. "Whoa Honey." He eased her to the floor. "Get a cool washcloth or damp paper towel. I think she fainted."

Marie was slow to come around. "What happened, why am I sitting on the floor?" She moved to try to get up. Still wobbly she remained sitting as she waited for her head to clear.

"Honey, you pass out." Her eyes were glassy as she tried to regain her focus. "I think you fainted. You toppled over in my arms, and I eased you to the floor. Sit still until your body stabilizes."

"I think I'm okay." With Brad's help she started to get up.

"Try sitting up sweetheart before you try to stand up. Here let me help you. Stop there for a few seconds we don't need you passing out again. You scared us."

"I feel stupid sitting on the floor?" He helped Marie to her chair. "You may let go now, I'm okay. I'll catch my breath and be okay."

"Humor me Honey and sit near me. If you pass out again I want you close enough I can catch you again."

"As I was saying your personal estate is increasing in wealth by leaps and bounds. Totaling over eight million plus the Burger Palace, your Seattle home and the new business you are about to start. I have no basis to put a value on your advertising agency. If you're past history means anything the business could be worth an additional million, for a total wealth near ten million dollars."

"All we ask Ms. Smith is you keep us out of any tax problems. We have the ability to make money. The ability we lack is filling out tax papers properly and on time. I think tax problems are what led my father to flee the country. Once you get behind on taxes to the point penalties kick in, the Government can break a person no matter what they have."

"We have a fine staff of accountants here at our firm. I'm not the only one watching your account. If I remember correctly from my conversation with Al Claymore you are working on new Wills. Sounds to me you are doing everything right. Treat your marriage the same way you do your business. Work at your relationship on a daily basis. Don't neglect your day to day lives."

"If there is nothing else Miss Smith we should be moving on to Mr. Claymore's office. He should have our business papers and our Wills ready to sign."

Out by the rental car Marie slapped his shoulder. "Why didn't you tell me how much money you were worth?" She questioned. "You allowed me to walk in there and get the shock of my life. How could I not help but pass out?"

"I had no idea what my net worth was. The ten million plus dollar figure was a surprise to me too. I was expecting four at the most. Judy and Sam were ribbing us about me having two million. Think what people might say if they know the true number."

"I can't phantom having millions of dollars. It blows me away."

"Nothing has changed we are the same people now as we were walking in the accountant's office. Long as we live a normal life we can do anything any normal family would do."

"I feel people are staring at us. Do we look that different now?"

"We do not look different. We better be moving on to our appointment."

Being a sharp, competent attorney, Mr. Claymore had their papers ready to sign. In two minutes the signatures were completed. "Congratulations Mr. and Mrs. Collins you are officially in the advertising business and your Wills are complete."

"We still need the local business license for the Ad Palace in Vegas before we can operate. At any rate we thank you for your help Mr. Claymore. We appreciate your timely work on our behalf."

By mid-afternoon they were back at the Seattle house. "Mrs. Collins would you care for a little hot tub adventure before a bedroom rendezvous?"

"I want it all. We won't be at this house often in the future. We should hot tub first. We have plenty of time before Sam and Judy come home. Let's use our time wisely."

"Your wish is my command." He winked and kissed her as he gently massaged her breast.

Three hours later Judy and Sam were in a glorious mood when they arrived home. "Sam's mother called with good news. We have two nibbles on the enhanced houses." She stated with pride. "She thinks these are serious buyers. Sam and I have our fingers crossed."

Sam quickly corrected her. "Prospective clients Honey, not nibbles, you need to learn the lingo. We are professionals and must act professional at all times, or we could slip up in front of a client."

"Come morning Marie and I will be out of your hair. She is going to her parent's house to start planning our official wedding ceremony while

I return to Vegas and get our business license. We must operate legally. Sam is there any chance you could get another set of house videos to take with me to Vegas?"

"I could have three maybe four houses videos picked out by ten tomorrow."

"I could hang around until you get the videos ready for me. Marie is leaving early. I don't need to be in the office until Wednesday morning. Honey, tell your little friend here what happened at our accountant's office today."

"I was so embarrassed. First off the office was warm and I had a sweater on. It was breezy when we left the house so I put on a sweater. To make a long story short, I fainted. I felt stupid lying on the floor. For the longest time they wouldn't let me get up."

"Marie, you never faint, what is going on?"

"I stepped into Brad's stressful tornado lifestyle that's what. Everybody but everybody wants some of our time. We were hounded all day long. We never had a moments rest until late afternoon."

"Not being used to Brad's fast paced life you need to be careful. Don't go get yourself run down so you get sick."

"Realizing we needed more rest we came back here for a long nap late this afternoon. We have so many things to take care of it is mind-boggling. I now know what Brad means when he says he is busy."

Brad added his thoughts. "One thing we would like to do is give you the car we have here in Seattle. We no longer need the car. We can't sell the car without creating ourselves a tax problem. We discussed giving you the car with our accountant." Marie went on to explain. "Giving our car away is the best option we have."

"Thank you, a car of my own will help me succeed in selling houses."

CHAPTER 34

The following day Marie flew off to her parent's house while Brad remained at the house waiting for Sam's videos. Judy was the messenger who brought six videos to him. "I can't thank you enough for all you are doing for Sam and me."

"No thanks necessary. It's more of a case we are all helping one another. Are you leaning towards marrying Sam yet?"

"I already told you I would marry him in a minute, if I knew for sure we could have children. I've seen him around his nieces. I know he would make a wonderful father. I also know Sam can't impregnate me because I stopped taking my birth control pills a month age. Marrying Sam would be a huge problem for me to handle. I would be giving up part of the life I so badly desire. I'm torn as to what I should do."

"You only live once girl, take a chance. Marry the man. Do the internet thing to find out how to increase your odds of getting pregnant. There are ways to solve your problem. All you need is to search them out."

"I checked two sites on the internet that were of no help. Now you and Marie have forced the issue and making me get pregnant fast if I want a child near your child's age."

"Whoa, slow down Judy. You are making no sense. You don't know how soon Marie and I will have children. We want to have two children, but we may wait a couples years before we start our family."

"Oh come on, you have to be joking. Marie has never fainted in her life. I'm betting she is pregnant now." His face went blank. "Think about it, she isn't real chipper in the morning, tired throughout the day and now she has fainted."

"Holly shit, are you sure about this, could she be pregnant?"

"Get real Brad, it all adds up. You and she have been doing more than playing footsie in the bedroom. Good things happen when newlyweds are enjoying themselves."

"Did Marie say anything to you about her possibly being pregnant?"

"She didn't have to say anything, look at her face her cheeks were flushed, she fainted, what more do you need than an Early Pregnancy Test Kit."

"Holly geez I should call her, but what do I say?"

"How about saying you are concerned about her fainting and then ask if she could possibly be pregnant. Usually asking straight out is the best way to find things out."

"Call me stupid. I thought she fainted because our accountant told her we were worth ten million dollars. I never thought she might be pregnant."

"You are worth ten million dollars! Oh my stars, maybe she isn't pregnant. A shock of that type could floor anyone. We were thinking your net worth around two million dollars at the most."

"I knew she was thinking I was worth two million dollars. It didn't matter because we married for love, not money. Money shouldn't mean anything. We will lead a comfortable life and be great parents for our children."

"No Brad, that kind of money means something. If I had several million dollars I wouldn't worry about getting pregnant. I could afford every procedure known to mankind."

"If you love Sam and believe he will be a good father for your children, marry him. You will be making good money very soon. The options concerning you now might not seem quite so expensive in the future. Do you really think there could be an outside chance Marie could be pregnant?"

"I'm not as sure as I once was. Of course she could be pregnant. That morning I woke you and you grabbed me. I wish it had been dark that morning, I might also be pregnant. Your little soldier was ready for action. I could feel him nudging at my core."

He gave her a strange look. "You shouldn't be saying such things. I don't know if I should wait here to call Marie, or call her this evening after I get home?"

"Waiting here would be best. You have time to kill while you are waiting how about you and me discussing how you might help me attain my goal of having children."

"What more can I do for you now?" She smiled at him. "If its money you need, tell me what you need and you got it."

"It isn't money I need. You have the ability to help me get pregnant. Better yet if the wrong people where to find out. You could do your memory block thing to smooth things over. The risk of doing any permanent damage to our marriages would be zero. Otherwise I can't marry Sam."

"Slow down Judy." He shook his head no. "You can't be serious. I can't impregnate you, it wouldn't be right. This can't happen."

"You and Marie both have had relationships before. You would be doing all us a big favor, Marie included. We want our children near the same age so they can grow up playing together. I know if I were to become pregnant Marie would be pleased. Think about the joy in your life if you had children your age around you when you grew up."

"We live in different states eleven hundred miles or more apart. How much playing together can our children do?"

"We are interlocked by business. The four of us Sam and me, you and Marie along with our children could vacation together each year. Our children could see one another six or eight times a year. As they get older our children could visit the other for a week at a time perhaps. Life would be perfect for all parties concerned."

He and Judy kept conversing about him helping her until he checked his watch. "I think Marie's airplane should be on the ground now. I better call her." Marie answered her phone on the second ring. "Hi Honey did you have a good flight?"

"My flight was smooth as glass. I wasn't expecting you to call until later this evening. Where are you calling from?"

"I'm still in Seattle. Judy is standing beside me. My real reason for calling is because of your crazy little friend is concerned about you fainting. She thinks you could be pregnant." There was nothing but silence on the phone. "Honey, Honey, did I lose you? Marie, are you there?"

"Let me pull over to the roadside." He listened as the car engine stopped. "Okay, now I can talk. What exactly did she say?"

"I'll let you talk to Judy. The little rat is standing beside me grinning like a monkey eating a banana."

The girls talked a good twenty minutes while he paced the floor. "Here you go Brad she wants to speak with you again."

After a brief discussion Marie announced she would get one of the EPT test kits. She indicated she would try to move the wedding ceremony up two weeks. "Don't worry about moving the wedding ceremony up we are married."

"I'll get a EPT test kit, and call you tomorrow."

"Bye Honey, I love you." Putting his phone away he stood looking a Judy. "Damn life changes in a hurry. I thought my life was busy before. If Marie is pregnant I'll need time to help care for her."

"Marie mentioned an upset stomach a few mornings ago. She could easily be a month along, meaning I'm a month behind." Small tears rolled down her cheeks. "I envy the two of you. Please reconsider helping me."

"Judy, I need time to think your proposal over. I will see you and Sam before long at our wedding ceremony. That will give me time to ponder if I should get involved in this hair-brained scheme of yours or not."

"Be reasonable, we shouldn't wait. How could we get together with so many people around for your wedding?" The tone of her voice was almost begging. "Once you leave here you won't give my dilemma a second though." More small tears began to trickle down her pretty cheeks.

"Please stop crying." He felt compelled to comfort Judy by holding her tight to his chest. "Would there ever be a safe time to do what you are requesting?" She nodded yes. "Sam could come home any second for lunch. I tell you what you are proposing is crazy."

"Sam has a lunch meeting. Two houses to video this afternoon and at six P.M. we show a house this evening. He won't be coming home early."

He could feel her heart beating against his chest. "I must be crazy for going along with your idea." Without further discussion he led Judy to the rear bedroom and began undressing her. "I must say you are a vision of beauty." He spent the next three hours making love and pleasuring her. "It's time I showered and drive to the airport. I hope your wish has been granted. We can maybe work out another time if necessary. My attorney and accountant are both here in Seattle. Marie did say I should keep a closer eye on my finances."

Brad took the liberty of kissing her goodbye and started to slip off to catch his plane to Vegas. She took the liberty of holding him back for a brief moment. "Thank you for being so considerate. I was expecting to have nothing but quick sex. We wound up making love, you are a true friend. When I get pregnant Sam will be thrilled."

He smiled. "I'll be honest with you. I received much as I gave from our love making. Now I must leave, I have a plane to catch. What we did is a secret we'll need to carry to our grave."

He waited for Marie's call the following morning. Her call came well after lunch. "Hi, I've been busy with a wedding planner most of the morning. Since we are in a family way, I decided it would be easier on me if someone else carried part of the load and did the leg work for me."

"Did I hear you correctly, you are pregnant?"

"You heard me correctly we are in the family way. What do you think papa, are you happy?"

"I think you have made me the happiest man ever, and I think you are smart to hire a wedding planner. Do your parents know you are pregnant?"

"I told my parents my EPT test was positive and they are thrilled."

"That's a relief I thought maybe your father might hang me by the gonads from a tallest tree in his back yard. This happened sooner than planned. Don't get me wrong, I'm thrilled."

"I'll see a doctor when I get back to Vegas in a few days. Our ceremony will still be on the small side. A hundred fifty people at the most."

"Spare no cost it's a once in a lifetime ceremony for both of us."

"A small and intimate wedding is what I always dreamed about."

"Go for it Honey. Wendy has a stack of papers for me to look at so I better get busy. Bye Honey, I love you. You might give your nosy little friend a call and tell her you are pregnant, you know how she loves gossip."

In a matter of days Marie returned to Vegas. The wedding ceremony was set for the third weekend away. In the meantime she mixed in with her work schedule, time to study Wendy's declining relationship problem. The two women withheld information from Brad about what they were planning to do, making him irritated at times.

"I don't understand why I come up with a good idea concerning Wendy and her husband. Yet you won't tell me how things are going or what you are doing. All I know is we are making Wendy a personal no interest loan to do something."

"We are creating a romantic play area. All other suggestions are not for you and Wendy to discuss. Since her sex life is none of your business you should keep enhancing videos. We girls will handle our ideas."

"Let me see if I have this correct. Wendy's sex life is your business but not mine. Honey sometimes you are no fun at all. Are you ladies forgetting this was my original idea in the beginning?"

"If you wanted to know about everyone's sex life you should have stayed in college and became a sex therapist."

"Now you suggest I become a sex therapist. Why didn't you suggest your sex therapist idea when I was in college? I may have concentrated in class more."

"For starters it never crossed my mind you were such a pervert."

"I'm not all bad. While we are on the subject of college we could after our honeymoon start taking internet classes and get our degrees. It would take time to finish our degrees but who cares. We have a lifetime ahead of us."

"I swear you are brilliant at times, what a great idea." She couldn't help but hug her husband. "My parents would love it if we were able to finish our business degrees."

"Did you have time to work on our honeymoon plans?"

"Indeed I have, we leave two days after our wedding ceremony in Oregon for two weeks of relaxation and fun in Hawaii. We'll bask in the mild sun, swim in the surf and have a wonderful time, if we ever get out of bed."

"Nice work Honey. A two-day pause would give us time to catch our breath before dashing off to Hawaii. I'll start calling in extra houses to enhance so people can continue working while we are gone."

Wendy interrupted the conversation. "Hey guys I almost forgot to ask. Are you by chance looking for a house to buy?"

Her question caught them off guard. "I don't know Wendy, we have been busy. We have little time for discussing where we will live. You are right to suggest we get a house, a baby can't live in a hotel."

Wendy's eyes lit up. "Marie, Are you pregnant?"

"Yes, I thought you knew I was pregnant. Brad can't keep anything to himself. I was certain he had told you or I would have told you myself."

"How far along are you?" Wendy seemed as excited as Marie.

"One month the doctor thinks."

"How wonderful, the two of you will make great parents. Having a baby will bond your family closer than you will ever imagine."

"My girlfriend in Seattle, the one you met when she was here. She and her boyfriend Sam were married last Wednesday. Their marriage sort of surprised me. They talked about marriage for some time. Sam isn't sure he can have children. She wants children in the worst way same as we do. I'm assuming they worked out some kind of deal if he can't impregnate her they will adopt or something. We talked about wanting our children to be life-long friends same as she and I have been all these years."

Wendy smiled and patted her hand. "Your dream of the perfect life is happening before your eyes."

"I am enjoying life to the fullest. Brad is spoiling me rotten though. Living in our suite everything is being done for us. No dishes, no laundry, no beds to make, life couldn't be better. By the time we move to a house I won't want to do anything in the line of housework."

"You will be fine Brad insisted. Having our own house will have many advantages. One advantage is we will have more room. Don't worry about the housework we will have domestic help for you, even a nanny for the baby. The difference is we will be there as parents the nanny will only be our helper not the sole caretaker."

"I don't mean to keep interrupting you but Joe's boss is talking about down sizing. He is planning to retire and turning the daily operations over to his son. They have a beautiful home. A home you might be interested in taking a look at. The house sits on a six-acre site not far from the city, a fifteen minute drive at the most."

Brad's eyes lit up. "We would be happy to look at any house. I naturally assumed we would opt for a new home. As Marie said we haven't discussed anything about the house we want. We have no reason to look at houses until after our honeymoon is over. We must honeymoon while Marie can still fly."

"I believe it will be two or three months before the Carson's are ready to move. The house was built four years ago. A very lovely home by anyone's standard. Well beyond what the average person can afford."

"Marie and I have been avoiding making a decision on our Seattle home. I'm thinking we should finance a more moderate home with a no interest loan for Sam and Judy and sell our big house."

Marie liked hearing Brad suggest a no interest load for her friend and her husband. "I don't think they would mind moving with an offer to help them buy house."

Over the following days the newlyweds began to gain control of their lives. The only hitch was the Ad Palace being in the same office as the Burger Palace there was no separation of the businesses. Having any type of private conversation was impossible. "Our office set up isn't working well. We need a separate office for the Ad Palace. I wonder if Robin would want to join together on an office. We could own the building and she pay the interior maintenance. Her expense could be shared among the other agents or however she wanted to handle it. Honey can you call Robin, and set a dinner meeting up with her and Bob. She can think things over our proposal while we are on our honeymoon. Nothing has to be decided immediately. It would be nice if our two offices were not that far apart."

"I better call now because in three days and we are out of here and on our way to get married again. We don't have time to waste."

"I'm thrilled everything is running smooth. Wendy can handle our two businesses while we are gone. We've laid in a good supply of enhanced videos. All she has to do is spread them out over the days we are gone."

"I'm so excited about having our wedding ceremony and going to Hawaii. Unless you need me here in Vegas, I was thinking I should fly up to check on our last minute wedding plans."

"By all means fly to your parent's house if you are concerned about anything. It never hurts to double check we don't need a hitch in our wedding plans."

"There is one more thing I need to mention. When you fly up for our wedding you will need a hotel room so you have somewhere to dress. Remember how it was in Vegas, the groom isn't supposed to see the Bride before the wedding."

"Honey I've seen you in your wedding dress."

"I want our wedding ceremony to feel authentic the way a church wedding should feel, pure and refreshing."

"I suppose I'll be sleeping in the hotel alone for one night."

CHAPTER 35

Brad flew to Oregon one day early for the wedding rehearsal and checked into the hotel. Once there he promptly called Marie to inform her of his arrival and ask how the wedding plans were progressing. "We girls are working on the bridesmaids dresses. Daddy, Ronnie and Sam are all golfing this evening. At nine we are meeting at the church for the wedding rehearsal. Please don't be late."

"Whoa slow down, I do not know the name of the church or where the church is located."

"Relax, I'll send one of the guys over to pick you up."

"Alright, see you later. Bye, I love you."

He found himself alone while everyone else was enjoying the pre-wedding preparations. This was supposed to be a joyous time for him too. His being alone didn't seem right. Around seven he went down to eat. In the hotel restaurant he was the only person eating alone. After a quick stop for reading material he strolled back to his lonely room. Stepping through the door his phone rang. "What's your room number Hon?"

"I'm in room three twelve."

"Thank you someone will be by and pick you up in a few minutes for our rehearsal." Marie cut him off before he could respond.

The book he chose to read didn't help. The book couldn't hold his attention. A loud knock on his room door caused him to jump. Going to the door he checked his watch. A little early for his ride but maybe someone came early. Opening the door he found the smiling friendly face of Judy. "I thought you girls were working on dresses this evening,"

"My dress is finished. Your lovely wife sent me to get you." She gave him a small hug.

"Where is Sam, I thought he would come after me?"

"The boy's golf game is running late, so I came to get you for the wedding rehearsal, are you ready?"

"Ready as I'll ever be. I'm almost afraid to ask how you've been since we last met."

"I have been excellent, no regrets what-so-ever. I hope you are not having second thoughts about helping me get pregnant."

"I have a twinge of guilt about keeping a secret from Marie. I keep thinking if she knew your complete situation she would understand. Who knows, she may have suggested I furnish the product for your needs. It's the delivery system she wouldn't like."

"I'm glad you saw my position and understood my limited choices. I can't afford any other delivery system. You are my only hope for a sudden pregnancy."

"I realized your dilemma. I worry what might happen, because I become attached to the opposite gender very easy. We must be super careful."

"Please don't feel guilty. Did you bring all the clothes you need for tomorrow?" Judy asked.

"I think so. Marie packed most of my things before she left for her parent's house."

"Marie asked if I would check your clothes to be certain you had everything you need. "Do you have your Tux, shirt, tie, socks, shoes, tie clasp and cuff links?"

"I have all those things and underwear too."

"May I see your cuff links?" She followed him to his suitcase. "Slide them inside your folded socks."

Brad gave her a sly grin. "I know that look, what are you up to young lady?"

"Follow my lead this evening if my plan goes right you will find out. There are way too many people at the house. They are all trying to give Marie advice. There good intentions are making Marie nervous."

"That is not what I wanted to hear. How is Mrs. Richards holding up?"

"She is great and I will give her credit, she is a smart lady. Susan sent the guys golfing to get them out of the way. Then she sends part of the ladies out on meaningless errands. She is doing everything possible to protect her daughter."

At the church he saw a glimpse of what Judy was talking about earlier. "Honey how can you stand this, can we leave for our honeymoon tonight?"

"If we left for Hawaii tonight we would be sleeping on the beach. There are no rooms available for three days in the area I chose."

"The weather is mild in Hawaii. Sleeping on the beach with you would be better than my sleeping alone in my hotel room. I keep telling myself in twenty four hours this will all be over. We'll move on and practice for our honeymoon." He sealed his words with a kiss.

"People are testing my nerves, here we are at the rehearsal and no guys except you. What's wrong with people today, why can't they be on time?"

"Take a breath deep and try to relax. The guys should be arriving any minute. If you want real relaxation come back to my hotel room with me later."

"You know I can't be with you tonight. I want our wedding to feel genuine."

The guys came stumbling in twenty minutes late and glassy eyed. Their golf game appeared to have stalled out at the nineteenth hole. Unknown to Brad and Marie, Mrs. Richards had called her husband telling him not to come back early because there was so much going on at the house. The actual rehearsal took a half hour. Again he turned back to his wife. "Are you sure you don't want to come back to the hotel with me tonight?"

"I can't stay at the hotel tonight. We have a few things to finish. I'll be lucky to be in bed by midnight. Judy can run you back to the hotel. The guys have been nipping the sauce. I don't need you riding with people who have been drinking. I want you here in one piece tomorrow. All the guys but you will have a headache in the morning."

Judy reached out and touched her arm. "Pardon me but while we were checking Brad's wardrobe for tomorrow we couldn't find his cufflinks. He and I can drop Sam by our room. Then I'll run Brad by the Mall and see if we can find one of the jewelry stores open."

"Thank you Judy." Brad and Marie kissed goodnight as they parted. "See you tomorrow Honey."

Driving back to the hotel he couldn't help but study Judy's actions. She was one smooth operator. He waited in the car while she escorted Sam to their hotel room on the first floor. She soon returned and motioned for him to get out of the car. "Pretty slick how you bought us some time together this evening."

"Do you mind spending time with me? I can be the entertainment at your bachelor party?"

Secretly he wished Marie was with him. Hand in hand they walk to his room. A few generous kisses ignited the secret lovers into the throws of passion. Slow gentle sensuous lovemaking consumed their bodies. "I better shower before I leave. Sam might sober up enough to miss me."

Brad helped dry her gorgeous body. "Thank you I wish Sam had your talent as a lover. Sam will sleep off his excess alcohol by morning. I will swing by and pick you up tomorrow evening, be ready at six."

"You were very comforting to me this evening. I dislike being alone and I do hope I will be successful in my services to you." Brad suddenly thought about his father. He had often cursed his father thinking about the life his father led. He was reasonably certain his father led a life of taking women anywhere any time. After becoming involved with Judy he now understood how his father may not have wanted to be alone either. He also thought about his father's words. "Your real test will be when the next temptation is standing before you."

The following day Judy helped tie his tie as they prepared to leave the hotel. "We must hurry Sam is waiting in the car for us. You did well this time. You didn't get your shirt caught in your zipper today."

"I suppose everyone at the house knows about that story by now."

"Oh yes, Ray was passing the pictures around."

"Oh great, now people think I'm a dork. Let's go before Sam drives off without us."

In the parking lot at the church Brad's cell phone rang. "You guys go ahead I'll only be a minute." The call came as a complete shock. Brad's father had passed away. "My father dead, what happened?"

"John passed away night before last at two A.M. I have few details at this time. You knew his health was deteriorating. He passed away quickly."

"Was mother with my father or was he alone when he passed away?"

"No your mother wasn't with John when he passed away. I thought you had been told your mother passed away some eight months ago. Didn't your father call you?"

"Damn it Bill, I thought you were my man. What the hell have you been doing? You weren't telling me the things I should have been told. Where and when is father's funeral?"

"Your father requested no services are to be held. His body will be cremated and his ashes spread at sea. More than likely his wishes have already been carried out. I'm sorry to be the bearer of bad news."

"I can't believe this, mother and father both gone. I wish someone would have kept me clued in better. I could have gone and saw my father."

"I was only a go between following orders from the people near your father. This is when I was told to call you."

"What did my father die from, for that matter what did mother die from?"

"Your parents were elderly and a person's health declines as they get older. No specifics were given to me as to the cause of death for either of your parents."

He looked up in time to see Judy walking towards him. "I have a feeling you know more than you are telling me. Very soon you and I need to have a serious talk, a long serious talk."

Brad motioned for Judy to stop. "I'm sorry I can only pass on the information I'm told to pass on. On Monday get with your Attorney, Mr. Claymore. Between Claymore and Darlene Smith you will have a mountain of legal work to do in the coming weeks."

"Damn it all. Alright, don't be surprised if I call you a few times with questions." Angry disgusted and teary eyed he flipped his phone shut. Then opened the phone long enough to turn the phone off. "I should have turned the phone off an hour ago."

Judy realized his call had been bad news. "Are you alright?" She asked with concern.

"I'll be alright. I'm holding up our wedding?"

"They are ready for you. My question is are you ready for the ceremony?"

"Do me a favor and go back inside, and ask people to give me a half hour to gather myself up." He wiped small tears from his eyes. "See if you can find a damp paper towel for my eyes."

"I'm not sure what is bothering you, but don't you dare go anywhere. I'll be right back." In her absence he used his deep breath routine to compose his thoughts. In a flash she returned with the damp towel he requested. "Am I at fault, has someone found out about our affair?"

"No one knows what we have been doing. I would never allow anyone to blackmail me. I would kill them first. My call brought news I wasn't prepared for today. Nothing you need to know about right now. Give me a chance to get a few more deep breaths and I'll be ready to go inside and get married."

"Something rocked you hard, are you sure it's alright to proceed with the wedding ceremony at this time?"

"Telling people about my call now would serve no valuable purpose."

The half hour delay sent Marie's nerves on edge. She couldn't understand why Brad wanted a short delay. "Mother, something is very wrong. This isn't like Brad. He never is late for anything. I'm scared something is wrong."

"Just relax Honey. He asked for a short delay. Maybe he broke a shoestring or got his zipper stuck again."

The peach and white church decorations were fantastic. A red carpet runner lay in the isle. The Bride wore the same beautiful white dress as she wore in Vegas. Having more friends and relatives around magnified the wedding procedure into beautiful exciting event. All eyes were glued on Marie as she walked down the isle wearing her long flowing white wedding dress. She was a vision of beauty. With pride Mr. Richards gave his daughter's hand in marriage. Everyone with the exception of Brad, Marie and Judy were having a wonderful time. Both girls were concerned knowing something was amiss where Brad was concerned.

Between the wedding ceremony and the reception pictures were taken. Marie and Brad created another delay as they lagged behind going to the reception area. "What's going on with you today?"

"I left my cell phone on too damn long. A disturbing call came just as I was about to enter the church, my father passed away."

"Oh good heavens, no wonder you are in such a down mood. You should have told me your father died. We could have postponed the ceremony."

"There was no reason to postpone our wedding plans. I spoke with Bill Barret, my father's business associate, and there is nothing we have to do except is to be in our attorney's office on Monday morning. My father was in his eighties and we knew his health was failing so this isn't a total shock. I don't want people knowing about his death until after the reception. We need to put on our game faces, and try to have fun."

He started away to join the others when she stopped him. "We can't leave for Hawaii as we planned if we are seeing our attorney on Monday. Does Judy know about your father?" Brad shook his head no. "I wish you had told me what was going on."

"No, for now let's keep his death to ourselves. No reason to put a damper on the festivities." Judy soon came back looking for the guests of honor. "Don't tell me, I'm holding up the itinerary again. We stopped to steal a few kisses."

"I can read your faces. Something is wrong, would you two care to share what is concerning you?"

"Later Judy, right now we need to go inside. People are waiting for us."

The buffet spread was second to none. People were patiently waiting for the newlyweds to start the food line moving. "We better fill a plate before they all leave. Your family is great."

"Our family, you are a part of this family now."

"Can you call your parents and Ray Junior over here? They should go through the food line with us." Marie's father was quick to compliment Brad on the fine buffet. "Your daughter did all the planning she deserves the credit."

Marie nudged him to move along. "Move along and fill our plates or we may have a stampede on our hands. People are hungry." Brad and Marie put little food on their plates. The news about Brad's father was disturbing.

Considering the circumstances the reception and dance that followed went reasonably well. Judy seemed to be the only person to continually watching the newlywed's actions. Eventually she asked Brad for a dance. Marie twirled around the dance floor with Sam. "I won't leave here tonight until I know what is bothering you. Be prepared to tell me something before the night is over."

"We'll talk about my situation later. There is no reason to spoil everyone's fun. It's best we let everyone have a good time."

Brad caught up with Ray Senior and asked if he and Susan could hang around for a few minutes after the dance. "Marie and I have something we need to speak to you about."

"We can't stay long. We have sixteen relatives at the house."

"Have your son entertain your guests until you return. Our talk won't take that long."

"We can stay a few minutes. Give us a chance to speak with our relatives first. Ray waited until Brad was out of hearing distance before whispering to his wife. "I think the boy may have over spent his resources. What do I say if he wants to borrow money from us?"

"Oh my word, do what you think is best but don't loan him more than five thousand dollars. We are close to retirement. We can't afford to give our money away."

"Okay we are in agreement then, five thousand dollar maximum we offer him. By the serious look on his face something is wrong."

Brad assembled Ray, Susan, Sam and Judy in a private room so he and Marie could speak without interruption. "As I arrived at the church today I received a phone call. Bill Barret one of my father's associates in Seattle gave me some bad news, my father passed away." The room fell dead silent for a few seconds. "The idiot further informed me something else I did not know. My mother passed away some eight months prior to my father passing away. No one bothered to tell me of her death. Only when I asked if mother was with my father when he passed away, was I told of her passing."

All four gathered close around him in a show of support. Their words of comfort were a blur as the death of his father began to settle in. "It will be impossible at this time for Marie and me to honeymoon in Hawaii. We have been instructed to be in my attorney's office on Monday."

Marie stood at her husband's side holding his hand as he spoke. "I wouldn't expect to go to Hawaii under these circumstances. There is no reason we can't have a delayed honeymoon."

"I wanted to explain what was going on this evening, so you wouldn't think I was having second thoughts about marrying Marie. She is the light of my life."

Ray rubbed his son-in-law's shoulder. "I noticed you were different this evening. I passed it off as being nervous around so many strangers. I apologize for being so insensitive. When are the services being held for your father?"

"My father requested no services for his death."

"No funeral service, I've never heard of such a thing."

"I was told he passed away two days ago, his body was cremated and his ashes were spread at sea. I had no say in the matter."

"How are you supposed to get closure, if they don't allow you to do so?"

"Father always had his own ideas. I asked what the cause of death was. I was informed me my father was in his mid-eighties and failing health. I'll hear what my attorney says on Monday. If I don't get any satisfaction I may seek some kind of investigation on my own. If you are sitting here thinking what can you do for me, the answer is you are doing it now. Your love and concern means a lot to me. Tomorrow morning the sun will come up as always. We'll all move on with our lives one day at a time as we always have."

"Susan and I hate to leave you. It is getting late and we have guests at the house. Keep the faith son, there will be better days ahead."

"You and Susan run along and tend to you guests. We will keep you posted on how we are doing and where we are. I have a feeling we may be in Seattle real often. If we are in Seattle will try to swing by for a short visit."

In their room words were not needed. Hugging and caressing dominated the night. "Thank heaven I have you. Tonight of all nights would be a bad time to be alone." Slow passionate love making continued to fill the night time hours. Near daybreak sleep came easy. Thankfully they had put out the do not disturb sign. Not until mid-afternoon did the newlyweds wake up.

While sitting in the restaurant eating he suggested their honeymoon trip be changed to allow Marie's parent's to take advantage of the trip. Although grateful for the generous offer her parents had used up their vacation time. "Are you sure mother?"

"I'm sure Honey, your father and I can't go to Hawaii but thank you for thinking of us."

"That plan went nowhere. My parents used up all their vacation time so they can't use the trip to Hawaii. Do we ask Sam and Judy if they can take advantage of the trip?"

"Go ahead and ask. Someone may as well use our trip."

Later in the day when they met up with Sam and Judy the trip was offered to them. They tried to hide their excitement about going to Hawaii. "I wish you guys were going with us."

Brad patted Sam on the back. "For now you and Judy go to Hawaii and enjoy yourselves. Someday the four of us may go to Hawaii for a vacation."

CHAPTER 36

On Monday they had no idea what to expect at the attorney's office. They sat quietly and listened as Al Claymore explained settling John's estate will take considerable time. "In the coming weeks you may grow tired of my office. Your father has vast holdings in several countries. His Last will and testament states you as the only heir. Since you are married, I should rephrase my last statement. You and Marie are the only heirs. I may need you in my office two days a week for the first few weeks. Later on one meeting a week might be adequate."

"Will we both need to be at these meetings?"

"It would be good if you both could attend these financial meetings. From a legal stand point either one of you could sign the money transfer papers. All deposits will be handled through Funds Vouchers directly to your bank accountant."

"Mr. Claymore do you have any idea what my father's net worth might be?"

"It would be unprofessional of me to guess at your father's net worth."

"Alright Mr. Claymore, we understand. Marie is pregnant with our first child. There may be days she won't feel like flying to Seattle. With our new business in Vegas, we can't remain in Seattle until these transfers are complete. We will do the best we can to be here when needed."

As one would expect flying back and forth from Vegas to Seattle soon became too exhausting a pace for Marie. She opted to remain in Vegas and help Robin Tilly set up the new spacious offices Robin would share with the Ad Palace. Wendy moved to the new facility leaving Carol and Rusty to man the Burger Palace.

While talking with Marie one day Judy learned Brad had been spending time in Seattle and not come by the house. "Marie, you and Brad own this house. Why isn't he staying at the house with us when he is in Seattle? Staying in a hotel makes no sense to us."

"He doesn't want to interfere with you and Sam's lives. After all you and he are technicality still newlyweds."

"I know but this is your house, and he is more than welcome to stay here in your house. Brad will not be in our way staying here."

"It may be our house but it is your home. The hotel he is staying at is near our attorney's office. He can walk to and from each meeting and rest between meetings or use the hotel's computer to conduct business. I know my words sound strange but his meetings are exceptionally stressing. I went with him on our first four meetings. Having a room close by makes it easy for him to rest and think between meetings. The down town Holiday Hotel is very convenient for him."

"You can bet we will be talking to him. The both of you are doing so much for us. We should be returning the favor best we can. I'm sure he would enjoy a few home cooked meals."

"You deal with Brad. I'm staying out of your way, girl."

Come evening they looked Brad up. "Hi guys, what brings the two of you here to my hotel room?"

Judy put her hands on her hips as she faced him in an angry stance. "Brad you should be ashamed of yourself. Why are you staying in a hotel rather than staying in your house, with us?"

"This hotel is convenient for my meetings. It keeps me from sitting in my attorney's waiting room half the day. I'm used to living in hotels so I don't mind staying here."

"You staying alone here is not right."

"Marie is busy in Vegas keeping an eye open for a suitable house for us. If something doesn't come up soon we will need to start building one. We do have one good lead on a house. Wendy's husband works for a guy who is considering down-sizing. We are told their home is fabulous with acreage. The house is supposed to be a paradise for raising children in a safe environment."

His rattling on confused Judy, when Sam excused himself to use the restroom she had her chance to whisper to him. "Are you staying away from the house because of our actions?"

"I don't believe so. I've been busier than you might think with our attorney and the accountant. The IRS paperwork never seems to end."

"Do you realize our efforts so far may not have been successful? More personal contact with you would be helpful?"

"Are you thinking a few stolen moments might happen if I were to stay at your house?"

She nodded yes. "Even Sam thinks you should be staying at the house with us. His reasons are different than my reasons, but he thinks you should stay with us. Visiting you in Vegas, Sam and I stayed in your suite."

"Alright, I will scoot over to the house later this evening. I'm not giving up this hotel room. I will continue to take my between meeting breaks here at my room during the day. I'm one block from both my attorney and my accountant's offices. Both are keeping me hustling back and forth."

At the house his old room was exactly as he left it. "Thank you for keeping my room tidy for me."

Sam turned to him. "Thank the cleaning people, they do all the work. How much longer are you expecting to keep this house?"

"We have been discussing this house. I believe we came up with something to benefit everyone. We haven't decided when to put the house on the market so you have plenty of time to think over our offer. The offer I am talking about is a no interest loan to you, and Judy, so you can purchase a house that fits your needs."

Sam looked at him with a blank look for a few seconds before saying anything. "How large a loan are you willing to go?" He asked. "We need a financial guideline before we start looking for a house."

"The size of your loan depends on the payment structure you guys want. We are in no hurry to sell. This is something the two of you need to discuss in private. Take your time and think about your future needs and where you want to be in five years, do some brain storming."

"In five years we hope to have a four year old child."

"Judy mentioned you wanted children."

"Along with the four year old child we may also have a two or three year old child also."

"You sound like a man with a plan. Now if you will excuse me I need my beauty rest I have more stressful meetings tomorrow. Sam you are on the right track. Lay out every scenario you can think of. Choose or build a house in a nice neighborhood. These are all questions for you to think about in to coming days."

"You and Marie are blowing us away with your generosity. We certainly will discuss your offer. We'll see you at breakfast in the morning."

While eating cereal the next morning, Brad enjoyed the conversation. "You guys make great coffee. This is the only time of day I drink coffee. Seems like all the daytime coffee makers make such strong coffee, I can't drink the stuff. The Burger Palace is the same way, espressos are over the top. I love the money we make on coffee, and espressos sales but in reality we sell a lousy product."

Sam laughed. "Apparently people don't agree with you, otherwise you wouldn't be selling so many espressos. If you will excuse me I have an early morning appointment. I'll see you this evening if you are still in town. Otherwise I'll see you on your next trip through."

"It's time I get ready for my meetings. I can't afford to be late for a meeting when people are pouring money in my pocket. You wouldn't believe the different directions my father's money is coming from. I doubt my father knew his actual net worth."

Sam patted the back of his shoulder. "What little I know about your father leads me to believe he was one of a kind."

"No doubt father was one of a kind. I may not see you tonight. I'm hoping to return to Vegas late this afternoon. Next Tuesday, I may return to Seattle."

"Please come to the house when you do return. I hate to run off and leave you, but I have an appointment with a builder today. We are working on an apartment complex of ninety-eight units. A nice project if we can put all the pieces together."

"I wish you luck Sam. I'll call and let you know when I'm in Seattle again."

With her husband out the door, Judy quickly approached Brad. "Can you spare a few minutes for me before you leave?" He gave her a questioning look. "Don't worry about Sam returning if he were to forget something he would call me so I could bring it to the office for him when I go in." She took his hand to lead him to the rear bedroom where Brad had slept.

"When you do become pregnant and our common interests stop it will be a sad day for me. I've grown to enjoy you more than I ever expected." He sealed his words with a kiss.

"Seems we both have been stupid to think we could just have casual sex without growing fond of one another. Let's not talk about the day we separate, it will be hard for both of us."

"I hope you realize you are making me late for my first meeting this morning. My attorney will be very upset."

"Relax and enjoy. I'm more fun than Mr. Claymore." Further words were not needed as he proceeded to pleasure her wanton desires.

As expected Al Claymore wasn't happy when Brad came walking in an hour late for their meeting. "I'm sorry to be late. I'm not a morning person, exhaustion caught up with me. Please accept my apology. I promise to do better in the future."

"Mr. Collins you have wasted half my morning."

"I'm sure you were doing other things and billing me for your time. Where do I sign today?"

"This Document gets signed here and again at the bottom."

"Is that it for now Mr. Claymore?"

"Yes, I'll see you again at two. More transfers will be coming by then. Try to be on time. I do have other appointments."

Outside he drew in several breaths of fresh air before calling his wife in Vegas. "Good morning Honey, I miss you. These meetings are boring beyond belief same as they were when you were with me, except I'm alone. I walk into Claymore's office sign my name twice, end of meeting. I'm walking over towards Darlene Smith's office now. I'll check transactions there and then hang out until mid-afternoon and do it all over again before heading home this evening. Thank goodness I love to read."

"I feel bad I can't be with you, but the best I can do is store up my love for you for when you return."

"Stop tempting me you little devil. I may skip my afternoon meeting and fly home early."

"Please do fly home early as you can. I'll cure your loneliness."

"There is only one thing stopping me from coming home early. I believe my father got in financial trouble not paying attention to business. We are growing our wealth right here in the states where we can enjoy life, and raise a proper family. Our children will have a complete family I'll see you this evening I love you, bye. We'll proudly walk anywhere we want."

"I love you too." She blew a kiss into the phone as if it were going somewhere. "See you this evening."

Arriving back in Vegas he found both businesses operating perfectly. "I can't believe how much help you people are to me. I come back and my work hasn't piled up. I'm thinking you girls don't need me anymore. I may as well buy a fishing pole or take up golf so I have something to do."

"Stop whining. We need you. Robin is asking about enhancing commercial property."

"So far our specialty has been enhancing houses that have a legitimate chance of moving fast. I wondered when someone might inquire about commercial property. What do you think, ladies, should we try commercial property or not?"

Marie pointed a finger at him. "Selling houses we pick out small details people often overlook when viewing a house. This in depth look makes the buyer instantly comfortable with the house he or she is shown. We tailor to the buyer's needs. I wouldn't know where to start to promote business property to move the property fast."

Wendy was nodding her head as Marie spoke. "I agree we should stay with what we do best."

"Then we should tell Robin we lack the experience to handle business property at this time. In the future I may look at business property while you guys concentrate on selling traditional houses. Until my father's estate is settled I need my schedule clear as possible."

"By the way, dear husband, you came home with lipstick on your collar."

"Hang me or tell your little friend to quit hugging me. Coming and going that girl is a hugging machine. I've never seen anyone quite like her. She is indescribable. She must have grown up with a lot of loving relatives. If someone looks familiar she hugs them."

"She messed up my clothes up with lipstick the same way when we were younger. I would dress for a date, and as I headed out the door she had to hug me goodbye. Sometimes I could wipe the collar clean and sometimes not depending on the material."

"Get a load of this Honey, Sam is hoping since you are pregnant Judy gets pregnant before long, I wished them luck."

"Considering Sam's condition, who knows when that might happen?" Marie added.

Wendy's ears perked up. "What condition are you talking about, is something wrong with Sam?"

"Maybe I shouldn't have said anything. Since I did mention Sam, he thinks he may have a low sperm count. He had mumps two years ago. I don't know if a doctor tested him or if he is guessing about his condition."

Brad suddenly felt the need to change the subject. "I did discuss their house needs with them. I suggested they do some time framing. Look ahead five years, and see where he wants his life to be at that time. Sam piped up saying he wanted two children in five years. Plus room for us when we visited Seattle. He was talking four bedrooms with a basement recreation room if I read him correctly."

"I'm happy to hear they are thinking in terms of getting their own house. I believe in the long run they will be happier in their own home."

"They have sold several houses and considering they have no living expense so far they should be saving lots of money. If they sell our house the commission there could be a hundred thousand dollars. I'm thinking at the most we would only need to kick in two hundred thousand to get the house they want."

The following morning Wendy's husband Joe was waiting at the office to meet Brad and Marie when they arrived. "Good morning, what brings you around this early in the morning?"

"Two things, my boss has moved his retirement schedule up. Meaning his house is for sale and I may be out of a job."

"That's not good. Joe may wind up long hauling again. Is there a chance we can see the house before it goes up for sale?"

"Mr. Carson said you were welcome to view the house and property any time you want by making an appointment."

"Then we should make an appointment. If you have his number I'll give him a call."

"I do and I would be happy to drive you and Marie over to their house for a personal introduction. That is if you want?"

"Thank you Joe. Today is Friday. I will be available anytime the next three days then I'll be in Seattle again for three days."

Joe placed a call to his boss. "How about you view the house Saturday at ten?"

"Perfect." Brad waited until Joe was off the phone. "Thanks again, now you said something about you may be out of a job. Correct me if I'm wrong but I thought Carson's son was taking over the business. Why would you lose your local trunk driving job?"

"The old man's son doesn't like me any better than I like him. He is a greedy little worthless no count shit. He is pulling a power play on his father. In my book the kid is stealing the company from his father."

"How long has this hot dog kid been working with his father?"

"That's just it; the kid has been around less than one year. He does absolutely nothing in the line of work. It may be the kid, Aaron Carson who you will be dealing with if you buy their house. Albert the father lost all control of his company and his property."

"Before we get mixed up in a family squabble I need to sort things out. Can you get your boss and his wife over to our office this evening?"

"Your request is somewhat unusual. I can't promise anything but I can try to get the Carson's over to meet you."

Joe came through and set up the evening meeting. Marie came to her husband with her concerns. "Brad we shouldn't get involved in a power struggle between a father and his son. We are busy people, we don't have time to fool around and get in the middle of a family fight."

"I don't know Joe real well, but I believe he has good instincts. If he says the kid is stealing the company from his father then it seems only fair I should steal the company from the kid, what goes around comes around."

Marie frowned at him. "This isn't like you, you are not a thief."

"Why don't you sit back and watch the real me before you go prejudging and thinking bad of me?" She starred at him with a blank look. "I'm serious, watch and learn."

"Marie, I've seen your husband in action." Wendy stated. "I'm not all together sure what he has in mind but this could be interesting."

"You can count on my watching him. I'll watch him from one side and Wendy you watch from the other side." While the gals discussed what might be going on. Brad ignored both girls as he busied himself making Albert Carson a subliminal message music C.D. "What pray tell are you doing now?"

"Honey this is called meeting preparation. Never go into a meeting short handed if you can help it."

CHAPTER 37

The meeting with Albert Carson was one of the sadist meetings Brad ever attended. Albert was a sixty-year-old man who looked eighty. He explained his current business problems. My son picked me clean, he set me up at a party we had when he came on board with the company. Sometime during the party he somehow convinced me to sign the company over to him. Aaron claims I signed my company away in front of witnesses. I don't remember signing anything but he has the deed in his name. I spoke to some of the party guests. They claim I signed the deed over to Aaron."

"Quite a son you have Mr. Carson. By what you are saying your son is rather greedy. That is very unfortunate. Greedy people usually fail in the end."

Aaron has always been a problem. I thought if I brought my son on board and gave him a chance to become a responsible person, he could turn his life around. What a fool I was. June and I will soon be looking for work ourselves."

"I'm sorry things didn't work out for you Albert. Joe tells us your home is up for sale. We happen to need a nice home. My wife and I may be interested in purchasing the house from you."

"Aaron has the final say on the house, he took everything we had. In six weeks he is auctioning off all our equipment and he is now after our house. We will wind up with little or nothing."

"Bummer, I know you are really down in the mouth right now. I see your future turning around soon. This greedy little son of yours needs to be taught a lesson. Can you get your son to come here to my office, so we can make a bid on your home?"

"If he thinks money is involved Aaron will be here. When are you thinking about seeing the house and property?'

"I don't need to see the property just yet. I sometimes buy things property unseen."

"Nobody buys a two million dollar property site unseen."

"I went on the internet and saw the sky view of the property. The property looks interesting. We sometimes buy things that appear to be a bargain price. Bring your son by sometime tomorrow and I will discuss my proposal with him. Please tell your son I am a practical man. A man that is willing to pay cash. In return I might want a discount of twelve percent on the property. I want your pea-brained son thinking about money, and calculating percentages."

With Albert gone Wendy smiled at Brad while Joe and Marie continued to frown. Wendy begged to be at the meeting with Aaron Carson. "Oh by all means I want you at the meeting, how about my two doubters, would you guys like to also attend our meeting?"

"Count me in. I can't believe you are serious about buying a house without looking at it." Marie's voiced echoed with anger.

"Joe you may also watch this dog and pony show too if you want. This kid needs to be taught a lesson. He is about to get the lesson of a lifetime. I need to do some special preparation before I'm ready for the kid."

"Aaron might not like me being at a business meeting of his. Judging by Wendy's excitement, I would love to see what you have in mind for this young punk. Will I be in the way?"

"We have a sneaky office. I talk to Aaron and spectators may watch form behind a one way mirror. You are welcome to join the party if you wish."

At two the following day, cocky Aaron Carson came to the Ad Palace office. "Hello Aaron, nice to meet you. Your father tells me you are taking over the family business since he is retiring. I think that is great when a father passes his company to his son." Brad patted the kid on the back.

"Let's get down to business. Father says you might be interested in buying mom and dad's house." Brad nodded. "Did they tell you they are moving to an apartment?"

"They did mention moving. Being a business man, I'm always open for a good buy. Plus I have cash to back up my offer. My wife and I will need a home soon and we hate financing anything. Your house sounds like something we should look at. My wonderful wife is in a family way. It's my understanding you have clear title to the house. A clear title means I can deal directly with you. I don't understand how you gained ownership of your parent's house. Your father passing the business to you I understand, but the house. Seems to me your parents would still have title to their own house, how on earth did this ever happen. It makes no sense to me."

"I know this may sound strange but when I returned to help dad run the business he gave me a big welcome home party. He invited many of his friends and business associates. During the party he signed all controlling interest of his business and their home to me."

"Oh come now Aaron this is hard to believe. No father willingly gives total control to his son on the day he comes home to join the business. Unless your father was dying, I still think it makes no sense."

"With a little help, my father did give up all control of his holdings."

"No way man, I've been in business long enough to know things don't happen that way. You are pulling my leg. I don't believe any of this."

"Skipper and I…"

"…who is Skipper?"

"Skipper is my lovely talented wife. Anyway we gave my father a special cocktail drink so he would relax enough to follow our suggestions."

"Like a double shot of Vodka?"

"Heavens no alcohol is unpredictable. We picked up the recipe from the internet. Skipper researched until she found the drug we needed." By now Albert was showing signs of anger, as he hid behind the mirrored glass with the others.

"So you drugged your father to gain control. I still have my doubts because I never heard of any such drug with the ability to do what you are claiming."

"Worked like a charm Mr. Collins. Skipper and I have ours names on the deed to the house to prove it."

"I'll need to examine the documents very closely to prove you are the owner of the property. I don't believe you have clear ownership. Did you bring the paperwork with you?" Brad questioned. "No one can drug someone and steal his or her property. You must think I'm a dork straight from the cabbage patch. If you want me to believe you, show me the web site and the product you used to drug your father. There is no flipping way to control people in the way you are telling me."

"Allow me to use one of your computers and I'll show you the website and the drug we used."

"You may use the computer on the end if you want." Aaron soon located the web site. "Well I'll be damned. You stole everything your father owned with the help of Skipper. This is the memory drug doctors used so a patient doesn't remember what was done to them. Marie this drug is often used on young children who are injured in a sensitive area, so the child doesn't remember the doctor repairing their private sensitive area. I'll give you credit Aaron you and Skipper are very clever."

"My father is a stupid man. All Skipper and I wanted was to be left alone. He kept badgering me get an education. I told him early on I didn't need college. Our family has enough money to hire all the smart people we need. My words upset the old man so he cut off our money. Short on funds Skipper and I retaliated by stealing his business. Now, I control the money. Skipper is a nurse so getting the drug wasn't difficult. We gained control of his business. His invited guests watched my father sign away a lifetime of work."

"This is so clever Aaron you should write a book. Have a seat there in the chair and stay put."

Aaron sat down. "About my father's house, on the tax papers the house is listed at two point one million in value. Houses sell higher than the price on the tax paper. For a quick sale, I'm willing to let the house go for one point five million. Skipper and I want to liquidate all our holding in Las Vegas, and get back to LA where we want to live."

"Your offer sounds very appealing except we have a problem Aaron. You don't legally own the house, you stole the house."

"You can't prove Skipper and I stole the house. If you don't want the house, I'm out of here." Unfortunately Aaron was frozen in place. He struggled but could not move. "Hey, what is this, I can't move."

"This is where you give your father's property back to him. I'm thinking this would be a good time to call Skipper to our meeting."

"No way, my father wouldn't leave me alone so now he must pay the price." Aaron watched as Brad dialed the police. "You can't bluff me."

"Wendy I can use your help now, would you mind joining us?"

Aaron's expression change as Wendy came in from the hidden office. "Help me clean up, while I continue entertaining our friend Aaron."

Wendy set about removing all his subliminal messages before the police arrived. Marie, the Carson's and Joe all remained out of sight until the police entered the front door. Aaron saw his parents walk in later. He was obviously surprised but tried to remain calm. "Hi mom, dad, what are you guys doing here?"

"We were hoping to get our business and property back."

In minutes two additional detectives arrived. Aaron willingly repeated the entire story word for word to the two detectives. "Aaron Carson, you are under arrest for grand theft." As the officers moved towards Aaron, Brad snapped his fingers to allow Aaron to move. He charged straight at the officers hoping to bowl them over and escape. His efforts were unsuccessful and taken to the office floor and cuffed. "You now have an additional charge of resisting arrest."

"Marie, see to it these officers have a copy of our security video. I'm sure they would like a copy. Albert, I believe you are about to get your business and property back. If you do decide to sell your house sometime in the future, we still may be interested in looking at it."

Albert Carson was one happy man when he left the office. Marie was quick to hug her husband. "You had me nervous, but you did a fine thing. Getting the Carson's property back was a wonderful thing. Albert and June were thrilled with what you did for them."

"My special advertising ability used properly is a powerful weapon. In the wrong hands my technique could be devastating. We must never talk about what happened here. By now Albert, his wife, and Joe will have no memory of what happened except he is getting his company back. We'll give Albert a few days and then approach him about the sale of the house. He may well not want to sell now that he is in control of his business again."

Later in the suite Marie cornered her husband. "You were marvelous in the office today. Your subliminal messages are very impressive.

"Too bad I needed to make a security video for the police. I wanted so bad to rocket up the intensity. I could have had him confessing in two minutes and begging for forgiveness. I knew Albert and June wouldn't want to lock their son and his wacky wife Skipper away proper. I had to take what I could out of Albert's hands and give it to the police. Now we'll see if the police can do the right thing, or if they will knuckle under to the little punk."

"You have so little faith in the police?"

"The police are idiots. They often do the wrong thing. They settle for small easy plea bargains. Aaron's case should be a slam-dunk. He and Skipper should be locked away for a very long time, but they may not. Judge and Attorneys like to recycle criminals and get paid over and over."

"You did a fine thing, but I'm somewhat disappointed. I was starting to get excited about seeing the Carson house. Now we may never see the house."

"You give up to easy Honey. When I get back from my next Seattle trip we can go see Albert and his wife. One never knows they may well be in a downsizing mood. This incident with their son took a heavy toll on the Carson's."

In Seattle the following day Brad was met with a surprise. Sam was on his way to Portland with his parents to attend a funeral. Judy remained in Seattle to man the office. "Who passed away?"

"Carmen's older sister, she died of cancer. Sam and his parents are driving to Portland. They left at nine this morning. I expect them to be gone two nights and three days." He stood staring at her. "Are you not talking to me today?"

"I'm not sure what to say, did you know Sam's aunt?"

"I never met the poor lady. Sam said she was nice."

"Do you expect her death to curtail our activities? I don't want to come off unsympathetic, but this may be our golden opportunity for us to move forward, and accomplish your goal."

"Sam's aunt dying touched him hard. I feel bad not being with him when he needs me. I didn't stay here in Seattle by choice. We have house sales in progress, Carmen thought it in our best interest to keep the office operating. Brad and his mother went down to the funeral. While in Portland they will visit the family."

"You feeling bad means we should proceed with caution tonight. How about we hot tub first, relaxation never hurts. Do we wear swimsuits?"

"What is the point of wearing swimsuits, wouldn't it be hypocritical at this point if we suddenly became modest?"

Two nights in a row the spare bed received a major workout, as efforts were made to impregnate Judy. Sam called saying they were staying in Oregon an extra couple days. Judy begged Brad to stay a third night. "I'm sorry, but we must not get careless. Sam and Marie know my routine well. Two nights and back to Vegas. Any altering of my normal activities while your husband is gone could prove to be our downfall."

"You are probably right. I'm asking for too much."

"I'm thinking my mandatory trip to Seattle may end soon anyway. My father's estate can't drag on forever. When my scheduled trips do end, I will miss our time together. As I feared in the beginning, I have grown attached to you." He avoided the word love.

"When you stated in the beginning how you often became attached too fast to a woman. I was naïve, and didn't believe you. I actually thought we could do this in a business-like manner. We failed in that aspect."

Two weeks later Judy called Marie to convey her good news. "Marie, I have good news, I'm pregnant."

Marie was thrilled at her friend's news.

Marie in turn relayed Judy's news to Brad that evening. "Judy called today, she is pregnant. Our childhood dream of having children near the same age may actually happen all thanks to you? If it weren't for our meeting you, she, and I would be unmarried college students. We wouldn't be starting our families now."

"Goes to show you if a person wants something badly enough they work to accomplish their goal. Things can work out good for everyone's best interest. I wonder if they are happy about having a baby as we are about having a baby."

"You better believe they are thrilled. I also have other news we have an appointment to see the Albert Carson property on Friday. They called while you were doing your paperwork thing in Seattle."

"Cross your fingers and be ready to give your honest opinion of the house. The house sounds perfect for our needs, but one never knows until we see it. I like the fact it has undeveloped land around the house. To some degree if we obtain the property we can control what is built around us."

The Carson Estate was magnificent. "What a place, I can visualize our children playing in the playhouse over there." A beautiful security fence incased the property. The guest house matched the main house in its Spanish stucco design. "Albert, do we dare ask how much you are asking for the house and property?"

"We are in the process of building a new condo. You did me a huge favor getting my company and property back for us. I'll sell you the property for two point one million, exactly what the tax assessment papers say."

Brad turned to his bubbling wife. "You make the call Honey, do we buy the house or not?"

"If the final decision is up to me, I say yes. We buy this house. This is the perfect place to raise a family. I like the fact we have security and room for guests to visit when they can."

Brad and Marie Collins bought the house and the surrounding open acre

Marie couldn't wait to tell Judy about the large spacious house they were buying. "Hi Judy, we bought a house. We can move in approximately six weeks. Our house isn't new but four years ago when it was built, the owners spared no expense. It is in a very secure fenced area and large enough to have plenty of room for your family when your family comes to visit."

"What a coincidence, we also made an offer on a house today. I'm sure our house is smaller than your house. None the less our house is a very nice house."

"I'm sure your house is nice, isn't it amazing how our lives parallel one another?"

"We planned our lives this way for the past eighteen years. Now our dreams are coming true. What could be better?"

During his next Seattle trip Brad was slightly depressed knowing his and Judy's affair was over. Sitting in his motel room alone gave him time to think. He had done what she asked of him. Everyone was happy except him. Come evening he would be at their home. How could he relax around them knowing the child she carried was his child.

The next eight trips to Seattle seemed like the longest weeks of his life. The Seattle meetings continued to drag on. Judy and Sam appeared to be happier than anyone could imagine. Twinges of guilt grew stronger each time he saw them. Marie was quick to pick up on the change coming over him. "Honey what is bothering you."

"Nothing is bothering me, why are you asking?"

"I can read you like a book. This money business of your father's is taking a toll on you."

"I am tired of racing around. I hate living out of a suitcase two days a week when I should be home with you. I'm starting to wonder if people are comparing me to my father. Chasing money and neglecting my family."

"I wouldn't worry about what people think. There is a big difference between you, and your father. Your meetings will soon end. Your father spent a lifetime away from his family."

"I suppose you are right Honey. I bet the Anderson's are tired of me being at their house anyway."

"They are not tired of seeing you. She refers to you as a man who can get things done, coming from Judy that is a great compliment. Sam is also happy to see you."

CHAPTER 38

Come spring Marie gave birth to a seven pound two ounce son they named John, named after Brad's father. Six weeks later Judy gave birth to a six pound five ounce girl they named Carrie. Nine months later Marie and little Johnnie flew up to Seattle to visit Sam and Judy before going on to visit Marie's parents. The women were thrilled watching the children play together. "Carrie loves to play with other children. Too bad we live so far apart."

"Brad and I have been talking about a little sister or brother for Johnnie. My wonderful husband refuses to raise a child alone. Our nanny, Emily is wonderful with Johnnie. She may only be our nanny but Johnnie thinks of her as his grandmother."

"Nannies are wonderful. I never expected Sam and I could afford a nanny. You and Brad enhancing extra houses videos for us made our getting a nanny a reality. We owe you guys more than we can ever repay."

"Our relationship is a two sided blessing when you guys make money we make money, we all benefit. You and Sam are a big help to us."

"It also appears great minds think alike. Sam and I have been talking about expanding our family again by having another child if we can. We may get lucky enough to have another baby."

"You have one child. Of course you can have another child."

"Having one child was a miracle. Can a person have two miracles in one lifetime?" Judy gave her a sad look. "Only time will tell."

"Of course you can have another miracle child. I'll pray for you to have a second child. It's uncanny how our lives are paralleling our dreams. Divine intervention or whatever it is called, I think this is fantastic. I hope we have a little girl this time."

"Allowing us to sell your big house here in Seattle is what set the foundation for our new house. We were able to get the house we wanted with a smaller loan than we expected. Sam wasn't keen on accepting your no interest loan at first. He thought Brad might put a lot of strings attached to our dealings."

"Your poor husband still doesn't know what to think of my guy. One thing I have learned about Brad, nothing he does surprises me."

"Sam and I miss his visits. We are starting to buy Mutual Funds. Most real estate agents seldom buy stocks of any kind. He and I are bucking the trend. Using your enhanced sales technique we are selling houses fast. We considered buying repo houses and reselling them as Brad suggested. Doing so would take away from our sales time of existing homes, and our family time. Mutual Funds looked to be an easy safe place to stockpile money. If we keep the money in a regular account we find ourselves spending part of the money on things we don't need."

"I'm proud of you and Sam." Marie stated. "You are responsible people taking care of your future. Theses mutual funds you spoke about can cover your later years quite well."

On day two of Marie's visit the girls took their babies and drove down to see Marie's parents. Ray and Susan showered the children with love as they marveled at how the children looked alike. The following day Susan came up with an idea. "Ray and I can watch Johnnie and Carrie if you girls want to go shopping?"

"Now there is an offer we can't refuse." In minutes Marie and Judy kissed the children goodbye. They were soon off to do some shopping."

"You are so lucky to have nice parents nearby."

"My whole life, I've been lucky."

"I wish my parents lived closer, they love Carrie. Unfortunately my parents moved to Alaska for personal reasons." She paused briefly. "My father had a mid-life crises, he had an affair. He had a brief relationship with a coworker and was fired. He worked at the airplane plant. Being good at what he did, my father was hired by an airline and moved to Alaska. "

"You never told me your father had an affair. Your mother must have gone bonkers. Talk about shaking up a marriage, they are lucky to be together. Affairs are always devastating to people's lives."

"My mother claims all marriages have problems concerning intimacy. She forgave my father. In fact she made forgiving my father sound so easy. Seeking comfort from a friend may be a natural instinct when one has a problem. I doubt people plan to destroy lives when an affair begins. Mother may be right when she said affairs can begin for many different reasons."

"I'm glad Brad and I work together as we do. With his money every little Twit with an itch between her legs could be after him. After the

Karen and Kathy's ordeal he had the good sense to hire an older more mature secretary. Wendy is fifty five years old I believe. How did we get on this gruesome subject of having affairs anyway? We are supposed to be out having fun shopping, not talking about cheating husbands."

"We were talking about my parents living in Alaska. Although my father did have an affair, deep down, he isn't a bad man. Mom doesn't hate him, she hates what he did."

"Small difference, how long did your father's affair go on?"

"I really have no idea how long his affair went on."

"Let's hope you and I never find out what it's like if our husbands stray. How did your mother accept the news of your father's affair?"

"Mother was very upset. She did consider leaving my father, but she didn't. I can only speculate the affair was the result of a pressure situation of some kind, something extremely unusual."

The girls made a few purchases of children's clothes before returning to the Richards home. "How were our little Angels?"

"The kids were good as gold, we'll give you a dollar for each of them."

"Oh my, a whole dollar, we better think this over before we accept your offer. Then again our husbands might object. How about I go home and have another child. When they get older, I'll loan both the children to you for short periods of time?"

"Now there is a plan your father and I like. It's a deal Honey. Do have more children, more the merrier."

As Mrs. Roberts suggested the girls have more children, Judy appeared very sad. "With Sam's problem having more children may be difficult. I was fortunate to have one child. It may take another miracle for me to have a second child. I do consider Carrie to be a miracle baby. I'm blessed to have her."

"Then pray for the same miracle." Marie's word's failed to make her friend smile. "Cheer up Judy. I'm certain you will become pregnant again."

Although tired Marie was ready to return to Vegas. She enjoyed her visit to her parent's house, and seeing Judy's family. Marie and Judy drove back to Seattle to spend one final night before returning to Vegas.

The following morning Marie said goodbye before taking a taxi to the airport. Being anxious to get home the plane ride seemed to take longer than normal.

Brad welcomed her home with a generous hug and a shower of kisses. Little Johnnie got his share of hugs and kisses too. "My visit to the Northwest was too short. I missed you so much I had to come home. I wish you could have seen the kids playing together. I do have pictures to show you later. Mom and dad wanted to keep the babies when we visited them. I told them you might object. I did promise to come home and have another child. When the kids were older we would loan them to my parents for short periods of time."

He snuggled hugged both Johnnie and his wife. "I bet this little guy would love a playmate. I hope your parents do see the kids often. I never had any family growing up. Our children will be very lucky to have extended family members in their lives."

"Judy went with me to visit my parents. When I mentioned having another child she looked sad. I thought she was about to cry. She has a child but for some reason she worries Sam can't produce another child for her."

"You can't fool me Honey. This is a conspiracy between you girls, you two planned this. You have been planning longer than I knew you to have at least two children."

Marie tilted her head as she gave him a sexy smile. "You could be right, all I'm saying is be careful and don't overwork yourself. I need your services of an evening. I want you well rested when you come home."

"What are you talking about? You get my services on a regular basis. I can do the job any day you choose to toss your pills away. I'm like a baseball player. When the time comes I'll step up to the plate and deliver."

"I get plenty of normal loving. Now is the time for you to step up and hit another home run. A little girl would be ideal this time."

"I'll check my schedule. Maybe I can fit you in somewhere, timed right we might get us a daughter." Marie gave him a playful slap. He took Johnnie from her arms. "Did you miss me little buddy, I missed you?"

"I'm certain Johnnie missed you."

"Your news of wanting a second child is good news. I too have news for you to. I received a call from Bill Barret while you were off gallivanting around. Bill made us an offer to buy the Import-Export Stores. I thought those stores sold before. I have no desire to own a business requiring me to travel more than I do now. We should go back to Seattle next week to work out the details for Bill to purchase the Import Export Stores."

"Please don't ask me to go back to Seattle this quick. I just returned from an exhausting trip to Seattle. You go to Seattle and handle the sale without me. Rest will do me better than additional travel."

"I can go do all the preliminary work if you trust me. Do you think Judy and Sam would be upset if I don't stay with them this trip?"

"Why would you not want to stay with them, they have a nice four bedroom house. I stayed at their house four nights. Sam and Judy were gracious hosts."

"I know they have a nice house. Their home is further from my meeting location than the house we used to own. It takes me longer to shuttle to my meetings and back."

"You can't insult someone over a ten-minute drive. I will call Judy and mention you have business in Seattle and see what she says?" Although he knew the outcome of Marie's call, he waited patiently for the girl's conversation to end. "They are thrilled to have you as their house guest."

"Being friends is worth the extra drive in traffic." The minute he heard Judy wanted another baby he was anxious to be near his illicit lover again. To look proper he wanted Marie to be the one insisting he stay with Sam and Judy.

"You will enjoy Carrie, she is a living doll. They too have a nanny. You staying with them won't be any extra work for Sam or Judy."

The minute Brad landed in Seattle a strange feeling come over him. Using great caution he met with Mr. Claymore and Bill Barrett. The slow takeover Bill proposed was beneficial to both parties. He secretly wished for his electronic equipment. The right message might ease the strange feeling in the pit of his stomach. The meeting adjourned with both parties agreeing to meet again at ten the following day.

At the Anderson house Judy met him in the driveway. She gave him a seductive smile. "Before we go in where our nanny might hear us, I have a question. Sam and I want another child, and Carrie deserves a sibling. Can your personal services be attained again?" Knowing Brad didn't believe in raising a child alone, she used the term sibling. "Because of our nanny, sexual activity at our house could be dangerous. Are you using the hotel room this trip? My schedule tomorrow is free and Sam is busy. A hotel room would be nice."

"After my early morning meeting, I can get a room. I'll call and give you my room number."

Brad felt nervous being around Sam all evening. Judy saw his nervous condition. "May I get you two men a beer to drink while you watch your Mariners baseball game?"

Judy's beer helped calm his nerves. "Sam has an early morning meeting with his apartment complex sale he was trying to put together."

Brad knew he was trying to sell the units without using his subliminal services. For some reason Sam wanted to prove he could sell property without Brad's services.

Sam stretched. "Well people, it's time for me to hit the pillow. Will you be here tomorrow night?"

"Sam, I'm not certain. It depends on how my meeting tomorrow goes. I do wish you luck with your property sale in the morning."

"Judy and I hope you can stay another night. We enjoy your company."

Brad's early morning meeting with Bill Barrett and Al Claymore lasted about an hour. All parties agreed to a slow takeover to purchase the four Import- Export stores. The uneasy feeling in his stomach faded once the papers were signed.

Marie called as he was checking in at the hotel. "There is a creepy guy hanging around the office. We informed him you were away on business. He sat down in the office and won't leave."

"Put Wendy on the line with you." He paused until Wendy joined them on line. "Ladies, I'm not there to help you. Pick out a distinctive trait this intruding idiot has. Use his trait to make a strong subliminal message for him. Give him an appointment late Thursday with me. Then turn on your message and blow his buns out the door."

"Brad, we can't." Marie protested.

"Start the intensity low, and keep working it up until you jolt the guys butt out the door."

"Alright Brad, Marie and I will see what we can do."

"Call me when he leaves."

Judy arrived minutes later. "You look upset. Are you against what we are planning to do?"

"I have trouble in Vegas. Marie and Wendy are being harassed in the office. If I were there, I could teach this clown some manners. Marie said he came to the office to see me and won't leave. Both Marie and Wendy are quite concerned."

"I bet they are concerned, there are a lot of weirdo's in the world. Should I come back another time?"

He pulled her tight in his arms. "If you can spare the time hang out with me." He began caressing her left breast. "Marie should be calling soon." His cell phone rang almost instantly. "Did the guy leave?"

"Did he ever, we rocked his socks. A pack of dogs couldn't have chased him out of our office any faster than he left."

"Nice work, I knew you girls could handle yourselves."

"Give Wendy the credit, she made the message and set the intensity. I was amazed at how fast the guy left."

"Wendy deserves a big hug, give her one for me. I don't mean to give you the brush off. I have another important meeting scheduled this very minute."

"Then I better let you go. Bye Hon. See you soon."

With a grin he turned to a more than willing Judy. Slowly he began unbuttoning her blouse as he tenderly kissing her lips. "I have missed our secret rendezvous. I thought maybe once you had a child Sam might give you your second child."

"I'm not on any birth control. It is obvious Sam can't impregnate me. I too missed our time together. We both must realize once I'm pregnant this time, it will be the end of our affair forever."

"Let's not talk about our dealings ending." Slow and deliberate Brad proceeded to pleasure his afternoon lover.

Near three PM Judy returned to the office to find Sam upset. "We have a house to show in twenty minutes. Where have you been?"

"If we have a house to show we better stop talking and get moving."

"I hope Brad doesn't get to the house this evening before we do."

"Our Nanny is at the house and Carrie can entertain Brad, it won't hurt anything if we run a little late."

"I have a house to video this evening. You may need to help Carrie entertain Brad until I get home? I can't rush videoing the house just to get home and entertain Mr. Money. It's your job to keep him happy."

"I can call Brad, and relay the information to him. Call me as you head home so I can call out for pizza, and have it there about the time to arrive home. I'll think of some way to entertain Brad until you get there."

She called Brad to relay the plan. "Pick up a half rack of beer to go with our pizza on your way over to our house this evening. You may get to the house before me. Sam should be home near eight. He will be calling when he heads home. I'll order pizza for dinner when he calls. Laura can make a nice salad for us. That will leave Carrie to entertain you until I get home."

As Judy suspected Brad did arrive at the house before she arrived home. This gave him plenty of time to play with Carrie. Judy came home to find her little bundle of joy riding him horsey style. The nanny helped balance Carrie on his back. He glanced up at the little tyke's mother. "What a sweet little angel you have, I love her dearly."

Judy beamed with pride. Sam called, he has been delayed. He thinks it might be nine or later before he gets home. He wants to video two houses in place of one house. We may as well make a sandwich and eat our salad now. Mrs. Campbell will be giving Carrie her bath around seven."

"Interesting, how long does her bath take?" He whispered.

"When Carrie goes for her bath. You might go to your room for a short rest." Judy whispered back as she kissed his cheek. "I'll be there in two minutes."

Later the heightened danger of having sex in their house excited Brad. He made love like an animal. After a hurried bedroom romp he and Judy both took a quick shower in preparation for her husband's arrival.

Sam found Brad sleeping in a chair when he walked in. "Hi, oops sorry I didn't know you were sleeping. Is my wife a bad host?"

"No not at all, your wife is a gem. I had a stress filled exhausting strange day. Of course your daughter romped on me for an hour taking my last ounce of energy before my shower."

"Knowing you will be in Seattle a couple nights. I'm trying to video extra houses to send back with you." Sam wrinkled up his nose. "One house is very unusual. I marked a large X on the video. If the house is not something you like send it back."

Brad relaxed during his second evening with the Anderson's making it an enjoyable evening. "I finished my business deal today. I'll check with my attorney in the morning to be certain we didn't miss anything. I plan to leave for home tomorrow. I'm missing my family. It wouldn't surprise me they are missing me too."

The following morning as Brad spoke to his attorney Marie called interrupting the conversation. "The creep is back."

"Damn that stupid shit. Is he in our office again or outside?"

"The guy is in the office arguing with Wendy. He thinks you are hiding somewhere and avoiding him."

"Put the son-of-a-bitch on the phone, and start yesterday's Subliminal Message you made for him." Brad paused briefly to wait for the phone change. "Hey dipstick, are you frigging crazy harassing my wife and secretary?"

"Whom am I talking to?"

"Brad Collins, your worst frigging nightmare. If you care to remain healthy get out of my office now. Come back at your scheduled appointment time on Thursday. Don't let the door hit you in the ass on your way out. Give the phone back to my wife."

Marie was quick to grab the phone back. "The guy appears to be leaving. I'm scared can you come home tonight."

"I'm on my way home. Go ahead and close the office and go home."

"We still have work, needing to be done."

"Let the work go, just go home. I'll take care of you untimely friend on Thursday. I'll tie up a couple loose ends here be home soon as I can."

CHAPTER 39

Brad took a private jet back to Vegas and went straight to the office. "Has the son-of-a-bitch been back?"

Marie crashed into his arms. "How did you get here so fast?"

"I flew on a private jet."

"The guy hasn't been back. He scares me to no end. He sits and stares right through a person. He has the eyes of a cold- blooded killer."

"He will think killer if he continues to screw around with us. Did the creep leave a name or a phone number?"

"No, he didn't leave his name?"

"I'll see him tomorrow after lunch and see what our mystery man is up to. How is everything else going here in Vegas?"

"Carol and Rusty are operating the Burger Palace well as anyone could expect. Profits are up and remain steady. Wendy is getting ready to take a vacation. We wanted to stock pile a few videos before she leaves."

"Marie, Sam sent you girls a challenge. This video marked with an X he thinks the video may be hard to enhance. Keep an open mind if this house is not to our liking, we can pass, and send the video back as is."

Thursday afternoon Brad watched the thin faced dark skinned man who had been harassing the ladies, enter the building. Not for a second did he take his eyes off the creep. He stood behind the door as the man stepped in the office. Brad's actions surprised Marie, Wendy. Most surprised of all was the little creep. Faster than he could blink an eye he spin the man, slapped him against the wall, and patted him down. A nine millimeter pistol was found and removed from a vest holster.

"You worthless shit, don't ever come to my office packing a weapon. Weapons make me nervous, sit down!" He slammed the small man in a chair, before quickly pointing the revolver between his eyes. "Now, why is it you think I'm trying to dodge you?"

The little creep straightened his clothes. "Mr. Collins we have important business to discuss."

"Then you best sit still and behave. I feel it only fair to warn you my friendly mood may change rather fast." He continued to point the confiscated weapon at the skinny little creep.

"I'm here to discuss your father. I think it would be better, if we talk in private. Send the ladies out for an hour or so?"

"Not your call dipstick, these beautiful ladies, and I are a team. You talk to me. You talk to all of us. If you don't like the format, there is the door right beside you, take a hike."

"Don't get excited. Now about your father, he was an evil man and he did me dirt."

"How convenient, you making accusations about someone who can't defend himself. If he treated you unfairly why would I care, it was none of my doing."

"Convenient or not he was an evil worthless no count bastard. I covered for him the past thirty years. I helped move merchandise all over the world. Drugs, diamonds, human traffic, he was into everything. Plus your father was a child molester." Brad sat quiet as he listened. "I didn't come empty handed. I have proof. I was part of his transfer team. We moved merchandise to various locations around the world, and collected cash for him. The Import-Export Stores were a convenient cover for his illegal activities. I should have been named in his Will. I helped amass your father's fortune on the promise I would be well taken care of."

"Tough luck buddy, father is dead. You were not part of his Will. Maybe you got a tough break, maybe not. Better luck next time."

"Not so fast young Collins, your father screwed me. If I were to tell my story to the authorities you will loose everything you have. I'm not a greedy man. I only want a small portion of what you have. Two million dollars will buy my silence. After you think over my offer I think you will agree with me. I deserve to be paid."

"Whoa, hold on. Two million dollars is more than chump-change my friend. In addition I fail to see where you deserve any money."

"Oh come now, you can't be that greedy. For someone who has a hundred million dollars, or more, two million isn't a lot of money. Open your purse strings and save your fortune." The little man was now grinning as if he were in control.

"I'll need time to discuss your proposal with my colleagues. Leave your name, and number, and we will get back to you."

"I'm not leaving my name, and number, with anyone. I'll drop by after lunch tomorrow. You have twenty four hours to have my cash ready."

"What kind of a frigging amateur are you? Moving two million in cash would bring the Feds down on all of us. We need a name, and a bank account. Somewhere to electronic transfer the money, preferably a foreign bank. The action must look like any normal business transaction."

"You must think I'm a fool. I'm not giving you my name."

"Listen Dipstick, I don't give a flip about your name. Use an alias or make up a name. The bank account number better be real, or you haven't a chance of getting one dime. You can use two bank accounts. We transfer the money to one bank account and you quickly flip it to a second account. Please don't get ahead for yourself punk. We haven't agreed to pay anything yet. Bring proof tomorrow, we need to see something. Wendy can you grab a towel from the restroom for me."

"My proof is in my brain." The smug little creep stated with a smile.

Wendy handed Brad the towel he requested. Slowly and carefully he unloaded the gun and wiped the weapon clean of his prints. He repeated the process to clean each shell casing. "If your proof is in your brain as you say. Bring a neurosurgeon when you come tomorrow, we need to see the proof." Brad walked over next to the little man. "Stand up. Here is your weapon back." As the little creep took his gun Brad's towel fell to the floor and his hand went straight to the man's throat. "Don't ever bring a weapon to this office again. You could die on the spot."

"I won't, I won't. Jose Lopez, Lopez Enterprises, that's my name."

"Not bad, a nice common name. Jose my friend it's time you left. You are wasting our valuable time and don't forget to bring proof tomorrow."

The women didn't speak until Jose cleared the building. "That guy is bad news he scares me. How much trouble do you think he can cause for us?"

"We knew money could bring trouble. This little guy is an amateur. Long as trouble comes through the front door, we should be clever enough to meet the challenge."

"You may think Jose is an amateur, but he looks dangerous to me. I doubt he will give up easy."

"I agree, he won't give up easy. Jose will be here tomorrow meaning we have twenty three hours to prepare for his arrival."

"What do you think we should do, pay him, or call the police?'

"Marie if we pay Jose he will spend the money, and come back for more. My father had many employees. He could be the first of a long line of people wanting a handout. Paying this Jose creep one dime is out."

"Could it be true your father's wealth came by illegal means?"

"No way for me to actually know without doing a major investigation. First we need information from Jose to handle this inconvenience. We need to know who Jose is working with. While I work on a special hot subliminal message for Jose, you gals should work on house videos so we keep the business rolling along."

"I have two questions actually. My first question is why did you give Jose his revolver back?"

"The gun may have been used in a crime at some time. None of us in this room need to be tied to his gun, anyway shape or form. What is your second question?"

"Are you planning to block Jose's memory?"

"I considered blocking his memory as we spoke to him. I get the feeling he doesn't have enough backbone to be acting alone. Have you ever heard of a little game called spin the bottle, that's what we need to do with our friend Jose. Spin him around and point him in a different direction. You ladies stop worrying about Jose and do your normal work. I'll take care of our creepy little friend." Brad stated with a joyful smile.

Brad's massage was simple and to the point. Jose would leave the bank account number, and then return to his accomplices for a strategy meeting. During the meeting with his accomplice, he would freak out, and kill all those involved in the extortion attempt before taking his own life. Marie looked over to see Brad smiling. "You seem pleased with your work." She then took time to give her husband a tender hug followed by a sweet kiss. "I'm still shaking inside. I love you and all your confidence."

"Here before me is the answer to a two million dollar problem. Our skinny little friend has met his match. He will soon learn not to mess with anyone named Collins. I do have a good idea who is after our money."

"I don't understand how you could possibly guess who is behind the extortion attempt?"

"Think about it Marie, who knows we are suddenly worth a hundred million dollars?" Brad asked.

"Our accounting firm knows our wealth."

"It could be Darlene Smith or one of her associates. I think we can pretty much bet the farm on our problems generating in the accounting office. Two million is not enough to share between more than two people. It's time to rock the firm. I'm confident somebody put him up to this little scam."

Marie shook her head. "Amazing how your mind works. You catch details others miss. I never thought about studying Jose's features."

"Girls, I will need your help on this. Jose must stay in the office long enough for my subliminal message to affect him. My message is strong but I don't want to take a chance on the little creep bolting fast. He left our office very uneasy. I'm thinking of having Carol come over for a meeting. I'll leave my door open just enough so he knows I'm in my office doing business with someone else. He has to wait in the office longer to see me."

"I'm sure Carol would be glad to help any way she can."

"Carol's help would be greatly appreciated. She must not find out anything about the extortion attempt. She would be coming for a meeting with me and nothing more."

The following day as one might expect Carol seemed nervous being called to Brad's office. "Hi Carol, thank you for coming to my office this morning we haven't talked in a long time."

"In the past we talked when you come by the Burger Palace. Your call for me to come here surprised me. Have we done something wrong?"

"Nothing is wrong. You, Rusty and Ernie are doing a fantastic job at the Burger Palace. We have been so busy here at the Ad Palace it's been difficult to get over to the Burger Palace. By your mother's accounting figures you are doing a good job. I'm very pleased with your work. I didn't want you thinking we were ignoring you and get nervous. Nervous people scare me. We want to keep you happy so you would not be looking for other work."

"I still don't understand why you called me to come over to your office. A simple cell phone call could have kept us in contact."

"Carol my dear you are helping me stall for time. Don't turn to look but I have another appointment with a gentleman who is annoying Marie and me. I have a special message playing for him as we speak. I didn't want him darting in and out fast."

Brad's words sank in fast. "Geez, is this guy a flipping idiot or what?"

"He is an idiot. I'm playing beautiful music for him as we speak. I want him to feel at ease when it becomes his turn to speak with me. A little relaxation music is setting the mood for our meeting."

"Now I get it, my being here delays your meeting. Your message is being delivered loud and clear."

"Right on Carol, I thank you for coming by. Keep up the good work at the Burger Palace. Tell Rusty hello for me, as I said the two of you along with Ernie, are doing a fantastic job with the Burger Palace." For a full half hour Brad and Carol talked as he stalled for time. "Thank you Carol, I will be by and see you soon at the Burger Palace, I miss eating there."

"Bring Marie with you when you come to eat."

The women followed Jose into the office. He appeared to be very uneasy glancing around all directions. "Sit down Mr. Lopez, you are among friends. If you expect to do business with us it's important we are friends. Now let's take a look at the papers you brought with you." Jose was hesitant to hand Brad the big manila envelope he was holding. "I'm waiting, are you going to show me what you brought or are you leaving?"

Jose kept looking about as though the police were about to break in. Slowly he opened the envelope. "These are flight schedules, hotel records, and phone records all indicating your father's movements. As you can plainly see this trip to Bancock was two people going, your father and I. Our return flight was eight tickets to Brazil. Does the term human trafficking ring a bell?"

"I wasn't born under in cabbage patch, and I learned to read at an early age. I've heard the term a time or two."

"This trip is from Columbia to LA, a common drug route. Here we have South Africa to France over to England on to New York and back to Mexico City. Can you guess what that trip was?"

"I can try and guess. Uncut diamonds to France where they were traded for cut diamonds and distributed in England and New York then back to home base in Mexico for a brief rest."

"Young Collins you are a sharp man. Here is the bank number you requested." Jose extended his hand as he handed Brad a small note.

Brad looked the number over before handing Jose his cell phone. "The third number here. I can't tell if it's a zero or a nine. You better call and make sure of the number we don't need any screw ups."

"It's a nine, make the transfer Mr. Collins."

"How can I make a transfer, I honestly can't tell what this number is. What does the number look like you Marie?"

"A nine maybe, I wouldn't want to say for sure."

"Wendy, take a look, do you think that is a nine?"

"I can't tell either. It could be a nine or a sloppy zero, I'm not certain. The hand writing is very poor."

"You better use my phone make a call Jose and get this straight. I can't be sending two million dollars to the wrong bank number. Let's get this right Jose so each of us can move on with our lives."

"I'll use my phone." Jose walked over to the corner with his back turned to make his call.

"The number is a nine, make the transfer." Brad opened up his laptop and proceeded to punch in the numbers. "Hold it Collins you jacked us around too long. Make it three million or your assets all over the world will be confiscated. You have been stalling from the second I laid eyes on you. Now you are going to pay, I want an extra million."

"Pay the man before he wants more." Wendy suggested as Marie nodded in agreement.

"You rotten worthless no good…"

"Shut up and transfer the money! I've been here long enough!"

"Then we come to decision time. Do I push one more number and transfer the money or do I kill you?" In a flash he had Jose pinned against the wall with one hand against Jose's throat. Using his left hand Brad removed a stiletto throwing knife from behind the man's neck. He slowly drew it around to Jose's face. I thought we discussed your bringing weapons to my office before. You are a slow learner. I'm not always in such a good mood as I am today. I don't want any blood on my carpet." Brad took a half step back as he tapped the sharp end of the stiletto on Jose's forehead causing an instant trickle of blood to stream down his face. "You will get your money." Slowly he backed away never once taking his eyes off Jose. He paused at the laptop. Using his pinkie finger he pushed cancel on the transaction as his hand swept over the computer he threw the knife two inches beside Jose's head. "Get out and don't forget your knife. Don't ever let me lay eyes on you again."

Jose ran from the office, as Brad turned and hugged Marie. "We did it Honey." He then reached out and pulled Wendy next to him and Marie for a three-way hug. "Did you see how scared Jose was when he left? When he turned his head and I saw the stiletto my brain clicked."

Marie was all smiles. "Where did you learn to throw a knife like that?"

"A Stiletto is a fine crafted knife made for throwing. You hook your index finger in the curl and fast as possible point your finger. The knife goes directly to what you are pointing at."

She gave a nervous laugh. "How did you know what a Stiletto was?"

"As a lonely child I read a lot of books, some of the books were Westerns set in the Southwest with Mexican Characters. Hispanics love stilettos."

"Do you believe your father was involved in any of these illegal activities Jose was claiming?"

"My father could have easily been involved in any and all of the things Jose accused him of. Had my father been anything close to operating legal he would have been living in the states, or allow me to visit him in Mexico. I have little doubt he was a very bad man,"

"What do you expect Jose, and whoever, he is working with to do when they realize your didn't transfer any money to their account?"

"Whoever is involved will have a big brew-ha-ha among themselves. I doubt they will bother us any more. I'm confident we've seen the last of Jose."

"Hon, I'm going on home. I will see you there in a short while. I'm in bad need of rest. It's been a stressful two days for me. No way could I take this kind of stress every day."

With Marie gone Wendy turned to him. "Marie doesn't realize what is about to happen does she?"

"She is a little innocent, but she will get the picture eventually. I'm not concerned about her. Marie will be so grateful the little man is gone. I think I'll go for a relaxing drive before I go home. I want to take a drive out and look at some of the new construction Pam and Bob have going."

"If you are leaving, I'm leaving. Jose might double back."

Driving around the city he called Judy. "Hello Brad."

"Hi lady, I ducked out rather fast on you the other day. I feel bad about ignoring you. Urgent business needed taken care of. Things are falling in place. I expect to be in Seattle soon for a funeral. I would like to see you while I'm there."

"I'm sorry Brad, who died?"

"No one has died yet, they are gravely ill. I would expect them to die this evening or tomorrow. It may take a day or two to make funeral arrangements. By this time next week you could comfort me for the loss of my friend."

"I must say you are taking the news of your friend's possible demise very well, what's the deal?"

"Everyone dies sometime, and these people we are talking about are not nice people. I once thought they were good people, but the world will be better off once these individuals are gone. It's your problem I enjoy working on, so coming to the Northwest is fine by me."

By mid-morning the following day Judy called Marie all excited. "Your accounting firm, the one you and Brad work with here in Seattle, what's your accounts name?"

"Darlene Smith."

"Yes Darlene Smith, that's the one. One of her assistants was murdered last night. It's in today's paper this morning. Some guy whacked her and then killed himself. Right in the firm's office no less. The authorities are calling in a lover quarrel that ended in an apparent murder and suicide."

Marie quickly realized what had taken place, she was speechless at first. "Did you just say one of Darlene Smith's assistants was murdered?"

Brad took the phone as he realized what she was telling Marie. "Wow, that's too bad, can you save a paper for me?" Wendy saw the expression on Marie face. A death in Darlene's office wasn't playing well in Marie's mind. As he continued to speak with Judy, Wendy made a quick subliminal message for Marie encouraging her to understand, and accept what needed to be done. "We should have transferred our accounting down to Vegas before now. Is there anything in the paper about a memorial service for Darlene's assistant?"

"There was nothing about impending services."

"My father before us and now Marie and I have worked with the accounting firm for years. I should attend the funeral out of respect for Darlene."

"I'll make some calls for you and find out when the funeral is."

"Thank you Judy. I have one more question. The strange house Sam videoed for us we are struggling with ideas. Is there any way I could personally view the property on my next trip to Seattle?"

"I can arrange a personal tour for you, with me no less. Sam may be busy videoing other houses."

By the time Brad was off the phone. Wendy's message for Marie to remain calm was beginning to take effect. "I was hoping Darlene's office wasn't behind the extortion attempt."

"Darlene wasn't involved. Some idiot hoping to pick up a fast buck was at fault. Darlene checked out clean."

"How do we know Darlene Smith is squeaky clean?"

"Darlene is alive. I hate doing what needs done at times, but what choice did Jose give us?"

"I don't know. I take no pleasure in this event."

"I take no pleasure in what I did either. Unfortunately now we have unanswered questions. He said our assets worldwide could be confiscated. It is possible some of father's assets were not transferred to us. Bill Barrett and Al Claymore we acting strange during the time money was being transferred to us."

"Brad, we have enough money. There is no reason to put ourselves in danger searching for more money we don't need. Any addition money we acquire should be money we earn."

"There are ways of snooping around without endangering ourselves."

On the weekend Brad spent a lot of time playing with their son. Marie came to join them playing on the floor. "Whoa little guy, take it easy on mommy. She has little playmate for you in her tummy. We must treat her nice, she needs kisses and hugs."

Johnnie squeezed his mother's neck as he kissed her cheek. "I love you mommy." Brad voiced for the little guy.

The entire weekend was a much needed relaxing weekend. Marie kissed her husband Sunday morning. "Mr. Collins we need to spend more time relaxing like we are this weekend."

"Mrs. Collins my dear, you are quite correct. We should invite your parent to come visit."

"I would love for them to visit us. Do you mind if I pay for their airplane tickets to fly here?"

"Honey, you don't need my permission to spend money."

"I'll call mother and see when they might be able to come for a visit."

CHAPTER 40

On Monday with Wendy off for her vacation Brad and Marie were met with a second shock. Sitting in the waiting room was a well-dressed dark haired gentleman. "Good morning Brad, I've been looking forward to meeting you, and your lovely wife. I take it this is Marie, your lovely wife I heard about."

"So you know who we are. I'm curious who you are. More important, what is it you want?" After dealing with Jose last week Brad was suspicious. His voice clearly showed irritation.

"It appears I've made an error. I should have called ahead and made a proper appointment. I wasn't sure what day I could meet you. Shall I come back another day?"

"You are here mister, what's on your mind?"

"I'm Burt Collins, your father's half brother." Burt produced a passport from his vest pocket. Brad looked the passport over before handing it to Marie for her inspection. "The passport is real, it's me, is there somewhere we can talk?"

"We can use the conference room on the left here." Brad was quick to challenge Burt. "It's easy to see by the suit you are wearing you have a taste for the good life, are you here for a handout?" Burt Smiled. "If you are here for a handout, you my friend are out of luck. I'm not a charitable person."

"First and foremost I wanted to meet my nephew and his wife. Until your father passed away, I never knew you existed. John never mentioned having a son. Al Claymore contacted me when your father passed away. For the past thirty years, I've been your father's investment broker. His investments have done well. You or someone on your behalf cashed out all John's stocks. I've brought you a printout of his account activity over the years for you to look at. I think you will find I've handled your father's money well. You on the other hand need better financial advice."

"We don't have an actual financial advisor. Marie and I prefer our money to remain state-side and pay taxes. My children will see their father as they grow up. My father living in Mexico to avoid taxes was wrong. Growing up I was neglected."

"I think you are mistaken, your father didn't live in Mexico to avoid taxes."

"Why do you believe my father chose to live in Mexico?" Burt looked at Marie. "We have no secrets she and I are adults you may talk in front of both of us."

"There were rumors why John chose Mexico as his home. My dealings with your father were mostly done by phone. It has been said he was a casual drug user who freely gave drugs to those around him, and in return he expected friendship and loyalty."

"Father stopped coming to visit me five years ago and never allowed me to know where he lived. I think he may have died from AIDS."

"Your father was up there in years. I heard complications from a breathing disorder, was the cause of death."

"Where do you live Burt?"

Burt laughed. "I live in New York."

"I have a million questions for you. How long are you planning to be in Vegas?"

"Five days, I have a traveling companion with me. Plus we have a couple friends with me here in Vegas."

"Great, most people eat while in Vegas. Check with your crew, and if you come up with a convenient time, I would be happy to buy dinner for everyone in your group."

"I'll check with my guests and get back to you. Look over the paperwork I left you Brad, I promise we will get together again soon. I would love to continue working with the family."

Brad extended a hand to his uncle. "You are the only family member I've met."

"Our family has a lot of dirty secrets. Sometimes family secrets are better left where they are, out of sight and never talked about."

"Do you know any other relatives I don't know about?"

"You have no other relatives that I know of."

"How well did you know my father?" Brad asked.

"I'm not sure anyone knew your father well. Your mother and father always had problems in their relationship. I believe people used your father much as he used them. It takes two people to make a deal."

"Are you talking about infidelity, drugs, or alcohol?"

"When a person is living an alternative lifestyle anything goes. Don't think for one minute your marriage will be flawless. In a moment of weakness you may wind up doing something you never thought you would do. It's hard for a person to plan your life before it happens."

Marie bristled up. "I respectfully disagree. We are marital partners and business partners. We are dedicated to our family unit."

Burt smiled at her. "Being young I thought you might disagree with me. You look to be a smart young lady. Let's say you have a child…"

"…we have a child." Marie interrupted Burt in mid-sentence.

"Congratulations! Let's say I come to you, and said look at this picture. Then show you a picture of Brad in a motel room with an unknown female in less than full dress. What would you do, throw away your marriage. Grab your child and run. Confront Brad, what would you do?"

Brad grew nervous as he asked the question about him, and another woman. "I don't know what I would do." Marie answered.

"Good answer, being upset would be normal. Your next move should be caution. Check your personal relationship first. Study if this person providing you with information is doing things for your interest, or their interest. Today's world is so different. We are constantly bombarded with sexual innuendos. Pressure comes early and comes often. Many people think being hundred percent faithful to your spouse is impossible."

"I certainly hope these individuals are wrong. I wouldn't like my husband straying for any reason. A scarred marriage is not what I expect in life."

"Is Brad the only man you have ever been with?"

"I don't think my sexual history is any of your business." Marie snapped back. "I love my husband, and he is all the man I need."

"Easy you two, we are getting sidetracked. I'm looking for information about my father. Do you know if my father was a child molester?"

"Your father liked his women. Living in Mexico I doubt he was fussy about age. Your father is dead now. Does it matter who he was or what he did?"

"I think it matters. Do you personally believe my father was a child sex predator?"

"Brad you need to move on with your life. You can't change the past. I need to be getting back to my guests. How about we do lunch tomorrow?"

"Choose a place, Marie and I will be there."

"I hear the Cesar's Buffet is excellent, shall we say one o'clock?"

"Marie and I will be there." Brad walked Burt to the door. "Thanks for stopping by. I wish we could talk longer. My head is full of questions. I'm thinking about hiring an International Investigator to learn more about my father. I have a lot of unanswered questions. "

"Hold on, let's go back to your conference room." Burt's sudden turn around came as a surprise. Marie was speaking to the receptionist when she spotted Burt's sudden return. She rejoined the men in the conference room.

"Brad, this investigator idea is a bad idea. You father was a no good worthless son-of-a-bitch, who would do anything to make a dollar. You name it, your father did it. He controlled one of the biggest drug operations in all of Mexico. He had worldwide connections through his Import-Export stores. His network was the distributing system for many illegal drug brought into this country. Am I making myself clear?"

"I never thought my father to be an angel."

"He was into prostitution, drugs, stolen diamonds, and human trafficking. You name it your father was into it. Your father didn't start out as a criminal. He was set up and used by a Mexican cartel. Before long he was in too deep to get out. His shipments were tampered with until one day he found some uncut diamonds. Being a good citizen he went straight to the Mexican Authorities. The so-called good guys were not what they appeared to be. Your father and mother were roughed up and told to keep their mouth shut." For their silence he and your mother could live if they continue his Import-Export business as usual and followed orders. Your father soon learned to play their game and managed to siphon off more money than due him. These unsavory characters did a number on your parents. There is an old saying if you can't beat them, join them."

"Are you positive about what you are saying?"

"In my mind, I'm certain. The money I handled for your father came from all sources. It has been shifted to you through your attorney and accountant. Other money your father had may remain with other factions. I feel you and Marie are better off leaving that money alone if there is money elsewhere. Did you happen to hear about your accounting firm in Seattle? Two people are dead, killed right in the office. Executed and made to look like a murder-suicide. I believe Bill Barret is the local Kingpin in the Northwest, a man you do not want to cross. He may have killed these individuals."

"You should have been straight forward with me from the start."

"I wanted to sugar-coat our meeting. Keep all your business dealing above board."

"You still haven't answered my question Burt, was my father a child sex predator?"

"There were rumors to that effect. Being forced into a Drug Cartel with no way out changed your father. He tried to hide his true feelings behind drugs and alcohol. He was consumed by his own success."

"Are we still on for lunch tomorrow?"

"Yes of course, one o'clock Caesar's Buffet."

For a second time Brad walked Burt to the door before dragging Marie back into the conference room. "Now that you have met my family what do you think?"

"I'm stunned, what are we supposed to do?"

"To be honest with you Honey, I'm not sure if he is related to me or not. As we eat lunch tomorrow let's play it cool and avoid talking business. Try limiting our conversation to the Vegas sites."

They approached the dinner meeting in a nervous state. Burt may have been in his mid-seventies while his traveling companion was borderline legal age. The second couple, a man and a woman in their forties did not appear emotionally connected. Brad read them to be bodyguards for Burt. Both Marie and Brad were relieved when lunch ended. Marie touched her husband's arm. "I've got to tell you Honey, I hope I never see my so called Uncle Burt again."

"I think you are right Honey. The couple with Bert and his lady friend appeared to be bodyguards. I still will be going to Darlene Smith's assistant's funeral."

"I'm not going to that funeral. I'll stay in Vegas. Let's talk about something else. Are you going with me, when I take Johnnie in for his checkup tomorrow?"

"I thought you took Johnnie to the doctor a couple weeks ago."

"I did, Doctor Mortiz is concerned about Johnnie being under weight."

"Our family eats healthy. Johnnie shouldn't have any fat on him. Fat babies grow up to be unhealthy children."

"Doctor Mortiz insists Johnnie is under weight enough to be concerned. A boy Johnnie's age shouldn't tire out easy as he does when you play with him. The doctor insisted we do a battery of test to be certain Johnnie is okay."

"Honey you are scarring me. When do we do these tests?"

"Some tests were conducted two weeks ago and more tests may be conducted tomorrow."

"Then I should be with you and Johnnie. I'm feeling uncomfortable about Johnnie's appointment."

Mid-morning the following day Doctor Mortiz looked straight into Brad and Marie's eyes as he relayed the bad news to them. "Your son has leukemia. He may require a bone marrow transplant to survive." Brad and Marie hugged one another as they sat in stunned silence holding their son. "We have modern drugs to use as a first defense. Rather than sit around waiting to see if these drugs work or not we should be looking for a bone marrow match for Johnnie in case he needs a bone marrow transplant."

"How could this happen to Johnnie?"

"I can't explain why some children are born with a problem. You and Marie are here today. We can take your bone marrow samples today."

"Of course we will test today. Let's do it, and stop wasting time."

Marie used a tissue to wipe tears from her eyes as they walked down to the lab to be tested. "This is unbelievable our son is so young. I don't understand, you and I are healthy how he can be sick?"

"Honey we must remain positive. You or I one should be a bone marrow match for Johnnie. If not we will search the ends of the earth for a bone marrow match for him."

Brad's words couldn't have been more wrong. They were not a bone marrow match for Johnnie. "If only our upcoming baby was born we might have a match there. As it is we will have to get on a bone marrow match list and hope something develops. There is also the possibility the medication will delay the progression of the leukemia until Johnnie's sibling could be born. Siblings are often a match."

Marie continued to wipe tears from her eyes as they sat waiting for the results. "Doctor, is the bone marrow list a long waiting period?"

"Yes Mrs. Collins the bone marrow match list is a long shot for Johnnie. He cannot continue to lose weight as he has the past month. We need to try every avenue possible to find a bone marrow match for your son. We can start Johnnie on medication today and see how he does. The fact he weighs a full three pounds less today than he did four weeks ago is very concerning to me. He must receive treatment immediately."

Brad did everything he could think of to comfort his wife. Nothing seemed to help. "Honey we will keep looking for a donor, we must have faith."

"How are we going to look for a bone marrow donor?" Marie paused. "Unless the baby I'm now carrying is born premature, what chance do we have to save Johnnie?" He sat staring off in deep space. "Brad, I asked you a question."

"I'm thinking we should take Johnnie home so he can rest. There has to be an answer somewhere. How about your brother and your parents will they agree to be tested?"

"I'm sure my family will be willing to test."

"Call them and get them tested."

Marie's parents and her brother were tested in Portland. The Roberts were not a bone marrow match for little Johnnie. "Our only chance seems to be our unborn daughter."

"Honey we must not give up." Brad drew his wife near for a comforting hug. "I need to go to the office and start a computer search for a bone marrow donor match."

While Marie stayed home with Johnnie, Brad went to the office. Wendy had returned from her vacation. She sympathized with Johnnie's problem. She vowed to take the bone marrow test herself. "I can get Joe and Carol to test also. Maybe some of our other employees at the Burger Palace will also volunteer to be tested?"

"That would be so wonderful. Do what you can."

Same as when Brad and Marie tested. Joe, Carol and Wendy were no match for Johnnie. "Thank you for testing." He was feeling squeezed from all directions to step forward, and admit Carrie was his daughter. Even with a low sperm count there could be a possibility Carrie could be Sam's daughter. He considered going to Seattle and take a paternity test. When Wendy went out for lunch he seized the opportunity to call Judy. He explained Johnnie's condition to her. "Carrie may be the bone marrow donor we need."

"Oh my stars, Marie may find out about our affair?"

"I know, everyone may find out about our affair. What else we can do, we can't allow Johnnie to die."

"Why don't Sam, Carrie, and I all be tested? If we act normal Marie may not realize Carrie is your daughter. If Carrie is a match Marie may be so happy to find a bone marrow match for Johnnie, she may not put two and two together meaning we still may be okay."

"You can test in Seattle. Keep in mind Marie isn't stupid. Don't count on things being easy. Life can get complicated very fast. Once she figures out Carrie could be my daughter. I may find myself alone again."

Made in the USA
San Bernardino, CA
08 June 2016